SHADOW

MATTER

SHADOW MATTER

S. W. MAYSE

TYCHE BOOKS LTD.

Shadow Matter
Copyright © 2023 S. W. Mayse

Published by Tyche Books Ltd.
Calgary, Alberta, Canada
www.TycheBooks.com

Cover Art by Niken Anindita
Cover Design by Indigo Chick Designs
Interior Layout by M.L.D. Curelas

First Tyche Books Ltd Edition 2023
Print ISBN: 978-1-989407-55-4
Ebook ISBN: 978-1-989407-56-1

Author photograph: Stephen Hume

This book was funded in part by a grant from the Alberta Media Fund.

Alberta ■
Government

For Annie Heledd, always.
Fy ngholau claer, seren y môr gorllewinol.
My shining light, star of the western sea.

ACKNOWLEDGEMENTS

Over the years as I worked on *Shadow Matter* between other books and editing jobs, I read, learned new skills, and asked countless questions. People from many backgrounds and specialties answered helpfully about virtual reality, air search and rescue, film, military life, cosmology, space flight, and a dozen other endeavours, and I'm grateful to them all.

Some I won't name to protect their privacy, but I specially thank those who trusted me with personal knowledge of defeat, danger, life in a war zone, and nightmare work situations. A few took a great interest and gave me advice, reading material, and encouragement; a few became friends. None, to my surprise, asked the obvious question: why in hell are you writing something you know nothing about? Maybe they understood there's no fun or challenge in writing what we know; it's more interesting to write what we don't know but want to learn.

James January helped me understand the psychology of a burn survivor. Eliza Rackham Edwards researched addiction for me. Gail Boulanger outlined the lasting effects of trauma. Daniel Kempling demonstrated the basics of aikido and iaido martial arts. Sandra Barta, Sid Sidhu, David Lee, and other members of the Royal Astronomical Society of Canada answered beginner questions on deep-space astronomy, as did the staff of the Centre of the Universe on WTIXES (its SENCOTEN name; sometimes called Little Saanich Mountain or Observatory Hill). Paul Hannah emerged from eighth-century Mercia long enough to send me astronomy news and wonderful eyepieces for my telescope. Matthew Petch and Marcel Poland taught me to fly a small plane. Karen Drysdale talked me through oceanography, climate change, rare earths, and geology, and read an early excerpt with a scientist's eye. None of these people are responsible for my interpretation of their information.

Long ago the fire marshal of the Northwest Territories told me of an experience at a ryokan bath house that I've retold here; his name vanished in a flood with my other files, but I'm still grateful.

Those who read all or parts of *Shadow Matter* in one of several drafts include Celu Amberstone, Jo Beverley, Marcelle Dubé, Claire Eamer, Kelley Eskridge, Mary Fishler Fisk, Ami Kingdon, Donna McMahon, John Pearce, Robert Runté, Kris Rusch, Alison Sinclair, and Dean Smith. Their insights were enormously helpful.

Nessa Ransom nudged me onward when I faltered. Annie Heledd Mayse provided art, ideas, and critical literary knowledge. Stephen Hume trudged every kilometre with me to the White Lake radio astronomy centre, Mount Wilson Observatory, Jodrell Bank, the Dominion Astrophysical Observatory, and the Centre of the Universe. It's been a long journey, but to quote Ursula K. Le Guin, we are always coming home.

PEOPLE IN THE STORY

Politaya

Anya—Claer Defence Force
Danek Arwyn—construction worker
Delun Qasri—senator
Ewa—labour-camp prisoner
Janin Kerkallec—Parvin's daughter
Lezig Milosz—Rozenn's daughter
Marek Cabral—labour-camp prisoner
Mihal Villandry Biron—medic, Claer Defence Force
Parvin Kerkallec—commander, Claer Defence Force
Pedr Kerkallec—teacher, Parvin's son
Radko—dispatcher, Proton Freight
Rozenn Milosz—pilot, Proton Freight
Lt. Seren Qasri—signals lieutenant, Claer Defence Force
Yasmin Kerkallec—Parvin's daughter

Pact

Anton Rethel—Wilm Nolin's chief of staff
Duri Balint—contraband runner

Gabriel de Jong—lifetime president
Wilm Nolin—deputy secretary of defence

Neutrality

Akiko Sigridsdotir—sculptor
Amelie—Helli Njau's second
Carlos Liu—MitraCorps Spartí
Galina Narain—MitraCorps Spartí
Halia—Tas's daughter, missing and presumed dead
Helli Njau—captain, MitraCorps Spartí
Inka Loukanos—scientist, CEO Loukanos BioGen
Jaime Riordan—director-general, MitraCorps Spartí
Kai Rivera—sergeant, MitraCorps Spartí
Lira—Tas's former wife, missing and presumed dead
Louhi Takahara—lieutenant, MitraCorps Spartí, dead
Maq Flett—head geologist, AnvilCo Mining
Mei—survivor of spaceliner wreck
Midori—cosmetic modification technician
Mitros—MitraCorps Spartí
Rav—chef
Renat Von—lieutenant, MitraCorps Spartí
Sunny—MitraCorps Spartí
Suva Cohen—survivor of spaceliner wreck
Tas Damou—dangerous goods pilot
Teak Kuhan—captain, MitraCorps Spartí, dead
Zari Lind—documentary maker, MitraCorps Spartí, dead

Other

Anubis—chimera
Baka-chan—vri host of a child's educational program
Cedar—augmented animal, Seren's childhood guardian
Doll Sorrow—chimera
Draken—chimera
Hasi—augmented animal, Maq's database and guard
Moulders—spacer myth, a nonhuman spacefaring race
Teak—avatar, Seren's virtual aide
Tŷ Coed—Seren's childhood sentient chamber tree

I
HOME

1

Hover 360-shot. A ragged oval of fused sand, empty canisters, broken crawlers. This moon crater was a nature preserve before the war, but now it was crusted with industrial waste. Rock and rubble slumped toward a rough horizon under scattered stars in a bronze sky. In the hatchway, Seren framed her shot and blinked, left-right. *Expand.*

The liar had grabbed her off her home station claiming it was a rescue. Now he'd dumped her in a desert.

Seren dropped from the landing ramp onto the gritty surface where the small ship rested on its stabilizers amid the trash. Cold air seared her throat through the flimsy breather.

At the top of the ramp, the dreg leaned inside his airlock membrane, grinning horribly.

"Safe passage to Claer, no questions asked. That was our deal. Otherwise, I'd never have come with you," Seren rasped.

"Work it out."

"Or take me back to Arian station," she said.

But Arian station was occupied territory now, dangerous for a Claeran. Her green uniform was in shreds in his ship cycler, and yesterday's bruises had bloomed blue and purple. The shabby grey softsuit he'd tossed her wouldn't retract to her size or warm up on command. Her hair was still spiked in fleet fashion. She

3

felt ugly and slow. She couldn't remember things.

Fighting wouldn't work. She'd fought as he wrestled her onto the ship—wrenched off a locker door and swung it at his head. All it got her was a sore shoulder and shoved into the hold with a cargo of premium art glass, probably stolen.

Seren crouched to grip a fist-sized rock. The stunted ship looked as unsound as its pilot; the starboard registration numbers were lost under a long scorch. Mitran patrol ships like this old Azande had their flaws, though. Aim for the forward sensor array. In the moon's light gravity, the rock would sail high and tumble lazily down into a satisfying slow spatter of broken glass polymer. *The Politaya at war: kneeling in the dust to throw stones at a spaceship.* But her orders were to deliver her data, not die in a waste dump. She dropped the rock into the sepia dust. The dreg read her glance at the sensors, dropped through the airlock membrane to the ground, checked his array, and shot her an evil stare. His face looked like a wax mask clawed open and melted at furnace heat. No sane man would choose that face. He vaulted back inside the membrane, all within twenty airless seconds. *Show-off.* Maybe he was sobering up.

"Go."

Keep talking. The words nearly choked her. "I'm on task. If I don't report in thirty-eight hours, they'll post me as a deserter. What's your price? Politaya Fleet command will pay."

"Your fleet no longer exists. Or your war."

"My family will pay." *Somehow.* Since the surrender she hadn't reached anyone at home.

"No."

"Why did you shove in, anyway? I could have dealt with the other two." *Maybe.*

"Your arm was all they wanted. Once they cut it off, you'd have bled out before station security found you." He moved back into shadow.

Useless. Seren rose to her feet and step-glided toward the low crater wall. Dust rose around her once she left the landing pad. The single-use breather should give her an hour's air, and then she would die gasping.

A tap on her wrist invoked her virtual aide, with a second tap for her retinal overlay.

<> Teak? <> she subvocalized.

<> Seren. <> The avatar took shape ahead of her, staying at arm's length as she walked. At last—she hadn't been able to invoke Teak since the station. His easy smile narrowed his eyes slightly as though he stood in dazzling sunlight. That was how she'd coded him, as a revenant.

Last time she'd visited the Outer Moons Preserve on Melusine, a nature interpreter's hut had overlooked the moon crater from its rim. No sign of it now.

<> Nearest habitation? <>

<> You're standing on it. <>

<> Never mind. <> His code must be scrambled. She'd given him a sense of humour, but not a deadpan.

<> How can I help, Seren? <>

Seren shook her head, resisting the old ache of loss. *Teak.* She didn't subvocalize, but some echo of emotion reached his invocation routine, and a crease of concern deepened between his brows.

<> Stand by. <> Wherever virtual ghosts waited for a summoning.

Teak clasped her shoulder, took a step back into his own brighter dryland, and faded through transparency to nothing.

A hundred paces on, she halted to scan the horizon. *Slow pan.* Double-blink, record.

It was an old habit, laying down useful shots for her stock image file. A sequence of this bare moonscape would reduce well to a grey-scale dropout for her next doc. Her hovercam pinged as it docked on her earlobe.

Another hundred paces, slowing as her air thinned—then she topped the crater wall and discovered what had amused the roach.

Beyond the Azande on the crater's down slope, four low domes rose glowing from the moon surface. Seren walked a wide arc past the ship. Eventually its ramp retracted and its hatch slid shut, but she didn't turn to watch. She wouldn't give him the satisfaction.

An open section of wall on the nearest dome shimmered with a transparent entry membrane, and a large apron of fused sand stretched out front. Inside, a few surface hovers and insystem craft and a small mirror-drive luxury yacht sat between engineering positions and equipment lockers. She walked into the transport bay, instantly heavier in the dome's standard gravity. The membrane stretched around her, then popped and reformed like a giant soap bubble.

No one here.

As she turned away, a flash of blue caught her eye. A small brown man sat in an alcove tossing a finger-sized blue stick from hand to hand. Weapon? But her sensors didn't ping. And the man looked old, not especially dangerous.

"Rough trip?"

"I claim right of refuge." She opened the softsuit hood and held out her hands, palms up.

"Christ in nirvana, another Politayan. Deserter or holdout?" He pocketed the stick, and his eyes refocussed as he viewed his heads-up retinal overlay. "Better work on that fancy Pol accent."

"What is this place?"

"Damou didn't tell you? Welcome to AnvilCo Melusine. I'm Maq Flett, head geologist." His own dialect sounded like a vintage clip from migration days, and his skin had a rejuv gloss. He got up and started toward a door. "Let's go, there's work to do."

"Work." Seren bit off a laugh, seeing he was serious. "I need to be on Claer soonest." *Tell them in Tirion.*

"Damou brokered you on a hundred-day contract."

A hundred-day contract to AnvilCo? She stared in numb dismay. A Pact industrial operation in the heart of the Politaya, so soon after the defeat. Grabbed by thugs in sight of the fleet docks on her home station, now dragged by Damou—if that was his name—straight to a Pact plunder operation, straight to the enemy they'd fought for four years.

Maq Flett palmed the door plate and looked back over his shoulder.

Seren didn't move. "My contract's not his to sell. He's a thief. Detain him. I'm laying charges."

"Later. Damou went to load station cargo soon as I paid. Hope you're worth it." He spoke to his hand, and a passenger cart stopped at the doorway. "Our data core's in rebuild, and he said you're a coder."

"He lied."

This wasn't how she meant to return to civilian life. Four years in disgrace, and one slight chance to redeem her name, turn over her data, and get back to her studio: she couldn't foul it up. Fear seized her throat again, but she forced herself to breathe. There had to be a way. Teak told her once, There's always a way.

Riding the cart around the dome's transparent outer walkway past a handful of men and women who nodded greetings, Seren spared one glance upward. Maq Flett followed her gaze to a bright pinprick in the dim sky.

"New station. Soon as they stood down, I bought a decommissioned Pol cruiser."

The Politaya was in ruin, Mitra and the Neutrality had gone dark, and a Pact war profiteer owned her contract. It was too late to fight and too soon to mourn. Seren searched the sky for Damou's ship lifting free of the moon's gravity. The bastard was probably laughing all the way to low orbit. Maybe he'd crash and burn.

2

Twenty-five degrees of night. A single human hand, stretched wide from thumb to smallest finger at arm's length, could span exactly that much of the cosmos. Seren spread both hands on the dome window, thumb to thumb, measuring a full fifty degrees of nothing. The glass curved her face back to her as she studied her home stars, unseen for so long.

Maq Flett nodded to the nearest worktop and headed for the door. "All yours. Readme in the prime index. Stay here where I can find you, Green."

Seren ignored his slur. Even Politayans called themselves Greens.

The darkened workroom was a tactical centre like the one where she'd trained—the sight clenched her stomach—except no Pol fleet signals and comms crew manned the worktops. Overkill for a mining operation, surely. Crossing the lush living carpet, she half expected to thumb the duty roster and start her watch.

The door slid shut. She needed to return to the hangar, get away. First, wake a worktop, not the one he'd showed her, and quickly open an offworld link.

The worktop she chose was locked down. So was the next, and the next. When she found one she could open, she gestured over the entry pad.

"Local access only," a pleasant androgynous voice said.

Above a big central table hung a zone for virtual reality imaging. Seren synched her wrist implant with a finger tap, and immediately the vri displayed human space. Lifeless Earth turned near the inward edge of the Pact's ragged reach, and the Pact was loosely enclosed by the Politaya, veined with the Grey space of its breakaway Neutrality worlds. Out beyond the Politaya lay the Tripline, for two centuries the limit of human space travel. Beyond the Tripline lay the Deep Outside.

Touching Claer's green spark in the display should open a link—but nothing happened. Seren bolted for the door—locked—and returned to the curved window. *Think.*

Warmth brushed her ankle, and she looked down to see a brindled mongoose crouching against her foot.

"Are you named?" Seren asked it. A natural animal would ignore her, but an augmented animal would answer.

"Hasi is named," the mongoose chirred from a throat speaker.

Its kind mainly used text or symbol scroll, not speech. Animals enhanced with artificial intelligence were illegal on Pact worlds, but AnvilCo had clearly lost no time introducing a high-functioning experimental type to help despoil this Pol moon. Seren turned back to the starfield.

"Looking why?" Hasi asked.

"Lost. Far from home." Seren's home orchard on cloud-wreathed Claer was out of sight below the horizon, and what was a Claeran without home and family?

"Find what you lost. Find home." Hasi's eyes glittered with starlight. "Hunt vermin now?"

"Yes, if that is your task."

Hasi flowed down to the carpet and became another shadow patrolling the dome's dim perimeter. If Seren ran for the hangar, the augmented mongoose would track her.

Damou still had her slate, stolen by the first two thugs. If she had it, she could jack a link. Maybe. Her fleet work had been mostly with image sequences and data captures, seeking patterns she never found until *a small spacecraft gleaming dark in the Deep Outside, a swirling blaze of white light*—the fragments didn't make sense. Her war had ended in a terrifying blur.

Seren checked the screens and vri stages lining the inner

walls. They woke to show dome interiors, the landing apron, moonscapes, several stations, and deep space traffic. Beyond the four domes, rock and grit stretched in all directions. Tarnished dust rose in a dissipating cloud. Somewhere on Melusine, AnvilCo was already mining the shallow ore veins for rare earths and natural alloys grown scarce on Pact worlds, tearing up the moon crust, vandalizing a Pol nature preserve.

Seren looked around. A wall niche held an array of ancient navigational instruments: a migration period transit comp in scorched and cracked plastic, a plain brass compass, a heavy bronze sextant that was beautiful even by Claeran standards. The ancients built tools that survived even dying Earth's rising seas and salt deserts and the Long Dark when they abandoned technology and nearly ended the human species. It had taken two centuries to redevelop science and technology once taken for granted on pre-migration Earth. These openly displayed antiquities were worth a fortune. Carefully, she touched the sextant. No stun field. AnvilCo might be overly trusting. More likely it had good security.

Seren had recorded a report subvocally for Fleet HQ aboard Damou's ship.

<> Teak, read me my report. <>

<> 2741.223 Earth Standard. Our transport docked at Claer Arian Station, and my crew and I mustered to shuttle downworld. A blond male in a black station guard uniform called me for an urgent message and led me to a work alcove, and a second man with facial irideco joined him. There was no message. Instead, they demanded my data. I ran, but they cornered me, stunned me, and searched me. A third man with extreme facial mods forced me aboard a small insystem ship. We landed on Melusine, where he ordered me to a new AnvilCo site. <>

Teak stopped abruptly. <> Your report ends there, Seren. <>

<> I'll finish it when I know more. <>

<> Saved and filed. <>

The central vri flashed an arrival warning, and text marched across the air beneath its display zone. Wall screens showed a small craft hovering down with its honeycomb lights ablaze, then settling onto the dome's fused-glass apron. Its faded port-side registration started with MC . . . an old MitraCorps ship, a survivor of its lost world of Mitra.

<> Teak? <> she subvocalized.

Teak stood smiling beside her for an instant. Then he shimmered and blinked out. *Why?*

A new screen lit. Maq Flett walked a corridor with another man, taller with close-cropped hair, nondescript clothes, extreme face mod. *The dreg.* She stared until she realized the door had opened silently behind her back. Too late, she spun.

"Still fighting your own war," Damou said. "Who's winning?"

Seren straightened from her defensive stance. *Not again.* He'd returned to afflict her, still surly because she'd fought him. What did he expect, grabbing her with some ridiculous tale?

"Meistr Flett, I need to go home." *Report. Turn over my data. Find my family.* No matter how outraged they were by her alleged act of treason. *Tell them in Tirion.* The words ran through her mind like a line from a song.

Maq Flett shook his head.

"You can go to Claer," Damou said. "You get transport and a new identity."

Why now? Why not an hour ago? It couldn't be that easy. Seren waited.

"First I get your data and comm implants."

Closing her eyes for a moment, she fought a dizzy wave of fear. *Think.* She could rebuild an identity, and her data files would self-destruct if he tried to open them.

"My data belongs to the Politaya Fleet."

"No fleet. No government. You want to help your people, turn over the data."

So you can peddle it to Pact intel? Seren managed not to laugh.

Hasi frolicked past her to sit on Damou's foot. Seren expected the roach to kick the little animal across the room—but perversely he picked it up and stroked its sleek head.

"My slate," she tried. "I want it back."

Damou lifted one shoulder in a shrug and reached into a pocket.

Seren took her worn old slate with an unsteady hand, and her eyes stung with relief. It held all that was left of her life. The dents and scratches came from that time in the war when—something happened. Details wavered in her memory.

"Take the implants," she said.

Damou told her to sit at a worktop and roll her sleeves. Flinching from the sight of his face, she looked over his shoulder as he scanned her forearms. On Claer people who looked like Damou, acted like Damou, got help. They didn't lurch around the Pol raising havoc.

"Why do you have bone pins?"

"Late in the war we ran out of medical supplies," Seren said. "No bone lattice, no regeneration agent. When I broke my arm, they used old-fashioned titanium pins."

Maq Flett tapped his hand display. Seconds later a black-veiled woman in black robes with hennaed hands—another Claeran—brought a tray and uncovered a surgical kit.

"Are you captive here?" Seren asked her in the only Tariqa dialect she knew, looking away from the small ceramic instruments.

"An exile like you, and grateful for refuge."

"You were in the fleet?"

"Station clinic. We fought in our own way."

"The war's over."

"Not till Claer is ours again, God willing."

A cold spray hissed onto Seren's left wrist and then her right. She felt only a slight warmth from the laser blade, not the painful slash and probe she expected. Somehow, they had acquired a registered bead extractor.

"Done."

Instantly, she knew her deep isolation. Her retinal overlay was gone, and now she lacked even her comm's faint background presence. Her hovercam lost its hold on her ear and fell. *Blind, deaf, touchless, scentless. Alone.* She'd been without her wrist implants for a few minutes when she received her adult upgrades, but that was among friends in a sanctuary clinic. Seren swallowed a cry of raw terror and forced herself to open her eyes on this empty world.

Then she felt a warm spray—nskin to start healing the incisions—and realized Damou had cheated her again. "Why did you seal me? Where's my new identity?"

"Now you're untraceable."

Alone. Silent. It wasn't his decision to make. *I didn't choose this.*

The Tariqan woman nodded to Maq Flett and left in a swirl of black robes.

Damou put his hand on the worktop's palm plate. When the screen lit, he slotted the data and comm beads they'd pulled from her arm and laid his slate on the data port, saying something quietly to Maq Flett. Then he was on his feet and heading for a larger worktop across the room.

"Maybe you're even trickier than he thought," Maq Flett said.

"Whose side is he on?" Seren's mouth had gone dry.

"Greys have no side." The geologist glanced at his palm scroll and dropped into a chair.

Maybe. Some Greys were well-regulated contractors on hire as security forces to low-population worlds. Others were predators backing up glitz runners or backworld despots. She could guess which category included Damou.

"Claer Arian—what happened?" Maq Flett asked.

Seren studied the vri zone, empty now that she had no implants to access it. She might as well answer. Damou had probably told him anyway. "We came in from the war zone travelling sublight for months on a disabled transport. Two thugs grabbed me on the station docks, but they got the wrong person. They wanted someone called Takahara. Then this Damou lurched in, drunk or spun up, and got in my way."

The small man's gaze took in her bruised and abraded face. He produced a green stick that was a good imitation of Claeran emerald and turned it end over end. Seren examined her arms. A narrow pink line on each brown wrist was all she had left of her implants.

In minutes Damou returned. "Nothing."

"Forget it, she won't help you," Maq Flett said. She still couldn't place his voice. It might tell her what he wanted from all this. Neutrality, or some Pact backworld?

"Maybe." Damou grimaced. "I need the data you carried."

Seren kept silent. *Why, when you just pulled my implants?* She'd already said too much. She didn't plan to tell anyone anything more, not until she reported in Tirion on Claer.

"You were on Gandhi Base."

Never heard of it. But any answer was dangerous with her memory full of chaff.

"Damou can protect you if you're carrying the treaty data," Maq Flett put in. "Mitran spooks say we're not the only ones interested in what you know."

Treaty data? Mitran intelligence? It hadn't existed for seven years since Mitra died. And she needed protection from Damou, not protection by Damou.

Maq Flett was silent as he viewed a retinal overlay, judging by his eye movement. "Try this instead. Tell me about Teak Kuhan."

So, they'd snooped her slate. Seren froze her impulse to lash back: it was all on record for anyone who knew how to look. "Captain Kuhan briefed my mother on MitraCorps mediation protocols." In her home orchard, where the bright rain fell like mist, she'd been picking russets with her guardian woodcat sprawled at her feet and winged unsects clicking in the apple boughs overhead, when he came to meet her. A man from a world of desert and ice couldn't know that Claerans in Tirion thrived on wet and cold; he'd pressed her hand between his warm hands—

They were still waiting.

"What can it matter? Captain Kuhan is dead." Even now she could barely say the words.

Maq Flett snorted. "I died at Come-by-Chance and again at Montane. It felt like hell, but not half as bad as getting dragged back to life."

Seren looked blindly away. It was a cruel joke to suggest that Kuhan had been revived. After the Pact acquitted him, he'd gone home to his family just before the plague swept Mitra.

"Why did you help him out?"

Seren gave the easy answer. "They were going to execute an innocent man."

"Most people thumbprint a petition—they don't record a vri to put forward new evidence, steal the prime minister's yacht, and run a Pol fleet blockade heading for a Pact mainworld."

"Who told you that?" Her documentary *Rain,* never seen on the vri grids, was an hour of raw images thrown together in one afternoon by a frightened schoolgirl.

Maq Flett nodded, and she realized she'd just confirmed a guess. They were playing her when she should be playing them.

Given time, she might drive a wedge, set them against each other, but there was no time. And Damou was a liar. He would never take her to Claer.

Find what you lost. But she had no implants to show her the way home. *So improvise.* At the open display niche of antique navigational instruments, she touched the bronze sextant again. No alarm.

Damou's ship sat outside on the apron. If he'd left his boards unlocked, she might have time to start the engines and lift. Maq Flett she could manage. All she had to do was get past Damou. He was close behind her again when she turned.

Seren's hand clenched on the ancient sextant. *Now.* She swung the heavy bronze piece at Damou's head.

3

Memory betrayed her, and again she was hunted in the wrecked station ringway on Claer Arian. Again, the predators cornered her. Again, she fought for her life against the blond station guard and his winger till Damou took over . . . Again, she got in one good blow. Then she sprawled face-down on the dome's living carpet with his knee in her armpit and her arm twisted up hard enough to break if she struggled.

"Friend, friend, love Seren, love Tas, nothing bad, friend, friend," Hasi cried, running back and forth in distress.

"Get away from me. You can't have it." The words came from Seren's mouth, but in another woman's raw voice. Behind closed eyes she saw black doors on a drab corridor that curved sharply. Not Claer Arian, some smaller station.

"Flashback," Damou said over her head.

Seren opened her eyes. *No escape.*

"Do I have your word not to attack me?" Damou sounded amused, damn him.

"No."

Tears sprang from her eyes as she tested his grip. His left hand rested beside her head; a code pattern was lasered on his wrist. Only the worst criminals went to prison. She shuddered.

At Maq Flett's command, wall and ceiling panels brightened

around the tac room, and the big vri display came to life. Damou released Seren, and she got back to her feet, shaken and sick. But she hadn't missed Damou completely. Blood soaked his collar and chest where she'd slashed the sextant across his ruined face. His shirt was absorbing the blood, and his face scabbed over as she stared. He had integral medical nano. A backdoor augment from some Grey lab. *Freak.*

She forced herself to search the twisted and discoloured scar tissue of his face for human likeness. Mud yellow eyes like some extinct wild dog, dark hair, dark skin. Either he'd needed full sun treatment to survive some high-UV world, or his ancestry was as mixed as her own.

"You're a liar and a thief." Somehow, she kept her voice steady. "You promised me safe passage, then sold my labour and ripped my implants."

"Your comm implant was corrupted, Lieutenant Qasri. Someone jacked your signal." He weighed her with open curiosity, and Hasi sat on his shoulder chirring and rubbing her glossy head under his chin.

"You can't mistreat a prisoner of war," she tried.

Maq Flett said, "You're not a prisoner."

So, she had no protection at all against a Pact that razed whole worlds.

"Green, you're adding it up wrong. And Tas, it wouldn't kill you to explain things once in a while." Maq Flett recovered the sextant and put it back in its niche.

How else could anyone add it up? He'd grabbed her on her home station and dragged her to a barren moon when she desperately needed to be in Tirion on Claer. Seren stood her ground, though behind her back her fists trembled.

"You intercepted a courier in the Bight off Gandhi Base." Damou stepped within arm's reach, and Seren tensed to fight. But he only folded his arms and said, "I need the data you took from her. You did the right thing. What happened wasn't your fault." He was almost polite when he wanted something. His voice had no discernible accent in Peel, the primary Pact language, but he spoke more exactly than a Pacter.

Liar. "Why do you need it?"

"Classified." But then, to her surprise, he went on. "War

crimes records. The courier carried data that was vital to negotiation of the Politaya-Pact treaty terms. Now the treaty's been written without that data. In three standard days it becomes law. Disastrous for all of us."

All of us? Human space revolved slowly in the vri zone. The Bight was a dim region of scattered dwarf stars and dust lanes in Politaya space out near the Tripline. Panic stopped her breath again; she'd been off Claer many times, but never to the Bight. And she'd never felt this urgent need to get home. "Why would a courier be out in the Bight?"

Damou hesitated but said, "Uncharted mirror transit nodes. A quiet route for a courier from the Tripline to Neutrality space if we can't trust mirror comms. I need that data. The war's over. It should never have started. We're not enemies." He held out a hand.

"I don't have any data. You took my implants."

"Your data implant was blank," he said.

"You're lying. Again." She ignored his hand, and he let it drop. Hasi slipped back and forth between their feet as though it could weave them together.

The Grey turned his slate to show her a screen that listed no indexes, no files.

"So? You razed it."

Damou shook his head. "Blank. You have another implant or bead. I need it now."

Seren looked up from the slate and winced at his terrible face; she couldn't help it. He looked away abruptly, showing her the more disfigured side. *If you don't want to be stared at, don't get a sickening scaremod.*

Maq Flett shot Damou a warning glance. Interrogation teams did this routine, one friendly and one tough. Maq was the friendly. Pact agent? Or another Grey like Damou? One minute they worked together, next minute not. Who were they? What did they really want?

"Let me tell you what started this war," Maq said.

Greed, obviously, and a history of aggression. The Pact had burned through its own easily exploited resources, settled its own marginally habitable worlds, and coveted the richer Politaya worlds. Claer system had vast deposits of rare earths and precious metals; Pamir had natural alloys and advanced mass drivers. Pact forces had occupied the backworld of Anansi on a pretext of aiding in a local dispute, and within a tenday launched a Pol-wide attack.

Seren eyed Maq Flett, recognizing a snare. "Let's hear the Pact version."

"Don't know it, don't care. Just the truth."

His offer made Damou scowl, so she nodded yes.

"Stupid bastards panicked. They saw a shadow on the wall and decided to fight. Never occurred to them to ask politely for help. You Pols were supposed to surrender the first day, but you fought it out to the last lifeboat. Your hired Greys warned you, but you didn't listen. Now everybody's wrecked."

"Really." She'd at least expected a believable excuse. "What kind of shadow?"

"Good question." Maq Flett turned to the big vri zone. "Where did you spend the war?"

Her fleet signals work was a vague memory. It felt years in the past. Not that it was their business. "Claer. Fleet headquarters. Shipboard."

Maq Flett persisted. "Remember Gandhi Base? Listening post back of beyond named after an ancient saint? Signals intelligence crew monitoring Pact transmissions?"

Seren covered her eyes with her hands as another fragment of memory rocked her. *Fire and blood. Ships blurring in from the Tripline and the Deep Outside. A blaze of white light.*

"Trauma?" Maq Flett asked Damou. "Or deep cover?"

"Memory block. A clumsy one, or it wouldn't trouble her. Leave her alone."

"Thank you." Seren pushed back her hair with shaking hands. They stood there discussing her like a lab specimen—and she had just thanked the monster.

"Lieutenant Qasri." Damou made another futile attempt at courtesy. "You'll suffer emotional bleed-through, reacting to stimuli you're not even aware of, until the block's removed. I can take you to a Neutrality neurological clinic."

"Go to Grey space with you, after you abducted me and ripped my implants?" Instead, she would seek her own cure at a Claeran sanctuary clinic that she could trust with anything she recovered from her fractured memory.

He lifted one shoulder and looked away.

The big ceiling vri zone brightened at Maq Flett's word to highlight Grey space, a breakaway silver vein glowing eerily through green Politaya space. A few stars blinked silver. He said, "Claeran refugees are heading for Grey worlds. You're better off there than Claer."

"My family needs me." *The fleet needs me. Tell them in Tirion. Tell what happened out there, somewhere, in the burning mist.*

"Too dangerous. What you can't remember makes you a moving target for whoever blocked and abducted you." Damou's expression was unreadable behind his awful mask. "Or do you plan to keep attacking people at random until you work it out?"

Seren tensed.

Maq Flett took a step backward from her anger, but the Grey only waited. Not many people excelled at the art of stillness. Actors, priests, assassins.

"We don't know who grabbed you on Arian," Maq Flett said. "Pact security detained Tas—"

"No." Damou cut across him. Then to Seren, "Wake your slate."

Seren's screen showed a message sigil that hadn't been there when they stole her slate. Delun Qasri's eyescan seemed authentic, and so did her voice. Seren listened three times through an ache of unshed tears before it made sense. Her mother said, "Do not return. Your name is on death lists. Trust the friend who carries this message."

"Why can't I reach her?"

"Unknown." Damou almost said more, then thought better of it.

Missing or dead. Seren might as well be dead if the data implant truly was blank. Never to go home again—but she had to go, had to report. "Another thirty-five standard hours absent without authority, then I'm a deserter."

"Tell us about Gandhi and you can go."

All she could remember was fear and danger and betrayal in the deep dark. The room grew hazy and cold, and somehow, she lay curled on the floor.

"What in hell?" Maq Flett muttered somewhere overhead.

"Worked it out, some of it," Damou said, "and knows enough to be afraid."

"Good."

"A Claeran pulled between sworn obligation and block-induced commands? Not good. Who knows what she'll do."

Seren pushed away Damou's offered hand and got to her feet, swaying until the tac room came back into focus. She folded her arms, trying to look more certain than she felt. "I'm going to Claer. You can't keep me here. You'll be liable under Claeran law."

Damou studied her for a moment and looked at Maq Flett. "Not alone. Under escort."

Seren nodded. On Claer she could lose Damou.

Maq Flett dropped his fake-emerald stick into a pocket and got up. "Sure thing. I'm going to Tirion anyway to bid on resource allocations."

"Why am I here? Why are you doing this?"

No answer. Who gave the orders, the Pact eco-wrecker or the Grey thief? Seren gripped her old slate, thinking of all she'd lost.

Damou opened the door into the walkway. "Claer."

4

In the dark between worlds, barely shielded from hard radiation by a fragile shell of carbonglass and titanium, human identity became fluid.

"Choose," Damou said, gesturing through a grid of portrait images that scrolled above his virtual comms board in the dim cockpit. In the navigation board images, the moon Melusine had shrunk to a pared-fingernail crescent orbiting an outer ice world in Claer system.

Seren unbelted and drifted forward to reach the list. As it scrolled down, she gestured to a woman with a freckled face under auburn hair. "This one."

"Inka, immediate global update," Damou said on voice-only comm.

Good luck. Global update was a high-level function that took hours or days even with top security clearances. But Inka, whoever or whatever that was, worked at AI speed far faster than a ship's brain. A second later the Azande's galley fabricator panel activated and spat out a small object. Maq Flett kicked back to the passageway galley and came back with a thumb-sized plastic card. He handed it to Damou, who slotted it on his board and called up the identity.

Marta Vuong was a Politaya Fleet transport pilot who'd flown backworld routes through the war. The file linked to Seren's own biometrics—DNA, iris prints, gait, fingerprints, voice and features recognition, breathprint—but should redirect any query to Marta's mythical bio file. The changes would spread as a carefully engineered virus across grids and databases, all but standalone systems that would update if she accessed them. Damou handed back the card, satisfied with his criminal list of false identities. *Global update. Impossible.*

Floating with her foot kicked into a hold-down, Seren examined the card's random wear. It would do, if she looked remotely like the image. "How do I synch appearance in this file?"

"You don't. We synch you," Damou said. "On Claer Arian."

Seren tensed but pushed away the memory of her abduction on the station. People who could call a global update in seconds could probably get her quietly through Pact-occupied Claeran customs. Then she could make her break.

Maq Flett was filling a coffee tube in the galley. She asked him, "Why am I a pilot?"

"Might as well be legal, seeing as how you like to steal ships."

Including this one, if you blink.

"Don't try it," Damou said.

Seren ignored him. "I'm a lapsed civilian pilot. You gave me a Class One rating."

"A civilian pilot who flew wartime missions," Maq Flett said.

Seren opened her mouth to deny it, but didn't. *I flew in the war?*

"We'll run you through basics." Damou unlatched and kicked away from the pilot chair.

"What if she has a blackout?" Maq Flett asked.

"Flashback. But she might be right. We can give her a safer identity. Clerk or cleaner."

Raze that. Seren eyed the chair and the stripped-down navigation and pilot boards. The Az lacked style and comfort, but despite its battered exterior, everything seemed to work. She checked the time on her slate. Twenty-one hours back to Claer. That left eleven hours to report in before she was posted as a deserter.

Damou latched into the nav chair. "Learn the flight manual

before mainshift. Should be easy for a Pol signals lieutenant. Or did you let your ratings pull the heavy work?"

Basic flight training again, but with the instructor from hell. Seren ran her checks and laid her slate on a data port to copy the flight manual. Then she suctioned the slate onto the viewscreen to record their passage through Claer's inner system; her eye cam and hovercam were dead without her implants. More images for her next vri, just taking shape in her mind.

"Take control." Damou pulled his hand from the navigator's glove. No warning, no transition with autopilot. Dangerous, to say nothing of bad manners.

Seren pulled herself down into the chair and muttered her acknowledgment of the handoff. "I have control."

The Pol fleet had recon and patrol ships built by Azande AirSpace on Mitra like this craft, and Seren had been backup pilot for Mam's small senate-leased Az. Still, she was a low-hours civilian pilot, and this was a highly modified ship in military configuration.

Virtuality swallowed her as she thrust her hand into the pilot glove and dropped the eyeband in place to check their status, badly missing the implants that could have linked her directly with the ship's brain.

The ancients dreamed of flying: this was their dream. Even the clumsy eyeband and glove let Seren fly within the vri display as part of the ship: another moving spark in space, gliding through the great void with a freedom and grace impossible to land-born creatures. Calling up near space, she rotated its image, and readouts scrolled across the cockpit. Her touch highlighted objects in the display—rocks, moons, scattered detritus—as they slid past beyond her eyesight. An asteroid expanded, then expanded again until she saw detail. The ship ran smoothly on an odd combination of ancient analogue tech, new tech that was still experimental when the war started, and heavy redundancy.

At first, she flew in raw panic, but her movements grew easier. She drew a virtual line of blinking blue dashes from their silver spark—a Neutrality ship in interworld airspace protocols—to the outermost Claer Arian nav beacons that flashed in red, green, and white. Text scrolled near the top of her field of view. Damou had been flying on subvocal commands and auto. Everything looked good. She hoped. Trying not to clench her glove hand, Seren stared into dark space that had become her greater self. It was like playing a vri game, she told herself. *Simple. Easy.*

"How does it feel?" he asked inside her brain.

Seren tensed as she sensed his presence in virtuality. *Only a lover should be in my head like this.* The right man, senselinked in virtuality . . . Quickly she said aloud, "Fast. Powerful."

A disembodied amusement. Some physical reaction to her thoughts had bled through her guard. Careless. Seren fumbled for the vri bridge control, accidentally turned up the cockpit light panels instead, and quickly damped the pilot-nav link as furious heat rushed into her face.

Minimal hand and eye movements and his slow heartbeat betrayed his presence, and an echo of strange icy music full of escalating chirps and booms like a symphony for glacial insects. Listening, it was easy to get drawn into the pattern. Finally, he nodded and sat back to watch her struggle with the unfamiliar cockpit. Seren puzzled over the board. Damou had rerouted all pilot, nav, weapons, and comms functions to both forward positions. Crazy, flying a four-crew ship alone; too much could go wrong. A solitary hunter. Men like him—privateers, pirates— were stock villains in lurid vri thrillers. It should be amusing, but the war had made their threat real.

On the virtual touchpad floating near her chair arm, the large bronze square should be autopilot. Labels and heads-up checklists on the surplus craft were not in Peel, the Pact language used throughout human space, but in Damotik; Mitrans had perversely used their own archaic languages and alphabets. Seren pointed to the sigil, and mercifully the actuators engaged. The craft yawed to match its programmed course. In virtuality she felt Damou's attention sharpen; he was probably wondering if she understood Damotik. Let him wonder.

Checking Damou's course on a virtual screen, she found a mirror transit neatly laid out in complete disregard for safety via a node that didn't exist.

Illegal. High-risk. A test. Permit the transit, end up questioned by a Pact occupation patrol—or kill the transit, dump them in a space traffic lane.

"Request reason for off-charts mirror transit."

"Speed. Security. Silence. Do it."

Seren left the transit in place, cursing him. "Course confirmed."

Displays rippled and rewrote above the boards when the ship declared its route, reporting no local alerts, and Seren glanced around the dim cockpit she'd barely glimpsed on her unwilling flight to Melusine. Most freelance Greys and privateers crusted their ships in decoration. Their bridges, passageways, even outer hulls carried heroic-scale murals, plunder, and semiprecious stones arrayed in exuberant Tripline deco. Instead, this ship was stripped to its struts and braces without a gram of dead weight, and its bare cockpit had the clean smell of a well-kept machine. Damou even ran low-gravity like the Grey companies, so the food fabricator was probably full of bone mass supplements. To a Pol, running low-G meant less eco-debt. To a scavenger like him, it meant less cost and more profit.

Damou opened his restraints and floated out of the nav chair, reaching to punch up schematics on her pilot board. His right sleeve was rolled up above his old-fashioned metal comm bracelet, exposing tan skin that looked as smooth as a child's, as though he'd also once had implants ripped and nanohealed.

Maq Flett reclined in his chair playing with one of his gem sticks; this one looked like opal. Hasi clung to his knee, grooming her barred tail.

"Lahal," he told Seren, seeing her curious glance. "A game of skill. You hold different carved bones or sticks, and the other guy's pointer guesses which hand."

Seren took the fake-opal stick from his outstretched hand. It feels real, she opened her mouth to tell him—then realized he'd spoken to her in her mother tongue. A Pacter who spoke Claeran Tavod? She said, "Good imitation."

Maq grinned. "Want to play?"

Damou was a standard-issue Grey thug, but she couldn't suss Maq. Yet. "Show me how."

"Set auto and swivel your chair."

Maq pulled out another lahal stick, opal with a dark band inlaid around its middle, and set a foldout table to local gravity. He tapped his palm scroll to call up vri, and suddenly they were surrounded in the cockpit by men and women in flower-embroidered shirts and jackets, clapping and waving their hands as half a dozen people behind them sang to the beat of flat drums.

Maq held up his closed fists. "Now you guess which hand's got the unbanded stick."

Seren pointed to the left. He opened both hands and showed her the plain opal rod in his right hand, the banded one in his left. When she watched more closely and beat him on the third round, he crowed in delight.

"Heya. Somebody new to play."

Till Claer Arian—then she could lose them forever in the station's familiar back corridors and service chutes and make her way downworld.

Damou guessed two hands, won as impassively as he lost, and returned to watching the viewscreen. Even Hasi got more excited over the game. No wonder Maq wanted new opponents.

Seren picked up a handful of the finger-length sticks Maq laid out. Clear green, blue, cloudy violet, metallic, black, all excellent copies of fine natural gemstone.

"Like the emerald stick? Bet you that against a five-minute vri on Melusine," he offered.

"Fabbed here?" It was a good copy, with the intensity of gem-grade Claeran emerald.

"Natural."

"You're on." Her slate held enough stock shots of Melusine to build a short vri. A Pact geologist wouldn't like what she had to say about his company's destruction of Melusine, but that was his problem. As a vri maker she sold her skills, not her ethics.

"Now you guess. Next, we play a full round with twelve tallies." Maq held up his fists and waved them while the drummers pounded and sang.

Seren pointed left again.

Maq won. "You owe me one vri. Give up, Green?"

"Hide it again. I'll have that emerald." Floating with one foot hooked in a hold-down, she eyed his waving fists carefully. Her next guess took it.

"One thing I don't get," Maq said, handing over the emerald stick. "Why you kept making vri dramas that got you in crap. First the protests, then the government banned you, then they threw you in lock-up. Why jail a producer of art vris?"

Seren bit back a sharp answer. Her dramas *Poison* and *Rain* and her other three docs, all banned during the war, were minor releases even in the Politaya. How did a Pacter know? "It was a needless war. If we'd kept talking, we could have found a peaceful solution."

"Cassandra complex, eh? You told the truth, and they didn't believe you."

"Orpheus complex." *But I failed—I brought Teak Kuhan back from the dead only as an avatar.* Seren shrugged. "Not prudent."

"I'll take truth over prudence any day. Your throw."

Something in the forward display caught Damou's eye. He grabbed a holdfast and somersaulted down, unnervingly agile in low G. A proximity alarm blatted.

Seren froze in shock for an instant, then glanced at the pilot board. An amber blip was closing fast on their stern.

5

In five pulses the blip resolved into an overtaking ship on visual display.

"Evade." Damou flipped over into the nav chair as Seren swivelled. Maq was already latching into the comm position behind her right shoulder, tapping the controls to read his implants. Hasi gripped the bulkhead netting, motionless for once.

Why evade? Another ship in visual range was unusual but scarcely threatening. When she pointed at its silver spark in the display, Damou's ship yielded full registration information. The other ship was blocking scan and running dark.

A chance to break free. Seren latched in and gloved her hand to claim control of the ship. She could lay a course for a free port, fab medication to knock out the others, drop them, and burn for Tirion—

"Get Qasri off the board," Maq Flett said quietly. "She'll do a runner."

"I trust her to do the right thing."

Seren bristled—but he'd accidentally invoked a bond she couldn't break. *I trust you to do the right thing:* Teak Kuhan's words in the dreg's mouth. Scowling, she activated full restraints, slapped on the eyeband, and hit the manual override. As

29

acceleration boosted the gravity, a shower of abandoned lahal sticks clattered onto the deck.

Damou's manual controls were so hair-trigger that a twitch sent the Az leaping forward all but out of control. After a jittery start, she steadied the ship within a moving image of near space.

Maq live-hailed the other ship, demanding identification. On her own comm pad, Seren watched him key through emergency frequencies and back to standard interworld comm in case they transmitted up-frequency like the Grey companies. High on her receive band, her sensors flashed, and she heard the faint hiss of an open link. Someone was listening, but no one spoke.

"Hold your heading. Let them match speed." Damou sounded insanely relaxed about an unidentified ship roaring in on their wake.

Why would another ship shadow them? Maybe Damou was worse than she thought, a criminal on the run from the Pact—but Pact enforcers wouldn't run dark.

Seren watched a hail of small white sparks fan out toward them from the other ship. Virtual decoys? Real drones? She couldn't risk a collision. As near space became a deadly three-dimensional hazards course, Seren wrestled the Az freehand, far beyond her piloting skills, barely keeping control. She couldn't do this. A careless tremor would kill them all.

The other pilot changed tactics, looped his ship into a hard burn past them and came back at blinding speed in a flash of dark metal and composites, swept under their hull, and streaked away. This was insane, impossible. Then Damou was in her head again. "Go."

Seren pulled back hard, rolled the ship onto its stabilizers, and burned after their attacker. A Mitran patrol ship could take Gs far beyond its rated stress load; she'd discovered that

in the Bight. In a dark place between the stars, dodging a black teardrop half the size of their recon ship. Her weapons hand disobeyed her order not to fire

The memory clicked into place as neatly as a DNA segment, freezing her hands on the controls, and she was back near Gandhi Base as the universe turned itself inside out, flying for her life.

"Stay on them," Damou breathed.

It seemed easier now, though local space gave them no nearby moons or rocks to slingshot or dodge behind, and Claer's star was only a searing yellow dot. Seren pursued until she saw the hostile ship streaking away. She accelerated and matched headings, but the hostile ship skipped in and out of visual range. *Get them.* This desperate ferocity was new. *Them or us.* Steadily she closed the gap.

"Lose speed."

They coasted barely slower even when her hand relaxed in the glove.

"Who are they?" she asked.

"Politaya pilot, maybe, all fire and flash. If it were about piloting, you'd have won the war."

"How would you know? You spent the war sitting dark off mirror nodes to hit unarmed freighters." As Seren had spent the war listening and parsing and coding, until a ship scorched in from the Deep Outside

at Gandhi Base.

Damou only grinned horribly at her insult and lifted his eyeband to study the viewscreen. "Now they'll come back. Tumble us."

Seren gestured randomly at the red virtual pads, and their ship shuddered into a dizzy lurch. She watched through slitted eyes, swallowing convulsively to keep her gorge down as they rolled and yawed crazily. This ship was faster and far touchier than the recon ship she'd flown off Gandhi Base that last terrible day. Behind her Maq swore in an unknown language, and Hasi moaned. Then Damou's hands were at his controls, correcting their tumble to a sluggish drift.

The hostile ship dropped speed and came about to investigate. Seren flew them within visual range, and Damou brought up the other ship in his navigation vri zone. Magnified, the larger craft was metal and composites under patchy black enamel, sharp-nosed like a freight rocket and raked at the stern like a Claeran offshore sailing yacht. Modified stabilizers and big actuator housings looked like Grey design. A specs scan turned up Landfall Aeronautics, early in the century. A Pact ship with Grey mods. Not unheard of in Pol space, but Damou looked puzzled, if she could read his occluded face. He slid his hand into the weapons glove. *Weapons insystem? Are you crazy?*

The Landfaller rested against the night, visible only as an elongated curve of reflected starlight and deeper blackness, until it emitted one brilliant spark that lit the Az viewscreen. Damou squeezed his hand and loosed a high-spectrum laser bolt that struck a shower of sparks off the incoming object. It seemed unreal till Seren saw the puff of glowing debris that marked a silent distant explosion. Live ordnance—*gods*.

Seren reached for her weapons glove. "Take them!" But Damou grabbed her hand away before she got near. Augmented reflexes. *Grey freak*.

"Bloodthirsty for a pacifist."

Seren met his stare. "I'm not the one flying a surplus patrol ship armed like a destroyer."

Shaking his head, he dropped her wrist. "We have an image. Go."

Seren burned away. It made no sense, turning tail. Most privateers would have disabled the Landfaller, boarded, and claimed it as salvage.

"What in hell?" Maq demanded.

"Hit. Heist. Who knows." Damou glowered at his slate, an old titanium-ceramic model that looked like MitraCorps surplus. So did the comm bracelet on his right wrist and the chronometer below the prison code on his left. And the ship. Maybe Damou himself was MitraCorps surplus. The best died, the dregs survived.

"Remember something back there, Green?" Maq looked out into the star-shot blackness that seemed to hang motionless around the ship.

Seren didn't move, didn't breathe. *Not yours to know*.

"Flying in the Bight?" Damou asked with too-deliberate patience, as though he'd rather shake the memory out of her.

Seren gazed out the viewscreen, remembering that other system where a solitary station orbited a brown dwarf among rocks and dust. *Give a little, get a little*. "No one cared about regs by the end. Our last pilot was recalled. He died at the Wairoa Cloud."

Wairoa was the Politaya Fleet's last-ditch action to halt the Pact fleets outside Pol territory, either a brilliant display of rash courage or a wasteful display of stupidity. Now it was a rallying cry for the damned Claeran globalists who'd clamoured for war five years ago.

"I regret your loss," Damou said unexpectedly.

Seren nodded as heat rose to her face, mercifully invisible in the dark. Did he know she'd lost more than a crewmate? A sweet man, and they'd spent good times together, to the disdain of her old schoolmate Mihal; before the war the pilot had been a fabricator tech. Gods, Mihal was on Gandhi too. *Mihal Villandry Biron, Medical Officer.* Her memory stencilled the words beside a dented black door in a narrow, curved passageway.

My turn. "How do you know about the Bight?"

"You sent a high priority mirror-comm message to Tirion HQ."

Seren had never sent a mirror comm in her life. "What did it say?"

"No way to know. Transmission was cut off."

What would a Grey know about Pol fleet comms? Seren turned to stare, but she couldn't read his ruined face. A small doubt tugged at her. Why tell such an unlikely lie?

The other ship didn't follow. After a while Seren put the Az on autopilot and relaxed enough to wipe sweat from her face with a shaking hand. When she spared Damou a glance, he was calmly keying in a log entry.

Seren tested her new memory fragments of Gandhi Base. Everyone there was in disgrace for one reason or another, serving time on a remote and useless outpost. Long shifts punctuated by meals and workouts and sleep. Cramped quarters. A dim alcove that passed for a signals office. So many jury-rigged repairs that by the surrender they joked about not having to walk out into space like poor Fazil; one day the station would quietly fall apart and leave them floating. Pawel and Yan, whose love flowered in that barren place. Others whose names she almost remembered . . . The harder she tried, the more her memory retreated.

Her slate chirped from the viewscreen. An hour of pilot-viewpoint recording would show a running chase between two Grey ships in Claer system. It could fit into a new vri documentary on the war's final days. But external links were maddeningly clumsy and slow, and vri production required full data and comm implants. *Never run a vri console again.* She had nothing else left to lose.

6

The pulldown berth on the cockpit bulkhead was hard and narrow, but it was an improvement over the cargo hold. They were still running in microgravity. Seren settled cross-legged, knees tucked under the straps, to check her slate. She stretched its screen to a double handspan and scanned her indexes. Damou had probably killed or corrupted her files.

But her image files looked all right: friends lost in the war, gatherings at home, the five-metre sloop she raced for her school cup in hard winds off Gwynfa, her art glass ovoid from Mam that the thugs stole on Arian, prewar sequences of Tirion and the native grass preserves, a forgotten still that looked like night fires in mist, blurred but weirdly beautiful. She could use that; found images and wild sound had provided some of her favourite effects in vri docs.

Even her Teak templates seemed intact. Her hand hovered over the gestural pad, but without implants she could no longer invoke her virtual aide subliminally; the avatar would be visible to anyone nearby.

The other two were discussing her in the passageway—did they intend her to overhear?—and Maq's restless intensity had an edge of anger. "Tell her."

Damou's voice was almost too low to hear. "Leave it alone."

Tell me what? Leave what alone? She badly wanted to know, but she wouldn't find out by asking.

Silence grew until Seren looked up. Damou drifted near the pilot chair, studying the void. Maybe he'd come to tell her—whatever—and changed his mind. He handed her a small copper oval pierced at one end. "Storage. Fabricator's not locked. Make anything you need."

Secure, high-yield Mitran memory beads were costly and increasingly rare. From another man it would be a generous gift. From Damou, it was a reminder that he knew the contents of her slate. Seren backslotted the bead into her slate as he went aft.

Alone in the cockpit, she opened the slate's back. Found her message still safely inside, folded small between nanocircuitry and plain titanium-ceramic shell. Smoothed the biopulp paper. Pressed it to her cheek. Traced the familiar words in a stranger's exact handwriting. *In your debt. Kuhan.*

In twenty-eight standard hours Seren Qasri would be a deserter. *What would you make of me now, Teak?* After their meeting over a handful of wet apples, even after his death, she'd tried to live by his standards. In the end it had cost her family and work and freedom, but she'd known she was doing the right thing. Until Gandhi Base.

Seren closed her slate and overhanded aft to the head through the dark passageway. Maq snored gently on a pulldown berth in the hold, but Damou lay with his eyes open and sat up in one swift movement. When he saw it was only her, he rubbed both hands over his face and his short hair, looking almost human. He didn't depilate his chest hair. *Primitive.*

When she came out of the head, he sat with his eyes closed, leaning back against the bulkhead. Floating in the passageway, she decided his face was like a cosmetic mod in reverse. Discoloured and overgrown scar tissue extended down past his right jaw. The left side was relatively unscarred, but even that twisted and pulled toward the right. Maybe it wasn't an extreme scaremod, maybe it was real accidental damage he refused to nano away.

Sickening, but like a good theatrical mask, it had a certain fascination. Shadow made it a death's head. Backlit or underlit, that face could be terrifying or tragic in the hands of a good vri director. Mostly he kept the scarred side toward her—unusual—and his body language shouted, Keep your distance. As if anyone wanted closer.

Sleep eluded her, and after locking the cockpit hatch, she settled in the narrow pulldown berth.

<> Teak. <>

<> Seren. <>

Running on her slate without implants or even clumsy skin-contact leads and eyeband, Teak shimmered out, then slowly regained shape and substance in the dim cockpit. She'd spent a long time crafting his simage as a work of art, highly detailed and personalized, more complex than any commercially available avatar. Seren motioned him to the nearest empty chair, the pilot's, and couldn't help smiling for the simple pleasure of seeing him again.

<> Teak, find Senator Delun Qasri. <>

<> Claernet is down, Seren, and your mother is not using any alternative service. <>

<> Try another grid. <>

<> Cantonlink is up. Senator Qasri has connected there in the past. I'll list her records. <>

The link pulled in prewar Claeran parliament records and a handful of Mam's senate reports, nothing else. Then the vri zone shivered, and the files blinked out.

Seren fought down panic. She would find her family, make things right; it would just take longer than she'd hoped.

<> Teak, find a man called Damou. Keywords are thief, criminal, Grey, abduction. <>

<> Nothing, Seren. New search? <> He frowned slightly.

Seren had coded that frown, remembering how the real Teak Kuhan had driven himself to solve problems, find answers, make things work.

<> Stand by. <>

The avatar shimmered again—what was causing that shimmer? interference from Damou's ship?—and blinked out.

In her battered old slate, one data bead lay stored apart, excluded from voice command, but Seren knew her way to it by touch. She gestured to open it index by subindex, and she laid down full encryption to leave no trace as she expanded it through the cockpit system. The Mitran code she'd gathered over the years should shut down any trouble from the ship.

Scents of unknown spices filled the air. Another world blossomed in her senses, a world of pale gold brick and tawny stone, ochre scrollwork around bleached ivory doors, shadows tight underfoot at midday: Tanna.

Seren smelled dust and tasted dried fruit, and Tanna's heat struck her like a fist. Then Teak Kuhan walked through an archway into the latticed shade of a dry garden in the lost village. He had been the youngest of Mitra's nine Grey captains, famous for his lightning campaign on Churinga and his peace negotiations on Alma. The heat hadn't troubled him, since his own world either scorched or froze beyond its great cities in a narrow terraformed belt.

As he walked, Seren stood closer than his skin, breathing with his breath, matching his steady heartbeat. His hair smelled of some lemon soap, and she felt the warmth rising from his tan face. He had paler creases at the corners of his eyes from working under a brighter sun, maybe from laughter. She isolated his image, rotating it as she gestured for editing tools.

Kuhan had always stood out. Beneath his ironclad Mitran rectitude, Seren had seen humour and warmth. Long before his arrest, long before Mitra died as a human world, she'd viewed everything she could find.

The Mitran Grey companies had evolved from a world defence force to deep-space rangers that could intervene on planetary surfaces or in the long reaches between the stars; their ships were fast and agile with fearsome striking power. Kuhan's company kept the peace on a dozen worlds and inspired a few breathless vri dramas. The Grey captains were tactical field officers as well as strategists. Often, they ended conflict before it began for a staggering fee that was still cheaper than war.

In their hands the Neutrality held balance of power between the first wave of emigrants that had settled the Pact and the desperate second wave that had pushed farther outward to Politaya space. Now the first-wave Pact had invaded the Pol, the Grey companies had deserted their second-wave allies, golden Mitra itself was a plague-swept ruin, and on any given day it was anyone's guess who held balance of power among the scattered suns of human space.

Teak Kuhan's simage looked soberly back at her, distinguishable from a living man only by the faintest marginal halo. Her restless hands colour-corrected it and lifted the hard shadows that a distant blue sun had slashed across his cheek and under his jaw.

Seren found an old clip of herself leaning on a grand fir, her feet crushing a scent of damp soil and slow decay from the moss, and with a gesture she set Kuhan's image beside her own in dappled forest shadow. Next to a rawboned Claeran like her, he was narrower, darker-skinned, and lighter-haired with startling eyes, not beautiful but striking; a son of many cultures from a brilliant lost world of the Neutrality.

Kuhan had never posted a senselink—he valued his privacy— but not long after they'd met, Seren had programmed her own. Now that was all she had, and she longed to touch him. Her slate deployed a virtual body mesh as she lay back, and she

<> leaned forward in a long slant of forest light to touch his warm shoulder. A scent of lemon and bruised grass rose around her as the senselink animated his portrait. He looked into her eyes as his warm hand touched her own.

<> Teak, I've missed you. <>

<> Long time, Seren. <> His voice was warm but precise, a Mitran voice.

In the cool morning light that slanted between great trees to the fragrant moss of the forest floor, Seren abandoned all other times and places. They

<> <>

Nothing. All virtuality vanished in an instant. His touch, the morning light, the woodland, gone. Seren sat up abruptly. *Gods.*

She scrubbed her face with shaking hands, staring at the empty cockpit that had been forest. Cold fire sprang up in its place: iridescent fractals that turned restlessly, formed and dissolved, twisted and inverted like flames in a wood fire. Or a dry river delta, or a ganglion . . . then the image coalesced, and a woman gazed out from a walled courtyard, a woman with light eyes and black hair curling over perfect golden breasts. Shocked to stillness, Seren met the other's stare for two seconds. Then the woman flicked one hand dismissively, and was gone.

In the globe of mist, a point of light tumbled and spun rapidly to a spark of light, a ball of light, an explosion of light so intense that Seren saw the bones in her own raised hands through her closed eyelids, and clear through both, saw lightning dazzle and arc around the cockpit with a roar that hurt her teeth. Voltage crackled through her body, throwing her off the pulldown. The dim lights winked into darkness.

"Qasri? You all right?" Maq Flett was hammering on the locked hatch.

Seren kicked over to open it. Her Mitran slate was hot to the touch, and a scorch flower decorated the bare composite of the bulkhead. The violent electromagnetic burst would have burned her badly if she still had implants. Shock was giving way to anger.

In the dark a woman's cold voice said, "We have enough trouble. Get out."

"Inka," Maq said. "Nice of you to drop by."

Damou swore in Damotik, gave Seren an indecipherable look, and turned back to the hold.

"Who is she? Why did she attack me?" Seren demanded, but Maq only shook his head.

Hours later the ship gave a take-hold warning on approach to mirror transit. Insystem? *Impossible.*

But Seren felt the ship's actuators engage. They would fold gravity wave on wave and thrust through a single point in space—marked by virtual beacons and trajectories on the nav screens—to an adjacent universe, and beyond that to others, finally emerging elsewhere in this universe. She felt an instant's complex dislocation, and the ship inverted itself at the uncharted mirror node that dropped them into Claeran high orbit.

7

ES2741.225

Slow pan. A cloudy green and blue world bracketed by two golden moons. A silver spangled backdrop of stars. Three glittering rings of a great station that spun on a kilometre-long core. Beautiful and unflawed from space, an optimal world of the Politaya.

Damou brought them in, sweeping past Claer Arian's upper-ring commercial and military docks to a private bay on the high hub. The docking membrane stretched and parted around them, and a crew ran out service pipes. Seren stopped recording to free her restraints.

"This won't take long," Maq said.

"Arian customs was the slowest in the Pol even before the occupation," Seren said.

But he was right. A Claeran customs officer and a Pact noncom came aboard for a minimal exchange of courtesies with Damou, barely glancing at Maq's card or even Seren's newly forged card with its image of a red-haired woman. She'd seen offworld diplomats endure hours of customs interrogation—and these two got through in seconds?

Maq led the way to an opulent corporate lounge. Four years ago, when she boarded her troop ship in hand restraints, even a day ago when the damaged transport disgorged her crew onto a wrecked military dock, she hadn't imagined disembarking to a discreet cosmod salon and boutique fab booths.

Cosmod felt like a frivolous waste of her back pay. Seren had kept her own plain appearance for years. Maq waited outside the salon, taking no chances on her bolting, until a convincing Marta Vuong emerged with freckled fair skin and rusty shoulder-length curls set off by deep green daywear.

Damou powered up the Az, and they drifted the ring for Claer. No shuttle ride for a Pact kleptocrat.

Seren's homeworld came into detailed view on their long descent across the southern continents. She monitored the nav board from habit, but her attention strayed to the viewscreen. They passed over the scrub deserts and farms of Tariqa, the Ayiti Archipelago in the West Sea, the pasture and croplands of Nevez, and finally Tirion city among the narrow valleys and wooded hills of Bryniau. In the southern distance the Gwynfa glaciers glittered in autumn afternoon light. *Home.*

Eleven hours still on the clock, plenty of time to report and demobilize—but the Az swept past Tirion's spaceport and roared on through deep atmosphere toward the northeast part of the city. Seren turned in irritation—was he drunk or spun again?—but Damou was talking into a hand pickup.

As they dropped, the devastation that was invisible from space came into clear view. The Bryniau region was badly scarred, and she glimpsed particle-beam melts, bomb craters, ruins, and more grievous damage. Several great groves and their sanctuaries had disappeared absolutely, without even stumps to show where the planet's oldest woodland had flourished.

Scattered farms punctuated the deciduous forests with their small houses and outbuildings of settlement-era whitewashed timber or tawny native Claeran hewnstone. The newer ones sprawled in grey grownstone.

Claer's vast prairie had become woodland centuries ago in an old-style terraforming project, long before full-scale nanoforming. The original second-wave survey team had found plants resembling sedges, bromes, and grasses that undulated for thousands of kilometres, broken only by topography and open water. The wind had swept the plants in kilometres-wide catspaws like the fur of a great golden animal. A few species of native life forms still survived in their own habitats, including the thumb-sized many-legged flyers called unsects. Even after terraforming, immense tracts of grassland survived as nature preserves—or had until now.

A huge new complex stood on a plain of bare red earth, sprayed against erosion with some shiny plastic. A few houses had burned, though their orchards were still green. A Pact fleet spaceport marred the native grass preserve. This occupation was more than a resource grab, it was cultural assault and ecowar.

Inexplicably, Damou headed for Tirion's citadel square. Landing there, even hovering, would break a dozen regs—but he talked steadily on comm as he slowly dropped the Az into the northeast corner, where data kiosks and street theatre groups had always taken advantage of the huge shade trees. An armoured Pact soldier waved them in to land, and Seren's heart lurched at the sight of broken paving stones and shattered stumps.

"I can find my own way from here."

"You wouldn't last two minutes," Maq said. "You don't know what it's like now, Green. Your friends are in labour camps, unless they resisted and got sent to the arena. Women and kids aren't safe. Hell, no one's safe."

Damou nodded once. Somehow that was more convincing than Maq's wild claims. Even before the Az shut down, Maq tucked Hasi into a cubbyhole, rummaged in a bulkhead arms locker, and tossed each of them a shock shirt.

"You can't be serious." Seren folded her arms.

Not answering, Damou stripped off his work shirt and dropped the shock shirt over his head. It shimmered and flexed as he moved, but it would harden in layers to repel any projectile or blunt weapon. Maq did the same, then pulled out two assault lasers. Seren turned away to pull off her top and drop the shock shirt, and it retracted neatly under her jacket sleeves and bodice. Quality, not like the coverall the thug had given her after she destroyed her uniform.

"Recolour your clothing," Damou said. "If you wear green, they'll think you're a holdout."

His expression froze any argument. She saw his face was ashen with a sheen of sweat, and his hand trembled when Maq handed him a weapon. A loser who profited from others' trouble, frightened at the sight of real conflict—but despite her contempt, his fear touched a chord with her own blind terror at her fragmented memory. Kuhan had always said fear was a friend, that it taught people caution. Seren touched her slate to rehue her clothes to deep grey; damned if she would choose Pact gold. It got her an ironic nod from Maq.

Tell them in Tirion. Time to report in at last, but now she'd remembered enough to know it would destroy her all over again. Had Kuhan ever grown tired of doing the right thing? The Bight wreck had happened on her watch; she was responsible.

Seren stepped off the Az ramp and down into Tirion citadel square. Two patrol ships and a few hovers were parked nearby, and Pact soldiers had checkpoints at the two main entrances. A few others were patrolling in pairs, but only a few Claerans were visible in the square or nearby streets. On one side of the square, the central maglev terminal now ended in a bomb crater, where a temporary wall of cellulose sheeting had torn and healed itself so many times it had lost all transparency. She stared in disbelief at the islands of burned-out flats and gaping cavities that had been shops. A Tavod scrawl in soap on an abandoned shop's window announced a workers' general strike two months ago; she wondered if any of the strikers survived.

Seren swallowed tears. Her city, famous for street music and theatre café-bistros and flamboyant festivals, lay in silent ruins.

Damou and Maq Flett flanked her on the pavement. A Pact lieutenant examined Damou's slate and passed them on—with weapons carried openly? Then, to her dismay, a detail of armoured Pact troopers fell in behind them, fanning out to the rubbled pavement margins. Seren bridled at having a Pact guard to walk her own city, but Maq warned her with a glance. This wasn't the time; she could raise her objections at Pol fleet headquarters. Protocols had evolved in other wars, other occupations, to allow for free movement of civilians, but she saw little sign here of Claerans going about their daily business. That would have to change.

Tirion citadel must have taken the worst hit. But as they walked three blocks south on Hafn Boulevard, she saw more ruined buildings that hadn't yet repaired themselves, standing amid broken grey grownstone. Movement among the wrecked buildings went still as they passed. Maq slung his assault laser under his arm once they left the square, but ridiculously in the late autumn sunshine, Damou kept his weapon at the ready and watched the shadows.

Maq saw her confusion and said, "Irregulars ambushed Pact troops when Wilm Nolin had his people clean out your museums and galleries. He ordered the city razed."

"Wilm Nolin?"

"Pact deputy secretary of defence. Greedy little bastard worming his way into power."

Picking her way around a wall of rubble, Seren must have overshot fleet headquarters. She turned back to see only a mound of broken grownstone that shielded a crater and spilled across the pavement. She put a hand over her mouth at the smell.

A woman hunched on the broken stone, silently rocking herself like the old water-seller Seren had cast so carefully for her vri drama *Poison*. Seren approached her in a rush of remembered feelings. Blocking out her scenes, she'd recorded herself or her friends as the water-seller and her daughter, the gang leader, the chorus of the dispossessed. Now all her *Poison* characters walked beside her in sensory memory.

Seren kneeled. "Mother, are you well?" The courtesy was meaningless here. "I seek fleet headquarters."

Damou took one step closer as though to intervene, but kept his distance.

"All dead." The woman raised her head. No older than Seren. She gestured toward the crater. "The Pack shot them as we pulled them from the wreckage."

Delphia Accord, 2532. Full medical assistance to be granted to prisoners of war. Had anyone recorded what this woman claimed, that Pact occupation troops had killed the Claeran wounded? Getting to her feet, she hesitated. In a small city the woman might know her family. "Delun Qasri? Her sister-friend Parvin Kerkallec? Rhian Qasri Janusz? Daoud Qasri Gwyn?"

"All gone."

Seren heard the words fall like stone chips, and the world blurred dizzily. *No.* But she forced herself to ask, "Who is in charge now?"

The woman shook her head. "No one. Do you have food?"

Maq offered her a protein strip, and the woman pocketed it, edging away with a wary look at the Pact troopers. Seren stared into the crater. Down among the tangled service tubes and fallen grownstone, a swarm of unsects quarrelled over something unrecognizable.

Damou said nothing when she returned, not even *I told you so*, but she avoided his eyes. She didn't need his pity. What a fool these two must have thought her, obsessed with reaching fleet headquarters in time and certain that she could report in, demobilize out, maybe pick up a civilian vri contract.

"You could have told me." Her voice was a rasp. "Damou could have explained all this on Arian instead of grabbing me."

Maq shook his head.

"I'll stay here." Seren stared blindly past them at the empty buildings. She could go to the family house, see if it survived.

"You'll die," Damou said. "Not in a good way."

"Who cares?" she blurted, one breath away from tears.

"I do."

"The things you want to know—I still can't remember." Her eyes finally spilled over.

"You will." Damou sounded almost sympathetic, and that was unbearable.

Seren got control of her voice. *Tell them in Tirion*. She couldn't report in, but she could try to recover her memory. "Derw Sanctuary. Is it standing?"

Damou nodded, looking away so she saw only the scarred side of his face. Strange man.

"Dark in an hour, Green," Maq said, checking his palm scroll.

Shadows deepened and ran together as they walked back to the square, climbing in eerie quiet toward the sunset. Their footsteps sounded clearly, and the hum of unsects in a broken tree seemed loud. Half a block from the graceful arches and spires of the Hafn Gate, a transport hover sighed down onto the street, and Pact soldiers wrestled crates out to the pavement. Seren raised her slate to record. The shadows disgorged swarms of people who fell on the crates, and in seconds all were gone. *Wide shot, enhanced light. Feeding time in the ruins of Tirion.*

Stunned to silence, Seren saw nothing as the Az lifted and flew the two kilometres northwest to Derw. Her home lay another kilometre west. The Pol surrender and Claeran occupation were common knowledge on her return from the war zone, but this she hadn't known, hadn't understood. *All dead.* Head in hands, she tried to absorb it all, checkpoints and ruins and food swarms, and barely noticed when the Az landed.

A good kilometre from Derw Sanctuary, they put down near a dirigible tower beside the main road. Flashes of light silhouetted the big trees on the northwest horizon. Three armoured hovers in Pact camouflage shot past, heading north. Maq was busy combing the comm bands, and Damou was talking into his hand pickup.

Seren unbuckled and headed for the arms locker—she still wore the shock shirt; now she needed a weapon—and lifted out an assault laser. When she turned, Damou blocked her way.

"They need my help," she said.

"No," Damou said, holding out a hand for the laser. "They don't need one more to bury."

What can it matter? Everyone I loved is dead. "I can go armed or unarmed. Your choice."

"Lieutenant, you're under oath and obligation. Stay alive, protect your data, wait it out. If you need to die, die for a good reason."

A Grey dreg, lecturing her on duty? Knowing he was right anyway stung her to fire back, "Who do you think you are? Roach." In low Tavod, she made a detailed anatomical suggestion.

"Good." Damou grinned evilly. "Keep fighting."

Seren flinched as another flash lit the sky, closer this time. Silently, she handed Damou the laser. He shoved it back into its niche and palmed the door lock.

"Coming this way," Damou told Maq.

"Time to go. You'll have to take the waters another time, Green."

Derw lay just beyond those trees, a five-minute walk, but Seren was denied sanctuary. Numb with her loss, she buckled in and sat silent as they flew southeast. By the time they overflew Tirion again, Damou was on comm arguing over a Pact takedown contract.

"Inka," Maq said quietly as Damou protested.

Seren's hand still stung from Inka's electromagnetic attack. "If Inka's his tasking officer, it's a wonder he's still alive."

"Nailed that one, Green."

Damou won his argument and turned down the job.

Maq told him, "Qasri is priority."

"Inka knows, she just doesn't want to know."

"Tell her to smarten up or screw off."

"Inka's crucial. She archives all that's left of Mitra."

"Dangerous."

Damou lifted a shoulder. "I can handle Inka."

"Let's hope so."

"I'll leave you at AnvilCo's hostel at Tirion port," Damou said. "Keep an eye on Qasri."

"Under escort for one day, that was our deal," Seren said wearily. "Not for life."

"Time to think carefully about your next step," Damou said. "I return in forty hours."

"Why are you doing this?"

"Some things we do over and over till we get them right."

What does that mean? Seren weighed her options. A Pact corporate hostel seemed more survivable than the alternative, struggling without family in a starved city. "Then you'll take me where I want to go."

"Yes." Damou wasted no words: it was the one thing about him she didn't loathe.

Seren nodded.

Maq tossed his gold lahal stick from hand to hand. "Sunny up, Green. Bet you this stick I can show you something to stop you in your tracks."

As if the last few hours hadn't already stopped her. A day ago, she'd been planning her future. Now she didn't have one.

"Who judges?"

"You judge. Fund your next vri."

"All right. Hide your sticks."

A Pact war profiteer funding a Pol deserter had a certain justice—but she guessed wrong, and he pocketed his gold stick.

What now? Everything had changed.

Leaving her world in ruins to hide on Melusine was

unthinkable. She would stay, gather images of the occupation, find ways to help restore Claer. A year from now she wanted to stroll a leafy Tirion boulevard, not a ruin. For the first time she had no refuge, no family, no friend, no plan. *There's always a way.* If only she could find that way.

8

Doll Sorrow crouched in the dank shadow of a bombed-out building. Her augmented night vision picked out her six other freaks, their powerful humanic shapes with brindled fur or glossy scales ready to spring, to kill. Doll was boss, the smartest and fastest. The shadows sheltered other fugitives like her—chimerai, manimals—altered from human infants or embryos to talking pets with fur or scales or wings by extreme cosmods and interspecies breeding programs.

An unlit dark hover slid along the littered back street, and Doll saw its infrared sweep pick a route toward her. When it slowed and settled on the broken pavement, two norms climbed out. Doll went to meet the brown man and a taller red-haired woman. The man smelled of fatigue, but not fear. The woman leaned on the hover, afraid but curious. The restless small animal chirring by her foot might be a bodyguard, but Doll doubted it. More likely a databank and vermin hunter.

Noob and another jackal cross drifted in from the dark to sit on their haunches beside her. Then the man gave off fear scent, and the woman at the hover gathered herself to attack or run. Numbers, not appearance, worried them. Smart norms.

"Doll Sorrow?" the man asked.

Doll showed her narrow, curved canines, and her fashionably

shredded clothing lifted in the stinking breeze. Doll needed no clothes—with fur she didn't feel the cold—but the shreds made her human. "You want?"

"Your owner brought you here from Walden and dumped you, I hear."

"Too big."

The norm stared at Doll a long time, making her want to tear his throat or run, but his curiosity carried no scent of malice. "Got work?"

Doll lashed her tail and kept silent.

"Brought you something."

"Man meat?"

"Cash card to buy work slates. Go buy a shirt with the change. I've seen enough half-naked women for a lifetime. Plays hell with my concentration."

"Fuck?" Doll offered.

"Consensual, thanks." He shook his head and sighed. "I hear you're a serval cross."

Doll hissed and flexed her claws, grinned to show her canines, and turned a slow vamp of her spotted fur and barred tail, growled, hissed, purred, the whole freak show. Then she crouched to leap an easy five metres in one smooth motion. A swift runner and fierce hunter had provided her gene splice, giving her an old Earth wildcat's spotted fur and clown smile. But Doll was no longer a captive child.

The norm nodded, impressed.

Biz time. Doll asked, "Work slates, what else?"

"Think. Talk."

"Do?"

"Later." He dropped a bead case and a cash card into a mesh bag, and Doll hooked a claw in the mesh to seize it. Someday she would buy hands.

"*Wassit bead?*" Doll lapsed into tox chat, testing the norm.

"Vri drama called *Poison*. Green woman who made it, they put hunters on her."

"*Sabat?*"

"*Sabat yoos*. Suffering humanity trapped in a toxic slum," the man said. The woman opened her mouth to speak, then shrugged and nodded.

"Why now?"

"Big trouble coming, but humans still fight each other."

"Your problem, norm."

"Your problem too. All humans."

"No more tricks. No more lies." She sniffed the case dangling from her paw, opened her mouth in disdain, and tossed it. Noob caught it between his crushing jaws.

"Time for humanity to grow up," the man said. "Time to work together."

Doll coughed, not a human cough, as their signal to go. In barred shadow ten metres away, she looked back. The small brown man stood smiling at the sky as his animal explored the dark crannies. Only the woman gazed wide-eyed as though she'd seen something wonderful.

Seren watched them slide back into shadow and dropped her slate into her pocket, unused. Doll Sorrow wouldn't take kindly to being recorded, but she'd be a powerful vri subject. Chimerai on Claer? Human-nonhuman gene splices were dismissed as myth on Pol worlds and only a rumour on Pact worlds. But here they were, intelligent and beautiful and deadly. Yet another thing she wished she could show Kuhan, not the avatar but the real man.

"You won that call," she said, wondering if she'd have another chance at his gold lahal stick. It could keep her alive for tendays. "Why are they here?"

"Hunters. Some track and capture fugitives, then fight them in the arena. Some are children's nannies or bodyguards or companions." Maq popped the hover's bubble, and the doors clicked open.

"Why did her owner abandon her?"

"Had her gene-spliced as a kid for his personal entertainment, probably, then couldn't handle her any more. I heard she outran a snuff."

Seren considered what that meant—slavery, rape, mutilation, and attempted murder, for a start—and felt sick. Some Pacters said chimerai lacked human feelings, but no one had told Doll Sorrow.

9

ES2741.226

A deep roar of operating equipment washed over the Claer Arian military docks in familiar waves as Tas worked, and an overheated gantry servo over in the commercial sector shrieked like a damned soul. Every time the station's atmosphere membrane parted to let small craft in or out, the dock breathed sweat and perfume and food. Today, samosas were outselling potstickers.

The starboard cannon mount had jammed open. Tas laid in lubricant and worked the hinge until the struts folded neatly into their storage slots; then he latched on a nanowire and lowered the assembly into its hexlock crate on the dock. He released his safety line and crossed the bow between bristling sensor arrays to the portside cannon, giving his full attention to his balance.

In the first years after his world died, Tas had grasped at equilibrium like a falling man. He took himself away from humanity to the wastelands or to deep space, where vast forces shaped creation and human flaws had no meaning. Now humanity was no longer unbearable, only a different species in which he'd let his membership lapse.

Once he'd laid hands on the old Azande command ship—infinitely adaptable, upgradable, rough-looking but smooth-running enough to meet his needs—he'd carved a niche transporting dangerous goods. One slip with hazardous chemicals or military-grade explosives would briefly blow an Az-shaped hole in this universe. So. Every day was a good day to die.

His aft laser and missile launch assemblies detached smoothly, and in an hour, he had every trace of ship's armament stowed in a MitraCorps lock-up. Tas rappelled down to dock level and retracted his safety line.

Fifteen hundred, station time. On schedule, plenty of time for his client meeting. He floated rescue equipment up his ramp, stacked medical supplies in his lockers, and stowed survival gear in the hold's cargo nets. When he finished, the Az was no longer an armed patrol ship but a long-range search and rescue craft.

"Taso. We've got a live one."

Tas sent the empty cart back to the dock and turned to find Renat leaning on his ramp, posed like a fashion spread. Today even an old friend wouldn't know Renat except for the swirl of inlaid gold and rubies on his command comm; his skin and long hair were deep-sea indigo, his face bore swirling blue irideco patterns, and his pants and tunic were midnight blue silk snapped with raw sapphires. He looked like a sea spirit from the masked theatre.

"Contraband seizure," he said. "Freighter inbound from the Tripline. We may see action." Renat lived for the rush; his pitches tended to stress the immediate, rich, and dangerous.

"I drift the ring in forty."

"Travelling unarmed?" Renat raised a brow at the empty weapons positions. "If you want the risk, pull the pay."

Tas tightened his cargo cords and tested them, backing up the inertial load stabilizers. Searching for the scattered Mitran survivors would reimburse only his supplies and fuel, but his last two contracts had paid promptly, so he could coast on his lease payment. His old company could handle a contraband job without breaking a sweat, and anyway, he'd seen enough action to make him a walking spare parts depot. "No. Thanks."

"Taso, don't cack me. I know you want back in." Renat always sounded cool, his voice at odds with hot eyes and incendiary temper, and he'd left his Evrotas accent somewhere on the hard road from Mitra.

Tas shook his head, not trusting words. There was no turning back. The new MitraCorps thrived on the postwar power vacuum. Things had been different in a strictly regulated corporation operating under old interworld law, but now Mitra was dead of plague and MitraCorps was in every way ungrounded.

"Frigate with fighters?" he asked reluctantly, ambushed by habit.

"Four patrol ships. Riordan balked on reasonable force. But four's enough, never fear."

Tas nodded. Trust Jaime to take the job, then release a fraction of the needed personnel and transport. How many would he kill this time? As MitraCorps director-general, Jaime Riordan liked to play hands-on with the companies, but he didn't grasp the post-Mitran reality.

"Dump the med kits and join the party. Easy money."

Generally true. Most smugglers were overarmed but careless. This one probably unloaded glitz on the occupied Politaya worlds and back hauled prisoners. Inner-world Pacters paid fortunes for exotically modified humans; robotics or nanotechnology would do most jobs, but offered no thrill of illicit domination. Shutting down even one of the slavers would save lives, preserve families. A step in the right direction.

"Not this time." Tas scrubbed his face, scouring away the passing temptation.

Renat stepped away from the ramp with fluid grace and flashed Tas with his slate strobe, blinding him for an instant. Then he threw a headlock on Tas. "Not last time. Not this time. Turned desker?"

Tas angled his shoulder to break the lock, and a foot behind Renat's knee put him down. They sprawled on the dock laughing and wrestling like the wild kids they were once. Renat got up, dusting off his silks. Tas glanced at his chrono. Thirty-two minutes till he drifted. In seven minutes, he met a client, and if he lost his safety margin now, he'd have to burn hard. Low energy reserves on his return could cost him the last faint hope of tabling Qasri's data at the treaty talks.

"All right, Taso?" Over folded arms, Renat gave him a long look tinged with concern.

"Turned priest, Ren? Good as it gets."

"We need to talk."

"You need to talk." Tas picked up the last supply crate. Renat meant well.

"I know about your hands. What's your game, selling identities?"

"Not what you think. Leave it alone." Tas managed not to look at his own hands, feeling his calm start to fray under Renat's jagged edge of anger. A few minutes with Ren were an emotional carnival ride—humour to horseplay to concern to rage—as changeable as his look. Thirty minutes left.

"You're going bad to worse. You like bad?" Renat tapped a puckered and ridged pattern in the irideco swirl on his cheek. It looked like a Claeran corporate logo. "Prisoner dissed me. I carved this out of her slow while she told me her life story."

Tas shrugged and hefted the last crate up his ramp. Ren loved to provoke shock and outrage. His stories usually held a grain of truth, but no more. He glanced back from the hatch. "Looks infected. Check it for virals?"

"Never change, do you?" Renat fingered the trophy on his blue cheek.

"How should I change, Ren?" But when Tas looked again, he was alone.

10

Mihal Villandry Biron paced the corridors of his family firm's Claer Arian bureau, waiting to learn his fate.

Some sleepless nights he let himself think she would dance into his clinic, back from recording vri out in the Bight, and tell some joke she'd picked up from the crew. But those days were gone forever. Though Mihal searched the faces in every crowd, he never saw hers.

The Grey security specialist arrived punctually for their meeting. A man in a threadbare flight suit was scarcely the ultra-tech MitraCorps officer of popular vri adventures. Irritatingly, he wore a null mask that blurred his features within a thin holographic envelope. Mihal wanted to read his expression; he lacked patience to play masked mystery with an overpriced watchman.

The MitraCorps booking clerk had apologized that rates were high for senior personnel, that he could find someone to advise Mihal at a more reasonable cost. *I need the best,* Mihal had said. It was safer than, *I need the man who thumbprinted a death certificate for Seren Qasri.*

Mihal led the way into a Villandry Biron EntreMondiale meeting room with a large time-corrected window on space, not the most elegant room but the most secure, and indicated armchairs near the window. The Mitran sat and folded his hands, waiting.

"I wish to see your face, Herra Damou."

When the Grey touched his wrist and the null mask blinked out, Mihal realized his gaffe. The Grey hid not only his identity but a terrible disfigurement. Discoloured and overgrown keloid tissue marred his face, twisting even the less affected side. It was quite inexcusably hideous.

"Chemical burn?" Mihal tried not to react. Claeran military hospitals had seen worse cases, long since discharged, but it was many tendays since the war ended.

"Fire and chemical."

"I can recommend excellent specialists. It would be an hour's work and a day's healing at minimal cost to normalize the facial damage."

"Yes," the Grey said. That was all.

Mihal shrugged. *Mitrans.* For an unwanted instant, he saw himself in the Grey's eyes: finely tailored in neutral blue and grey linens that complemented his fair skin and hair, freshly groomed, subtly augmented, sitting at his ease among the room's beautifully executed full-vri paintings that murmured details of Villandry Biron EntreMondiale's most famous and costly projects. None of that mattered to Mihal now.

"This station reports the death of my fiancée Seren Qasri in an apparent abduction." Fiancée was not quite the word, but it was only a matter of time: eventually Seren would have understood, would have accepted. Mihal took a breath and continued. "You may have been the last to see her alive."

"No." Damou let that hang for a moment. "I found her body."

Mihal fought down a wave of panic. Then tears stung his eyes. Seren dead? All he had ever wanted was to keep her close. "How did she die?"

"Energy weapon. A laser shot to the head. There were signs of a struggle. That is all I can tell you."

"Why did you find her, not station security?" Would he really have to pry out each painful detail?

Damou studied him as if deciding how much to say. "Lieutenant Qasri's family was high on the death lists. I came here to extract her. Pact security intercepted me for questioning, and while they detained me, two unidentified contractors seized her. I arrived too late."

"Who hired you?"

He shrugged in the Mitran way, with a quick lift of one shoulder. "Client confidentiality."

"Why you?"

"Extraction is one of my specialties."

"Perhaps the body belonged to another woman." Even to Mihal it sounded like wishful thinking. This was an eyewitness, or as close as he would get to one.

"I matched her genetic identity and implants."

"Would you know her in person? Had you ever seen her alive?" It was hardly the moment to ask about his missing data, so dangerous to lose even with its unbreakable encryption.

"Yes."

"Your work for the Pact must require you to lie."

"To save a life I might lie. Lies don't help the dead."

"I don't believe it," Mihal said, surprising himself and perhaps Damou. "Maybe it was a cosmetically modified look-alike. Seren's alive. I would know if—I want you to find her."

The Grey folded his hands. "Tell me about the interception off Gandhi Base. I viewed the cockpit records. I went there. An unknown ship crossed the Bight."

This man was supposed to answer questions, not ask them. Sweat prickled under Mihal's arms. He had destroyed the patrol ship records with his own hands. "I was off Gandhi by then. I heard later."

"I decline your assignment." The Grey stood and looked down at him, amused. Insufferable. "I could search for Seren Qasri forever with no result." After a moment he added, "It's too late to change anything. And what you found could never be what you lost."

"You have no idea what I lost," Mihal said.

The Grey checked his chrono and walked out.

Mihal wiped his eyes carefully. It might take him some time, longer than he'd hoped, to recover from this.

11

Two shot on vri projection. Calling the bones in the hostel room to the beat of a dozen brightly clad drummers in the big vri zone, Seren won Maq's gold lahal stick and predictably lost it before their caffe brewed, then won it again. Hasi curled asleep in her lap, ignoring the drums.

"I quit." Seren pocketed the gold stick and dropped the twelve peeled-willow tallies in the middle of the table. It was only a matter of time until she lost again. Lahal wasn't really a two-person game even within a vri-generated setting, and Maq had been polishing his skills for a long time, judging by his deeply rejuv-stained skin.

"Play for points then." He handed her two iridescent sticks that could be bismuth.

Seren hid the sticks—plain left, banded right—but he called left in seconds. She pushed one of the tallies across the polished table top toward him.

Maq tapped his palm scroll for higher volume in the vri zone. As intended, the waving arms and drummers distracted her enough to call wrong. She pushed him another tally and sipped her excellent Tirion-style caffe, thick with cream and apple-blossom honey.

AnvilCo's hostel was nothing like a Claeran-style hostel with bare dormitories and commons. She and Maq rattled around in a grand suite with a handful of opulent bedrooms, a four-star food panel, and gallery-curated Claeran art glass and murals that she explored in vri for a fascinating hour. Its gym had good equipment and ten offworld gravity settings, and the huge library listed even *Poison* and her three other minor dramas. Everything was madly encrusted in a highly ornamented Pact style, but someone had put thoughtful design into the comfortable lounge and airy daylight solar. Maq travelled light and made whatever he needed, like most well-heeled people with fab subscriptions and implants, and he left his eyescan active for Seren to make anything she wanted.

All she wanted, though, was to escape this luxury detainment cell. If she could get back into Tirion city and sell her gold stick, she could see what survived and how she might go to ground.

Dropping her hands under the table, she arranged the sticks by touch. Maq pointed left.

Seren showed him the banded stick in her left hand. Sometimes she forgot they were enemies, at least not friends. "Beginner's luck," she said as he pushed her a tally.

"Beginner's luck yesterday. Today you're getting to be a tricky hider and a hot pointer."

Now was the time to suss out what Maq Flett knew and gain control of this situation. Damou returned in a day and a half.

"Why are you playing jail guard, Meistr Flett?"

"Sorry you see it that way."

"What's your interest in Claer?"

It took two rounds—one loss, one win—for Maq to answer. "Reminds me of home."

Her ambivalence to him hardened a notch. "And it has resources you can plunder."

"Thank your saints it's AnvilCo, Green. I hire Claerans and run a clean operation."

"Like Melusine?"

"Melusine's a lifeless moon."

"A nature preserve."

"I do what I can. You'll see worse." He got up to pour more caffe.

I do what I can—not, AnvilCo does what it can. Head

geologist, he'd said on Melusine. AnvilCo was a Pact interworld corporate, but she knew nothing about it. Seren tapped on her slate's virtual keyboard, "AnvilCo, key personnel."

Nothing came up in her grid search—nothing, not one hit, from billions of potential hits. Either it didn't exist or its vast power and wealth had hushed all grid data. Quickly she called up the Mitran code she'd used on Gandhi to bypass Pact security, and accessed the Pact department of industry on Walden. One hit, no detail: AnvilCo, sole proprietor Maq Edzo Flett.

Later, after Maq collected all twelve tallies and activated a privacy cone for a business call, Seren irised her bedroom door shut. The room was lovely, once she'd swept away its decadent rococo scrolls and fluting and worked out the subtle Mitran technology that ran it.

An oak leaf drifted down over her shoulder, caressing her senses with its cool, dry autumn fragrance; more leaves rustled under her feet. She'd set her living space to a sun-dappled Bryniau oak meadow beside a swirling stream. It morphed at a word to other Claeran places: the hikers' stone hut at Hafoty overlooking the Gwynfa glaciers; a starlit evening in the Tariqa desert; a cabin on a windswept northern beach on the Ayiti archipelago; a studio opening onto a tree-shaded Tirion square.

At her touch the desk's control surface tilted and glowed faintly green.

"Virtual reality imaging is now on. Choose input method," the vri set announced as it blinked to life.

Even without her implants, using the clumsy skin-contact leads and an eyeband, the system was better than anything she'd used in the Politaya Fleet. She ached to call up her virtual aide in the room's big vri zone, but that had gone badly wrong on the Az. Instead, she maxed her slate's screen and used 2D to evoke him.

<> Teak, a woman in Tirion said Delun Qasri was dead. <>

<> Seren, a woman in Tirion said you were dead. <>

Seren ran her hands through her unfamiliar shoulder-length curls. Her Teak avatar had been scatty ever since she returned to Pol space, shimmering out at any hint of signal loss. <> What does that mean? <>

<> I see no evidence for either your death or your mother's, Seren. <>

Seren gave up on that debate. <> A man called Maq Flett has me in detainment. How can I make a break? <>

<> Recover your memory. Learn what you can. Wait your chance. <>

Good advice, probably, but not what she needed. <> How exactly? <>

<> Hide your actions in plain sight. <>

A Teak Kuhan answer. One more question. <> I need to know about a man called Tas Damou. <>

<> No record exists for a man of that name. <>

<> Does Damou have a meaning? <>

<> One of the people, one of us, everyman. <>

<> Language? <>

<> Damotik. <>

Seren shook her head. Trust a criminal to use an untraceable name.

<> Next query? <>

<> Nothing. Thanks. <> Thanking an electronic impulse was foolish, but she'd coded the avatar with deep nuance and detail, and sometimes she forgot.

Teak was silent for a full two seconds, then spoke uninvited in his beautiful voice. <> Keep talking, Seren. Do what you know is right. <>

His familiar words stayed with her long after she signed off.

At dusk Maq asked the food fab for local fare. It produced galettes stuffed with cheese, onion, and salt pork that Seren would have savoured at any Tirion café-bistro, but wrestling with Teak's advice, she barely tasted the fine food. How could she do what was right? She had no idea what was right, now.

"Tomorrow let's fly to the Cantons," Maq said as they ate in the suite's balcony garden. "I'll show you something you need."

"Refugee settlements? I've seen enough suffering."

"Mitrans don't sit on their hands for long. They did a fast nanoform, raised some grownstone and livewood buildings, brought in your horticulturists for accelerated plantings, and settled in to produce vri and develop tech."

Mitrans? There couldn't be all that many survivors. "What do I need in the Cantons?"

"Friends."

"Grey friends?" Seren looked out over the night-scented gardens that surrounded this Pact corporate hostel. "When things got bad, the Grey companies withdrew and left the Pol fleet to fight alone."

Maq sighed. "You understand Greys, unlike most Pols. You know they had to quit, or they'd have gone down with you and fallen a lot harder. At least you still have a world."

"Do I?" *What good is a world if you have no family, no friend, no lover, left to share it?* Seren calculated her chances of breaking free in the Cantons: better than her chances here, and she could work on Maq. Her promise to wait for Damou didn't bind her. Whatever he claimed, she was a prisoner.

"Also—"

Seren sharpened at his hesitation. "Yes?"

"We might get you help with your memory."

Recover your memory, that was Teak's advice. Seren said, "But what?"

"But Tas won't know."

Good. A secret. Now she had a weakness to exploit, a way to wedge them apart.

The door chimed, and a slim parcel tube dropped into its delivery tray. Maq scanned his palm over it, shrugged and handed it to Seren. It was addressed to Marta Vuong.

One white rose with a silver cast to its petals and leaves slid from the tube. Seren touched a petal, releasing its scent of exotic spice. Cardamom, she thought, remembering to breathe again. Maq had been snooping her history again. Was this his idea of a joke?

But Maq denied any knowledge of it, gave her one uneasy glance, and went off to sleep.

Years ago, someone had anonymously sent an armful of these burnished white roses to her *Poison* opening night, shocking Mam and inspiring her cousin-friends to joke about her secret admirer. She had pressed one rose into a book and forgotten it— until now, breathing the same spice and admiring the same silvery petals.

Seren sat for long minutes with the rose across her palms, silently waiting for her heartbeat to steady. She breathed in the scent she'd missed for four years: flowering plants nourished in worldbound soil. Her orchardist and silviculturist ancestors had been among the few chosen for the second wave of emigration from humanity's ruined homeworld. Seren thought of her botanist father—Delun Qasri's dear friend who had died years before her own conception—and called the botanical garden in Tirion, hoping it still existed.

A senior horticulturist on night shift carefully noted her description and said, "We never acquired a silver rose, sadly, and the sequence is lost forever."

"Why?"

"Quarantine. In a century the engineering will probably revert or fail. They were bred that way." He added hopefully, "You wouldn't know a local source?"

Seren regretted not. After she ended the call, she held the impossible rose for a long time. Then, with a silent nod to her ancestors, she sealed a single petal into a message capsule and addressed it to the senior horticulturist. Not every good thing had to be lost.

Thoughtfully she compiled a two-minute montage of the artworks in the luxury suite and keyed an intro under a heading, "Claeran art in Pact hands: preserved forever or lost forever?" She posted it to the *Singularity* arts site as a beta, and before she signed off with an old grid name, smiled to see that a comment war was well underway. Even deep in defeat and ruin, Claerans loved an argument.

12

ES2741.227

The next day Maq signed out an AnvilCo runabout, a small mirror yacht with a flash cockpit in grey and silver like a top-end game pit. Its style was all Pact, grandiose but endearing, with its arabesques and motifs in thinly disguised composites. The tech was all Grey, with powerful converters and mirror cloaking over vat-grown sensor skin. Hasi looped around them in excitement for a few minutes, then went to sleep on Maq's shoulder.

As they lifted, daylight illuminated the mostly empty northern continent from low orbit. Scattered barren islands came into view ahead as they flew northeast, then the pale coastal dunes of southwestern Matawin. The Cantons grew into a green haze on the eastern horizon. Spring was well along in the northern hemisphere.

On their descent Seren glimpsed the Cantons' new city and scattered villages in late afternoon light, and Maq flew slowly enough for her to see the settlements below. She'd thought hard-headed Mitran refugees would draw straight roads and square islands of housing, but the Cantons looked chaotic, like a collection of neighbourhoods that hadn't quite grown together. Dogleg streets ran in every direction through city, woodland, and even farms. Cities on old Earth had supposedly been like this, organic and accidental.

Over a lake with a floating township of rafted gardens and houses, they dropped through the lower traffic lanes. On the far shore the land rose steeply to fall away in deeply shadowed ravines green with spring growth. Maq checked his dashboard map and descended toward a crease where cobbled streets of wood or adobe houses climbed crazily in every direction.

As they landed in a square, flame and smoke rose through an eerie reddish light, and Seren covered her face, refusing more destruction. Pact reprisals?

Craters and energy-weapon scorches scarred the cobblestones, and a house was in flames. No one was fighting the fire.

"We shouldn't be here. Let's go. Now."

But Maq had already climbed out, heading for a sheltered passageway. She followed reluctantly. It was no place for her new sandals and dress, but there was no time to fab boots and body armour.

A small girl ran into the centre of the street alone and stood lost. Barefoot and soot-smeared in a torn blue shift, she was four or five standard years. Her family had to be dead or injured to leave her wandering alone in a combat zone. Primitive explosives roared from another building, sending a huge billow of light and debris into the street, and there was a high whine as combat lasers speared red tracer beams around the child.

Small-arms fire came from an open window high under the overhanging eaves of the brown house opposite. *Sniper*. The tracer swept in the other direction. *Now*. It took no thought for a Claeran; children were too few. Seren launched herself to run.

Maq grabbed her arm, but Seren furiously shook off his grip. She ran straight out into the street, somehow ducking laser bolts, and swept up the struggling child. "It's all right, treasure."

Then a man in grey combat dress ran from another doorway and covered her and the child to safety under the flash and roar of high explosives. Mitran Greys? Three soldiers ran out to kneel in the street. One danced horribly when laser fire caught her and flung her to the cobblestones, where she now lay still. Another launched a heavy laser bolt at the window. One truncated scream, and silence.

Seren set the girl down in the corner of a doorway and crouched in front, sheltering her. The door behind her was locked and its palmplate hung out by its torn circuitry. She drove a heel into the door panel, and when the lightweight plastic gave way, she nearly plunged through it—onto a neatly raked stone garden.

"Cut," someone shouted out in the street. "Break for ten."

The small girl wriggled away and ran across the street, past the dead Grey soldier now climbing to her feet. A tall woman with scaled silver-blue skin brought the child a pair of fuzzy yellow slippers and led her skipping through the debris. Banks of red-filtered set lights blinked out, leaving the street in fading daylight.

Seren straightened, noticing for the first time that the grey uniforms and assault lasers were years out of date. *Fool.* She of all people should know better. She'd just crashed onto a vri set and ruined the scene.

Maq stepped out of his passageway, shaking his head. "You're not here to find a job, Green. Seren Qasri's dead."

"So why am I here?" she demanded.

"Later," he said, and went to touch hands with an actor and the silvery woman. Her skin was lapped in small fish scales, Seren saw up closer, blue-black with rosy streaks between her shoulders and paler silver on her arms and chest. A makeup woman who was working on an older actor had mauve and blue feathers. Transgenic mods on that scale were strictly black market in the Pact and rare even on Pol worlds.

Seren slunk toward the director, fumbling together an apology. His scaremod of parasites trailed glowing tracks under the skin of his face and neck, and a black cat in a jewelled collar followed at his heels. But as soon as she was in range, he slapped her arm.

"Great improv. Once a year casting calls it right. You're done. Print your card."

Seren took a deep breath. *Leave it alone.* "Thanks."

"Talk about throwing yourself into the spirit of the drama," Maq muttered.

"Just be glad I didn't capture their laser cannon." She wanted to stay, record images for her own future sets, compare notes with the director, but her work was stolen along with her family and her life.

"Ayuh. I can see the screamers—'Claeran attack on Mitran-exile vri industry.' No wonder Damou thinks you're a dangerous woman."

"Damou. Why does he call himself that?"

"Some Greys call themselves Damou on assignment. It's a high-risk life, being an assassin. Let's go. You've rescued enough Mitrans for a while. I should have told you they were shooting *Greys*."

"Shooting Greys," Seren repeated stupidly. She pushed hair out of her sweating face with shaking hands, close to hysterical laughter as her pulse finally slowed to its normal rate. *Damou is an assassin?*

"*Greys*. A vri drama series produced for Pol markets. Hell of a good story. This episode's the evacuation of New Honshu in the plague and attacks. Things got rough. Anyone who thinks Mitrans were all pacifists never saw a meeting of the focal, the world council."

A series called *Greys*, and the terrible death of Mitra re-enacted for vri. *Gods.*

The director called the actors and crew for their next take. Maq turned toward his runabout, but Seren could have watched all day. This was her culture, even if the crew flashed extreme Mitran mods and the actors spoke Damotik. As they climbed in, Hasi greeted them and went back to sleep. They lifted from the vri set as the action resumed.

"Who does all these mods?"

"Grey labs. Mitrans," Maq said absently, checking the dashboard map.

"I thought there were only a handful of Mitran survivors."

"Some people were offplanet when the plague hit. Students, techs, diplomats, MitraCorps companies on offworld contracts. Great travellers. God knows there wasn't much at home besides rock and dust and ice." Even aggressive terraforming had created only a small habitable area.

"One thing I never understood," Seren ventured. "If the plague was engineered as the task force said, how did it get past all that Mitran biosecurity?"

"Insider knowledge. The Pact needed a war and bought some Mitrans to help."

"I find that hard to believe."

Maq shrugged. "They screwed up—didn't plan to wipe out the

whole world."

Landscapes and architectures slid past below them at dizzying speed. They skimmed over stone villages, adobe villages, shining bezels of glass and carbon set among woodlands. A knot of spires and pyramids could be a commercial district, but it lay among farm fields and gardens.

"You saw Mitra?" Seren asked.

"Back when I transported rare earths and metals. Mitra was resource-poor, barely made it through the first century. That's why they started selling tech and defence offworld."

"Survival," she agreed. "We'll be doing the same now the Pact owns us."

"The Pact isn't anything like you think, Green. It has more minorities and religions and wonders and evils and pissant power struggles than you could imagine in your wildest dreams. But it is easily as wicked as those old Earth empires, and it needs to change." Maq spared her a sombre glance from small brown eyes creased deep in burnished dark skin.

Seren opened her mouth to argue and closed it again, chastened. She'd said similar things about the Pol. "I never expected to hear that from a Pacter."

"I'm not a Pacter."

"I wondered." It explained his accent and odd archaic slang.

Maq grunted. "The last frigate off Sitkum, the one you see in all the vris—I was comms three. We blasted our own wrecked station right into a Pact carrier, blew them all to hell, but it was already too late downworld, so we ran for Grey space. It really happened that way, for once the grids got it right. Now they make endless dramas . . . the Pact loves to mourn its enemies once they're tragically dead."

It was nearly three centuries since the Pact backworld of Sitkum declared for the new Neutrality and a Pact fleet nuked it to glowing cinders—and still they'd failed to halt the Neutrality's expansion. But rejuvenation could extend a human life only to a hundred and forty years, maybe a hundred and fifty. Longer-term rejuv was a myth or a failed experiment, depending on who you asked. Human trials had killed more than half of the conscripted participants. Who would risk those odds even if the treatment existed?

Seren turned to stare. Could he be telling the truth? It would make Maq Flett a living artifact, not only sole proprietor of a Pact megacorp but one of the original Grey rebels.

"The Pact is greedy and arrogant—don't worry, the runabout's clean, or three different alarms would be going off—and it's getting worse. Maybe your Pol can knock some sense into the shitheels."

"Knock sense into them with what, spears and clubs? They flattened us."

"You're out of touch," Maq said.

"We're not strong enough alone."

"Who's alone? You don't know your friends from your enemies. Figure out the difference fast if you want to survive. It's a greyscale universe."

"Why are you helping me, Maq?"

"I help lots of people. Money, job, medics, transport home, depends what they need."

"Commendable. Why me?"

"Damou left you on my doorstep."

"So why is Damou helping me?" Seren asked patiently.

"Common ground?" He shrugged. "You both lost family, you're both under obligation. And he needs your data. Pols and Greys both have to recover and rebuild, so you need a treaty that doesn't grind you under forever."

"And you?"

Maq looked aside at her. "My job is to straighten out the Pact. It's bent out of shape pretty bad since Gabe took his hand off the wheel."

"Gabe?" Seren asked. He'd said it as though she should know.

"Gabriel de Jong. Lifetime president of the Pact." Maq nodded at her confusion. "When we were kids, his name was Gabe John. Got a fair ways for a backworld boy, eh? Gabe was always smart. First chance, he bought into Han rejuvenation and Mitran mirror drives. Hang onto the right shares and the right idea for three hundred years, you can buy about anything you want, including the Pact. Not many living people know that story. But you can keep a secret."

It was an invitation to spy if she'd ever heard one. *Plant this detail, see how it travels*—but Seren wouldn't touch it. She didn't even know who she could tell. Anyway, her intelligence work had been mostly analyzing visual and data files. Then, late in a mind-numbing watch, she'd tracked a small iridescent blur, hardly bigger than a drone probe, crossing the dark and empty Bight. They had flown out to intercept, Seren and—who was her weapons hand? Her memory failed, and she could see only the found image from her slate, a blur of night fire and mist.

"Why did you bring me to the Cantons?"

"Grey friends. And I thought you might remember more. About Mitrans. About the courier and why she died."

"No." Seren dropped her face into her hands. *Tell them in Tirion.* She needed to get to Derw or another sanctuary clinic and get help to reclaim her memory. She pulled up her wrap to cover her head in mourning and clasped her hands, but she could find no solace.

Maq touched a new destination on the map. Houses passed below them now, set among stone gardens and twisted pine trees in a district that sprawled across dry hills. Maq brought the runabout down in a village of tawny plaster houses with tile roofs. Twilight was falling.

Seren dropped her wrap from her head, rejoining the world. "What now?"

"One hour, then back to Tirion." Maq rummaged in his pocket. "Here, keep this safe."

Seren took the whorl of pearl grey composite he held out. It fitted perfectly into her right hand. Or her left. Its design was simple and intuitive—Mitran, like most of Maq's tech. Artwork? Recording device? Then she found the touchpad recessed into the bottom edge.

"I don't need a laser."

"You don't want to need it, you mean. Tell you what, Green. Send it back in a tenday if you've never drawn it. It's unscannable. Untraceable. Doesn't exist."

"I could shoot you and steal the runabout."

"Ayuh. And then you get real Pacters extracting your minerals. They won't leave you enough of Claer to stand on."

Seren swallowed her objection and palmed the laser into her pocket. Maybe immediate escape wasn't her best plan.

13

The runabout hissed down onto a stone pavement shaded by trees and vine-draped arbours. When the hatch opened, she smelled pine woods and herbs and lemons. In the roof garden of a house like a Mitran souterrain, built underground to deflect oppressive heat, Seren followed Maq past a hideous extruded carbonglass sculpture that looked like two scorpions mating. A staircase led down to a landing where the rough earthen plaster smoothed to a glossy grey composite wall. At an unmarked door, Maq palmed the handplate.

"I told you not to come here," a woman said in a hard contralto. "Or your companion."

"Missed you too, Inka." Maq shoved his thumbs in his belt. "Want the word from Tas?"

Inka. The deranged woman who'd attacked Seren on the Az. Maq had lost his mind, bringing her here.

The souterrain's door hissed aside into the glass wall, and warm air breathed out from the dim interior. Maq touched Seren's elbow to direct her in, whistling under his breath. Hasi followed at his heels, unusually quiet.

Wall panels glowed on as they walked into a lounge in subdued retro style. A niche held a sculptured hand, twisted as though in agony, and a painting near an inner door might be an emigration period Jiao-Long. Under their feet, the carpet displayed a sinuous branching pattern of fractals that looked like a great coral or a river delta seen from space. Seren had last seen it on the Az before Inka's lethal-force data storm.

In a freestanding vri zone, a woman stood in a garden, gazing at blue hills that stepped up toward dark mountains. Her back was turned, but Seren recognized her. Maq walked over to palm a wall data port.

Inka spun. "Get her out. She's a thief and a murderer."

"Bullshit. Tas showed you the courier's cockpit record. A Pol weapons hand panicked."

The Bight. Seren shifted uneasily. Everyone but her seemed to know what had happened.

"Qasri is trouble. I don't know why Tas bothers." Her accent was Mitran but unfamiliar. Wildly mixed cultures on the dead world had produced many subtly different regional dialects.

"Sure you do." Maq looked taken aback by Inka's performance. "That's why you're throwing a tantrum."

The garden's ambient light brightened, showing Inka's pale blue eyes in a stunning golden face, black hair knotted on her neck, a white dress under a mauve wrap. She was in the roof garden; they could have talked upstairs.

An inner door became a screen where a double helix of genetic code rotated slowly. Over the image scrolled text: *Seren Mirlande Qasri, born Tirion 2715.14.08, Claer Defence Force seconded to Politaya Fleet Intelligence, Lieut., active, MIA.* Images followed. Medical records from childhood, graduating papers, dramatic productions, civilian licences, friends, lovers, Seren and a cousin-friend in traditional dance robes showing off their hennaed hands, Mam with her sister-friend Parvin, her cousin-friends, Teak. Every detail that Damou promised to suppress when he set up her new identity. That was their deal. *Liar.*

"Your information is safe, Lieutenant. As you discovered, it's not easy to break into our grid." Inka spoke in a lighter, differently accented voice—Seren recognized it with a shock of anger as her own—and her face morphed to Seren's natural blue-eyed, dark-haired appearance.

"Querying a worldnet isn't jacking a grid," Seren shot back. "But emping a spacecraft in flight is criminal assault under interworld law. You could have killed three people."

"Prove it."

Taking a deep breath to rest her irritation, Seren asked, "Shall we come to the roof?"

"Tell her."

"Doctor Loukanos lost her mobility in an accident. She doesn't meet in person." Maq settled among the embroidered cushions of a livewood armchair.

Loukanos? Seren keyed the name on her slate for a bio. *Loukanos, Inka Li-Ling, inherited Loukanos BioGen research institute in Thessaloniki, Mitra, molecular information systems, genetics, xenobiology, missing and presumed dead in collapse of Nueva Chiapas space elevator, Mitra, 2735.*

Inka gazed into the night, secure in her flawless beauty. A breath of air stirred her hair and the leaves overhead and every fold of her dress, shadowed and textured in the faint light. Subtle facial expressions, perfect hair and hands, all projected into the roof garden. Even with the finest equipment, Seren could never match this simulation, perhaps indistinguishable from the real woman. Few people troubled to create such perfect simages.

"Come closer," Inka said.

Seren glanced at Maq and walked up to the vri zone. The smart carpet writhed in fractal red and purple, and though she tried to calm it, she achieved only a roiling indigo.

"Why did you image Tas?"

Seren opened her mouth to deny it, but remembered—after their encounter en route to Claer, she'd recorded an establishing shot. "File footage. I make vri docs."

"Destroy the images."

"If he asks." Why should Inka care?

"Leave Tas alone. He has enough on his hands." By her tone, Inka was Damou's lover.

"Rest assured, I want nothing to do with the man." Seren didn't try to keep the revulsion out of her voice. She blinked as though a bright light had flashed in her eyes for an instant, but when she glanced around the room, nothing looked different. Retinal scan? Nano sweep? The virtual Inka glanced down at the slate she held, maybe checking a readout, and frowned up again.

"As he detests you," she hissed, sounding quite mad. "Leave

the dead in peace."

Damou had a bloody nerve judging her, after deconstructing her life. But Seren shrugged.

Inka spared Maq a glance. "What do you want, Maq?"

"Thought you'd never ask." Maq grinned. "We need to know everything that happened in the Bight. You can help unblock Qasri's memory."

"Let her scream out everything? Qasri killed Takahara and stole urgently needed data that's no use to her. And she reeks of Pol intelligence."

Takahara. The roaches that first grabbed her on Arian shouted about Takahara. The courier pilot? Seren closed her eyes and saw a tiny ship against the dark dust lanes of the Bight.

"Crap." Maq got up to look at the tortured carbonglass hand. "Think it through, Inka. Claer Defence charges a pacifist vri maker with treason, throws her into the Pol fleet, and shuts her up by sending her out to Gandhi Base. Qasri does the right thing, goes out to challenge an apparent intruder, gets attacked by her own crew, and sets off an interworld crisis. She's a Claeran, for God's sake, she just wants to go home to her family and her trees and her art."

Seren bit the inside of her cheek. Dismissive, but mostly true.

"Tas says on Arian station she was raving about a black teardrop and rivers in a wall of mist," Inka said.

"Takahara's ship was a black Az Abhaya. Teardrop shape," Maq said. "The wall of mist is Claeran mojo from their New Grove rites. The living and the dead are separated by a wall of mist. We can pass through it, but not lightly and not for long."

"Do you believe that?" Inka demanded.

Seren said with unshielded disdain, "It's a metaphor."

"Could she have seen an uncharted mirror node just as it opened?" Inka asked Maq, as though Seren weren't in the room. She had the manners of a scorpion, even worse than Damou.

"Crossed my mind."

"Then what came out of the node?"

"Rivers."

"Exactly. Nonsense."

Maq shrugged. Seren held her silence.

Inka returned to her objections. "Why should I help a useless

Pol dissident?"

"Qasri's anything but useless. She knows—"

"Doctor Loukanos," Seren cut across them both. Time to end this. "Meistr Flett overlooks one detail. The last thing I want is you prying around in my memory. I don't want your help."

Inka hadn't expected that, Seren guessed; she'd wanted to hear them beg. Now she stared from the vri zone with a chilling absence of expression. "Then you'll die, Lieutenant."

"Is this another threat?" Seren asked coolly.

"A probability."

Seren allowed herself a smile and a jab of provocation. It was ages since she'd enjoyed gloves-off improv. "Surely you don't think Meistr Damou will harm me? He's been remarkably kind." Not quite the truth, but not an outright lie.

Inka's stare shadowed through uncertainty to anger, and Maq looked as though he didn't know whether to protest or applaud. Pity that Damou was such a shipwreck. It would be a pleasure to come between Inka and almost anyone.

"I need fresh air," Seren said to Maq. "I'll be outside."

Seren climbed in darkness to the landing pad. The surrounding garden smelled wonderfully of green growing things, drier and more aromatic than Tirion. Soon she'd be at Gwernant, maybe even at work in her home orchard.

II
SURVIVAL

1

ES2741.227

Tas drifted the ring and took his time outbound. The Az had a new high-efficiency mirror drive, but its old insystem plasma drive was still an energy glutton; in Claeran airspace he had a long haul out to a legal transit node, then a second rougher transit through the erratic Dead Gate node. Returning he could burn hard, in the unlikely event Maq secured any data to stay the treaty.

Grit rasped his eyelids. Last night he'd gridded search patterns in virtuality, charting the plague survivors' outward movements from Mitra in expanding spheres. When he finally slept, he dreamed again of dogs standing in the moonlit river and woke in a cold sweat with his heart pounding. A cloud of glitz would keep the dreams at bay, but he wasn't so far gone that he flew spun. Besides, why prove Qasri right that he was an addict?

Eight moons circled the largest gas giant of Claer's system. Tas pulled down his eyeband to track them. He would pass near the third moon, where liquid water boiled up through a fifty-kilometre ice crust and steamed in arabesques far out into the night.

Beyond the last beacons, Tas pulled his softsuit out of a locker and hooked it to his chair back. Three times in seven years he'd needed it underway. Once a rock took out his forward screen.

Another time, pirates from the notorious freehold of Xanadu tried to board—he'd warned them to stand off, but they'd mistaken his warning for fear; their dead hulk was still drifting off the Broken Cluster. They were probably still cursing him after limping home three to a two-person life capsule.

The third time he'd met a Pact warship that had no business running dark in the Deep Outside. Unarmed, he'd tried talking them down, but they'd razed his shields and closed in for the kill. Then space turned inside out as though every particle and wave of light that ever left this universe surged back from beyond. Fixed in its writhing heart of brilliance, he knew all times places lives—The mirror flaw passed, and he sat alone amid a spreading cloud of dust-fine debris. Strange things happened out in the deep dark, and human science explained only a fraction. When he limped back to Grey space, the Pact ship was listed as lost.

Six hours to his transit node. He pulled down a virtual screen and called up his reading list. Recently, having reread the texts he'd cursed long ago in his sleep-deprived MitraCorps training year, he'd moved on to science, literature, performance arts, and philosophy. Another century and he'd be an educated man, but he'd never make a century. The surgeons and their nanobots had rebuilt him with relentless skill, but only what they could see and touch and measure.

Emigration history today. The system cross-indexed for him, and he pointed to a sigil. Images and text scrolled up smoothly as he settled to read—but instead he ignored the screen and looked out at realspace.

The ancients imagined infinite universes, each one tangential to every other universe, each with slightly different history and physical laws. Their physics hinted at travel through this multi-dimensional space, but the ancients couldn't send physical objects through near universes. Finally, they learned to focus the immense tides and fluxes of energy to permit physical transit.

In major gravity wells, these focussed nodes were erratic and washed by hard radiation, potentially dangerous to use. Intersystem transit soon relied on nodes beyond planetary gravity, though, marked only by virtual navigation beacons in the solar systems' empty outer reaches. One early scientist had described the multiverse as a hall of mirrors, inspiring generations of great artworks, and the newsgrids soon referred to interdimensional transit as mirror transit.

Tas stirred himself and reached for his comm pad. He should call Maq, make sure Qasri hadn't bolted—*No. Leave it alone.*

As Earth died, the first-wave emigrants from its rich nations had left in huge ramjets, laser-sails, light-pushers, and plasma-driven generation ships for rocky worlds within a few hundred light-years. Their colonies coalesced into the Pact of Human Worlds, a minuscule bubble lost in the Local Arm, in turn lost in the vast home galaxy. A century later, in Earth's last dreadful years, the impoverished survivors developed mirror transit. The second wave left a world of barely habitable islands in storm-lashed seas that steadily rose above underwater landslides and volcanoes. Driven away from the Pact worlds, they found richer planets out beyond the Pact and called their federation the Politaya. There was no third wave.

Even most insystem ships had mirror capability by the time the Neutrality split from the Politaya three centuries ago. Mirror transit routes skirted the quarantine zones around old Earth and Sitkum and now Mitra. Officially they linked the Pact, Politaya, and Neutrality, respecting invisible boundaries drawn by convention or treaty. In truth they were only ideas sketched between lonely beacons and distant stars.

Tas leaned back in his chair, hands linked behind his head. Charted in a vri zone, interworld politics looked remote and abstract. He had known the bloody reality of Tanna, where all diplomatic abstractions failed, and Mitra, where twelve million died terribly in a few days. *River Evrotas in moonlight.* If he slept, he would dream again of his brother's dogs.

Ice music penetrated the humming stillness of the old ship— Tas thought of it as music—in the rising sequences that still defeated his understanding. He glanced at his comm board and met Inka's pale blue eyes in her simmed image. She'd found a new way to override his security.

Her simage flickered out, and the comm screen rotated a three-dimensional object against a scattering of stars, ovoid at one end and tapering to three curved points at the other. Its length was just over a metre, according to Inka's text scroll below the image, and its surface was a silvery grey solid. Every centimetre bore ridged fractal designs as though moles had colonized its subsurface. Tas stared at its image, shocked silent.

"No contemporary or ancient analogue exists," Inka said.

Tas knew otherwise. Years ago, he'd seen the same pattern on an artifact in a backworld village square. "Where is it now?"

"On a freighter near the third moon." Inka's simage leaned toward him, becoming subtly more beautiful and seductive. "Renat's closing on it."

"That's why you set this vector." It wasn't even a question. Tas knew her too well.

"Back him up. Board the freighter. Seize the object." Inka hesitated, a long time for her. "Please."

Tas killed her signal. His cochlear relay buzzed, and he jabbed the comm pad.

Renat grinned. "Join the hunt."

In the background he heard the high-pitched artificial scream that a weapons board assigned to incoming fire. Space was inhumanly silent, in truth, and Tas had long ago disabled his ship's assigned-sound system. Over Ren's shoulder he glimpsed the patrol ship's bridge, painted and encrusted in 'Line deco, and winced. Renat was still playing Tripline runner.

"Come on, Taso, get live. You'll be good."

Tas kept silent, too angry to speak. Ren knew his true weakness: false courage that kills a world and then like a fool tries to make it right.

"Easy, no rough stuff," Ren prompted.

Tas punched his comm pad hard enough to drive his fist right through the virtual board and sat back scrubbing his face. His hands shook, and his clothes warmed as they worked overtime to mop up his clammy sweat.

After a moment he pulled on his softsuit and pushed back the open hood.

Five ships hung near the gas giant's ice moon when he motored his port-side cams and sensors to pick up distant ship signals. Tas boosted his magnification until he had a visual image.

Four MitraCorps patrol ships flanked one larger craft. Tas bracketed the freighter's registration and brought up screen after screen from MitraCorps's known-offender files. The owner was

Duri Balint, a contraband runner from Xanadu. A man's head rotated on his display: fair hair, elegant features, far removed from the street criminals' preference for exotic cosmetic mods. The smooth planes of his face were almost too perfect. Tas told the screen to enlarge detail and enlarge again until he located a trademark on the nano scale. It was a sim, a remarkably good one. Balint could probably afford it. He'd had a handful of arrests but not one conviction.

Why did Riordan drop MitraCorps into these no-win contracts whenever Pact customs and revenue put on a show of enforcement? Without a conviction bonus, the task fee would barely cover costs. And Renat in command raised a new nightmare.

Numbers flashed on his screen a moment later, quickly transforming into icons and objects. Not far away. He pulled down his eyeband, and the ships' deployment came clear in the grid. Slow on its insystem plasma drive, Balint's freighter passed against the distant green gas giant. Tas scanned deeper, waited while the long rays penetrated and bounced between hull and bulkheads, accumulating a scan profile. It was a former Politaya Fleet transport, vulnerable at communications tower and laser arrays and too lightly armoured on the bridge. Bad design. If the Greens had built to Mitran specs, they might have won their war. If they'd heeded their Mitran strategists, they'd never have fought a war.

The scan read armed ordnance, shielded holds, converters badly out of phase and in need of maintenance, and a skeleton crew. Still, it seriously outclassed all of the smaller ships together.

His hand was on the nav board changing his heading even before he'd consciously decided—left to himself Renat would screw up. He slipped on the vri glove and rotated objects onscreen: freighter, rocks, moons, scattered smaller craft. Touching the freighter object expanded it, then expanded again until he saw detail. A word activated his augmented vision and heads-up retinal overlay, and his speed and course scrolled before his eyes. He waited till one of Renat's ships briefly blocked his signal, then stealthed the Az.

Tas tracked the freighter with a flex of thumb and fingers in the glove and called up his visual deceptions on split screen. The left panel showed his own stealthed ship; the right panel showed the one toothless weapon his stripped Az could deploy, a freestanding simulation that could ride a virus into their nav and pilot boards. He selected a Pact destroyer destealthing a bare kilometre from Balint's ship.

The freighter reverse-burned to dump speed. Tas pushed his throttle and drove straight in for the bridge, close enough to see two duty officers flinch as the destroyer sim passed above their viewscreen. Then he flipped a one-eighty down the freighter's port flank—a blur of pitted composite hull with expensive new equipment welded in among the slagged cannon mounts and twisted comm receptors—and came up to the starboard docking ports. A glance showed him Renat's patrol ship already docked. Auto took him closer, and his ship matched hatch rings and grappled in. He pocketed a stunner, then sealed his flexible helmet and told it to cycle air. Balint's crew wouldn't offer a friendly welcome. Pushing into his airlock, he irised open his outer hatch and punched control code into the freighter's docking keypad.

Tas kicked through the opening hatch into light artificial gravity and nearly collided with a composite case the size of a one-man life capsule. Inside lay the strange object Inka had showed him. Up close it gleamed dully in the dim light, looking smaller but suddenly more real, and his slate calculated it at twice the weight he'd guessed. He ran a gloved hand across the linear ridge patterns that made it unmistakably an object from the Deep Outside. A smooth layer of clay had masked the pattern on the object in the backworld village square years ago, but once the Tanna elders removed the clay, it looked much like this. No obvious controls, no obvious function. The latches clicked shut when he dropped the lid, and he lifted the capsule toward his hatch.

A red priority bar flashed across the top of his hud, and his cochlear relay buzzed. Renat said urgently, "Backup needed on bridge."

2

Ren was in trouble. When was Ren not in trouble? But Tas didn't have to read him the regs any more. He stood for a moment with the case ready to transfer, but he'd hesitated a moment too long. The hatch behind him hissed open, and he carefully set down the object.

Three of the freighter's crew kicked into the docking port. When they saw his grey softsuit, they opened fire. No one gave orders, typical for a hired-on runner crew. No marksmen either. Tas flattened to the bulkhead and let laser bolts fly wild around him, though a few spots of warmth betrayed hits. His softsuit wasn't combat-grade, but it deflected light laser fire. He stunned one crewman, then the other two, and fanned the beam across them again to be certain.

Tas flung himself through the hatch into a dark passage. Empty. The passage illuminated as it sensed him, and he followed the handholds around the hull's curved contour to the lift. Another two crewmen met him as the lift opened on the bridge deck, but he stunned one and the other fled aft. No loyalty, no cohesion. *Good.* Tas kicked for the bridge. The last guard took one look and surrendered.

The bridge portal was irised shut, which meant the duty watch had seen everything on the bridge security feeds. Tas punched in override code and handed in to find a stocky man in heavy cosmod lounging against a wall. Balint himself, his ID scanned. His captain had his hands on his head and a no-argument-here look, and the duty watch of two men and a woman did the same. Two of Renat's people guarded them, Carlos Liu and Galina Narain. Everything seemed under control. What was Ren's urgency?

Balint stood with arms folded over his black silk robe looking amused, if Tas could read an expression behind his green and copper lizard scales. So much for his bland simage. His brown eyes looked oddly without depth but fully human.

Near the runner stood an overarmed bodyguard, a little man with a liveware snakeball tattoo that writhed across his face and neck. Some people didn't know the liveware's essential component was maggots. This man probably did know. Hyped and raging with artificial courage, clearly a glitz spinner—his name meant nothing, but Tas's memory clicked into place despite the man's new subskin larvae and glazed hair. *Claer Arian.* He'd taken Qasri from this man and another spinner with a bad case of glitz jitters. It was a windfall, first the object and now this dreg. Once they wrapped it, Tas could question him about Qasri's data bead.

"Weapons on the deck," Tas said. The guard deposited an assault weapon, a hand laser, and an ugly shiv near the bridge bulkhead, where a riotous 'Line deco mural sparkled with trophies and ornaments. Narain and Liu should have disarmed the crew. Sloppy.

Tas spun as another man stepped from an alcove, but it was Renat. In that instant the tattooed bodyguard yelled and straight-armed Narain, who flew back across the bridge to slam into the bulkhead. Tas moved in, and fire ripped his upper arm. He took a step backward for balance. Renat dropped the bodyguard with laser fire, and Liu covered Balint, who shook his head in disgust. The assault wasn't his order, just a glitz frenzy.

Narain got to her feet unscathed; she'd had the brains to wear a shock shirt under her self-healing softsuit, unlike Tas. He checked the guard. Dead.

"You're in Pact custody on suspicion of transporting contraband," he told the captain, since Ren showed no sign of

handling the formalities. "A MitraCorps crew will guard you in to
Claer Arian station. Run and we disable your ship."

The captain nodded glumly and told his bridge watch to start
damage checks. They'd lose their pay and bonuses, but they were
alive, unlike Balint's guard.

Narain showed Tas a slate with the ship cardwork. The
freighter was registered on the Pact backworld of Kasumi, a
trouble spot that Pact justice departments could have cleaned up
years ago, but too much money passed through too many hands.

Balint finally found his tongue. "Mitran pirates, that's a new
bubble. You know the deal. Ten percent of the cargo, pure organic
alkaloids."

Tas stared and felt his own people hold a collective breath.

Balint misread his hesitation and bared his jewelled teeth.
"Well, captain?"

His rank insignia was still legible on this softsuit. Tas unsealed
the helmet and pushed it back off his head, blackly amused to see
the muscles beneath Balint's eyes tighten in shock through his
gaudy scales.

"Ask again and I'll stun you."

"Fool. I'll be free tomorrow. Glitz is nothing to what we
trawled off the Tripline. Big man himself gets this one." Balint
eyed him. "What's your problem? You got the girl on the station.
Too hot to go for my taste."

Balint had a hand in Qasri's capture? Tas reached left-handed
to grab him by his black silk robe. His right glove was full of
blood, though the softsuit slowed the flow, and his arm burned.
He slammed Balint back and pinned his throat with a forearm,
feeling the man begin to choke and panic, and saw Narain white-
eyed in shock, probably thinking he'd finally slid over the edge.
In twenty years not many people had seen him lose control.

Tas let go abruptly, and the runner slid down the wall. He said,
"Who got the data?"

"Everyone's asking that," Balint smirked.

Swallowing a last temptation to knock him senseless, Tas saw
the bridge through a blur. He'd make a worse fool of himself if he
didn't get out now.

"We'll take him in," Renat said in a roaring distance.

Claim the object and drift. Tas made it back to the docking bay, but when the light panels brightened, he saw only the object's case. Open. Empty. A search of the other docking positions turned up nothing like the object, and the patrol ships were now standing off.

Balint's lead on Qasri was the key thing, whatever Inka might say. He'd question the runner at the port lock-up. But if Balint didn't have the data, who did? They'd be signing the Pol treaty in hours. Time was running out.

In his cockpit Tas pulled off his softsuit, found his med kit and peeled on a bandage. Thirty centimetres farther left and he'd be a bad memory. The laser had sliced skin and muscle to the bone, a day or more's work for his med nano. And now he needed to return to Arian to question Balint. His search pattern would have to wait.

Ren hadn't needed backup. Maybe it was power he craved: Taso comes at my call. Ren could be so much more. Inka he understood too well, but not Ren, not any more.

One thing puzzled him: why a glitz runner like Balint would go after data and artifacts. They were hard to fence. A commissioned job? Inka would know. He set his nav for the Pact's new docking level at Claer Arian and let his eyes close.

Tas slept badly and dreamed of Seren Qasri, not in the ruins of Tirion but walking among rain-scented trees. He clasped her cool fingers—but she was wholly Claeran in her careless beauty, accustomed to perfection and disdainful of the flawed. Tas woke stiff and cramped and angry at the betrayals of sleep.

An hour out of Arian, every alarm on every board went wild. A massive explosion somewhere back near the gas giant's third moon. He scanned the MitraCorps ships, all intact, but near the freighter's last known position he saw only a spreading globe of debris that glittered like metal confetti. Go back, seek survivors, find the object? No point. His scan said nothing larger than a rice grain survived the blast.

At Meath port on Claer, where he finally thumbprinted his arrival at the MitraCorps terminal, Tas flagged a public hover pod that dropped him at Inka's house before dawn. A runabout waited on the pad. Unusual. But Inka did not encourage visitors; whoever they were, they would leave soon.

In the garden he folded onto a bench to wait, one knee up to prop his chin on his forearm. No one came out, and Tas felt the chill even with his old jacket over his shoulders.

His eyes closed, raising the old nightmare. The Mitran plague was a hemorrhagic fever. Everywhere the dead lay alone or in each other's arms in pools of clotted blood.

Mitrans had boarded any ship that could cycle air as labs raced to sequence code, seeking an antigen for the unknown man-made plague. Mitran engineers had even stripped an old light-pusher and an ion-drive ship from a low-orbit aviation and space museum, making them operational in four days as the plague swept across the southern continent of Ithaki, across the island chains in the shallow equatorial sea and through northerly Mikkeli.

By the time Tas came insystem, labs had sequenced the plague virus, and the vaccine code was in home and automat fabricators—days too late. He had dropped downworld into Mitra's deepening silence. No space traffic control, no comm activity. He'd landed the commandeered ship illegally at Pronoia in his farm's river meadow with his fear freezing to dread—*No. Don't remember. Don't think. Don't feel.*

Two great stations infell, and four others with their space elevators soon became orbiting mortuaries. One by one Tas blew them to plasma, giving thousands the decency of a fiery grave, and torched the down stations. Downworld, he had buried towns and incinerated cities until the bodies fell apart in his hands, knowing he would never find his own people alive. Millions still lay uncovered beneath clear Mitran skies when he released clouds of nanoscale mechanisms and spores to uncreate his world. Then he lifted for the last time. Within his natural lifetime, Mitra would no longer be the hard, barren planet his ancestors had settled. He had ended that world to recreate a paradise nourished by twelve million deaths.

Thousands had fled Mitra. Many were found and resettled in the first year, a handful in the second and third years and none since. The official MitraCorps search stood down after four years. Tas mourned the loss of his daughter Halia and her mother, but pursued every rumour and trace of any Mitran survivors. *Tomorrow.*

Scents of juniper and lemon and thyme rose to him from the

warm garden, and music drifted from distant cafés and windows. Fragrant evening, springtime, even a few stars showing, but it was far from Mitra.

3

Moving shot, hover. Seren walked the roof garden, avoiding the ugly sculpture. In Tirion tomorrow she could consult a clinic about her memory block, then search for Mam. Dark grape bunches hung on an arbour that led into shadow, and she stopped to squeeze a ripe grape. Inka probably poisoned them or wired them as data pickups—Seren froze, hand to mouth.

In the dim starlight, a still body lay face-up on a bench at the end of the arbour. She turned to leave, but what if someone needed help?

A man lay with his left hand trailing in the grass, and there was enough light to see his right sleeve was soaked and dripping. Seren stepped closer and kneeled to take his left wrist. Warm. A slow steady heartbeat. Too heavy for her to carry, but maybe he could walk if she got him on his feet. Better still to call for help. His face was turned, but he had a fine straight nose and brow. She put a hand on his shoulder, slowly and carefully, well acquainted with the startle reflex.

"Finished?" He shifted slightly and turned his head.

Seren found herself looking into the small aperture of a stunner held in his right hand, then into the last face she wanted to see anywhere. Half a face. She flinched away.

"Have a good look. Then go."

Evil-tempered lout. Probably bleeding from a tavern fight. Seren overcame a temptation to tip the bench and dump him onto the dew-soaked grass. Instead, she thought of Teak Kuhan and tried for his patience.

"You're hurt." Clearly, he'd lost the fight. Good.

"Not much," Damou snapped, but the weapon vanished. Then he sat up, trying not to catch his breath. *Stupid.* She'd seen enough brave posturing in the war.

"I'll call a medic."

"No. I'm all right."

"I can see that. Grab the wrong woman this time?" Get him down to his lover, then escape before Inka decided this also was her fault.

"Defended a woman's honour and declined a bribe, not that it's your business."

As she stood, Seren lifted his jacket from the grass, a grey and silver uniform jacket with most of the flashes stripped off. *MitraCorps.* A poignant end. She noted his torn sleeve and the pale bandage beneath, and guessed he'd been waiting for Inka's guests to leave.

It was cool in the roof garden, and Seren draped the jacket over his shoulders. He pulled it straight and glared at her. Anything she did, in Damou's eyes, would be the wrong thing.

When she started back through the grape arbour, surprisingly he came along. She took his elbow, ready to steady him, but he pulled away. Still, she stayed in arm's reach, and once near the bottom of the stairs, he stumbled against her and recovered. This time he didn't shrug off her hand.

At the door an overhead light woke and glowed dimly. He lifted his hand to the wall but stopped short of touching the palm plate. On the shoulder of his jacket the faint light picked out a silver rose. *Sparti.*

"Thanks, Lieutenant."

Seren swallowed her shock and managed a nod.

4

"Playing with fire, Inka." Maq drained his akvavit and set the empty glass back on a shelf, which slid silently into the wall. He'd as rather drink herb-flavoured ethanol as akvavit, if anyone could tell them apart. "Why in hell do you want to shop Tas to Nolin? You'll get him disappeared."

Maq watched Inka drop her illusion of the beautiful woman in the rooftop garden now that Qasri was gone. Her simage leaned on a counter, looking older and wearier, in a stained lab smock that Maq had seen her wearing before her accident. With selective editing, it was how she'd looked twenty years ago on Mitra; this time she was angling for respect, not seduction.

"Nolin runs Gabriel de Jong. In other words, he runs the Pact."

"Better hope not. You really want Nolin at the controls of a Pact that's busy swallowing the Pol and eyeing the Neutrality? What's left of the Neutrality, anyway, since you dropped the ball on Mitra." Maq went back to pacing the salon. "Nolin will burn you down. My dad told me, 'Never mind how many sticks you're up, never gamble what you can't live without.'"

"I don't need advice from a man who's eaten the hearts of his enemies for three centuries," Inka said with silken malevolence.

"No, you need advice from a man who knows your dirty

secrets. Level with Tas."

"I work for the best interests of Mitrans." Inka's sim turned and walked away.

Delusional. Maq rolled tension out of his shoulders. "A while ago I got this high-powered new bio rack that gave me nothing but problems. Froze. Crashed. Garbled data. I pulled the panels and let it sit overnight. Once it lost its juice, it smartened right up."

Inka's lab-coated sim walked back into the zone, attentive now.

"I want to keep funding your survivor search. Wish someone funded mine after Sitkum."

Maq stood silent at the centre of her salon, hands clasped, letting her attention sharpen. The room was stylish, expensive and heartless. Her carpet, sensing his anger, morphed from calm green landscape to a sinuous red-gold fractal design of shifting, hypnotic beauty. It made him think of the branch coral they'd tried to introduce on Sitkum after the native extinctions.

Inka looked at him obliquely. In the past she'd been coldly analytical, but lately she'd developed a wobble that was anything but reassuring. Her outburst at Qasri was like a kid's jealousy— or a last flicker of human emotion in a mind steadily losing touch with human ways.

"If you want to tell me something, say it straight," Maq said.

"Another Pact cruiser vanished Outside."

"Yeah. And it doesn't make any better sense than the last one. Fleet ships vanish. Survey drones come back wiped. Manned ships return if they manually navigate a mirror transit. Why?"

"Moulders. Moles." Inka frowned into her simmed night sky.

"Spacer myth." Forgotten Mitran drones might have zapped the ships, still enforcing the old Neutrality-imposed treaty. Right now, he had more immediate concerns. "Inka—don't push Tas." *Or you'll regret it,* he didn't add. Inka could work that out.

"Make your point and go." Inka was still in a combative mood.

"I want you to help Qasri lose the block." Maq dropped into the elegant livewood chair, where Hasi perched on an arm. It looked better than it felt, like most of Inka's stuff.

"What's your interest?"

"Lahal. Qasri's a skookum pointer. I hate to kill off a good opponent." Maq sighed at Inka's stare. "The Pol's our key to reunity. Claer's our key to the Pol. Qasri's our key to Claer. We need Qasri up and running."

"Everyone wants our help suddenly."

"Pol courting you again?"

"The Politaya has nothing to offer Mitra."

"Not since it took the brunt of the Pact attack. You didn't spurn the Pol then."

Inka ignored that. "We make the decisions now."

"Hard work, saving humanity without its consent." Neutrality and Politaya needed each other badly to avoid being ground under by the Pact, but he didn't waste his breath telling that to Inka. "So, you won't help Qasri."

"Qasri doesn't want my help." Inka looked far too pleased at this excuse to refuse him.

"Too bad about your next million."

"You truly are a demon."

"Look who's talking. Ancients would have burned you at the stake if they found enough to burn. What are you these days, Inka? Electronic impulses glued together by malice?"

Inka simmed back to the young woman in the garden; she must be feeling defensive. "I've lost him three times. MitraCorps. Lira. Piñar. I'm not losing him to Qasri."

"You don't own him, you never did. Dead he's no good to anyone. He's endured everything so far, no thanks to you."

Seconds later the door slid open, and Tas walked in with Qasri. He looked like he hadn't slept in a tenday, his old MitraCorps uniform jacket was slung over his shoulder, and his other sleeve was soaked dark. *God.* Inka would overclock.

Maq levered himself out of the uncomfortable chair, feeling his years, and told the liquor shelf to pour akvavit. "Thought you were heading Outside."

"Tomorrow."

"Sit down before you fall down." Maq offered Qasri a glass, but she shook her head. Propping up the wall beside the door, Tas took his glass left-handed. Blindsided? Anyone who messed with him was crazy.

Tas tossed back the akvavit at one shot, a bad sign in a man who rarely drank since his year-long bender. Qasri frowned as he wiped the scarred side of his mouth. Then he was silent, gazing downward. The carpet at his feet writhed with shapes like gorgon snakes, then it calmed to a forest floor spangled with flowers like fallen stars. It liked him.

"What got you?" Maq quirked an eyebrow at all the blood.

"Pact contraband op. Duri Balint."

"You do have a death wish." Immediately he regretted his words.

"Nothing so easy."

"Need a medic?"

"Med nano has kicked in. Give it a day."

"If you say so." Time to stir things up, Maq decided. "Inka, you're too hard on Qasri."

"What's going on here?" Tas stood away from the wall.

"Probabilities," Inka snapped. "Sixty-three percent that Qasri will kill you within a year."

Qasri shot Inka's sim a look that should have fried it.

"You know what it means to have your life stolen," Tas said mildly.

Inka weighed him for a moment, and blinked out of existence. Swirls of colour twisted and grew in mid-air above the vri stage where her sim had been. *Crazy.*

"That god with all the arms, the scary one, what's her name?" Maq asked.

"Kali." Tas had a hell of a deadpan, ought to play more lahal.

Maq had made his point, earning a rare smile from Qasri. Inka would be watching, irritated by his reference to an ancestral culture that she scorned as irrational. She'd always been literal-minded, lacking a grasp of metaphor and the arts of illusion. He clasped Tas's shoulder and watched him through the door to Inka's inner sanctum, walking too carefully.

In prison the Pacters had put him back together from the inside out, but left his face in ruin as a heavy-handed reminder that the ancients branded criminals. Tas called their bluff by leaving it that way. Every day for a year after they convicted him, he'd waited for his lethal injection. Then the cynical bastards inoculated him against a rumoured new hemorrhagic fever and released him the day the plague hit Mitra. Now Inka in her bioware fortress wanted Tas to work for Nolin, the man who'd ordered his death. *Halo mesachie.* Hell of a mess.

"Guess we let ourselves out," Maq said. "Let's go eat."

Qasri already had her hand on the doorplate, and she was unusually quiet as they climbed to the roof garden. She pulled her wrap over her head again; among Claerans that meant she chose silence to mourn, so Maq shut up. A breeze lifted tempting aromas from cafés below, and Hasi frisked around them all the way to the carved wooden gate onto the greenway.

5

Cut in. Seren swirled her untasted wine and watched the village come to life around their table. Musicians started their second sets as people flooded into the greenway from a theatre, and chefs wheeled out their carts to compete for business.

The village sizzled with raw energy even in mid-evening. Night handcarts rumbled in to loading docks, and merchants displayed a rainbow of clothing and linens outside their shops. In Tirion she'd be strolling in the cool spring evening between the fragrant herb market and the bakery stands, touching the silk scarves and rough baskets. Seren realized what was different here. She dropped her wrap and asked, "No Pact soldiers?"

"So far the Pact respects the Cantons as a Neutrality leasehold," Maq said over his frybread, then paused to study her face. "Don't take Inka personally. She's a shit to everybody."

Hurt feelings weren't her worry. "Will it cost me, standing up to her?"

"Damou can talk her down." He licked a finger. "Her rant about the Bight is all chaff. Mostly she hates that you saved Teak Kuhan's life when she was sitting on her hands feeling sorry for herself, wishing she was dead."

Good. Seren took a wedge of frybread. The prospect of vexing Inka restored her appetite.

"Coffee, black," said someone standing behind her.

Seren turned as Damou took another chair. He looked less deathly now that he'd cleaned up, halfway presentable in an ivory shirt and tan slacks. She thought of telling him he should get some rest. Not her business. Instead, she asked Maq, "So Inka knew Kuhan?"

"Ayuh."

Holy fire. "Too bad I can't record her for a vri."

"Inka's not your most reliable source anyway." Maq eyed Damou, who scowled into his caffe. "Maybe we can find you someone who knows—"

A chair crashed to the sidewalk in the next café, and a tall red-haired woman who'd leaped clear was protesting hotly to a white-haired man. Jealous lover, Seren had time to think, before the man fired a hand laser at point-blank range. People drew away screaming or rushed to the fallen woman. A few ran after the shooter, already far down the greenway.

Seren got up to offer help, but Damou was already on his feet and blocking her view.

"Let's go." Maq pushed back his chair and tucked Hasi under his elbow. "Inka's place?"

"No." Damou held out his hand. "Lieutenant?"

"Right here suits me."

"Not an option."

Seren licked honey from a finger and contemplated telling him to leave her alone, but maybe it was time to go. She ignored his hand but followed him through the crowd on the greenway. Maq, deep in talk to his hand pickup, soon fell behind.

At the next greenway intersect they climbed to the top floor of a mixed-use building. Seren looked around in an entry full of flowering trees, trying to decide whether this was a business or a private home. She turned to ask why they were here, and saw Damou retreating down the stairs. *Damn him.*

As Seren turned to go, a woman asked, "Laure Prakash?"

Iridescent mauve feathers smoothing to pale blue plush—it was the makeup woman from this evening's vri shoot. She had the delicate bones of a bird, but not a brassy little songbird, maybe a graceful wading heron.

"No. That's not my name."

"It is now. Check your slate."

Glancing to prove her wrong, Seren saw a text line: "New bio below. Cosmod soonest. Trust Midori. Damou."

Two cosmods in two standard days? She headed toward the door.

Midori held up a hand. "Wait. I'll sweep you. Tas said you were probably dusted with surveillance nano."

Cloak-and-dagger silliness. But Seren stood and extended her arms.

Midori's wand flashed and chirped impressively as it disabled the nano. "You're all right now. It would have entered your bloodstream soon, and then someone would know every move for days."

Inka. No one else here cared what she did, and Inka was unhinged enough to do anything. *Laure Prakash.* A cosmod might be wise after all, though it irked her to agree with Damou. She followed Midori out to a roof garden with a pair of wicker chairs near a life-sized vri zone.

The cosmod tech scrolled through selections on her vri stage, head after head, and stopped at an oval face. No resemblance. "This one's good. Leave your nose, reshape your cheeks and chin. I'll show you."

Midori lifted circles of cultured skin from a dish and stroked them onto her cheeks. Only a neutralizer would remove the treatment once it melded in a few minutes. In seconds the margins smoothed into the skin below. At a command the vri scrolled skin pigments from albino to jet.

"Too light, it looks like a UV treatment. Anyone would know me," Seren dismissed one choice as Midori scrolled. When the skin tone cycled from walnut to mahogany on her vri image, she nodded. Stretched out on a lounge among unfamiliar plants and murmuring artworks, she waited for the cosmod to take effect. Laure Prakash, whoever she turned out to be, had to pursue Seren Qasri's urgent need to reclaim her memory and work and family.

The sheltered rooftop garden overlooked narrow streets. Stirring leaves, birdsong, and a murmur of voices were the main sounds below. The only hovers and ground cars were a few public vehicles, and the greenways were slow rivers of pedestrians. The open pine forest was as different from her own misty Tirion as two temperate landscapes could be, but Seren recognized a kindred love of craft and detail in this Mitran enclave.

Midori cultured her hair and spliced it to her mid-back, longer than she'd worn it in four years, and settled her to wait for the skin colour to finish its chain reaction through the pigment switches of her epidermis. When a timer chimed, she whisked off the cooling towels and examined Seren critically. "Pigment's good all over. How about breast inserts?"

"Just the cosmod. Forget about improving me." Seren felt her colour rising. In the mirror her brown face deepened to a twilight rose, gentler than her usual glaring blush.

"Now your eyes, or you'll look Mitran. Everyone in my family has that colouring." Midori's skin was golden beyond the violet feathers, but her eyes were pale. She applied live lenses to Seren's irises for an uncomfortable few seconds, and it was done.

Laure Prakash, dark-skinned with amber eyes and long straight black hair, gazed silently from the vri. Seren handed over her new identity card, fresh from the salon's fab panel, hoping cosmod wasn't wildly more expensive here than Tirion. "My credit should transfer."

Midori waved it away. "Tas is family, so you're family."

Seren cut off a protest that she was in no way related to Damou; an insult to family was unforgiveable anywhere.

"Not my genetic family," Midori added, misinterpreting her look. "He saved me and my brothers and parents from a lifeboat off Mitra Penta during the plague. We'd been drifting for days without supplies on emergency power after the station infell."

Seren thanked the cosmod tech and made her escape. Rescued people after the Mitran plague—interesting. Unexpected behaviour from a Grey dreg.

In the lift her slate buzzed with a new text line: "Wait with Midori. Damou." Seren killed it and walked outside.

On the greenway Seren didn't recognize her own reflection in late-night shop windows. In a moment of frivolity, she bought a wisp of a handmade lime-green silk dress. Second glances as she walked on told her the dress was a mistake, but at least it was something Seren Qasri would never wear. The unscannable palm laser weighed her hidden pocket, fitting neatly against her thigh.

Carrying a weapon felt wrong—she'd hated her fleet sidearm—as Kuhan said, a failure to disarm conflict.

A new text arrived from Maq with a marked guidesite map: "Meet Ryokan Bara soonest."

Her belly growled as she passed food carts and cafés. She followed the map to an inn farther down the greenway in Izu village, which the guidesite said was named for the canton on Mitra.

One moon had set, and another had not yet risen. In the dark the grassy path climbed through woodland that screened a deceptive number of dwellings, some detached and some in multi-storey islands. The village could have been transported to these hillsides from abandoned Earth, before its last poisoned centuries. She passed rock outcrops tufted with small twisted shrubs, but ahead the greenway curved up toward open pine forest.

At the foot of the hill a tall wooden gate stood open on a night-fragrant garden. Her path became broad steps up to a wooden building with great roof beams and deep overhanging eaves. The wooden doors were mostly a design feature; they led her through a Mitran entry membrane, the kind used on station docking hubs. It stretched and popped, and she came into a warmer and slightly more humid atmosphere.

Inside the inn the reception area was quiet and formal, but the dining room had the air of a neighbourhood café-bar at home. Families and couples ate at tables or in private rooms along a side wall, and across the room a crowd clustered near a bar to watch players in a game pit. A faint sound of running water came from the open back wall, where a garden stepped up the wooded hillside. Seren headed that way.

The problem with neighbourhood café-bars was that everyone noticed a new face; the room fell watchfully silent as she crossed, then buzzed with renewed talk. At one table she passed a woman with three small boys. A nursery class? No, all three carried a strong resemblance. Seren tried not to stare, caught their mother's watchful eye, and looked away, embarrassed. Among Mitrans, with their higher birthrate, these could be true siblings, not brother-friends. On Claer and other Pol worlds, second-wave emigrants still carried a mutation introduced as a minor genetic mod to lower birthrates in desperate times. Rumour said the Neutrality worlds had repaired the damaged sequence.

Seren claimed a corner table near the garden and stretched her slate screen to its double-handspan max. The only Claeran news stories were occupation propaganda—nothing on the Claeran government, let alone Delun Qasri. She shoved her slate across the table and gestured in an order, brought by the robed innkeeper, a square man with a blond topknot. The egg-lemon soup was excellent, and the galettes as good as anything in Tirion.

Over her meal she viewed her found images and file shots on the war's terrible end. So many needless deaths. Time to start her vri, once she reported to whatever fleet senior she could find. But when would that be? Her memory of Gandhi Base was slowly filling in, but some things still lay beyond memory, dimly sensed. Recalling Gandhi made her wonder how any of them had survived. They'd been on half rations in a dying station until the Pact-crewed transport arrived to take them off. Then it had taken many tendays to return to Pol space from the remote Tripline bases, sometimes by sublight, standing off their own nodes for days for Pact military traffic to transit, while other ships died hard around them from failed life support or mutiny or starvation.

Her vri on the war's end came first, then she would compile her material on Kuhan. Two brilliant documentaries covered Piñar, but there was no biography. No one had fully explored his background, his influence, what went wrong at Tanna. She couldn't bear to see him forgotten.

Finally, Seren sighed and slotted her new identity card. Laure Prakash was a Gilgai pilot with a Pact licence—an ex-Pol Fleet fighter pilot? Damou was mad to give her that bio. Combat experience wasn't something she could fake—but she had piloted the Az at Gandhi and knew the comms protocols. *All right. Maybe.* Laure's cardwork might get her a job flying insystem transport to the Claeran moons and rock belt, more likely dispatch or other ground work.

Laure. Seren was ready to be Laure. No one would expect anything of her; behind a stranger's face she could be whoever she wanted. Maybe Damou felt that way behind his mask of scar tissue . . . Where was Maq, anyway?

"Help us out?" A man stood by her table. He wore pearled grey vat suede with the look of hot fashion and had gold wire braided into his long red hair. Not bad. "I'm Ren. My friends and I need a fourth for *Sphinx*. Never fear, you don't have to play, just mark position."

Seren glanced toward the game pit. Expectant faces turned her way. Maybe they needed a fourth, or maybe they'd bet on whether the redhead could score. Mihal had cured her forever of pretty boys, but it would pass time, better than fretting over her new identity. She got up, smoothing down her too-short silk dress.

Cash cards changed hands as she approached the game pit. Ren showed her the setup; hyped for the game, he could hardly sit still. The other two, Galina and Carlos, synched their implants and settled into their chairs. As they talked, Seren heard the slight accent Ren was trying to cover. Galina and Carlos had it too. Over the wooden bar among the banners and flags hung a bas-relief gold sun with a silver star rising radiant on its horizon against a black starfield: the old Mitran emblem. A shiver walked down her spine. A Mitran bar, immeasurably distant from dead Mitra.

Seren tried the controls. *Sphinx* seemed to be a slick update of *Dragon's Gold*, which she'd played to a standstill in Gandhi's mess. Two teams took turns to race each other, dodge flying rocks, blast mines, and grab nuggets from between a dragon's claws until the timer rang. The sequence ran faster and faster until the inevitable collision, but after four years of practice, Seren didn't collide. Kid stuff, but fun.

Seren tested the pit's almost-familiar cockpit and controls enhanced onto a vri stage. This might be a bad idea. If she washed out, she'd look like a fool. If she won, they'd remember, and she didn't want to be remembered in the Cantons. But Laure was disposable; she could walk away from being Laure anytime. And for now, she could enjoy life.

What would Laure say? Laure would like improv. *Play hard. Live now.*

Carlos led, then Ren. The redhead dodged every rock and killed every hostile, but the timer caught him two gems short. *Hotshot.* By the end a few people had gathered to cheer and lay bets. Galina trailed him by five gems. Then it was Seren's turn.

"Take a trial run first or let me handle it," Ren offered.

Seren shook her head. "I've played."

"So, show us how it's done," he said, earning a few laughs.

Seren smiled and settled the eyeband they kept for unimplanted players. Sight, sound, and vibration enfolded her senses, even the ship smell of metal and plastics and cycled air. She lifted. Off and running.

Go out fast, she'd learned on Gandhi, and slow for obstacles. She accelerated furiously past the rocks, blasted all the mines and missiles ahead, ignored anything aft or flanking—no one got away with that realtime—and finally landed on the smaller moon. She'd clipped a couple of rocks, which cost her points and seconds, but she had all three hundred gems in her hold and a score in the thousands in time to cancel the timer. When she pulled off the VR set, Ren was collecting bets.

Seren breathed carefully, unexpectedly close to tears. It took her back, not to *Dragon's Gold* in the mess but to the deadlier game in the Bight. Not kid stuff. Not fun.

Ren gave Seren a long, measuring look from shrewd blue eyes before he smiled and congratulated her. He held out a hand to help her out of the chair, and the dress rode high on her thighs, drawing a low whistle from someone in the crowd. It was a very Laure dress. After four years of being nobody nowhere, being Laure was sweet. *Live now.*

The innkeeper set a steaming decanter that looked like Nevez bubble glass on the table nearest the game pit with a nod to Seren. A lemur with a striped tail bounded after him and leaped onto tables to collect cash cards.

Ren poured their small cups as Carlos bitched about their duty roster and their supervisor. Old friends, with their own jokes and slang. Any of Seren's friends who survived probably thought she was dead, thanks to Damou's paranoia. The rice wine warmed her, and Ren leaned closer than necessary, seething with jumpy, raw energy. Glitz? Probably not. The Cantons banned it; too many people spun up and spun out.

Something changed abruptly in the main room, like the subtle shift in noise level that greets the first actor on stage. Why? Seren's neck hair lifted—gods, she'd grown trouble sensors.

Near the door Damou spoke with a blonde woman and headed for the bar. She'd never noticed his slight limp; he'd moved better in micro-G.

Damou stopped at the bar, leaning to talk with the innkeeper.

Seren looked down at the heavy glass decanter, at the tabletop, anything, not wanting to see him and not wanting to be seen. Seren Qasri wasn't here, Laure Prakash was here, and Laure wanted a good time.

"Never quits," Ren muttered. He stood abruptly and headed for the door.

Trust Damou to wreck the party, Seren had time to think as the lights dimmed and died.

A chorus of protest rose from the game pit, and a few slate lights flickered on around the main room. Smoke drifted over the tables, and a child wailed. People headed for the exits, not in a rush as Claerans would, but with purpose. She should follow the crowd, contact Maq to meet her somewhere else—

A hand seized Seren's right arm above the elbow, hard enough to make her wince, and a harsh voice said in Mitran-accented Peel close to her ear, "Get up. Walk toward the front door."

"Not a chance." Seren gripped the table with both hands.

"Now. Don't try anything." *Damou?* But his voice was rougher and darker than Damou's. It made her skin crawl. It was a voice she'd first heard in terror when two men grabbed her on a wrecked station. *Claer Arian. Again.*

Something hard pressed between her shoulder blades. Not sharp like a knife, blunt like a hand laser. Could she pull Maq's palm laser from her pocket? Not without standing up. Instead, Seren stretched just far enough to grab the heavy glass decanter by the neck and swung it with all her strength at the hated voice. Connected.

The cruel grip on her arm lightened. Seren jumped to her feet and stumbled toward the open wall and the wild garden.

6

Continuity cut. Cool air brushed her face, and she dimly saw large shapes, trees or rocks, that loomed by starlight. She would be too easy to track in the garden. Up into the pines—but as she gathered herself, a warm hand closed on her left wrist.

"This way," Damou said.

"Leave me alone."

Damou tugged her away from the inn's black bulk, and she felt gravel underfoot. Seren hadn't evaded one captor to let another take over, as on Arian. In the dark she slammed a fist at his head, but instead she punched empty air and staggered forward.

"Quietly." He pulled her uphill on a narrow gravel path between long-needled conifers, pungent with evening scents of warm sap and other plants she couldn't identify.

"Don't give me orders. I don't answer to you."

"If you did, Lieutenant, you'd know when you were in trouble. You're bound to damage yourself or someone else, and God help you if it's another of our people." Surprisingly, he spoke in her own Tavod, with a distinct Mitran accent like her voice synthesis for Teak, except she'd coded Teak to sound a lot friendlier.

"What does that mean?"

"Someone wants your Bight data."

I don't have it. You stole it. But she'd already said that enough times.

In a curve of the path, a small building nestled against the hillside, overhung by conifers and broad-leafed trees. Its roof rose darker than the night sky as they stepped onto its wooden porch. A sensor post near the door lit and murmured, "Welcome to the moon viewing hut." Damou dropped her hand, then slid open a door and stepped inside, while Seren paused on the porch to kick gravel out of her sandals. She angrily rubbed her sore wrist.

"We'll go out the other side," he said.

"Why would I? You turn up every time that dreg from Arian grabs me."

"The same man? Are you sure?" He sounded shocked enough to give her pause.

"No. But he sounded the same, acted the same."

"Inside," Damou said. "Now."

Seren took in his body language—wary, not threatening—and stepped into the dark building that smelled of disuse. In Bryniau it would be crawling with unsects or luzards. A raised alcove in an end wall held a flower arrangement in a vase, but she was in no mood to appreciate the minimalist beauty.

Across the room, Damou slid another door to look out. "Someone's out there. We'll go back the way we came."

"You can go where you want. I'm going down to find Maq," Seren said.

"Maq's not here. An AnvilCo emergency. Don't risk it. Please." He sounded less peremptory in Tavod.

"Talk first."

"Not this time."

A crunch of gravel sounded faintly outside the back door. Damou nudged her out onto the porch where they'd entered and silently slid the front door shut behind them, staring uphill between the dark trees. Seren saw only a quarter moon sailing above the hill's eastern shoulder. He pulled her back against the wall of the moon viewing hut, waited a long moment, and led her forward up the rocky hillside.

Seren stumbled, knocking down loose rock with a wake-the-dead racket, and a second later, a laser trace from below them streaked red toward a conifer just overhead. A lower branch hissed into flame. Then a bolt from above sizzled past close enough that she felt the heat on her bare arm. She and Damou dropped to the ground and froze. No escape that way.

Then he caught her wrist again and tugged, and she followed him down and across the hillside with as much haste and care as she could manage, knowing that a single hoverlight or flare would illuminate every pebble and make this a shooting range.

Beyond a knot of closer-growing trees, he tapped her wrist and pointed downward. The shingled roof of the viewing hut was just below them. A quick descent of the outcrop put them in deep shadow under its eaves. Seren leaned against the hut's end wall to catch her breath, and felt more than heard the door slide open just metres away. Even before Damou's warning tap on her wrist, she froze at the sound of quiet voices.

In the narrow passage between the hut's end wall and the outcrop they'd come down, Damou felt along the rock face, searching. Seren saw nothing but the black hillside, ragged treetops, a starry sky, and the faint glow of his pale shirt.

"Here." He guided her hand across the outcrop, and she felt a rough wood-plank door faced with grownstone, now slightly ajar.

Seren edged in cautiously sideways after Damou, but the niche was so small that she collided with him trying to turn around. He pulled the door shut.

Rough rock underfoot sloped toward the opening, and rock walled them on three sides. Her hands found garden tools on rustic metal hooks. A gardener's storage shed carved from the bedrock, or maybe created with grownstone, to blend in with the site.

She heard the moon viewing hut's door slide closed a few metres away, and the men talked quietly as they moved away across the slope.

"They'll be back," she said over her shoulder in a bare whisper.

Damou didn't answer right away, busy with his slate. "The hut blocks any scan. Even heat seekers would need to strike the opening at exactly the right angle."

Seren tried to find a foothold for her sandals on the sloping floor. Damou's steadying arm came around her waist. Angrily, she shoved his hand away, and her feet slipped on the rock.

Seren chewed her lip and let the silence grow until it collapsed.

"Who are they?"

"Pact hunters. Pol spies like you. Who knows. If they get the data, millions will suffer."

"You must know I don't have your data."

"Someone thinks you do. Tonight, they nearly killed a Spartí rating in a greenway café. A tall woman with red hair and blue eyes—as you were a few hours ago." He managed to sound stiffly offended, a tone she'd heard more than once in her undistinguished military service.

Seren recalled the woman they'd seen shot in the next café— then it struck her. *Spartí.* Kuhan's old company, still operating? She'd thought Damou's jacket was a relic of lost Mitra. She closed her eyes a moment to dispel the grainy image of men and women in grey uniforms lying motionless in the dust of Piñar village.

"A full ground search will find us."

"No. My people will come for us."

Seren's feet kept slipping, and she couldn't get a purchase on the sloping rock. She'd been too hasty in throwing off his arm, but damned if she would let him hold her like a rag doll. She leaned away, even then feeling the warmth he gave off. She touched the storage nook's wall and felt ragged protrusions. If he leaned back, it would shred him. Better him than her.

"Why don't we just call them?" Mitrans were insanely secretive, that was why.

"My comm is jammed. They have up-to-date Mitran tech."

"I thought you'd have more practice at grabbing strangers."

"Qasri—" Damou tangibly controlled an impulse to snap at her.

Good. It was satisfying to get under his thick skin for a change. She slid Maq's palm laser from her pocket.

Damou took her hand and closed it around the laser. Seren shivered. Their niche seemed to trap cold rather than warmth.

A sound of approaching machinery, muffled by the rock around them, might be a high-powered hover. Searchlights probed the rock face, and their reflection lit the niche. She gathered herself to reach for the door.

Damou held her back. "Those aren't my people, they'd have hailed. If a searchlight angles in here, you'll shine like a snowfield in that dress. Recolour it."

"I can't. It's natural silk."

"What colour are you wearing under it?"

"A rather pretty cocoa brown." Warmth climbed Seren's neck to her face.

"Take off the dress."

"Are you crazy?"

"Roll it small. We have about twenty seconds before the hover clears those trees." He pulled off his pale shirt.

She grabbed the laser from her pocket and peeled off the dress, banging both elbows on the storage nook's rough walls. Rolled into a ball, it disappeared into his hand.

"Push as far back in toward me as you can."

Turning to face him as the first searchlights probed through the trees, she saw what Damou had missed, the glaring white bandage on his arm. She put both brown hands over it and leaned close against his chest. A sharp exhalation, as though she'd slugged him in the solar plexus. She bit back terror and laughter. His chest hair tickled her breasts, which felt indecently good, and his warm hands on her back raised an electric tremor. Too bad it was Damou.

Frozen in a minute that crawled like an hour, they waited as a searchlight passed back and forth across their narrow niche. Seren slitted her eyes as its glare pierced chinks in the door and illuminated every crystal in the rock, every pore on her hands, and Damou's shoulder.

Finally, the hover roared off above the moon viewing hut. When darkness and quiet flowed back in, she shivered against Damou's warmth.

"Quick thinking."

"They teach us in spy school," she said.

Damou snorted. "Among other things. Good thing I'm immune."

Coarse hair curled between her spread fingers on his chest, and her hands—Laure's hands—wanted to explore. In fleet training Seren had blushed her way through the classes on seduction, knowing she'd never use those tawdry skills. But now he had challenged her. *I'll show you immune.* She shifted her hip and let one breast brush his arm, and felt his breath catch. His warm hands rested on her back under her long fall of hair, and she swayed to the slightest pressure. *Oh.* She stood quite still for a breath while warmth flooded her. *Yes.*

Then her brain started to work again. *Bad idea.* She stepped back and folded her arms over her breasts, not that there was much to cover. "Take off your dress or we'll die, he says. Does that line usually work?"

"Grow up, Qasri." Damou was having difficulty breathing. *Good.* At least she wasn't suffering alone.

7

Damou handed back her rolled dress, and she pulled it down over her head. As she dropped the laser in her pocket, Damou's shirt settled around her shoulders from behind. She said, "You'll get cold."

"No. Higher body temperature is a Mitran mod. I'll show you."

His hands were warm on her shoulders. It was true, he was always warm, now that she thought about it, as though some internal thermostat were set higher.

"Huh. You say that to every naked woman," she said. Another exhalation. Getting him to laugh, and twice in two minutes, was more entertaining than making him angry. She'd made Kuhan laugh, too, to his surprise.

"Are you drunk?"

"No, you spoiled my party." Laure said things Seren would never dare.

"Wrong party. Lean on me."

"This is the right party?" Seren leaned back, and his arms came around her again. Warm. The hair on her neck tingled. "You invited me, you entertain me. Tell me a story."

"I don't know any stories," he said over her shoulder, warm breath on her cheek.

"Make one up." Seren yawned and put her arms into the shirt

sleeves. His skin or his shirt gave off a subtle aromatic scent she couldn't identify.

"Do you remember the men who grabbed you on Arian?"

"One was short with liveware tattoos."

"Dead. What about the one who ran?"

"Long blond hair, taller than you, with a lot of irideco. Angry. Violent. He was the one who grabbed me again tonight." Seren swallowed dry, unwilling to revisit her terror. She watched a satellite flash across the sliver of night sky that she could see by leaning to the right. Smoke drifted up from the inn through the fragrant pine trees, but it didn't smell like woodsmoke. Maybe they'd used a smoke bomb to clear the inn.

"Difficult to lay charges for an offense committed under martial law. Pact lawyers will brush it off. But under civil law I can bring him to you for *sarhaad* so you can settle the insult."

Seren nodded. It was a generous offer. "You know Claeran law?"

"I worked in Tirion during the war."

Seren hesitated. If Damou was a working name, as Maq said, he must have a real name. Until now she'd never cared. "Who are you, Meistr Damou?"

"A passable dangerous-cargo pilot."

"Is that a joke?"

"If you're laughing."

"Why is it you're almost human in the dark?"

"You have a natural gift for abuse, do you know that? I'm almost human in the light, but you can't see past my face."

"You have a problem with your face. I don't." It was mostly true. His abrasive manner and his arrogance bothered her more than the twisted scar tissue that drew her eyes less often. It wasn't like any scaremod she'd searched on the grids. She pulled his shirt closer, feeling its sensual slip and catch against her skin. Silk. "Meistr Damou, I don't know anything about you."

"You know as much as you need."

Seren counted on her fingers. "Mitran survivor. Onetime MitraCorps officer or noncom. Angry with everyone, especially yourself. Worked on Claer. Good with languages. Solitary."

"Not bad. Now drop it."

And a strong sense of justice, she didn't add. Her life was littered with debris for the same reason. Seren guessed uneasily she was some of Damou's debris. "And Inka's lover?"

"A lifetime ago."

Inka didn't seem to know it was a lifetime ago. "I don't understand you. Behind that face you're a kind and honourable man."

He tensed as if she'd insulted him, but kept silent till curiosity won. "But?"

"Why don't you act like you know it?" Seren smiled in the dark. Leave it alone, he would say. Time for a pre-emptive strike. "If you were Spartí, you knew Teak Kuhan."

"I was Spartí." A long pause. "Your vri *Rain*—why did you do that?"

Damou knew about *Rain?* The vri was never released or distributed outside the Pact appeals court that finally admitted it as evidence under diplomatic pressure. Maybe Kuhan told some of his people before he died.

Seren took a shaky breath and risked the hard answer, the one that wouldn't make sense. "He looked the wrong way."

"What?" He went still.

"Were you at Piñar?" Seren felt him nod against her hair. A Piñar survivor who knew Kuhan: suddenly Damou looked more interesting. Maybe she could interview him for her vri doc. "Kuhan looked north across the square when the insurgents entered the village. What he saw brought him down. It wasn't just the Pact weapons, though I focussed on them in *Rain* to get him acquitted."

"Saw what?"

"A rock. I don't know why it mattered. A stray shot knocked chips off it, and it pulsed with light. It shook him so much he abandoned his command. He couldn't tell anyone. Their comms were jammed, and the Tannans didn't have the tech, so Pacters or an insider must have jammed them."

"How in hell do you know that?"

"I studied Zari Lind's footage, trying to make sense of what happened. I built a sightlines analysis program, not knowing that better ones were already available. But mine did what I needed—it exonerated Kuhan."

"Why?"

"Everything worth knowing I learned from him. 'The only true victory lies in shedding no blood.'" She never talked about this. For some reason it felt easier to tell a stranger in a surreal nonplace.

"Don't romanticize. Spartí was never pacifist. One thing we learned the hard way—peacemaking is only as powerful as the threat that backs it."

Seren bristled. "There's nothing romantic about it. Spartí accepted mostly warfighting jobs until Kuhan took over and steered it toward peace building. Four other companies followed his lead, and it deepened an old split in MitraCorps. Maybe that's what brought him down—someone in Spartí knew about Piñar."

Damou shook his head. "You worked this out alone?"

"I viewed grid files. I read. I listened. My mother headed the Claeran senate committee on Mitran liaison. No one noticed a gawky, tongue-tied kid in the corner."

"You're wrong," he said, "about some things. Right about far too much. Keep it quiet."

Seren nodded, distracted by his voice. Over the last hour it had become less raw, more Mitran, even in Tavod. Maybe Damou also talked more easily with a stranger in the dark. "You're giving me orders again. What was your rank?"

"I made warrant officer."

"And then?" All MitraCorps officers rose through the ranks.

"Tell me why Kuhan."

"Can we open the door?"

"No."

Seren sighed and leaned her head back on his shoulder. She could see deeper black where two door planks and their stone facing didn't quite meet. Above the hut roof and the black treetops, stars floured the night sky. They must be facing the galactic core. The galaxy's vastness neatly put her own small concerns into perspective.

"My cousin-friends teased me that it was the flash uniform." She shrugged. "I liked how he looked and sounded and moved, but the worlds are full of handsome men. How he thought was more interesting. He told stories, and people listened."

"Twice your age?"

"It seemed like a lot then. Now, when I view the Tanna images, he looks so young."

"A vain, arrogant kid with fool ideas about saving humanity from itself."

"He did exactly that, time after time." As a strategist he'd studied his enemy and struck decisively with minimal loss. As a negotiator he'd sensed flaws and applied leverage to draw opponents together.

"You read too much into one flawed man." His voice was almost too low to hear.

"All of us are flawed, Meistr Damou. To believe one man's flaws are greater than others is the ultimate arrogance."

That made him smile, she felt it. Strange man.

He said, "I need to tell you—"

Seren turned her head on his shoulder, but instead of speaking, he rested his fingers lightly on her mouth. Then she heard it too, a faint rustle and scrape. Someone climbed across the rocks down to their left, stealthily coming this way. Two people, she thought. Seren froze, not daring even to breathe deeply.

Damou shifted slightly, and she felt the small weapon in his hand. He tapped her pocket until she drew out Maq's palm laser. Someone whispered almost in arm's reach. What if they had high-end nanobot DNA seekers? Then the game was over. But if they had off-the-shelf pheromone sniffers keyed solely to fear hormones—she had to be giving off waves of fear—maybe they could be misled. What was stronger than fear?

Seren dropped the laser back in her pocket and turned to slide her hands around Damou's back and down, making him catch his breath hard. She murmured, "Pheromones."

Then she stopped thinking as his hand smoothed her long hair, down her shivering spine, down and up . . . *Oh. Gods. Yes.* She brushed her lips across his warm shoulder and up his neck to the less damaged side of his face. Salty. His hair smelled good.

A few minutes later, the voices and scuff of feet sounded more distant. She let out her breath. So did Damou. It was perversely reassuring, his fear.

Damou smiled against her cheek. "Claeran spy school."

"Huh. We're alive."

His knowing touch still had her full attention. She let her own hands explore, and they told her he was very fit, very fine. His face didn't matter to Laure. What mattered was his hands touching her where she lived, and her body lifting to meet him. She let her fingers drift down from his navel, quickening his breath on her cheek.

No.

Time to stop.

Damou knew it too. Before she could form a coherent thought, he eased away.

"How did you know me in the inn?" she finally thought to ask.

"I'd know you anywhere. Beauty surrounded by chaos."

"Liar."

"Just this once, how about rescuer and friend?"

All right. Seren smiled. He brushed back her hair to cup her face in his warm palm, and she leaned easily. Later, drifting into a restless dream, she asked, "Why?" His quiet words stayed with her, "I had a debt."

Seren. She stirred at her name. Warm arms around her . . . it was a good dream.

"Qasri. Wake up. They're bringing a hover."

Early light found the chinks in the gardener's shed door, and when he opened it, trees stood black against a golden sky. Damou spoke into his wrist comm in an unknown language. Both her hands clasped his forearm, and she felt the play of muscle as he tapped the comm bracelet, signing off. His movements were sure, and his warm breath was sweet on her cheek. Learning a man by touch was a new experience, but the lesson was over.

Seren slid out of Damou's shirt and twisted carefully to face him. He'd bled through the bandage on his arm, but otherwise, with his face half turned, his hair and skin and eyes were all golden in the morning light. She lifted her hair off her neck, momentarily surprised at its length until she remembered her cosmod, darker than Damou—Damou who called her a beauty. *A joke.* Maybe he liked to provoke her as much as she liked to provoke him. In another time and place, they could have been friends.

Damou braced one elbow on the rock beside her shoulder, looking at her much too closely. For a moment she thought he would lean to kiss her, but kisses were for lovers, not survivors.

He opened the shed door and walked out, pulling on his shirt.

"I thought of a story."

"About time." Seren followed him out to sit on the front step of the moon viewing house. The sun sent dusty shafts between the trees in the lovely garden. What kind of story would she hear from a man who barely said five words together?

"Years ago, when my friend Kai built this inn, I came here for the hot springs," Damou said. "Over there in the pine grove."

Steam rose from a small building's shingle roof. Seren would do anything for a hot bath. She yawned and leaned against Damou's shoulder.

"I stayed in for a long time. When I came out, I put on the long bathrobe and walked back to the main building."

Damou was good to lean on. His voice was beautiful when he wasn't giving orders. Seren let the Mitran accent flow over her senses like warm water. When she realized what she was doing, her eyes flew open.

"I had my clothes under one arm and my kit in the other hand. I wasn't used to wearing a long robe."

Kai and his elderly grandmother had stood on the porch to welcome him, and he'd climbed the stairs toward them. And without noticing, step by step, Damou had walked up inside the front of his bathrobe.

"By the top step I squatted like a duck at their feet, trapped inside the robe. Kai's grandmother looked down and said that humility could be a virtue, but that kneeling showed excessive pride in humility."

Seren looked aside at him. Deadpan. Then she started to smile, and the good corner of his mouth twitched. That gave her unreasonable pleasure.

"Don't go back to Tirion alone, Seren. Let me take you."

"I will." But she wouldn't. She regretting lying to him—Damou was all right—but she needed to go. In a few hours she could be in Derw clinic rebuilding her memory, and this would seem like a strange dream.

"Seren-Tas! All happy!"

Hasi bounded up and leaped onto Damou's shoulder as an armoured hover in MitraCorps colours dropped to the gravel in front of the hut. Maq crouched in it like a leathery brown gargoyle, looking angry enough to spit nails.

Ren leaned out to hand them in. "Good thing you called. We thought you went over the ridge, but we couldn't find you."

Damou clasped his shoulder and turned to Seren. "You met Renat Von."

Renat Von? A must-have interview for her vri bio. Seren tried not to stare. The flashy dresser who'd challenged her at *Sphinx* had been Kuhan's second at Piñar.

Later, soaking in the hot springs pool, she recalled Damou's amusing story. Excessive humility was pride, and pride led to a fall. The story was his oblique answer to her romanticized ideas about Spartí and Kuhan. She had never been taken down a notch quite so subtly.

8

ES2741.228

Cloudy light flowed down the sword blade like sleet. It was the only thing that moved in the practice zone for a long moment before Tas shifted his balance, and the blades slid onward and apart with a cold hiss of steel on steel.

Kai gestured: Again. Take the opening.

Tas found his stance and lunged, and Kai blocked his sword at mid-blade, holding him there on his own strength. If he turned, Kai could cut him in half. If he pushed farther, he would be face-down on the mat. Kai sighed and let his blade slide free.

An edged wind blew in through the open walls of the practice area, cooling Tas even after an hour's warm-up and making him shiver when they paused for more than a few seconds. Beyond the wide roof overhang, the new yellow-green maple leaves were still small on their branches. Cottonwood silk drifted down from the height and across the broad porch.

Step. Lunge. Push against Kai's block. Relax and turn. Let the blade slide. Angle the hilt up to the left, pivot and slice down. Kai defeated every move he made.

Balance eluded him. Instead of sliding flexibly, his thoughts dragged. What had happened last night? Nothing he knew as reality.

Step. Lunge. Deflect. Tas found it hard to concentrate on an exercise they'd done for twenty years. They did it first as boys learning not to damage each other with wooden staffs, then as young men pushing their own limits with wooden swords, then as seasoned fighters with unsharpened steel. Now Kai was probably Mitra's best surviving teacher of edged weapons, far exceeding any skill Tas would attain. Their practice was a long-established construction of mutual trust, a moving meditation on death.

Reality surrounded him but it too stayed just out of reach. Tas rubbed his bare feet on the coarsely woven cotton mat, no warmer than his cotton shirt and pants, and breathed out hard to see his living breath rise as steam. That was real. The cedar roof posts were real, and if he slammed into one, the pain was real. The cottonwood silk drifting across the porch was real. But he couldn't shake his own sense that this was someone else's world, someone else's life. He feared this illusion, even knowing it was mostly exhaustion.

"Again. This time slowly."

Concentrate. He needed to stay present in himself or cease to exist: that was the truth of his own fragility. Kai could kill him with one blow if his mental calm wavered, or worse, he could kill Kai. Sometimes that made him want to drop the sword and walk away.

Tas found his stance and brought up his sword point two-handed. Right foot forward. *Lunge.* Kai blocked the blow forcefully, and their blades slid shrieking until they hung suspended in exact opposition. Tas turned sharply, too sharply, raised his sword overhead and sliced down in anticipation of another hard parry. Instead, it skidded over Kai's sword, and the hilt caught the teacher brutally hard across the back of the hand.

Only then did he register Kai's instruction. Slowly. Instead, he'd made a full-speed attack. Tas opened his mouth to call a halt, apologize, concentrate for God's sake, but Kai's blade swept around behind him in an icy blur. Tas's sword flew up out of his strong grip and far across the mats. Kai set his own weapon aside and stood open-handed, inviting his attack with a calm face. Tas stepped in to seize his arm. Long before he could frame a thought, he was pinned face-down on the mat with his right hand twisted up hard. He bore it as long as he could, then slapped the mat.

Enough. Kai released him, and he rolled to his feet quickly.

Again, Kai offered the opening, and again threw him hard. And again. Anger finally flooded out Tas's calm, and he fought back with all his strength. Kai accepted the attack and put him down abruptly, and on the mat, he pressed down on Tas's elbow harder and harder until tears sprang from his eyes. Kai helped him up, finally, both of them sweating rivers and breathing clouds of steam. They sheathed their swords, bowed, and left the mats.

"All right?" Kai finally asked as they walked past the reflecting pool. Each of its five boulders represented one of the five traditional virtues.

"Yes." Tas looked across the garden rather than meet Kai's eyes. The trees overhanging the pool were late coming into leaf, and the grass was still green. Kai was his oldest surviving friend, apart from Renat. What else was he going to say? *No, I'm deep in trouble of my own making.*

Kai pushed blond hair out of his face and retied his topknot. After a long look, he nodded. That was all. He didn't need to say anything. *Don't go off the rails again. Ask for help if you need it.* Tas didn't need help.

"How's your hand?"

"All right tomorrow."

Tas knew otherwise, having felt bone break under the sword hilt. It was worse to feel in another man's body than his own. Kai still looked at him, not quite frowning, wanting to ask something else. Kai also had quit Spartí except for special tasks, and they were both sole survivors of close families. His fourth thema sergeant never lost his temper and never dealt twice with a problem. They'd learned each other well as they searched for Kai's five boulders in desert Haram. Kai was able to let go of the past by the time they found his five stones, having absorbed their five virtues.

Kai clasped his shoulder and walked away. Tas followed the cottonwood silk drifting toward the pool and sat, acknowledging the aches Kai had bestowed in teaching him to pay attention.

On Earth long ago, the artist's garden had flourished within a house courtyard. This garden recreated in the Cantons of Claer lay between Kai's porch and the wilder growth that spilled up the hillside into the pine woods.

Wisdom. Benevolence. Justice. Courtesy. Fidelity. The five boulders rose from a rectangle of water to define a space no larger than the moon viewing hut. One of the overhanging trees would bear white flowers, evoking the purity of life. Justice was the greatest virtue, or was it benevolence? Wisdom was his own favourite, low and rough and solid underfoot. But the harder he worked, the more dramatically he failed. All the virtues eluded his efforts.

Tas sat cross-legged on the stone step, seeking his balance, seeking nonattachment. But his mind was irresistibly drawn back to chaos. Quick, resourceful, and ruthless, she had all the qualities MitraCorps sought in its own intelligence people. Her plan to defeat pheromone sniffers—if they'd had sniffers—dispelled any illusion that she was an idealistic kid thrown in over her head. Someday he might laugh about spending hours wedged in a shed with a Politayan spy, but this morning he still felt concussed.

In the morning quiet, a fitful wind caressed the hillside and carried down a dry aromatic scent of pine. Unsects in their iridescent gossamer stage floated across the garden pond. Few native species had survived Claer's rapid terraforming, and these flyers were now among the planet's highest native life forms. Hardier than they appeared, like Qasri. His arm throbbed from hours of holding up a woman who wasn't as slight as she looked.

Lira had been everything he admired in a woman, lovely, calm, a fine technician, and yet before he left for Tanna, they'd amiably agreed not to renew their contract. Everything he disliked, Qasri distilled to its essence. She was volatile, undisciplined, arrogant, armed with merciless wit, pitiless in her beauty, a maker of inflammatory vris, a traitor drafted into her fleet, who tried to kill him on sight. A splinter under his thumbnail.

Concentrate. Unknown men with a stolen industrial hover, Ren said, knew Qasri's identity and pursued her. How had Ren lost them so easily? Inka hadn't yet traced anyone. The inn and the moon viewing hut yielded DNA only from him and Qasri.

Tas had missed every move. He should have dropped their pursuers and climbed the ridge, where Ren could have found him. Instead, he'd gone to ground and tried to protect Qasri.

A Claeran girl from the misty hills of Tirion y Bryniau who probably wore woollen socks to bed . . . It didn't work. She was also a lithe young woman with a spill of silken hair and deep eyes that saw straight through his defences. When she forgot to hate him, he glimpsed the girl she had been: passionate over her causes, quick to laughter, full of life as he was full of death.

Tas imagined courting her as Damou, getting her to accept him as he was, becoming her lover, but his face was an acid test she failed over and over. He could repair the damage—but that was madness, a threadbare plot straight from the vri dramas.

Courage had failed him when he wanted to tell her. Her vri plans put his identity at risk, given her skill at assembling overlooked fragments. Now he needed Louhi Takahara's data—safely hidden, he was certain—and Qasri's memory of the Bight encounter. As long as Tas got the intelligence, it didn't matter if she told her superiors, who couldn't use it anyway. Time was running out, and Qasri exponentially complicated his only way to contain the threat.

Once she was safe again on Melusine, he would run for the Deep Outside to finish his survey. Write this off as extreme provocation under bizarre circumstances. Forget it. But the feel of her stayed in his bones and her jasmine scent lingered in his shirt, and if he closed his eyes, he saw her small breasts haloed in starlight. It was intensely erotic and adolescent, and his body betrayed him in adolescent fashion. So much for nonattachment.

9

When his comm vibrated, it felt like a reprieve.

"I had Spartí rebook you. I need you on Walden, working with Nolin," Inka said from his wrist; he didn't bother switching to his cochlear relay here in Kai's safe garden.

"No. Kill the contract. Nolin is trouble." Tas swallowed an angrier reply, in no mood for Inka's imperatives. She still hadn't turned up the patterned moulder object from Balint's docking bay airlock. He tapped his comm twice, severing the connection.

Tas got to his feet stiffly and walked around the garden from the stone of courtesy, in which he had just failed again, to fidelity—it was what the Spartí rose stood for, keeping faith. Faithfulness he had in good measure, searching for Lira and Halia beyond all hope, returning to extract Seren Qasri from the fate she'd drawn down in the Bight.

His comm vibrated again as he walked toward justice. Inka had pressured him to fit an implant, but he refused her a permanent place in his brain. Inka knew no boundaries.

"I need him," she said more calmly now. "He's my conduit to Walden's six families."

"Send someone else. I'll be gone." His search task was more important.

"The six families plan a Pact coup. We need to safeguard

Mitran interests."

"The six families have planned a Pact coup since old Earth. Let them conspire. In the end they'll keep the devil they know. Gabe de Jong holds the Pact on a sane course." *As long as he controls Nolin.*

Tas stepped from the wooden walk onto the stone path. Bright leaves brushed his cheek with a scent of growth and life. As a restorative between deep-space jobs he often walked in Kai's garden, which looked and even smelled like Mitra, as he chose to remember Mitra.

"Nolin has backdoor links to the Xanadu cartels. I need to know their movements." Even on voice only, Inka sounded anxious. She knew she asked too much.

"You have better sources." *Yes. A Nolin link explains Balint's swagger.*

"I need a way to deal with Nolin."

"You can't deal with Nolin, only neutralize him."

"I know you want to settle old scores, but if you kill him—"

"Not kill him, contain him." Enough people had died, too many by his hand.

"You can contain him better on Walden."

"No."

A tremor started in his left hand and quickly travelled, tensing his shoulders and stiffening his back. His regeneration was good but not perfect. The Mitran surgeons at the prison hospital on Mesa had saved his life, even improved it in limited ways with his augmented senses, though more than once he had cursed them as torturers.

"What does it take, Taso?"

Justice. Tas studied the pool's still surface. Benevolence. When he could move again, he resumed his pacing. Fidelity. Rarely did one get a true chance to make things right—and his only leverage was Inka's fear.

"Qasri."

A long pause. At last Inka answered. "She'll bring you down."

"No," he said. Qasri would come to harm if they kept her in the dark any longer. He knew that after last night.

"Does she have Takahara's data?"

"No." Maybe. Someday she would tell him what happened in

the Bight. Qasri was as honest as circumstances allowed, unlike Inka with her many small, cruel secrets. Tas knew far more of those than he wanted.

"What do you want?" Inka sounded subdued.

"Qasri needs to know everything. Far worse if she goes looking for answers and puts it together alone. You can rebuild neurons and stimulate her amygdala to heal the block." Once she knew, she would hate him again.

"It would be unethical. She refused my help," Inka said, taking the high ground for once.

"So, give her all the Pol senate and surveillance files and a full set of grid control codes."

"What happened last night?"

Tas had no answer. He'd walked around all four sides of the garden as they talked, and now again stood on the corner stone of courtesy. Golden carp were schooling around it, hoping for something more tangible than virtue.

"Forgive me. I know. Lira." She actually did sound contrite.

Lira had been gone for nine years. This had nothing to do with Lira, but the answer showed exactly how little Inka did know of common humanity. Tas didn't want this job—Nolin was dangerous—but he had to try. "You'll help Qasri?"

"I'll give you the Pol files and control code. You owe me. And I shall certainly collect." Then Inka was gone in a storm of manufactured static.

His bracelet flashed an alarm. His damned meeting with Jaime Riordan at HQ. All he wanted was sleep. No, all he wanted was to find Seren Qasri, clasp her cold hands, and say, Come away with me now.

Instead, Tas fought a yawn and palmed through his hair. His vision was shattered, his credibility was in ashes, his judgment was unreliable and—having attained none of the virtues—he was exactly the brute Qasri thought. Damou.

At the morning-shaded side of the garden, he spoke a few words and walked through the window membrane into the room Kai kept for him. Table, chair, narrow bed, a cluster of stills on the wall: a large family group in a barren pale landscape; a fair woman and child smiling in lost sunlight; a borrowed miniature of Seren Qasri.

He would tell her everything. Soon.

A hideous stranger stared back from the mirror when Tas stepped out of the cold shower. He depilated by touch, avoiding his reflection. His shirt hung loose and the slacks gathered at his waist until he told them to adjust. Either he'd lost mass or the Pact's Mitran surgeons had rebuilt him a size smaller. Jaime liked him to report in uniform. Not today, not around Qasri.

The inn was quiet at this time of day, mercifully, and Tas walked from the southwest wing to reception without passing anyone. On the cantilevered mezzanine he slowed to watch birds and lizards dart among the leaves in the warm interior biozone of waterfalls and vines. Kai had built and grown his inn from nothing in seven years. The hand-adzed timbers and hand-plastered walls enclosed subtle tech, and Kai's rescued animals wandered freely through the public rooms and gardens, safe in the Cantons from the Pact occupation. The textiles, porcelains, and sliding screens were real art objects from old Earth. Someday he could show Seren—No. Put that aside. It would be hard enough to keep his balance when he took her to Tirion.

Detaching a platform, he floated down through the tropical garden near the waterfall to a reception area that overlooked the greenway. In an armchair near the big phoenix screen, Maq sprawled with Hasi chasing dust motes in the sunbeams at his feet.

"Emergency over?"

"False alarm. Getting me out of the way, I guess."

"Qasri?"

"In Kai's hot springs," Maq told him sleepily.

Tas nodded and walked on, fighting the temptation to check on her. Outside in the north door courtyard, he lifted his face to the scented breeze and sunlight.

Visitors to MitraCorps sometimes searched Izu for an ugly administration block, but the airy building was all light-drenched wood, stone, and glass that stepped down beside an eloquent waterfall to a quiet garden pool. Years ago, he'd ragged Kai about designing it purely for the entertainment of watching outsiders revise their ideas about the uncultured Grey companies.

MitraCorps HQ, like most Mitran buildings, contained more than met the casual eye. Its reception areas and offices opened onto the gardens, but twelve underground levels held communications and training areas that few outsiders saw. The building, like the spaceport compound, was large for a force of ten thousand plus support. Even in exile the Mitran Grey companies remained a professional core designed to stiffen a larger force of reservists or volunteers. At the war's outset Tas had advised aiding the Politaya in that way; the Pact assault was a serious setback, and losing it would be ruinous. Jaime had cast the veto.

Tas turned at the waterfall and crossed the garden. People in the offices looked up in surprise as he passed. It had been a while.

Jaime Riordan sat at his desk lost in thought. As soon as Tas entered, he got up to measure coffee beans and pour water, instinctively turning his back on trouble. Even when they sipped sweet coffee from Claeran glass cups, Jaime looked anywhere but at Tas's face. His light eyes and UV-treated mélange features showed mixed second-wave ancestry, making him a darker version of Tas, back when Tas looked human.

Jaime had been a brilliant field officer, but never the diplomat MitraCorps needed as its director-general. If he'd acted on Spartí intelligence about illegal tech and the artifact at Piñar, there'd have been no massacre. If Jaime had protested, Tas would have been exchanged out of the Pact prison in days. On the other hand, if Tas had died tragically in the line of duty, Jaime would have been spared the awkwardness. It was an old impasse, but Tas had long ago let it slide from his shoulders.

"Wilm Nolin. We'll accept his contracts." Jaime lifted Tas's report from his desk and moved it precisely ten centimetres to the left. Then he steepled his long, elegant fingers to support his chin. He'd dried out as much as he wanted to dry out. Alcohol and glitz were favoured routes to self-immolation for diaspora MitraCorps officers.

"Why?" Tas wanted to hear a plain answer for once. And why was Inka interfering when Jaime had already agreed?

"MitraCorps has a proud old combat tradition. In settlement days we defended every square metre of every world from Pact incursions."

Tas didn't correct him. Politaya planetary defence forces had held off the Pact in settlement days, not MitraCorps. Mitra

Defence had started as a tiny volunteer force, evolving into MitraCorps after the Neutrality split from the Politaya over its murky ecoethics.

"Nolin's battles aren't fought on any ground we want to know," Tas said.

"We're not a charitable organization. We're not here to do good works."

We do good works if our survival depends on it. But pragmatic altruism was another thing Tas didn't discuss with Jaime Riordan. A military corporation in exile could easily disintegrate into an overarmed, unprincipled mercenary force accountable to no one; most of old Earth's free companies had fallen to unchecked greed and violence.

"Inka says you have a rare opportunity with Nolin," Jaime said over his fingers.

"One job only. Then we should cut him loose. He tramples interworld law—unlawful confinement, torture, and murder for a start."

"You handled his other requests without complaint."

"Necessary evils." Tas shrugged, hoping Jaime hadn't installed biometric security that could track eye movements and blood-flow patterns—and detect his lie. His last contract had been to terminate an Anansi econophysics professor who analyzed Pact occupation resource transfers for the Pol resistance, but Tas had altered the plan. After a major cosmod and a new identity, with Inka's reluctant help, the professor was now running an institute on Rustam.

Jaime nodded dismissal. Was that really all he'd wanted? If Tas were director-general, God forbid, he would work to strengthen the old Interworld Accord, push clients toward peace building, maybe even disband MitraCorps. The worlds could raise their own forces again, solve their own conflicts before wars broke out, instead of carelessly spending Mitran lives.

"Take Von," Jaime called after him. "New challenge. I want to keep him sharp, on task."

Tas kept silent. He and Jaime both wanted to encourage Renat, help him to expand his strengths and options, but Ren wasn't the man to finesse a quiet and subtle matter.

10

Freeze frame. Seren found Maq waiting outside the inn. It was barely noon, only a day since she left Tirion, but everything had changed.

In Maq's runabout Seren activated her belts, and they began to lift. She'd booked a silent retreat in a New Grove sanctuary that ran a native biozone in Palikir, the westernmost Canton, still untouched by the Pact occupation. It had no neuro clinic, but no one would doubt that she needed some time to sort her thoughts.

A hover pod dropped nearby with a hiss of decompressing air, and Maq let his runabout sink back onto the flagstones.

Damou got out of the pod, looking exhausted even in his flash daywear.

"Never thought I'd see you in those fancy rags again," Maq said.

"Same." Damou walked to Seren's side of the runabout. "All right, Qasri?"

Seren collected her wits. "I thought maybe you'd wait at the inn and show me that number with the bathrobe."

"Don't push your luck." He reached in and lifted a fallen strand of hair back behind her ear, an oddly intimate gesture from a stranger, maybe thought about saying something else and didn't. On impulse Seren raised her hand to touch his wrist.

Warm. If she'd learned to read his expressions at all, he smiled.

"Palikir sanctuary, tomorrow noon."

Seren nodded. *It's a lie.* She couldn't say it and wreck her plans, but remorse ached her throat. She'd have helped him rescue the Pol treaty he cared so much about if she could, but the things he needed to know still lay beyond her grasp.

Halfway to Palikir village, Maq said thoughtfully, "Qasri—Ah hell."

"Leave it alone, Maq." Realizing she'd used Damou's expression made it all harder.

"You need to know." He concentrated on reaching flow altitude for a minute, then keyed the runabout's comp to the traffic grid and punched up autopilot. "He's no more human than Inka. Drunk. Glitz spinner. Bad rep with women. All that holds him together is his damned pride. I say this as his friend. Take my advice just this once, Green. Run."

"You're wrong." Seren had almost managed to forget last night, but she couldn't let this pass.

"Mitran survivors are post-traumatic as hell. Suicide rate's sixteen times the interworld average." Maq sounded serious now. "Inka and MitraCorps are no damn help, pushing him into high-risk jobs. Yesterday he got shot taking in a Xanadu glitz boss. Today there's a price on his head. Run like hell."

"Thanks for the warning." The landscape below became a green and tawny blur.

Maq hunched around in the pilot's chair, scowling. "Forget this stuff about debt of honour. You can't make people whole again once they break."

"Last night he was good under fire." Hasi crept into her lap and stuck her head into the angle of Seren's elbow. *Debt of honour? Something he said last night . . .*

"Ah, crap. You're just like him. Can't tell him anything either."

"I can." Seren tried for Damou's unreadable expression. "He listens to me."

"Claerans. Mitrans. You never learn. *Mahsh siah,*" Maq said. It sounded like a curse, though her slate translated it innocuously as "send far away."

In the silence, Hasi lifted her head for a cautious look around. The mongoose reminded Seren of her guard cat Cedar, an old lady now for a woodcat. Was she still at Gwernant? *Home.* Would Mam or her cousin-friends be there? Now that the war had gone as disastrously as Seren predicted, they might accept the family traitor.

Maq dropped her outside the sanctuary gate. "Tomorrow tell Damou what you remember. We can work together. You've got data. I've got connections. He makes things happen."

"What do you gain from this, Maq? What do you want?" Seren asked as she climbed out of the runabout. What she might gain— money, pull, safety—now meant less than getting away.

"Reunity."

"Reunity's a broken dream." Kuhan's dream. He'd talked about it over dinner at Gwernant.

"Reunity. And faith, hope, and kindness. And Damou's five virtues. Time for humanity to grow up, like I told Doll Sorrow. That's what I want. Anything else, either I got it already or it's long dead and gone."

"You really are from Sitkum."

"Ayuh."

On impulse, Seren leaned in to clasp his hand. "I hope we meet again."

"Sitkum's like bird crap, you don't rub it off that easy. I get around." He stroked Hasi, who clung to his shoulder looking manic. "Sorry about Inka."

"Don't be. This time she didn't even try to burn me alive," she said to make him snort.

Seren scritched Hasi's ears and walked quickly under the gate. Damou's five virtues? She could ask him—but she would never see Damou again. When she looked back from the carved wooden door, Maq raised a hand in farewell.

Now for her deception. Feeling only slightly guilty, she spent an hour in the sanctuary library and then took a public hover pod to the spaceport.

The Cantons domestic terminal was a superb work of soaring architecture, designed and built by Mihal Villandry Biron's family empire, but Seren barely glanced at the grand concourse or its art galleries and shops. She tapped her wrist to call up her Teak avatar for directions before she remembered she had no implants.

Searching signage in four languages and three alphabets, she discovered the walkways were colour-coded and harmonically tuned. Someone had a sense of humour; D minor green led her to the ClaerSpace desk. She couldn't risk a slow dirigible trip, and a suborbital ticket to Tirion nearly wiped Laure's funds.

"Half-hour to lift. Gate 143. You'll make it."

Seren caught a ringway tube pod, and as promised, Maq's unscannable laser raised no security alarms. An illegal weapon would have shocked her before the war, but after last night she didn't plan to travel unarmed. Maq had been right after all. She exited the pod opposite Gate 141—and stopped abruptly. A man stood reading his palm scroll, glancing up often as people floated their bags into the small ClaerSpace lounge.

It raised a prickle between her shoulder blades, and just to be sure, she walked on past her lounge. At a mirror-walled display of Tolm skystone and third-rate Claeran glass, she watched the reflected man study female passengers. He was tall and black-skinned with metalled features. No one she recognized. Still, Seren strolled onward to a tube platform and climbed aboard the pod. Her legs shook so badly she could barely manage the ramp.

Seven or eight stops blurred past before Seren could take a deep breath. Soon her pod would arrive back at the terminal entrance. *Think.* A map above the pod's front window showed terminal delivery bays, security offices, passenger services, and commercial gates. She got off at the next stop and pushed through the first door out of the terminal—no alarms screamed—and was outdoors in a commercial zone.

Out on the apron, three sleek Dauphin couriers in Reprise Express colours perched like birds of prey. Beyond them an old Umiak freighter marked Proton Transport squatted on its maglev hydraulics with its cargo ports open. Could she fly a Dauphin? Maybe, with time to figure it out. But she had flown an Umiak years ago. The ships were humble, plain and as durable as Mitran tech could make them for backworld traffic.

As long as the crew stayed inside the port buildings, maybe she could lift the Umiak and talk her way past traffic control. Seren walked toward the craft as though she belonged—and slowed at the sound of a woman's angry voice.

"Not bloody likely," the woman said. "You're still hours away and we're lifting now, screw the regs. I called Radko. You're fired." The woman was invisible on the starboard flank of the small transport, but her voice was a rising cadence straight from Nevez Claer.

Seren glanced over her shoulder. A tall black man stood inside the terminal door, looking out. *Trouble.* She strolled around the Umiak. A dark-haired kid sat in the open hatchway kicking her heels and playing a slate game. The woman who secured the cargo wore a Claer Defence jacket over her coverall, and her hair was spiked in Pol fleet fashion. *Welcome home.*

"*S'mae. Dwi'n y criw newydd.*" Seren reported as crew, trying for an air of distracted haste.

The terminal door hissed open.

"*Na fo. Hude.*" She looked Seren up and down doubtfully but tossed her the manifest slate. "Radko moved fast on hiring for once. Want to double-check?"

"Radko said trust your checks, lift immediately."

Mercifully they were bound for Taupo in Politaya space, then back via the outer moons to Claer Arian. She handed back the slate, wincing at the wrongness of skipping her checks.

"Let's go. We can still make our dispatch bonus."

Seren sweated until the woman dogged the hatches, got the kid into a pulldown, and took the right seat. So Seren was pilot. She said crisply, "Hover us out and take the comm, if you please. I want to check the manual. He hired me straight off vacation."

"You usually holiday in hell?"

"With the right man. This time it didn't work out."

"I see that. He doesn't look happy."

A glance out the viewscreen showed a tall black man, angrily shouting up at the Umiak. The Nevez woman blatted the klaxon at him, and he retreated to the terminal door.

Seren's hands shook wildly as she paged through the system manual, checking hover and lift speeds. "I may be rusty. Back me up."

Her nav got their clearances and hovered them out to the lift zone. Seren didn't take her eyes off the boards till they passed the last beacon, with the dock lights of Claer Arian blinking furiously as the triple-decker station spun past and astern. Then they were out in the deep and dark. Seren slumped back in the pilot chair in a wash of rank sweat.

The woman leaned and held out her hand. "Rozenn. My girl is Lezig."

Seren touched her hand. "Laure."

"I'll send in your cardwork," Rozenn said. When Seren handed it over, she slotted it and read it twice, then tapped her slate with a forefinger. "I guess you can explain why a Gilgai fighter pilot has a Pacter class-one licence and speaks Bryniau Tavod with a high-Tirion accent."

One breath and another added up to a long silence. What could she say now? She had Claeran relatives? It wouldn't work. Seren locked auto and twisted in her chair to meet hard black Nevez eyes narrowed in suspicion.

"Classified. Politaya Fleet Intelligence."

Rozenn caught her breath and snapped a salute. "Ma'am. Orders?"

III
GROUND

1

ES2741.240

Mihal tasted the cold like a crystal on his tongue. At minus fifty and dropping, the temperature was too low for new snow, and by sunset, ice fog lowered close and grey over Claer's ravaged northern city of Reprise. The dome was long gone, its membranes ruptured by the Pact's final aerial attack and brutal ground war.

Walking away from his volunteer clinic in a looted art museum—his last patient had a protein-deficiency condition not seen since old Earth—he set out across the city on a now-stilled walkway. The snow pack creaked under his feet, and he breathed out a cloud of ice particles that turned and fell glittering through the air. Steam rose in tight columns from a few intact commercial buildings. His gloved hands were numb even in his coat pockets. Walking in cold weather was a new experience, like hunger and poverty.

In Yenisey Square he paused at the scattered wreckage of the hastily armed, volunteer-manned freighter *Annelise Brekhov*, destroyed in the last hours of Claer's defence. Part of its bridge had crashed down in a recognizable mass, and three candle flames flickered in the cold twilight under an overhang of fractured composite. It was a significant sacrifice of lighting materials, since parts of the city still had no power or water. Two teenagers kneeled hand in hand, heads bowed. Reprisiens had quietly made a shrine of the *Brekhov*.

Mihal bent stiffly to light his candle from another, then set it under the twisted bulkhead among the melted stubs. A few tendays ago he'd lit his first candle trying to find some peace of mind. Now he stopped here every day. Many people committed this small act of defiance, keeping alive the idea of Claeran independence. It was an old tradition; in three centuries the Pact had occupied Reprise not once but several times. He tried to think of Seren, of all the other losses, but he was too aware of his freezing hands and the breath that burned his lungs.

His route onward took him through a nightmare obstacle course of broken and abandoned vehicles. Burned-out Politaya and Grey military hovers lay among wrecked private craft from the last desperate battle to defend golden Reprise. Volunteers from the new Cantons had turned up, a bitter irony after their Grey companies betrayed Claer. Now beggars and thieves had occupied alleys and gaping shops among the ever-mounting layers of garbage. Wind shrieked between the parks and government buildings in the famously beautiful city. The public spaces were no longer lit at night, and much of their art was now on its way to Walden or Prospect or Seneca. In the distance, a plume of steam rose from the lovely Reprise Beaux Arts theatre, now stripped of all ornament and housing a soup kitchen.

Villandry Biron EntreMondiale could soon be a bare hulk like the *Brekhov;* the Pacters were seizing assets on occupied Politaya worlds. Villandry Biron was taking hard blows, but in time it might recover. Mihal knew of certain long-term investments, family secrets that not even other board members knew. They included a mothballed transport fleet and a handful of Pol fleet warships, salvaged and refitted late in the war, now secured deep in the outer rock belt orbiting Claer's yellow sun.

Mihal found unexpected liberation in losing much of a lifetime's wealth and privilege. Seren's disappearance, on the other hand, entrapped him. He could find no convincing proof of her death on Arian station. The Grey he'd consulted didn't answer his calls. A body had been rushed to cremation, but whose body? No forensic report was available. The Claeran cleaner who saw the body and two station guards who witnessed her abduction proved impossible to locate. And the industrial-sector crime scene was too apt, like a virtual set that Seren herself had programmed for some noir murder vri. All this added up to a vague suspicion that somewhere Seren was alive.

When a clinic on Claer Arian posted an opening, he decided he'd seen enough of malnutrition, unhealed wounds, mutilation, and oozing sores, and threw in his name. Now the job offer sat unanswered on his slate.

His hands felt like frozen blocks by the time he opened the weathered door of Survival, the bistro-bar in the Old Quarter that attracted the artists of dispossession.

Pact occupation officers had quickly discovered the bistro. Most had expected rustic Green insularity and found a cosmopolitan after-dark society more daring than Havre's. Survival offered them wines and brandies, excellent live music and poetry, and risqué political satire that titillated the Pacters. Many found a welcome in Survival's candle glow and soft neoarchaic jazz. Some found lovers. None so far had found the fifth-floor closet—squeezed between the garbage cyclers and the lift—where Survival's resistance cell hid safely under the nose of the occupation.

Just before opening time, the empty bar was unromantically bathed in artificial light that exposed its mismatched furniture and crumbling brick walls. It had taken hard work to transform a featureless, hygienic automat to Survival's air of immigration-era poverty and ennui. Now it was quite convincing, right down to bot roaches and an elderly Mitran AI-enhanced ape pressed into service as a door guard.

Mihal was an irregular at Survival after his clinic hours. Occasionally, he recited terza rima to a house larded with Claerans coming and going from the communications room upstairs, collecting their orders and checking the illegally shielded transmitter for unofficial—thus reasonably accurate— news of other Politaya worlds. It was his only interest in the resistance cell, which had been depressingly easy to infiltrate. Seren would have laughed to see Mihal on the stage side of the house lights, and in turn it gave him a glimpse into her world of radical politics and avant garde arts.

Three tendays ago the arts collective *Singularity* posted his terza rima cycle *City of Gold*. Its bittersweet lyrics of lament for his broken city were simple, but someone had written a haunting melody. Now people were singing it in bars.

Mihal surveyed the room. Too often a woman would be waiting for him with an untouched drink and a slate full of bad poetry about joining the Pact fleet to escape her dull backworld of Landfall or Yizhou. Rarely he passed on information to remain credible with his inept cell. Secretly he'd feared these enemies might charm away his cold rage at the Pact, but most were insolent fools that Mihal detested. He wasn't Seren Qasri, raised on daydreams of interworld harmony and Grey propaganda.

No one yet. He claimed the best corner table and settled to wait for the man who'd requested a meeting. Mihal cycled his raw Ayiti red after a few swallows, checked his subskin timepiece, and watched the entry. Another quarter hour. He would not wait past the agreed time. Impatiently, he tapped through vri channels on the table sigils, skipped the glossy infotainment that passed for Pact occupation public affairs programming, and paused at a documentary.

Mihal reached to cancel after one glimpse of barren, dusty Tanna. Seren Qasri had told him enough about what happened there to last him a lifetime, and he would never forget that the Grey companies withdrew their services to the Pol in the war; even the narrator's raw Mitran accent raised his hackles. But the famous sequence in the table's vri sphere froze his hand over the sigil. He tapped his wrist to activate his own vri implants.

Boards creaked under Mihal's—the cam operator's—step as he entered a village school hung with childish paintings of green growth and blue lakes that didn't exist on this Pact backworld. In a classroom the drylanders greeted Seren's captain, her childhood hero, a young man with a deep desert tan and light eyes who already commanded a full MitraCorps company—he would be a colonel in any world defence force, but Mitrans had clung to their own ranks and traditions.

Tanna had no surface water and no rain. A hard drought had touched off conflict between ecotopian Dries and corporate Dippers—data contractors and subsistence farmers on both sides—and the Pact hired MitraCorps to mediate. A lightly armed peace-building group arrived carrying gifts for the elders. Then the Dippers acquired unsanctioned energy weapons despite the

Pact blockade, and the resulting massacre ignited an interworld war.

Teak Kuhan arrived on Tanna as a reluctant celebrity, fresh from two brilliant settlements negotiated without bloodshed. His reluctance only strengthened his appeal, and his good looks and eloquence couldn't have hurt—exactly the kind of man Mihal distrusted on principle. An ordinary man, Seren had approved; under her haute Tirion founding-family manners, she was charmingly egalitarian.

No sign of his appointment yet. Mihal called up Kuhan's bio on his slate implant, and screen after screen scrolled above his palm. A mongrel. Mitra had never produced an aristocracy, only an obnoxious meritocracy. Insignificant family in Mikkeli, Spartí, New Oraibi, and Bihar. Sciences and arts honours, a prestigious research internship, then inexplicably he'd quit to join MitraCorps, rising quickly through the ranks.

In the vri zone, now a young woman smiled into the clear desert light, the cam operator herself captured on cam. She pushed back her broad-brimmed hat to demo her custom vri gear covering her right eye and ear. Portrait of a Mitran Grey: hair in many small beaded braids, blue eyes bright in a brown face, cam gear slung over her combat gear. A drama series about her short life still aired on backworld grids. Zari Lind was another of Seren's romantic heroes.

Tanna's golden plains rolled away behind her to a dark horizon. Dust stung in Mihal's eyes, and he breathed the heat of parched trees, heard children yelling in Piñar village square where Kuhan negotiated construction of a precipitation plant.

The crisis unfurled slowly in the vri display. MitraCorps hovers moved by night into a village of rammed-earth Dry houses. It was outside their assigned zone, but the Dippers had attacked it, and that called for quick intervention. Their transport was in low orbit; the Grey companies preferred agile smaller craft to heavy warships. Even near midnight Tanna's air was warm against Mihal's face, laden with scents of withered fruit and drought-stricken crops. Drylander refugees straggled toward them in vehicles and on foot. Everyone watched the sky, occasionally lit by flashes that could be lightning. Empty streets flickered with the strange light when they entered Piñar from the south through the grove of stunted nutrient-adapted piñon pines that gave the village its name.

Pale dust coated his skin—in fact Zari Lind's skin; she had recorded this vri—and blew everywhere as the wind shifted, and a few human shapes darted across the night footage. Now small-arms fire traced through the dark, and flames and sparks roared up from burning houses. Heat and smoke, a grit-laden wind, and the pounding thunder made his heart race. Eight years later and many parsecs distant, Mihal sweated and swallowed dry, hating every second, angry to be sucked in yet again with the same helpless fascination.

"Zero-seven to command, armed insurgents two klicks north." That was one of the scout hovers.

The cam op stayed close to her captain. Her vripac picked up voices from the perimeter, the patrol ships overhead, a woman undercover in a shelled-out house. Bedlam. The calls fragmented, overlapped, broke into static, faded under thunder.

"Artillery north and east," his second in command confirmed. Not thunder.

"Shelling the clinic."

"Zero-four to command, indigenous air support estimated twenty klicks east."

"Evacuate houses north of the square."

Information overload. The data barrage was dizzying and deafening. Artillery fire closed in, and now small-arms fire seemed to come from every direction. Heat grew quickly as the Dries set fire to the rubble piled in their three main streets. Blisters rose painfully on Mihal's face under the cam op's vripac, on his arms and shoulders not covered by the heavy combat gear, on his bare hands—*her* bare hands. He tried to distance himself, but it never worked.

"Send backup to Piñar." The captain kneeled behind a low wall bordering the market, taking reports from his second, using positioning data on his slate to direct his troops through the blocked and burning streets.

Dippers swarmed the village, firing their illegal high-powered energy weapons. Dries returned fire with primitive projectile-throwers from the still-standing houses.

"Zero-seven to command, you have a clear route from the

market square west."

"Fight your way out!" Mihal barely realized he'd said it aloud. The Mitrans were a lightly armed mediation team, but they wouldn't leave the remaining drylanders to burn with their village. They'd thought they could hold out, till the captain's act of madness.

"Zero-four to command, backup one klick south, ETA three minutes."

Disaster blossomed slowly at first. A human flood seeped between the eastern houses to overflow the village. Heavily armed Dippers broke through the street barricades and surrounded the Mitrans. More flames sprang up, and screams came from burning houses. The vri's field of view jolted to a pine tree overhanging a rock on the north side of the village square.

The captain looked east to the thickest knot of insurgents, then north. Then he made the fatal error that the tribunal had named dereliction: he stood, spoke to his wrist, raised his open hands, and walked straight toward the insurgents.

Small-arms laser fire splashed across a hover overhead. It tilted dangerously and crabbed toward the square, exploding before it touched down. A great flash of white light caught the captain and flung him down, and he was lost beneath the fireball of the burning craft.

Zari Lind lurched forward, and her cam view skewed wildly and fell into darkness. There was no pain. No feeling at all. Nothing.

A hard transition to the street at first light in flat video with no sensory input. Villagers and grey-clad soldiers lay shrouded in the same pale dust. Pact troopers walked from body to body, counting their hired dead. At the southern side of the square, where the Mitran casualties lay deep, they found Zari Lind with a projectile wound above her left eye. Toward the centre, they uncovered the captain's body. Mihal rubbed his face, reassured that his own skin was whole. He took a long breath, shaken by second-hand terror. It was far too much like dying.

The camera shot pulled back from dusty street to arid countryside, to the curve of horizon glowing with atmosphere, to the ochre ball of Tanna hanging in space, to three Pact cruisers poised in the darkness like spears aimed at the planet's heart.

End credits, and the vri zone emptied to star-flecked black with Mitra just visible at the margin. It had been radiant once, a barren world transformed into a rich, populous jewel. Mihal remembered his first voyage there in a Villandry Biron yacht, his first awed glimpse of the famous elevators and huge stations glimmering against the night, and downworld, the brilliant collage of cultures and arts and technologies. All dark now.

A blast of cold air dragged Mihal back to Survival. A tall man stood near the table with legs braced apart and arms folded. Dark hair, freckled skin, pale blue eyes.

"Biron? Revo." He dropped into a chair.

Mihal nodded perfunctorily. Was this Revo interested in trade? Investment? His olive daywear was shockrave fashion fabbed in an automat knock-off, and a dark streak under his jaw suggested a hasty cosmod reversal. Watching the bar too closely, he didn't look like a man with a mercantile fortune to invest in a stumbling Claeran interworld corporation. So, what did he want?

Revo wasted no time. "You come from a prominent family that owns a famous Claeran intercorp. You supported the Globalist party before the war, so you're a loyalist. You travel, unlike most Pols these days. You still hold a reserve commission in Claer Defence Force—"

"In a force that no longer exists," Mihal frowned, uncomfortably aware that he knew nothing of this man's allegiance or affiliation. "As a medical officer."

"—and the word's out that you want Seren Qasri. I can help."

"At what price? If money were all you wanted, you wouldn't cite my politics or family."

"Straight to the point. Good." Revo gestured over the sigils for a drink, a garish red and orange concoction, and leaned back with an elbow crooked over his chair.

"Where is my fiancée?" Mihal asked.

"Fiancée?" Revo smiled slowly, but Mihal stared him down. "I have a client, a corporate herra much like yourself, who's getting nowhere with the occupation. He needs information on Claeran funds transfers, offworld stock purchases, corporate bonds."

Mihal shrugged. "You're talking about commercial espionage. I can't help you."

Still, Revo could turn out to be more useful than the

overpriced security expert who'd printed Seren's death certificate. He had an accent not unlike Damou's but masked under colloquial Peel. Another damned Mitran. First, he got an arrogant snot who offered him philosophy, not compliance, and now he got a thug. Revo's corporate herra was probably Pact intelligence in some guise. Agree to anything, give him nothing. It was easy to handle stupid men convinced of their own brilliance.

Revo lowered his voice. "And I'm talking about Claeran resistance. Waving banners in the citadel just gets people shot. Revolutions are about money."

"Certainly." God's name, the man truly was a fool. It was all Mihal could do not to laugh outright. Why would he talk Claeran politics of any kind with this man? He had no time for a futile resistance movement—but he did need to follow every lead to Seren Qasri. Every lead cost more than the last. In a few short days he had burned through his laughable salary and pillaged a trust fund with few results.

"Can I meet this client of yours?"

Revo pretended to hesitate. "I'll do what I can."

"You have proof that you can deliver Seren Qasri?"

Revo handed something over, and the clammy chill of his fingers raised Mihal's curiosity. Unless he'd just come in from a cooler biozone, he was a glitz spinner.

In his palm rested the small blown-glass ball that Seren had always kept in her cabin or her pocket, never out of her sight. Could he really produce Seren? Mihal was about to ask when Revo said, "You were sensing that vri doc on Piñar. I heard Qasri had something going with Kuhan years ago."

Mihal opened his mouth to deny it. Seren had barely known the man, she claimed. Then logic overtook his disbelief. "Why? Couldn't keep his hands off women?"

"Other way round."

One last betrayal. Seren always had a taste for the outré. Mihal nodded. "Naturally I would be desolate to learn of Seren's death, but I would pay well for her remains. She deserves the proper New Grove rites."

Revo said, "Never fear, you'll have the same rites soon if you don't get more cautious."

Mihal stared in shock.

Revo nodded. "You have a hunter on your track."

Unlikely, but still. "What do you require?"

Revo recited a list of impossible requests that only deputies in the finance ministry could fill. As they talked, Mihal thought about Seren. Dead or alive? Where? He needed to know.

2

ES2741.242

Extreme wide shot. Lifts clung like bright unsects to the outside of Claer Arian's central hub. The station spun perpendicular to Claer's surface and followed the ancient convention, with the inner end designated as down. As she descended, Seren glimpsed her cloudy blue homeworld through the lower windows. Both moons were out of sight on the Tariqa side of the planet, now the night side. Somewhere below her feet, Tirion city—a village by Pact standards—hid under cloud. Outward, away from the nav beacons and station lights, Claer's home stars shone dimly.

After six days in Taupo system and the outer moons, Rozenn had dropped her on Arian and taken a cargo down to Ayiti with a new pilot. By that time, she'd trusted Seren to take Lezig to a station crèche, and they'd compared their wars over hard Nevez cider. Call on me anytime, Rozenn said as they parted, anything to strike back at the occupation. Now Seren would find her own way to Derw sanctuary clinic, and from there to some remnant of the Pol Fleet.

First, she had an errand. A one-room station flat and a shuttle pass were among a Claeran senator's few privileges in return for endless work, travel, midnight crises, and a political debate every time she entered a Tirion shop. Seren needed to know what she would find in Delun's flat, whether it had been reassigned,

whether it even still existed. Mam had warned her, *Don't return.*
But Mam likely hadn't known her final tasking.

Residential and industrial levels flashed past the descending
lift, giving her glimpses of a station plundered of its comforts and
adornment, struggling to survive. Braided vines and waterfalls
still marked the ecology zones. Arian's beauty and cultural
pleasures had been famous across the Politaya until the war. Now
the station looked desolate with parts in charred ruin.
Everywhere she saw faces stamped with anxiety and caution,
unusual in a Claeran crowd, and many Pact uniforms.

Seren kept her head down as she walked, keenly aware of her
forged identity card and the laser slightly weighting her pocket.
She half expected a Mitran thug to lurch up and, guessing she
would never believe his explanation, manhandle her into a
battered old ship. On Glas 3, Seren stepped out into a corridor
tangled in Earth-origin vines and deciduous trees that were thicker
and leafier than she remembered but still alive with birdsong and
the whirr of wings among the branches. Almost over Seren's head,
a capuchin climbed a vine to watch her from glittering bead eyes,
nibbling its citrus. She greeted it but got no answer; it was a mute
natural animal, not an augmented working animal.

The Glas 3 residential sector looked better kept than most,
with its light panels and service booths operational and its
biozones intact. The lounge alcoves and café-bistros and shops
were all empty, but the apartment doors she passed still had their
murals or bas reliefs. Above the carved door of Glas 347, her old
mobile of West Sea driftwood and volcanic glass still turned
gently against the silverleaf interlace on the door.

Seren glanced into the service hallway next to the flat—both it
and the main corridor were empty—and scanned the door with
her slate. No explosives or alarms on the door or frame, nothing
on the walls in either direction, nothing on the ceiling or floor.
Taking a deep breath, she palmed the handplate. After long
seconds it glowed green, recognizing her biometrics, and the door
slid soundlessly into the wall as though she'd only stepped out for
caffe with a friend.

Lights brightened inside as the wall sims came alive, and the
wall censer breathed out scent: heather, juniper, thyme. She was
on a ridge above Hendy, looking down into the streets at dusk, as

a kestrel wheeled a last slow hunting spiral overhead . . . Wasting time. She palmed the inner plate to close the door.

"Welcome home, Seren," the flat greeted her. That meant Inka's global update hadn't reached this closed system.

The flat was unchanged. A resort card—for a planned trip with three cousin-friends—lay forgotten on the desk. The closet still held clothes and costumes and props that she'd meant to take home to Gwernant after a station theatre performance of *Poison*. Vacpac ingredients filled the cupboard above the food fab, quilts hung to air over the lav shower tube, linens covered the pulldown beds, and her woodcat Cedar's blanket lay folded in her favourite corner.

Seren longed to roll up in a quilt and breathe its memories of old vri dramas, midnight cocoa, and fierce debates with Mam and any visiting friends. If she turned quickly, surely she would see Mam at the desk arguing with her exec down in Tirion, reaching blindly for the tea mug Seren brought. Jasmine green, orchard-blossom honey, no milk. Seren checked the garments in the closet, but there was nothing she couldn't fab at an automat.

The flat's sole luxury was a spin-corrected window on space where most flats had only a wallscreen. Her hand froze halfway to the control pad to rotate the opaque blinds. *Careful.*

<> Teak, check security for breaches. <>

Teak materialized at the window, briefly transparent as the blind opened. <> Nothing, Seren. All clear. <>

She'd half expected to find explosive putty lining the frame, ready to detonate on touch and suck her out into vacuum.

<> Stand by. <>

The flat felt eerily trapped in time. The nanobots had eliminated dust, and the ventilation cycled fresh air, but it looked as though no one had stepped inside for a long time.

At the desk Seren scanned the screen and gestural entrypad. Mam had insisted on high-security data systems with standalone power, immune to global updates and undetectable, in their station flat and at home. When the screen blinked to life, Seren called up recent entries to the flat. Mam, her sister-friend Parvin with her children, Senate Security, cousin-friend Rhian, cousin-friend Daoud, Senate Security again—why was security here so often? Seren filtered and cross-indexed. Mam's last fourteen visits coincided with Senate Security number S470198 for five minutes, seven minutes, never longer. Their last visit was time-stamped from the war's final days, many tendays ago now, when Seren's shattered arm was being rebuilt in the Gandhi sickbay after the Bight disaster; when Claer Defence had scrambled every ship to the asteroid belt, even small pleasure craft crewed by cadet volunteers and students, even Mam's small senate ship, to stand against Pact destroyers that lasered them and burned inbound through their debris. Only when the Pact threatened to raze the planet did Claer surrender.

Frowning, Seren tapped the sigil for her personal cache—and looked into her mother's face, frozen in the instant of starting to speak. She sat down so hard the chair rocked. *Mam.*

Leaning forward slightly, lips parted, Delun Qasri looked ready to deliver some coup in the Senate. She was oval-faced and blue-eyed like Seren, as graceful as the Qasris, as intense and eloquent as the Gwyns. Almost every soul on a world of two million knew her face, her family, and the best lines from her passionate speeches.

Seren gestured play. Mam sprang to seeming life, and her satsuma perfume blossomed in the still room. She wore her old green Claer Defence uniform. Called up on reserve? Things had been desperate toward the end.

"Seren darling, love of my life, there are things you need to know."

Seren froze the screen to catch her breath at the onslaught of Mam's ferocious love.

"Offworld communications have been down for three days, but we think this relay will work in case you stop at the station flat," Mam said. "Listen well, sweet. Naturally you'll plan to report to the fleet. Do not report. Wait. Tell no one but our trusted friend what you saw in the Bight."

How could Mam know about the Bight? *Mist and starlight.* Seren closed her eyes so tightly she saw sparks, and another memory splinter surfaced of

her own bandaged hand, keying data on the highest-security system in her Gandhi Base alcove, sending out files so heavily encrypted and fragmented and multiply relayed that she feared for their integrity, but there was no other way. Sent them—not to fleet headquarters, but to a commercial site. *Shut down quickly. Leave no trace. Get to safety. Out in the passageway his shadow fell across her back, no surrender, a sharp pain stabbed her arm, a scream died in her throat*

<> Seren. <> Teak's voice barely pierced her concentration at first. <> Seren, caution. <>

A bleep sounded in the flat. Mam had forgotten to shut off a timer. Strange to think it had quietly alerted an empty room every evening all this time. But she found nothing in the galley. Then she saw a red light flashing on her slate.

<> Seren. Proximity alert, <> Teak said calmly.

<> Description? <>

<> Four armed personnel approaching. <>

"But here's the most important thing, treasure," Mam said from the desk screen.

<> Leave now, Seren. <> His tense voice mirrored the warning.

Quickly. Seren dragged all the recent files to the card slotted in the reader and shut down. Delun's face froze, then the screen greyed. She pulled out the card, dark green with seven silver stars across the bottom. Why was Mam's senate data card up here in the flat? Seren backslotted the card into her slate.

<> Proximity alert. Emergency, <> Teak said urgently.

<> On my way. Quiet now. Stand by, <> she told the virtual aide, and a double tap darkened her slate. Once for on, twice for off. The Mitran tech came naturally. Seren had grown up with Mitran security, a Mitran cat, Mitran guests.

In the silent flat, the ceiling light panels faded one by one, dimming through twilight to a state she knew from starless space in the Bight, absolute and measureless black.

By touch Seren found her way to the closet, lifted the old water-seller's costume from its hook and pulled on the ragged tunic and shawl. The street sweeper's bristle broom leaned in a corner, and she grabbed it as she fumbled for the recessed latch. The flat's concealed back door let her into a supply room, and she stepped out into a side passage. No time for cosmod or makeup, just a temporary overlay on her identity card. Then she stooped and shuffled wearily into the main corridor.

Invisibility came with age, Seren had discovered years ago

when she first tried out her *Poison* costume and stage makeup to roam Tirion's shops and parks, where she was usually greeted as the senator's girl. In one hour, she'd been brazenly robbed of a cash card, served after every other customer in a shop, and offered a hostel bed by a kindly Gautama Quaker. Mostly she wasn't seen at all.

Invisible again now, the shabby old woman sweeping the leaf-strewn floor didn't look up when four young people strode past her to the door of Glas 347. The woman and three men in casual daysuits ignored the elderly cleaner whose ID card scanned as a Matawin guest worker. The Pact occupation had ended elder and medical support, creating a large hungry Politayan labour pool, and even old women had to eat.

Whoever they worked for, station security or the occupation force, had neglected their training in practicalities: no one sweeps a smart carpet with a bristle broom.

The four held a small device over the palm plate and stepped into the flat. Minutes later they returned at a brisk walk and disappeared up the corridor's curve.

Seren counted out another three minutes. Her hands clenched with icy sweat as she slowly swept her way to a washroom, overrode the supply cupboard lock, and abandoned her broom and her *Poison* costume. Heading for the main lifts to the shuttle docks, she finally let out her breath.

In a residential plaza she passed the station's huge old kinetichron, too massive to plunder. Graffiti in vulgar Peel defaced one of its outer probability vanes, and a litter of crumpled food wrappers lay beneath it. A drink carton bounced off the vintage kinetic sculpture, and two Pact ratings passed by, jeering each other's aim. Seren ducked between two slowly turning vanes to avoid them, and walked quietly to the giant artwork's centre. They would see her feet if they stooped; the three-storey vanes hung nearly to the floor. But the Pacters didn't see her or didn't care, and walked on, cursing their sergeant in a backworld twang.

Seren stood among the gently swinging vanes at the sculpture's core, seduced once again by its sweet C-major drone. Interactive kinetichrons had been wildly popular three centuries ago in the first exuberance over the mirror-drive, when it was hailed as humanity's coming of age. Then the violently anti-intellectual Long Dark knocked the sciences back to pre-emigration levels for two centuries. Vri dramas now swarmed with fantasies of lost sciences, lost arts, lost contact with aliens, and lost colonies of old Earth.

As a girl she'd loved the old kinetichron, but it was years since she'd stood here to listen and meet herself coming and going in its time-shifted reflections. It always seemed to contain more panels than she could see, as though it really did exist in extra dimensions. This was how she'd always pictured mirror space. She let her breathing slow as the probability vanes blurred and glittered around her, and another forgotten memory fragment rose to

Mist and starlight. In the umber glow of a star veiled in dark gas bands, two unfamiliar shapes moved. One was a dark iridescent teardrop shape hardly bigger than a probe. The other was a great many-armed tree, a shape from deep ocean or dream or nightmare. *What is that ship?* she'd asked, but her weapons hand shrugged. Ship identification quickly matched the teardrop as an Azande Abhaya. *What's a Grey courier doing in the Bight?* she muttered. *It can't even charge its converters out here.* Someone answered, *Grey ship doesn't mean Grey courier. It's a Pact scout. No surrender. Take it.*

Deep space opened beyond the courier like a flower in a slow wheel and dance of great vanes. The courier hung dark against a vast twisted knot of faintly glowing matter that grew in their viewscreen as Seren fought for control of the weapons pad. Alarm klaxons screamed and swallowed her own scream when her arm broke. A flash of brilliance and the glow was gone, and the courier's twisted debris expanded slowly in near space. The pilot's greeting repeated through the comm board translator in a woman's precisely accented voice, *Neutrality diplomatic mission, urgently request escort.*

Standing now within the kinetichron, both hands pressed to her face, Seren wept silently. Remembered. How she salvaged the pilot's sealed diplomatic capsule among the terrible charred debris. That was what everyone wanted, the data she'd uploaded. But it was lost.

3

At the communications room door Mihal took an untidy sheaf of tearoffs from Sylvie, who was brunette again, two nights running. She was more interested in her appearance than in doing her job, like most of the Claeran resistance dilettantes. They'd made a few futile gestures, mostly childish pranks. An Ayitien cell had glopped Pact intelligence offices with old-fashioned deconstruction nano, dissolving the walls to grey goo and leaving data tanks and banks of vri monitors standing out in the rain. The farce had Claerans laughing in their hands until the predictable shootings and arrests.

Mihal sorted the tearoffs and read the most recent—then he saw his silent visitor leaning in the corner, arms folded. Mihal recognized his height and his nervous edge. Last time they'd met, he'd been red-haired. Now he was black with a shaved and metaled head.

"What do you want?" Mihal snapped. The man unnerved him.

"It's time." Revo straightened and sauntered closer. "We need your help. And soon I can bring in Qasri."

In other circumstances Mihal might have walked away and found ways to live with the occupation, but Seren had left him no choice. As long as this gave him what he needed, he didn't care if it also helped the resistance. He turned, dropped the tearoffs back in the wall file, and listened uneasily as Revo briefed him on his client's task.

At midnight the security clerk at Pact occupation headquarters strolled back out to the checkpoint with Mihal's new ID. Mihal hefted the toolkit and yawned, trying not to overplay the lazy local tech called out on a late repair job. The clerk touched slates to give him a map of the Pact HQ for the northern continent. A few tendays ago it had been a school complex. In minutes a siphon code would take over the clerk's slate and copy several hundred others to a resistance system, but that was a secondary objective.

Data storage was in Building 7, once a children's theatre with colourful painted animals still frisking across its facade. Mihal strolled the main corridor to a lav where he sealed his sterile gloves, then walked down the hall to a utility cubby and slid in with his pilfered code. He shifted uncomfortably in the sterile suit that masked his geneprint.

"What kept you?" Revo's small voice snapped on his comm.

"Security," Mihal said quietly to the slate implant in his left palm. Let Revo sweat.

The utility room door slid open soundlessly, and the resistance woman—a girl really—slipped inside. Her shapeless service smock made her nondescript, and she had twisted her wonderful auburn hair into an ugly knot. They touched hands to exchange data.

"You're beyond viral," she told him as each of them scanned instructions. "I heard their CO humming *City of Gold* in his office. Too bad you didn't implant some subliminals in the online lyrics. We could have the whole Pack dancing gavottes in the street, and they wouldn't even know why."

"What makes you think I didn't?" Mihal pretended to check his timepiece. "Look out your window in three hours."

The girl laughed as he'd hoped. She was a Gwynfa girl from a stony farm on the high moors, with an accent that reeked of goat cheese and garlic, but she had a pretty smile and loved a joke. Soon perhaps Mihal would invite her to a private dinner, just the two of them in his flat. She'd mentioned a beau, but he probably had dung on his boots, no credit, and no way with words. Once all this was over, they would laugh about it together.

Mihal maxed his virtual screen from his implant and called up the secure data room's blueprint. The targets flashed yellow at his touch, three big bioware tanks of almost his own mass separated by worktops. She had already infected the backups with siphon code to draw off the data Revo wanted and a timed attack on the border gateway protocols to infect the occupation grid later. The Pact would face days of rebuilding its grid connections.

"Every watch ends the same way," she said, already back at the door. "The techs run system diagnosis, scan and remove backups, count equipment, and count heads. Then the lieutenant signs off. Don't hurt him, he's my best source."

Mihal found it hard to meet her gaze, wondering what her beau thought of her work, and was glad when she left. On Claer their best agents were women, playing to Pact prejudices. In a few tendays this woman would get herself transferred to another menial service job, another highly skilled undercover task. Her beauty easily got her hired in occupation offices, he'd heard, and produced schedules and passwords.

Deploying the device was easy. The cubby's wall, insulated and nanowired but not blast shielded, backed onto data storage. Mihal opened his toolkit and carefully lifted out the charge. It had to be preset, since a remote trigger could leave a traceable dataprint. Shaped like a microlith scope, it was in fact a lightweight mould packed with a polymer that was invisible to infrared scan at room temperature; it would remain inert until a coded pulse reached its implanted fuse. Its low-yield focussed blast would neatly remove the three bioware tanks and the backups stored at the worktops, crippling the Pact's northern HQ. Not a silly prank, a professional job.

"Hurry," Revo said, safe in his refuge.

Mihal took his time warming the fake scope between steady hands and sprayed on glue from the toolkit. He pressed it onto the wall—and it fell to his feet with a clatter. Revo swore distantly, but he should know the substance was harmless until triggered. Mihal picked it up, resprayed it, and held it against the wall until the surfaces bonded. Easy.

He felt calm when he packed up and left the building. But his hands were shaking.

Soon afterward he found Revo pacing a bare room in a

labourers' hostel near the compound entrance. They sat side by side on the sagging bed to pore over Mihal's maxed slate screen, watching the main data storage from a fibrecam the woman had planted high on a side wall.

Twenty minutes. Two clerks in Pact uniforms and a smocked service worker—the resistance woman—walked in past the bored guard. A third clerk began checking bioware tanks. The lieutenant came in with a checklist. All according to plan.

Sixteen minutes. Three clerks went out with the guard. The slate image dimmed as though the lighting had dropped, but it compensated. No one was on screen, only the bioware tanks.

Twelve minutes.

"Why the hell is she still in there?" Revo was watching from his own slate.

Mihal gritted his teeth. The woman was alone in data storage with the lieutenant. *Don't hurt him, he's my best source.* He should have asked why. They hadn't told her the schedule, it was too risky.

Eleven minutes. Mihal said, "We'll lose her. I'm going back."

"Too late." Revo's face betrayed no expression through the cosmod.

"I can make it." Mihal jumped up and pulled the used sterile gloves from his pocket. Compromised, probably, but he would take that chance. A story about leaving a tool behind in the centre might get him past security.

Halfway through the door, Revo caught him. A hand seized his shoulder from behind and flung him against the wall.

"Don't be stupid. No time for sentiment."

"Get out of my way."

Mihal swung at him and reached for his stunner, but size and strength were against him. Revo easily blocked his fist and shoved him back inside the room.

"Who do you think you are?" Revo's hand on his shoulder tightened to the point where Mihal felt bone strain at the joint, a millimetre from dislocation, and it was all he could do not to cry out. "Shut the fuck up and do what you're told." He thrust Mihal into the nearest chair, rocking it so hard that his head slammed the wall.

Mihal hunched over his slate, ignoring the brute, doing

everything possible to hide the trembling of his hands. Five minutes. Three minutes.

"Crap. Will you look at that?" Revo laughed.

In the slate's image two people finally moved into pickup range. The young woman's lovely hair curled to her waist, and her lieutenant had his face buried in it against her bare shoulder. They made love on a worktop desk with an ease that suggested many such rendezvous. For a moment the woman looked directly at the fibrecam, fingers linked around her lover's neck, and smiled. Defiance, Mihal thought, not apology or shame. He watched helplessly as his slate screen became one brilliant flash of white and went dark.

"What have we done?" he whispered.

"What we needed to do. Accidentally." Revo's slow smile creased the cosmod. "She would have betrayed us. Never trust a whore in love."

Mihal stared blindly at his empty screen where the woman's perfect miniature image had smiled moments ago. Unbearable. But still easier than looking at the Mitran; now he was this man's creature forever. Maybe Revo had even planned on this. Mihal's mind writhed back and forth over it, seeking a way out.

Claeran independence meant nothing to Revo; Mihal had no illusions about that. An hour ago, he too might have said he cared nothing about Claeran independence—he could always adapt, with his few solid investments and his open invitation to the Pact CO's receptions—but he needed the High Gwynfa girl to have died for something.

Love crosses all borders, Seren had told him once, no doubt thinking of her Mitran lover. If she'd still been alive, Seren would hate what he'd done. And there was no going back.

4

ES2741.245

Medium shot, follow. Surface shuttles to Tirion port ran irregularly now. The bored Pact troopers on station duty had grown careless with their weapons and their procedures, Seren noted as she handed over Laure's identity card at the gate. They passed it without a glance and scanned her sloppily, but she was still tense with delayed fear as she strapped in for her descent.

On the shuttle she wrote an awkward apology to Damou for leaving the Palikir sanctuary without him, but she found no locators for Damou or Inka Loukanos or even Kai's inn, and a message to AnvilCo bounced. The trip to the Cantons was already receding into unreality.

In West Tirion she saw less war damage and more people going about their business than she'd seen in the high city core. Café-bars were serving at outdoor tables, though most of the patrons appeared to be Pacters. She kept her distance from them, and the Pact patrols. Ragged cleanup crews repaired the pavements. A white-haired arbourist on a floater platform trimmed broken branches from a venerable elm as Seren passed. But few Claerans her own age were on the streets. Many had died trying to hold Claer system, and more in the final ground war. The only children she saw walked hand-in-hand in a queue under a teacher's close supervision.

Derw was an easy half-hour walk northwest up the valley where Qasri and Gwyn families had grown tree fruits and run woodlots for three centuries. As Seren turned in at the great livewood gates of the sanctuary, the twined trees welcomed her with a low A-minor chord, and she returned an octave-higher answer.

Inside at the livewood reception desk, a braided and homespun novice asked, "House of men, house of women, nonbinary house, or house of joyous union?"

"Women."

"Water rationing," the novice warned as she thumbprinted, "and sunset curfew."

"I may be later than sunset," Seren said.

"Don't be!" The girl looked horrified.

"Who'll stop me?"

"Hellhounds. Manimal patrols. Predator chimerai. If you survive your arrest, you fight them later in the arena. They've already hunted all the augmented house animals, and they've run short of people to call criminals." She lowered her voice. "Now they take anyone they want. Don't be out after dark."

Predator chimerai? Hunting criminals for sport in an arena? She couldn't begin to count the Interworld Accord infractions. The Pact had followed the accord, when it suited them, even after the Neutrality's balance of power died with Mitra. Something had changed. A shadow of shifting timevanes passed across her inner vision, and even in her newly fabbed outdoor clothes, she shivered.

"I know. It's terrible," the novice said.

"When are the patrols?" If they'd killed the house animals, she might never again see her old friend and guardian Cedar.

"We never know."

Seren paid by unmarked cash card and asked no more questions, unwilling to raise suspicion. The novice showed her to a bare room overlooking the grove—and Seren's jacket slid from her hand to the plank floor as she stared in shock at the torn field of stumps outside, replanted with livewood seedlings, each carefully supported and marked with the name of its lost parent. Two sanctuary brothers worked among them, heads bowed. The trees' grief and confusion, plus the brothers' own grief, must make it a heartbreaking task.

The novice followed her gaze. "Logged and sold as prime lumber for their construction. Some they just burned in bonfires to terrify the other trees. Right here. They made us watch."

"They butchered sentient trees?" Seren sat heavily on the narrow bed, fighting tears.

The novice silently gave the ceiling light panels a glance that needed no explanation. But on her way out, sliding the door shut, she laid her hand over her heart and clenched it into a fist. Even the New Grove had changed.

Seren sat by the window with her slate, then glanced at the light panels. This wasn't the place to check Mam's senate card. *Soon.*

And now that it was time to get help with her memory block, she found herself dragging her feet. What if she learned things she couldn't bear to know? What if she'd panicked and fired on the courier? Finally, she gathered her courage, pocketed her slate, and headed for the clinic.

In the wild garden, Seren paused on the path, lulled by birdsong and the murmur of water. A tall golden-skinned boy in a volunteer's smock came toward her, floating an empty supply cart.

Pedr saw her in the same moment and started to speak. Seren motioned him closer and said quietly, "I'm a friend of the family from Tirion. Don't react." This was no place for a reunion.

Pedr was her brother-friend, the closest she'd ever have to a younger brother, the son of Mam's sister-friend and Seren's second-mother Parvin Kerkallec. Curly brown hair, amber eyes under long lashes. In her years away, he'd grown from a beautiful boy to a handsome young man.

"Glad you're alive." Pedr smiled despite the warning, showing the two crooked front teeth that his mother Parvin could never get him to straighten. No surprise to see who won that battle. His mother might turn a hard face to the world, but Pedr and his sisters owned her heart. Three sibs were rare on Claer, but their father was Mitran.

"I'd better not be that easy to recognize," she said.

"Your height and your voice, even with the Mitran accent," he said. "Mam said to keep my eyes open."

Two novices and a priest emerged from the chapel, and Seren put her finger to her lips as she would have ten years ago, when Pedr was a young explorer in Gwernant's orchard and woods. She murmured, "Parvin's alive? What about Delun?"

"Mam can tell you everything. She'd love to see you." Pedr grinned, unable to resist. "How many Mitrans does it take to program a light panel?"

"Twenty," Seren guessed. "Nineteen to conduct a feasibility study, one to program."

"Wrong."

"Three? Two to stand guard and one to program."

"One."

"Why?"

"Sorry. Classified." He even did a passable Mitran accent, and Seren smiled ruefully at his teasing. Since when did she have a Mitran accent? Blame Inka and Damou.

"Can I find you here?"

"Mostly at a backroom school in Kumun Arvorek in Dinan. I volunteer for the hours and training. No one's hiring teachers now they've closed the public schools."

Seren gave Pedr a quick hug, and he floated his cart off toward the healing grove.

So Parvin Kerkallec was alive. That would be Seren's next task, finding her second-mother.

As the afternoon cooled, she left the wild garden and walked past the sighing House of the Winds and the dim House of Night to the healing grove. If she explained her memory block, a neurologist would assign her a healing cell overlooking the waters and guide her through assessment and medication within a sequence of healing dreams. Years ago, the process had eased her grief when she understood that Teak Kuhan was dead and could never keep his promise to return.

But in the clinic reception, a Pact officer with medical flashes on her uniform sat beside the sanctuary sister who handled admissions, questioning each patient. Seren nodded as though she'd lost her way and fled with her heart pounding. This wouldn't be as easy as she'd hoped.

Shaken, she walked a wandering woodland path home to Gwernant. When she finally crossed the worn flagstone landing pad, her shadow stretched before her onto the front verandah. It had rained earlier, but now sunshine struck a familiar perfume from the tall cedars and firs and the thyme between the flagstones.

In a blow crueller than outright destruction, Gwernant was partially burned, and now the house looked abandoned. As she circled it, unpruned roses and honeysuckle sagged from the walls to slap her face. The big old hawthorn guarding the door was a ragged and solitary sentinel.

No one answered her greeting or door chime. Inside she could see the dining room table laid with two settings—Mam had expected a friend. How long ago? Seren had sat at that table most evenings, listening to Mitran and Pol outworld guests debate whether Mitra should lead Rustam, Vritra, even Xanadu, back into a greater Politaya informed by Neutrality ethics. Now they were unlikely ever to see reunity.

Fire and water damage had ruined one corner of the old house. Someone had grown cellusheet across the open roof and walls of Mam's study, but wind or falling branches had ripped a section free, letting the weather in before the house could fully heal. Seren lifted a loose corner to see blooms of black mould on the emigration-period furniture, and with its code destroyed, the livewood desk chair had reverted to a twisted young oak. Moisture swelled the old biopaper books in Mam's bookcase like bloated corpses. She spoke a command to turn on the vri wall projection and transform the study into a sunny corner of their orchard, but nothing happened. The mould-blotched livewood bookcase moaned in pain at her intrusion, and she quickly dropped the cellusheet and backed away.

Her footsteps sounded hollowly on the oaken boards as she followed the south verandah to the livewood chamber tree where she'd grown up. In her first delight with Tŷ Coed, she'd taught it to welcome her whenever she returned. On leave once from fleet training, she had also taught the tree intelligence-grade security—and forgot to tell Delun. It was the only time she remembered Mam swearing, after shivering outside in a rainy midnight trying to convince Gwernant that she wasn't a Pact spy. Now her tree was dying: strips of its bark lifted in the valley breeze. Would it recognize her now? She palmed the plate beside the outside door, and lights glowed on softly as she stepped inside.

Her chamber had been ransacked. Not theft but a hasty search. Her green quilt lay rumpled on the floor beside her bed niche. Books, bead cases, and jewelry were spilled everywhere. Drawings she'd gummed to the living walls were torn. The wardrobe door stood ajar, a jumble of clothing on the floor. Everything she'd ever owned seemed to be here in this chaos. Seren stood stunned amid the ruin of her childhood treasures. What had happened?

"*Croeso'n ôl, Seren,*" her own voice greeted her when she closed the door.

The tree's closed data system still operated, to her relief, unaffected by any remote intrusions. Her palmprint still IDed her as Seren Qasri.

Seren sat down at the living desk and laid both hands on the embedded control surface, which obligingly tilted and warmed to her touch. Her wall vri transformed the chamber to her default choice, the cockpit of a racing yacht. Unwilling to leave aural prints, instead of immersing herself in the system's full sensory architecture, she keyed in Laure Prakash as a self-erasing guest identity with full access.

"List all files modified the day Delun Qasri last left this house." The last day Mam paced her study, probably answering comms and composing senate reports, many tendays ago now.

"Denied." The word flashed yellow across the vri zone.

Seren re-entered her pass codes. The system confirmed—and again shut her out. She keyed furiously, "Denied why?"

This time the vri flashed Claer's tree-of-life interlace logo with the senate motto *Truth and Justice* in graceful ta'liq calligraphy and five official languages, all rotating dimensionally. Then the zone scrolled "Senate Security S470198."

Why was Senate Security all over Mam's business? All of those access files at the station flat had a security number too. She searched her pockets for Mam's senate data card. Not there. Not in her satchel. Surely she hadn't lost it on Arian. Trying not to panic, she finally found it backslotted in her slate. In her haste she dropped it on the living carpet and kicked it far under the desk. *Holy fire.* Seren forced herself to stop and breathe, then retrieved the card.

Skimming index after index on the card, she found nothing useful and keyed, "List personal correspondence, Senate Security." More than a hundred files carried the number S470198. She scrolled, silently cursing the slow text commands, to the Senate Security lists she'd downloaded at the station flat.

And stopped with both hands on the board, shocked to stillness by a file titled "Lt. Qasri urgent immediate attention." The message was dated hours before the preds had grabbed her on Arian, just before midnight in Claer's twenty-three-hour rotation, days after Mam disappeared. How did that get into the station flat system? Impossible, unless someone physically placed it there, and only family had access to the flat. Family— and Senate Security S470198.

Seren pulled the card and reslotted it. A vri globe shimmered in thin air over the stage, and Seren grabbed her eyeband from its branch.

A familiar face resolved in deep shadow in the vri zone. *Damou.*

"Lieutenant Qasri, do not under any circumstances descend to Claer." Damou had used his real face, not a simage. With the heavily scarred side turned away, she might not have noticed the damage if she hadn't known. He looked sombre, serious, not at all like an addict. His hair was longer, well cut, and he wore dark business clothes that hadn't come from any automat fabricator.

"If you wish to confirm my status, enter 'Claeran Senate security, MitraCorps/Spartí, personnel number S470198,'" Damou said in his provocative Mitran accent, stronger than she'd known. His voice kindled a remembered—better forgotten— warmth at the base of her spine.

Seren's hand flew to her mouth. All of those entries were Damou? Then Mam came in-frame in her old fleet greens, leaning forward. "I hoped for a more suitable introduction to my aide and dear friend Tas Damou. By the time you read this, he'll have met you on the station."

Mam's image froze and resumed in a slightly altered stance; usually her messages were seamless. "My life has been threatened since I drafted the peace initiative. There have been two attempts in a tenday."

Delun Qasri had designed a Claeran peace initiative—but there had been no Claeran peace offer. Unopposed, the Pact had now imposed harsh treaty terms. Seren's eyes were leaking, and she wiped them angrily: no time for that now.

Mam looked off-cam again. "I must leave Tirion now, but I have an expert advisor. Seren, Tas Damou has already saved my life twice. Trust him absolutely."

Delun had Mitran security, with its legendary high fees? Even though she was poor and the Senate was bankrupt? None of this made sense.

Damou said, "Your mother leaves tomorrow with a security escort. I will meet you on Claer Arian station when you return. I'll need your cooperation." He turned, then looked back at the cam and almost smiled. "Careful. We want you alive." His image froze in the vri zone.

Cooperation . . . Instead, she'd fought him and spent days wishing he'd die horribly. Why hadn't he just given her this card on Arian? If she'd known, she wouldn't have fought him every step to his ship. His appearance had frightened her, but was he even drunk or spun? Or was he just roughed up from an encounter, according to Maq, with Pact station guards?

Delun's message from the flat said, *This is important.* When she opened the file, Mam appeared in the small vri zone, leaning over her desk in the station flat. "Seren, Claer's peace offer depends on getting your data into the right hands. We need your help."

So, Mam had known about the Bight. Thinking hard, Seren dragged all the recent house files onto Mam's senate card. As they transferred, she programmed a nutrient boost for her livewood tree. At her wardrobe she shrugged on the old thermal coat she'd worn hiking the Gwynfa glaciers. She gathered drawings and scattered jewelry, dropped favourite hard-copy books and her vri doc and drama beads into her school satchel. The tiller pin from their old sailboat. A palm-sized vri cam that nano'd to near-invisibility against skin tones. Things that mattered.

A small rhythmic beep and flash caught her attention, and this time she recognized her slate's emergency alert.

Teak warned, <> Seren. Perimeter breach. <>

Quickly she checked the tree system. A light blinked at the

upper margin of her vri zone, then went out. It might be nothing, just a glitch caused by the fire damage in Mam's office, but she couldn't afford to ignore it. Seren paused Delun's file and keyed for an outside security report, and a honeycomb array of views came up from cams around the house.

A wind stirred the leaves outside, and its movement shook the hawthorn by the front steps. When she zoomed, she saw a pair of nuthatches flirting around the branches, Earth-origin birds that Claer had unpacked. Not an intruder, just the birds that often triggered Gwernant's security. But she'd let time slip past, and the daylight was fading. *Sunset curfew.* She needed to go now.

<> Perimeter breach, <> Teak said again. <> Caution, Seren. <>

Seren double-tapped her slate to cancel the alert, dropped her slate and Mam's senate data card into her pocket next to Maq's laser, and palmed the data system's power pad for a last check on house security. Nothing.

Lights out, hand on door plate, she was ready to go when Tŷ Coed said, "Lonely. Come back soon, Laure. You and Cedar and Delun?"

A transgenic livewood tree thrived on purpose and affection. "I will, treasure. But Delun and Cedar are far away for now." Her voice broke on the last words. Let it be true.

The door slid silently open on a windy dusk.

5

The shadow hunter Doll Sorrow stalked the pylon arrays above Tirion, where hurricane winds blasted over the city's communications and transportation fields. Up on these barren travelways and platforms no human form moved, and even the sleek composite bullets and lances of maglev transit lay still. Her self-powered hovercam briefly surveyed them, dancing and dipping on the strong winds, as she piloted her tiny drone with one blunt paw. If she had human hands . . .

Here on this strange green world of big trees and tall grasses, unleashed chimerai walked in and out through open gates. Back in her old life, her leash had snapped her big jolts when she went within three metres of a wall. The owner had known every time she tried to get out, and his punishments were cruel. But Maq had asked politely if she would like to work here for a while and earn a new hand. It still felt strange to be asked and not told.

At her controls in a dark cube kilometres away and deep underground, Doll choked back her humiliation. Why did she have to be here tonight while others went down to the Twll and talked with the new council of the toxic poor? Last night Captain said Doll's eyes were the best, but others said when Doll Sorrow smiled, full-human children screamed and ran.

On Tirion city map sites, the tox quarter was called

Willowbrook. The working poor, the jobless poor, the uncarded illegal poor, and all the other poors inhabited the last remaining sinkhole of toxic inner city. Down among the moulds and rats and roaches whose ancestors stowed away from old Earth, it was the Twll, the hole.

In a few tendays the Twll would become a new Pact commercial enclave, and the tox would become refugees in their own city. A few people were ignorant or trusting enough to take the Pact's Ministry of Opportunity ticket to developing worlds or underpopulated Pol worlds, but most wanted to stay.

Doll Sorrow sent her cam drone along Hafn Boulevard up to the citadel and back to the Twll. Nothing good to tell. Captain's orders, nodded true by Maq, were to watch the high city, especially the mansion her old owner occupied till his own house was ready. She descended her drone over a leafy avenue to the mansion. It was quiet and dark tonight, except for one light in a lower discipline room. Doll tensed. No light was on in the nursery in an overgrown corner of the garden where the fiercest predators patrolled at night.

"Got?" she said to Noob in the next cube. Noob also scared norms and pulled drone duty.

"Not got," Noob rumbled. Speech was hard for him, and few beside Doll could understand unless he voice-synthed. He was smart but he used baby words. "Now got."

"Remember nanny?" When she was small and alone, Doll had called her *mama*.

"Gave us honey cake." Noob had belonged to the same owner. "Miss her."

Noob raised a paw. "Look now. It goes in."

A military hover descended to a service bay out of sight of the mansion's front entrance. Finally, a thing to tell. Warms coming? Colds going?

Doll drifted her drone probe in close to the man who stepped alone from the hover, floating a composite chest ahead of him toward the house. She couldn't scan the contents, so either it was well-shielded or the case was empty. His fish skin glittered blue-silver under the security light. She detached a nano from the cam and rested it for three seconds on the palm of his hand.

<> Ident? <> she queried the expensive new control. Maq had

bought it, and Captain showed them how to use it the same day he taught them nanoglops.

<> Duri Balint. Tolun City, Xanadu. Art collector.<>

<> Contents of chest? <>

<> Artwork on offer to Herra Nolin is statistically probable.<>

A second discipline room light went on in the lower level. Doll shifted restlessly in the dark cube and heard Noob whine under his breath. Who was in discipline tonight? *Pain toys. Fear.* Maybe new Baby was big enough to play. Doll had watched the sprite toddling with a nanny in the daylight, struggling to keep his awkward new wings from dragging on the ground. Her mouth drew back to a silent hiss. And deliberately relaxed. Captain said they had to be human now.

"What is human? How do I be human?" Doll had asked one training night.

"Don't jump long," Maq said. "Don't growl. Don't snatch food. Don't scare."

Captain glanced up from his slate to Doll. "You are as human as I am. Learn how other humans eat, dress, and work. Read gridsites. Watch and understand everything that happens."

As human as I am. Learn. Read. Understand. Doll held his words to her heart. Remembering gave her enough pride to swallow tonight's duty.

Someday she would be full-human again, even if she had to buy back her own hands and her own skin a centimetre at a time. Or maybe she would keep her fur. Noob said it was pretty.

Carefully, she filed a good clear report on the owner's visitor, the art man, pretending that it really was important.

6

Cut in. Fallen leaves flew around the neglected garden as the smaller moon cast racing shadows under the trees. Glad of her boots and coat, Seren shouldered her satchel and stepped out. She took one step toward the front of the house and froze.

Moonlight silhouetted the verandah overhang and the hawthorn tree. Near the tree, looking up at the house, stood a tall man—or a manimal.

Seren eased back against the chamber tree's rough bark. Risk a shot? It might just be a curious neighbour. Sneak into the main house? She could get trapped. Instead, she slid toward the back of the house, ducking the untended roses that clung to the stone walls, all the way around to the shuttered summer kitchen.

Slipping away from the back wall, she darted to the nearest tree, a neodar with branches cascading almost to the ground. She watched the southeast corner—the man didn't follow—then chanced a move to the next tree, and the next. She folded up small beneath an overhanging dwarf plum still in leaf near the stone orchard wall. Mercifully the untended grass had lodged flat under last year's fallen leaves, and her footprints barely showed. The unmortared drystone wall was too high and would rattle if she climbed over, but a few metres away stood the big russet tree that overhung the gate.

As she lifted off her heels to move, she heard voices. Not one man. Two.

Strangely, she felt calm now. She leaned back behind her screen of plum branches until the sharp stones dug into her shoulder blades, and eased out her laser. They might have sniffers and infrared sweeps. She pulled her thermal coat hood over her head and tucked her hands into the sleeves, the best she could do to mask her body heat. An unsect walked slowly across her leg. The neuters had nasty stings, but she didn't dare brush it away. Finally, it flitted. The two men walked across the back of the house, then out into the open toward her shadowed corner.

"No one. My intel got it wrong." A Mitran voice, rougher than Damou's.

"I'm dealing with you to get results, not rumours." A cultured Claeran voice, with the narrow vowels of Reprise. A stocky man of average height.

"Someone saw her heading this way," the Mitran muttered. "Should have sent a drone and saved ourselves the trouble."

"Clearly. I wasted hours on this adventure." Irritated, the Claeran gazed around as though he'd lost something.

The smaller moon sank behind the trees on the front boulevard, leaving deeply textured blackness. Seren didn't dare to shift weight, but from slitted eyes she watched him look into the orchard, then lean on the wall to study the house.

"Something here?" The taller Mitran joined him.

"Nothing." The Claeran turned, and moonlight moulded his face.

Mihal?

Seren gathered herself to get up, greet them, and admit they'd startled her, but the plan brought an unexpected wave of nausea. Something about Mihal and Gandhi Base, something she should remember . . . she fought down an unknown terror. Instead of showing herself, she kept her head on her knees between the cold wall and the branches, laser cradled under her breast, not moving a muscle, willing them away.

Mihal and the Mitran finally turned the house corner just as a small voice from the tree above her head chirred, "Seren. Love you."

Seren's heart stopped and kicked double-time as the Mitran

looked around and started back. By then she was through the orchard gate and running in a crouch along the wall's shadowy far side, with her arm clamped over a struggling, wet, burr-coated, wildly purring animal. Any cat could stage a showy entrance, but none did it like an augmented Mitran cat. Seren caught her breath and whispered, "Love you too, Cedar."

At the Gwernant streambank, Seren vaulted the orchard wall. Just outside, almost hidden among the alders and willows, someone had piled stream-rounded rocks into a small cairn and planted flowers. A candle had burned out on a flat rock. A shrine? No time to look. The path east through the wildwood was open overhead and firm underfoot, not the tangle she expected, and she let out her stride.

Cedar leaped down to frisk ahead, a brindled woodcat almost invisible in the dappled moonlight. As a closed-system entity, impervious to global updates, she'd recognized Seren and not Laure. It was full night when they jogged to the fork at a folded outcrop of bedrock. She had bolted this way many times, running up to the sanctuary, late for evensong—

Cedar stopped and arched on all four legs, spine bristling, tail bottled, and ears back in her ancestors' instinctive fight-or-flight response. Seren nearly ran over her cat and halted so suddenly that her knees locked.

Two tall shapes glided to a stop and moved wide to block the path. Moonlight curved on round eyes and backswept ears, furred shoulders and muzzles that looked inhumanly powerful. They walked upright, slightly stooped, and turned their heads to snuff the wind with feral interest. Hyena and ocelot genes, Seren thought, swift pursuers with deadly jaws. Each wore a metal cuff on its right wrist.

The larger manimal snarled silently.

"Intruder. Arena meat," Seren's slate relayed their message from her pocket.

"Friend." Cedar's voice came from the speaker implant under her chin, but she growled softly for emphasis. Every matted hair stood on end. She looked huge. "Mine."

The chimerai regarded the enhanced animal with predatory curiosity. Cedar was a quarter their size but probably near their intelligence. Then the larger one snuffed side to side, lowered its head, and shuffled a thoughtful half-step sideways.

Seren inched her right hand toward her laser. She could probably hit one before the other fell on them with crushing jaws and tearing fangs. Cedar took a dainty step forward, sniffing at the grass, looking everywhere but the manimals.

The second manimal also shuffled sideways.

Cedar said, "Mine. Tell others."

A show of strongly curved fangs in a face that was a fearsome mockery of the human. Then the moonlit path was empty, and a clump of willows along the track swayed and fell still.

Cedar sat and licked a paw, a Cedar she'd never imagined. Two patrolling chimerai had respected the small animal's claim instead of hunting her. Why? Groomed to her satisfaction, her cat got to her feet. "Hide now."

Between the trees ahead glowed the lights of Derw sanctuary. She'd have to smuggle Cedar inside, make an early start tomorrow, find somewhere safe, ask a hundred questions—but when Seren turned, her cat had vanished, and she stood alone in the dark woods.

7

Inka dreamed of birches in early spring on another world long vanished from her living memory. The five pale trunks leaned together under a high, light blue sky that stretched to forever. Around the trees, small white flowers nodded in grass newly emerged from snow. A west wind stirred around her, and she spread her arms to rise through the green woodland. As a golden eagle she breasted the wind over the expanse of sky-mirrored lakes. Effortless, weightless, timeless, beyond existence. Then a thought of her beautiful young lover drifted her down into a warm sensual sea of pleasure.

A harsh alarm signal shattered her virtual dream. She plummeted shuddering and sick into the painful dark, incapable of flight or ecstasy, without even the common senses that savoured a bread crust or brushed the nap of velvet. Here in nowhere, she had only knowledge.

Awake, Inka searched her banks. Few worlds had successfully adapted Earth-origin trees to soils full of voracious native enzymes and bacteria. This was not her own buried memory but a recorded fragment seeping into her consciousness from lovely Mikkeli among the northern lakes on old Earth, before all complex organisms died in the earthquakes and floods and fires.

Troubling, this bleedthrough of external record into personal

memory. Losing her acuity. She subtly altered her
neurotransmitter balance to regain tranquility.

Time to run her checks. Inka searched all known worlds,
dividing billions of electromagnetic signatures by the few
thousand genes of human DNA. She captured images on slates,
implants, cockpit screens, orbitals, and hidden security pickups.
A few held her attention.

<> Tas drifted in a dark corridor at abandoned Gandhi Base,
en route to a nameless world by way of the Bight. From here
Louhi's ship had auto-transmitted its cockpit records to Tas as it
disintegrated; he'd launched the wreck into the brown dwarf.
Now Louhi's data bead was in heedless Politayan hands—or since
chaos had not yet erupted, maybe Qasri's idiot abductors had
destroyed it.

Gandhi was already deep in infall, but the brown dwarf's
gravitational pull was slight and its radiation low. Inka quickly
calculated that Tas was safe on the dark station. A cautious man,
mindful of his task. Once her plans bore fruit, she would free him
from his pain. Inka followed his helmet sensor's view as he
explored. Why was he wasting time on a dead station?

<> Seren Qasri traded a gold rod to a nulled black marketeer
for unmarked cash cards at Tirion's dirigible depot. Then she
demanded a transport map from her virtual aide—Teak Kuhan at
her bidding. In a rage at Qasri's travesty, Inka thrashed in her
nutrient tank. Let the dead rest.

<> Gabriel de Jong swam laps with his bodyguard in an
echoing dark pool. Where? He'd barely been seen since Nolin's
rise to power. Inka checked her most obscure watchers and at last
located him as a guest on an island estate. He was unlikely to
leave soon. The security that kept brigands out also kept Gabriel
in.

<> Tas hung motionless in the station officers' quarters. His
helmet sensor showed a room's narrow bunk and desk, still
images and drawings stuck in a mirror frame, words scrawled
across its clouded surface. A woman's room, abandoned in haste.

Carefully he wiped frost from the mirror to read the Bryniau
Tavod: *Long the sun's road, longer my memories.* Words from
an ancient poem by another armed pacifist. Tas would like that,
with his irrational love of literature and drama, the arts of

falsehood and deception. This was a Bryniau Claer officer's room, and the only Bryniau Claer officer serving on Gandhi when the Pact fleet shut it down was Seren Qasri. Recognition wrung Inka's heart.

< > Duri Balint watched a captive opera company perform in his lovely formal garden amid Tolun City's squalor. In his private sanctum lay an object, not unlike the object he'd delivered to Wilm Nolin, that could raze worlds and destroy polities.

< > Tas brushed frost from the still images, revealing faces and scenes. Delun Qasri with a boat tiller under her elbow. A Politayan pilot in a combat hardsuit, helmet in hand. Seren Qasri sitting on a stone wall with a Mitran cat at her feet. Tas in a Spartí group shot, not quite smiling. A younger Seren Qasri outside a theatre, holding an armful of silver roses. Damn him.

< > Jaime Riordan tapped an order into his medical fabricator. Inka skimmed his prescription database and made a minor adjustment.

< > Renat Von paced outside Riordan's office. Inka had never forgiven Renat for dragging Tas after him into MitraCorps years ago, abandoning all his potential, abandoning Inka.

< > Tas freed two of the still images and pressed them to his chest. Inka was denied even the comfort of tears. Never again could her hands touch him, and in a greater cruelty, nor would he allow her. In her nutrient tank she fell still, making herself small within her measureless grief.

< > Maq Flett left his hover on a quiet street of Bulawayo village in the Claeran Cantons. In a lawyer's office, he punched his fist through a vri display of new surface-mine regulations. Inka breathed relief. She'd feared he was up to his old tricks.

< > Wilm Nolin kissed a young naiad who convulsed in glitz frenzy. Inka's rewards to Wilm were soon spoiled; she must seduce him to less costly pleasures.

< > Delun Qasri remained unlocated. Her implants had been dark since the invasion. A dangerous woman, if she lived, like her sister-friend Parvin Kerkallec. Claerans with their fatally low birthrate formed pseudo-familial relationships that defied definition. Sister-friends, brother-friends, and cousin-friends were personally contracted to aid and support each other. To Inka's irritation, every relationship seemed unique. Delun and

Parvin had been lovers and business partners, but the war had kept them apart for years, even when Delun passed through AnvilCo's domes on Melusine. Was her apparent disappearance accidental or Maq Flett's good security? Inka needed to know. She had plans for Delun.

<> Tas passed skeletal gantries on Gandhi's docking level and kicked toward his command ship. The one time Inka flew with him, in agony after he pulled her from the twisted ruin of the elevator pod, she begged him to let her go. You'll live, he told her. You have work to do. In time she understood he'd also been ordering himself to carry on.

Nine hundred nanoseconds of Inka's life had passed. She forced herself down, and down, to a human timescale and started her day's work.

8

ES2741.347

Slow pan, spatial wild sound. A sprawling township that looked like a vandalized construction site. The religious group that had settled Alluvion had planned for only basic needs, and beauty wasn't high on the checklist. The sole public attraction was a faltering botanical garden, now scoured by the ash and eroding topsoil that blew through the town since the Pact burned its woodlands and drained its lakes for industrial use. The town's main revenue source—extruding foam crates for Claer's famous blown art glass—was in a postwar slump. In the wake of the Politaya's defeat, Claer's remote lake district crumbled deeper into obscurity.

Closeup. Anti-Pact graffiti livened the drab walls, but no one had the energy for any real protest. If there was a Claeran resistance, it wasn't in Alluvion. The Pact would leave anyway, people shrugged, as always when the plunder ran dry. But Seren knew this time the Pol was on its own; the Neutrality was staggering from Mitra's death, the Grey companies had abandoned them, and balance of power was non-existent, leaving nothing to hold the Pact in check.

Seren burned through her last cash card a tenday after arriving on the midnight dirigible and took a night desk job at the town's failing automat overlooking a dry lake bed. In the quiet hours of darkness after cleaning and repairing the fabricators, she searched the grids, replayed Delun's messages, pored over her vri production notes, compiled clips about the war and occupation, erased them in frustration, worked to reassemble her life.

Gwernant stood stark in her dreams, burned and abandoned, a sad mockery of all she'd come home to find. Cedar had risked a terrible death to appear and vanish again. Delun and her cousin-friends might be lost forever. *All gone.* Every morning after her shift, as she fought sleep on her hostel cot, Seren tried to believe they lived. But in unsought dreams she mourned Mam, Kuhan, all the Claeran dead, as she stumbled through a charred and ruined garden.

A sanctuary clinic lay beyond her reach now; at the automat she logged in with the admin card to research *Amnesia, induced, treatment of.* Her memory of the Bight encounter was slowly coming into focus, all but the face of her weapons hand in the Bight and whoever jabbed her in a Gandhi corridor. The same person, maybe, protected from her recognition by posthypnotic suggestion and meds.

It had to be someone on the shutdown crew. She listed everyone she could remember, but always came up short. Mihal might know, though he must have left Gandhi by then. Perhaps he had been looking for her at Gwernant that night to seek answers of his own. She would contact him when it was safe.

Since Alluvion had no Pact garrison, Seren also risked research in the regional archives. She blended in with the data workers, fashionably turned out in this season's multi-pocketed vests and jackets—clearly inspired by Pol fleet uniforms—and long colourful silk scarves. Her warm clothes, the backup identity she'd painstakingly created during slow spells in the automat, and the essentials in her satchel were her emergency plan.

One day in the archive Seren had the luck to discover that an absent-minded researcher, a botanist from the public garden, had failed to sign off in his data booth. She copied his archive identity to her own card. Every two or three days, usually in understaffed lunch hours or quiet early evenings, she used the data booth in the corner farthest from the check-in. Its gestural array stuttered over too-sudden movements, and the symbols had worn off its control pad, but it delivered full gridstream.

For hours Seren called up documents on the history of Claeran silviculture, following the identity owner's research pattern. Once or twice a session she contrived a bibliographic trail to her real searches. The Pact occupation forces made a pretence of upholding local government departments and documents; she crunched through their files for anything on Delun Qasri, but security on Claer had tightened after some fool bombed the Pact data service in Reprise.

Alone in her hostel cube, she worked backward from the stab in the arm that ended her Gandhi memories. She'd been uploading files at her worktop in the cramped signals alcove but left quickly. *Panic. Dread.* Someone had ghosted up beside her in the passageway, someone she couldn't trust.

Image fragments and random emotions didn't add up to memory. Seren paced her three-metre square room and walked the cracked pavements of Alluvion for hours without breaking through her wall of mist. She viewed all the files from their station flat and her Gwernant chamber tree; most were routine correspondence or records of Delun's senate committee meetings to plan the peace offer. Damou, attending for Senate Security, spoke rarely but knowledgably on Claeran and Mitran defence and diplomacy. Seren studied these sequences, but his formality defeated any attempt to understand him. *Friend. Rescuer. What else?*

<> Teak, can you help me find my file backup? <> She'd asked more than once, hoping she'd left herself waymarks to recover her data.

<> Hidden in plain sight, Seren. You asked me to forget. <> So, she hadn't risked leaving directions even with her virtual aide.

Seren examined her slate and scanned every centimetre of her body but found nothing unusual, and she'd wiped her grid storage account years ago during her intelligence training. If she'd been rash enough to send files to Gwernant or the station flat, they no longer existed. Finally, she concluded there was no backup, just wishful thinking.

Late one evening, as rain slapped the automat roof tiles and flattened on the window membranes, two neon-haired shockrave boys strutted in to demand help uploading an oversize file to *Rax,* an entertainment kidzone the Pact hadn't gotten around to closing. Seren leaned over their shoulders into their clouds of neon hovertunes, hand sweeping over the gestural entrypad—

"You spun?" one boy nudged her elbow. "That's not my loot."

Seren stared in shock at the vri zone, where an image of an art glass ovoid rotated dimensionally. A blue glass ovoid swirling with crystal bubbles and a small landscape of gold and silver, a small perfect world that would fit in the palm of her hand. A gift from Mam. She would know it anywhere. Unhindered by conscious thought, her hands had entered the locators for her own file storage, the one that had eluded her memory for the past year.

"Sorry," she said, working to control her voice. "Wrong entry." She gestured the correct access with a hand that barely trembled and, to distract them, showed the boys how to jack the size limit. They left her a small tip, her only tangible gain from her Pol fleet intelligence training.

Three days later she decided no one had taken any special interest in her or the seedy automat. On the fourth day she returned to her corner booth in the archive, entered the botanist's identity, read a paper on root propagation in Earth-origin temperate zone herbaceous perennials, started an archive search, and finally gestured for her old screen on *Rax*. On Gandhi she'd hastily chosen the least obvious gridsite she could access to upload her data. *Hidden in plain sight.*

Her art glass rotated in the zone, and she blinked back tears at the image of Mam's gift, stolen by the roaches who'd grabbed her on Arian station. Then she took a deep breath and called up a virtual entrypad to tap out her pass code; she'd used the geographical coordinates and local date for the day she'd met Kuhan.

Seren smiled, reading through her indexes—named in keeping with *Rax* themes—*Brother-friends. Belles. Birthdays. Vri.* Most contained random files lifted from other sites: chat, festival pranks, vri clips of lovers, holidays with friends, technical how-tos. But the index named *Study prep* contained one large file that a cautious nonintrusive view revealed as locked and heavily encrypted. Image? Data? It was huge. If she could get in, she might remember . . . but she didn't dare open it in a public data

booth, and her slate didn't have space. Then in the backslot she
felt the extra bead Damou had given her en route to Claer many
tendays ago, and felt a warm rush of gratitude. One last rescue.

Seren fitted the copper bead into her slate and downloaded
her file from the gridsite. As it finished, her earlier search turned
up results. The Pact system, she'd discovered, turned out to be an
inefficient straggle of linked grids and nets, and there were
backdoors. A painstaking file-by-file crawl through two-year-old
surveillance records produced a file that looked promising, with
keywords *Qasri Mitra hostilities cessation threat*—Seren called
up a summary, and the monochrome sigils of the Pact file list
turned slowly in the air fifty centimetres before her eyes.

A second motion caught her eye. In the upper left corner of
the zone, a small file-share box had activated. It was the first time
she'd coincided with another user in these obscure files.
Cautiously she touched its whois sigil, but the profile was
blanked. In the query zone at her left elbow, a stylized question
mark rotated and tumbled as the remote user demanded her
profile. It should give the profile of the careless botanist who'd
loaned his identity.

Then the Qasri file opened, though she hadn't called it up or
even tried, and she stared at a high-speed flood of images. A
flurry of faces, a handful of council rooms, explosions in a city
that looked like Tirion, burning buildings, screen after screen of
images and text. Her document winked out of the zone, taking
down the file list and file-share box.

Instead, a second box opened and announced, "Alluvion
Regional Archive, Data Wing, Third Floor, Booth 16. Guest.
Female." Seren shied back from the booth, stung with shock.
Somewhere deep in the building an alarm sounded. Seren signed
off the botanist's identity, shouldered her satchel, and left. Before
she was out of range she heard the data booth warning, "Security
breach in progress."

Emergency plan. Seren's legs shook so badly she nearly fell
descending the archive steps. A pale-haired man looked up from
a bench near the dry fountain, but he didn't follow. Abandoning
her hostel room and her few anonymous possessions, she strolled
up shabby Hawking Boulevard past the botanical garden to the
grownbrick Sunfire shrine. At the altar she knelt and dropped

Laure Prakash's identity card into the eternal flame dancing in a shallow brass bowl. She waited on a shadowed back bench for ten minutes. No one entered. Then she walked to the maglev station and burned out a low-value cash card on fare to the end of the southern line.

Night came down before Seren left the maglev pod at its terminus. She wrapped her scarf around her face—silver-grey silk, a treasure from a backstreet charity shop—and for three starlit hours walked south.

A steady east wind erased her footsteps and drove the long-haul freight dirigibles sighing high overhead on their way to the deep south. They wouldn't touch down till Dinan or Tirion. As she went, she sucked water from a vacpac and chewed a protein bar. When she was too tired to go on, she told her slate to alarm a close perimeter near a wind-smoothed boulder and stretched out. Her nanosilk sheet floated in the cold wind until she told it to warm and cling. Sleep evaded her, so she lay back with her head cradled on clasped hands to gaze into Claer's starfield.

Her life had gone missing. In one way the fleet owned it until she finished her task—but in truth a dead man owned it now and forever. Her eyes strayed across the bright band of the home galaxy toward once lovely Mitra.

Kuhan had barely crossed her mind in tendays, she realized with a small shock of regret. Betrayal in a minor key. But Kuhan was certainly beyond caring, and anyway would have advised her to forget the past and live now.

<> Teak, what can I do? <> she queried. <> Someone's after me, but I don't know who, and there's no one who can help. <>

Teak wavered into life as a small image floating above her hand. So young. He'd never had the chance to realize his full strength and his gift for right action.

<> Head down. Eyes open. Keep moving. <>

Good advice, but generic; that was the problem with consulting a lost oracle. Damou would probably say something much pithier. Where was her Grey shadow now that she needed one? Damou had probably forgotten her, as she'd forgotten him. But that wasn't true. Everything about that night in the Cantons had been too disturbing to forget. Damou had been a different man once, by the way he moved and talked. And by the way he touched her.

Seren closed her eyes. She could summon Teak as her virtual ghost lover, but it was better to remember Damou. When he was around, it was like having a realtime Teak to answer questions and come to her aid. For a few hours, Damou had been a man she wanted to know.

Kuhan and Damou were both blunt, generous, smart, pragmatic. Damou would deny any similarity to Kuhan; he hadn't much liked the man. What would Kuhan make of Damou? Probably tell him to quit fighting his personal demons and get on with life. Kuhan had an answer for everything. Damou was better in that one way. He didn't claim to know all the answers.

En route to Claer her slate had recorded Tas at the controls of his old Az. She propped herself on her elbows and called up the sequence on her slate, watched him turn to face her—not angry but wary—and froze it to copy a clip. She lifted another image from a senate committee file and merged the two. Her slate's sim tools were rudimentary, but she patched and shaded until she'd lifted the scars and corrected the twisting of his face.

A stranger looked mildly back at her. Damou. Everyman. One of the people. Next Seren copied a sequence from Delun's files of Damou walking across a senate chamber with that slight halt in his step.

<> Teak, search this man's face and gait in Mitran civilian and military files. <>

<> Processing, Seren. <>

Damou's estimated vital stats scrolled in the darkness above her slate: male, healthy, fit, forty to fifty standard years, fractionally taller but somewhat slighter than the Mitran average.

<> No match, <> Teak said after an endless few seconds. <> Next query? <>

No one she knew. What had she expected, someone she recognized? But she still didn't understand why an unknown Mitran had taken such trouble to help her family.

<> Stand by. <>

Half asleep, Seren smiled. Maybe the rumoured resistance would give her letters of marque, and she could talk Damou into privateering. Could anyone talk Damou into anything? Not a hope. It was pure romantic fantasy anyway, straight from the vri dramas. So was Damou, a shadow man driven by a shadow debt of honour. In a vri drama, of course, the producer would cast him as handsome, charming, and dull. Damou was ugly, abrasive, and contrary.

Seren woke shivering. She washed her face in freezing water and walked on south. At midday she came to a maglev track just west of a stop and burned out her next-to-last cash card heading home, but not to hilly Bryniau between the glaciers and the wild western sea. She couldn't lead pursuers straight to Gwernant; instead, she took a chance on a neighbouring city.

Dinan crowned a peninsula jutting northward into the East Sea from the green farmlands of Nevez. At small Dinan port, Seren found a bare automat that overlooked Proton Transport's apron. Four days she sat by the window working on her slate, unremarked by the few regulars, and laboured over the file she'd uploaded many tendays ago to *Rax*. Her pass codes were lost in the mist. Obvious keys, keys that she knew she'd recall how to reconstruct. *Hidden in plain sight.*

On the fourth afternoon she looked outside to see a dark-haired woman in a Pol fleet jacket helping a child down from an old Umiak freighter. Her gamble had paid off; Rozenn had finally passed through here. Seren quickly pocketed her slate and went outside. At the dispatch office door, she handed the woman her fallback identity card.

"Tara Hassan from Taupo." Rozenn handed back the card, taking her cue flawlessly. "I remember you. Long time. Another holiday in hell?"

"No such luck," Seren admitted. "Looking for work."

"Marika's at seven local." Rozenn and Lezig ducked into the office.

It took Seren some time to find the small café in one of Dinan's old historic wood-timbered boulevards, undamaged by the occupation. It overlooked a back garden that must be pretty in summer. Her instincts distrusted its dark dogleg entryway, and her instincts were right.

As the door sighed shut behind her, a man stepped from a recess and put something cold and hard to the back of her neck. She might disable him long enough to seize the weapon and run— but run where? Better to stay and turn the tables on him, learn what he knew.

"Step three paces forward." At least he had a Claeran voice.

Seren walked to the centre of the shuttered room, where he scanned her with a handheld. It hadn't been a weapon after all. Rozenn watched from the window table, silhouetted against the filtered evening light.

"All I want is a job," Seren tried.

Instead, they had questions. Who did she really work for, since Pol Fleet intelligence no longer existed? And what good was she to those who wanted the Pact off Claer? They asked quietly, even politely, and that was more unnerving than fists or blackjacks.

Seren answered each question with silence. It was none of their business that she worked for no one, had fouled up her one major task, and couldn't even jack her own memory. Finally, she said, "I'll talk to your senior officer."

The man sighed. "Soon. Who can vouch for you?"

Time for a delaying action. "Maq Flett. AnvilCo."

"A Pacter?"

Seren said nothing. Glances met, and the man went outside talking into his comm implant. When he returned, he nodded to Rozenn. Seren managed a straight face. They were enjoying their cloak and dagger games.

"What can you do for us?" The man joined them and clasped his scabbed hands on the table. The scars suggested he'd been doing manual work he wasn't particularly good at.

"Nothing." A job was what Seren wanted, and a chance to probe her retrieved file, not a rebel's death at Pact hands by arena battle or torture.

"You flew combat."

"Hardly. And not in the war." Seren pushed on before she had to explain. "I worked with signals and images. Not what you need." They wouldn't need a pilot anyway. High-hours ex-fleet pilots besieged every scarce flying job.

"We need our world back. Our families are starving or dying in labour camps. Our children are brainwashed or stolen." The man sounded more like one of her milder art college teachers than a revolutionary, and he lacked the beady-eyed intensity of some politicals.

Seren shrugged and folded her arms. Without asking a

question, she now knew more about them than they knew about themselves: well-organized, motivated, empty-handed, desperately seeking resources and personnel. And she knew how to use them for her own purposes. "You think you can fight the Pact with small arms and farm-made bombs? You'll never win, you'll just kill a few homesick draftees, destroy materiel, and do everything you detest in the occupation. You'll become the Pact's mirror image. Why give them an excuse to tighten down? You don't need a guerrilla war, you need to remediate the terms of peace."

"How?" the man demanded. "We have nothing left."

"By diplomatic means."

"We tried diplomatic means. Now we have a treaty that enslaves us in perpetuity."

"Try again. The Pact rushed the treaty into law without the required Pol data or depositions. Gather evidence to reopen the treaty. Find the senator who headed the peace committee, Delun Qasri, and put her to work." Maybe they had ways to find Mam. "If she's dead"—Seren caught her breath, remembering the cairn and flowers she'd glimpsed at Gwernant—"tell the world, make her a martyr, and find someone else to do the job. Weapons and threats create only chaos. Remediation creates hope."

It was all straight Kuhan with adds from Damou, but it worked. Seren might even have relevant data, once she found a way to open her file. Rozenn and the man exchanged glances again and walked out.

So much for finding a job. Workers' collectives or the toxic poor might have helped her go off-grid before the war, but now anyone she contacted could die. Instead, she headed back to the New Grove shelter and soup kitchen in a burned-out school. In the morning—gods knew.

Her slate buzzed, and she stared at it. No one knew Tara Hassan's locators. But when she touched the sigil, the message told her, "Proton Transport, Dinan port, 0400 local."

9

It took a bunch of tendays for Maq to track down his old friend Gabe on Walden and toss him a line. There was nobody home but understaff and bots at the grand presidential palace in Havre, and there was nobody at all in the lifetime president's lovely villa overlooking the Sea of Longing. Maq had to call in a century's worth of favours to locate Gabe on a remote Barrier Sea island. From the air it looked a lot like a prison.

Gabe didn't want to be rescued, Maq quickly found out. He'd fumbled his sticks but he wasn't ready to admit it.

"You screwed up, Gabe. You burned up everybody's ready resources, and now we're shit out of luck if any rodents turn up. Your old lady used to whack your hand when you grabbed the last bannock. Didn't you learn any damned thing? Don't take what's not yours. Ask politely."

"Last time I ever get talked into a resource war," Gabe admitted.

"Nolin." Maq made it a curse. "You're crazy, letting him run things."

"The Pact runs itself," said the oldest and richest man in human space. His skin folded like dry parchment, and his big hands trembled, but his dark eyes were still shrewd.

"Hell it does." Maq sipped superb brandy from a chipped tin

190

mug. "You promised to harpoon that pervy shitheel."

"I can spike Nolin anytime I want," Gabe said, a little too querulously for Maq's liking.

"Now would be good. He's running crazy since he married that six-families heiress." Maq took a swallow. "Your brandy's crap too. This stuff isn't five hundred years old, it's younger than me."

"You didn't come here to bitch about my brandy. Shut up or drink beer."

Beer was all they drank back when they were pissant blackware studs on industrial Hell Seven, the most radioactive site in human space. Why freeze down the half-life, the Pacters reasoned, when you could burn a planet to its core and move on? Maq could still see Gabe stagger out blinking into the Glow's fractured firelight with a data monocle bruise around his eye, cursing the day they left Sitkum, though in truth Sitkum had left them.

Gabriel de Jong scowled into his brandy, clearly pissed off at hearing straight talk from his one last friend. Someone had to tell him, Maq figured. Nolin was locking down the Pol occupations, tossing scraps to his cartel goons. Soon they'd get tired of scraps and go after Nolin, and then who would grab power? Maybe that greedy prick Balint.

"How?" Gabe finally asked after his third shot. His fancy lahal set still waited unused on the table under his elbow.

"Pay attention. Listen to the rad sites. Get your hand back on the wheel. It's not too late."

"Nolin's rubbed out everyone I trusted. Nothing left but mud sharks."

"So, sharpen your hooks and get fishing."

"Lay off, Maq." Gabe set down his mug with a clatter. "Mend your own nets."

"You bet I will," Maq said. "Sell off AnvilCo, pack up my domes and crawlers, prayer to Saint Jude, and I'm gone. Always wanted to be a space nomad."

"What's Jude good for? I forget." De Jong poured them both another snort.

"You don't forget, you're a heathen that never knew. Jude's the patron saint of lost causes." Gabe still made a skookum straight man. It was probably the only time he got to be real. "Thought I'd give you heads-up before I mirror out."

"When?"

"Few tendays."

Maq's internal calendar still ticked off the long days and short years of a world no longer on the charts. The day Sitkum declared for the Neutrality, they discovered too late, it had exactly one standard year to live. No diplomatic censure, no hostilities, until a Pact fleet coasted into high orbit and launched its nukes. Now his calendar was ticking off tendays until Nolin ordered his heavies to discipline AnvilCo the same way just for the hell.

Maq's intercorp would soon consist of three freighters that strikingly resembled Politaya Fleet warships, decommissioned and brilliantly retrofitted thanks to his Mitran aerospace engineers. The Pol's flagship carrier was already in service as an ore hauler based on Rustam's barren moon Sohrab in Neutrality space. The freighters would take short-haul jobs within easy reach of wherever AnvilCo might be at the moment. Greys might be spear-up-the-ass righteous post-utopians, but at heart they were also anarchists that did business his way. *Screw the licence fees, screw the bribes. When you show profits worth taxing, we'll be around to collect.*

"Good claims opening up on Mesa."

"No more prison worlds. I've done my time."

As Grey company POWs, they'd been exchanged out after surviving a mortal year in the Lorelei strip mines. De Jong's colourful past caused little excitement in Havre; he'd been a respectable Pacter longer than most people had lived, thanks to his rejuv cocktail of ancient mojo and Mitran genetic mods. Fed up with living way too long, tired of watching his great-grandchildren get old and die, Gabe had cashed in his wealth for power and took a run at reunity.

"Pack your crown or whatever a tyee wears these days, and let's hit Havre. Show the flag, throw a party, hold a giveaway. You're not doing anybody any good on this rock."

"Safer here." Gabe wouldn't meet his eyes.

"Bullshit. You're a sitting duck. Come on, I'll give you a ride."

"Not this time. Thanks." Gabe handed over the half-full bottle. "How's the rehab business? All those Pol yahoos must be driving you bush crazy."

"Politaya governments in exile is the diplomatic term. Happy as clams now they have something new to argue about. Some were in rough shape, but my Mitrans stitched them up. Jerk Nolin's leash, drag him off the pillage, and they're good to go."

"Retaliation. Crap." Gabe had seen it too many times, like Maq.

"*Cultus wawa*. No way. Damou pounded dharma into them years ago. Carry it, and it owns you. Forgive. Forget. Move on. We all got better things to worry about is the bottom line."

"How's his tox?"

"Shaping up nicely." Maq raised the main purpose of his visit with his last swallow of brandy. "Just keep your goons off their backs a little longer."

"Sure thing. More than one way to split planks, eh?"

Not a bad deal, Maq thought as he left Gabe's luxurious suite under ridiculously heavy escort. It took a lot of effort forty years ago to enthrone Gabe instead of some other rich bastard who could buy the infinitely buyable Pact, but it paid off pretty good.

As Maq strolled out to the island's landing zone, the hair on the back of his neck prickled a warning that unfriendly eyes watched from cover.

His new ship *Emerald Star* was fail-safed all to hell, so he wasn't surprised to find a medic working on a Pact trooper's scorched hand. *Do not attempt unauthorized entry,* read the Peel block letters on his cargo hatches, but some folks didn't take a clear warning at face value. The Pacters had only Pact tech to get them in, but he had his massively funded Mitran tech to keep them out. Not a fair match, but this was war.

"Contents of cargo holds?" an overdecorated customs official challenged when Maq strolled toward his cockpit ramp.

Maq had spent a world's ransom in unmarked universal cash cards on a few new toys, loaded into his hold an hour ago. He held up Gabe's brandy bottle. "Gifts from the president. He's way too generous."

Never lie when the truth will do, Maq's dad had always said. It worked especially well if the truth involved the lifetime president of the Pact of Human Worlds. As a result, Maq's spectacularly illegal cargo was still intact when he boarded. Sixteen orbital laser cannon, ten particle-beam cannon, and a handful of plasma cannon were snug in his hold's inertial nets, but that was only the sharp end. Their housings and platforms could ship later as communications satellite parts. There were also two miniaturized mirror-synch transmitters, one for his ore hauler and one for his number one freighter, space-space and ground-space missile systems, and enough portables, small arms, and personal shielding to give his crews some peace of mind.

Once Maq got outsystem, he called his bank on Xanadu to transfer another million to the tox fund, then called his Mitran engineers to discuss design flaws in the communications and weapons arrays of his freighters. Hasi crept out from her hidey-hole—the mongoose knew when to duck and roll—as he finally propped his feet on *Star's* main board. Maq downed more of Gabe's brandy straight from the bottle, set the transmitter to maximum encryption, and called his military adviser.

"Destroy all of it," Tas said after Maq brought him up to speed. "Launch it into the nearest sun or loft it into orbit and forget it. Weapons invite conflict."

"Sure. I can do that." All according to plan. That took care of business—but Maq waited for the inevitable question.

"Where is she, Maq?"

"You asked me that exact same question three times now. Why do you think the answer's any different this time?" One thing was different. Tas was straight and sober. He hadn't missed a step for ten tendays, maybe longer. Maybe it was time.

"You'll know if anyone does. She trusts you."

Edgy concern was as close as Tas ever got to full-blown panic. Maq hesitated long enough to make him sweat. "Last I heard, Tirion and then Alluvion."

"Gone. Her identity's static, no comms, no searches, no charges or deposits. Either she's someone else or she's dead."

"Guess she doesn't want to be found, eh?" So even Tas's slick surveillance network hadn't tracked her. Good to know.

"I have something she needs."

"True," Maq was lubricated enough to say. "Does she know that yet?"

Chilly silence. Tas gave him the Mitran stare, light eyes in a ravaged dark face like some extinct raptor, scary as hell. Maq wasn't fooled. Neither was Seren Qasri.

Maq tried exploration. "Damned woman drove me crazy on Claer trying to green me up. So, I comply with insane Pol ecolaws, pay out my ecodebt, and does she thank me? Hell no."

Moving operations into Grey and Green space was a pain, it was true, but he could lower his costs and charge the same rates for certified green zero-impact ores and tech.

"Qasri is all right," Tas said.

A major concession. Satisfied, Maq told him, "Don't try to run her life."

"Someone needs to run her life, or she won't have one."

"You can't carry it all forever. Tanna. Mitra. Qasri."

"I don't leave a task half done."

"You Mitrans make my head hurt. You can't legislate brotherly love." Maq had tried a few times.

"We don't need brotherly love. All we need is to tolerate each other."

Maq was sobering up, to his regret. "It's a sin of pride to burden your life with a debt of honour. And all this nonattachment is crap. I tried it for twenty years or so, and it didn't make me any better or wiser or less horny. God, I hate martyrs."

"I'm not a martyr." Stung. Good. Got his attention.

"Mostly you're an arrogant, smart, stiff-necked bastard who knows what's best for everyone but him." Maq knew when to quit. Qasri and Damou would find each other blindfolded in a blizzard anyway, so it didn't hurt to make things easier. "Few tendays ago I got a reference call on a Taupo pilot from a freight service on dryside Claer."

Tas was tapping his nav board when the screen greyed out.

Maq didn't have any business in Claer's desert zone, but he could find some. He had to wonder if it was sacrilege to cast himself as *spiritus mundorum*, but the archangels seemed to be slacking on the job. First, he'd get the tox on cleanup. A person might love to hate the Pact, but Walden still looked like the big player in the last years of humankind. The Pols had no capital world, just treated government as a travelling songfest and carried on a good-natured squabble over precedence. The Greys did the same but soberly called it democratic process and, until its death, quietly agreed Mitra was the Neutrality mainworld for business, tech, and policy. Walden was almost sane by comparison, but that was the Pact's loss.

Instead of burning for Claer, Maq decided to stash his new insurance policy, namely Gabe's gift. With any luck, archaeologists wouldn't pull it out of orbit for a thousand years.

IV
DUST

1

ES2742.077

Two shot, full sensorium. Today's freight manifest was the usual nightmare tangle of last-minute changes. Seren leaned on the Umiak out of the cold wind to read the data pad. Dust stung past her, heavy with eucalyptus and tired old buildings, the scents of Samun's industrial spaceport.

<> Teak, what's our weight so far? <>

<> Ninety-nine percent of legal limit. <> The avatar gazed from her slate screen, awaiting her next request.

<> Let's keep it there. <> Seren made an effort not to look over her shoulder at the dome and asked, <> Any progress on opening the file I downloaded? <>

<> Working on it, Seren. <> Teak looked regretful. Not a good sign.

Every offshift hour she spent trying to open the big file. At Gandhi she now recalled seeing numbered indexes of many numbered files on the courier's bead as her code froze its auto-destruct routine. But those files were all small. If the file wasn't the courier's data, what had she uploaded to her unlikely *Rax* storage?

<> Teak, what about Mam and Cedar? <> Every day she checked the grids, but Delun Qasri's name had eerily disappeared even from archival records.

<> No leads. But your cat may be safe. Some chimerai don't harm animals. <>

Radko darted like an unsect from his lair just inside the dome's big portside doors, waving a handful of tearoffs. "One more for Arian. Eighty kilos. Let it go, she's easy on weight."

Seren ignored him to calculate her legal weights and balances, checking them with Teak. She guessed the Proton dispatcher took bribes and skimmed the accounts, but she needed a job. Radko guessed her ID was forged, but he needed a pilot to overwork. Mutual blackmail kept them both quiet.

In the past hundred-days of Samun's northern-hemisphere early winter, her research had slowed to a crawl. She couldn't risk approaching fleet officers with someone hunting her—Delun had warned her not to report anyway—and so far, she'd found no keys to open the massive file.

Seren moved into the thin winter light, seeking its scant midday warmth, and the cold wind found her again. Samun clung to a landscape of extremes. Its long midcontinent winter was cold and dry, but bearable if she dressed for the climate. In another two hundred-days a hot wind would roar in off the dryland, plucking up sand and pebbles to reshape landmarks from one day to the next and sending the tough-skinned native vegetation into heat dormancy for many tendays. She didn't plan to stay long enough to experience a Samun summer.

Teak blinked out. Glitching again? Lately the avatar had worked perfectly—

A moving shadow fell silently across her back onto the ship's flank. She spun, and her data pad flew clattering under the Umiak. A man stood behind her, only a dark shape against Claer's distant yellow sun.

"What in hell are you doing here?" Her heart still thumped when she straightened.

"You always welcome old friends this warmly, Qasri?"

"You'll never know."

"Slow. You should have seen me sooner. Careless for someone who doesn't want to be found. And learn to tell your friends from your enemies." Damou looked troubled. "I lost you."

"You don't worry about me, I don't worry about you."

Seren retrieved the data pad, glancing up once. New clothes in well-cut black, a wide-brimmed MitraCorps field hat pulled down low, same terrible face, same sawtooth manners.

"We need to talk."

"Sorry. I leave in"—Seren checked her chrono, bought in a Samun surplus shop; she couldn't risk an implant when any update could expose her ID—"three minutes. If I wait, Radko will load us over the legal limit again."

"Now."

Seren studied his face, impassive again as usual. She had planned what to say if they met again: *Thank you, Meistr Damou. I know now what you did for my mother and me. I'm in your debt.* Maybe even, *I missed you.* Instead, she'd snapped at him. Again.

Dust drove into her mouth and nose, gritted in the creases beside her eyes, sifted into her hair. The cold wind streamed out her long silver-grey scarf and floured her blue clothes. Not a comfortable spot to talk. Three minutes and counting. She folded the manifest data pad and swept flying hair off her face.

"Talk fast."

Damou was looking at her wrist, and the four dark finger bruises.

Not your business. Seren sighed at his expression. "A docker on Han Three."

"All right?"

"Probably. I didn't hit him too hard."

Damou flashed his death's head smile—metal teeth gleamed along his burned right side—and was abruptly serious again.

"Don't travel in Pact space. You don't want to come to security notice with forged papers and a Pol intelligence background."

"Telling me what to do again."

"Let's go."

Seren tossed the data pad through the hatch before she turned. "Why?"

"Delun," he said. "Comm your dispatcher, claim three hours' sick time. We're going for a meal."

Radko nearly deafened her when she called. "Are you crazy? I'm not paying demurrage so you can screw around!"

"My nav's not even here yet. What's your breakeven?"

"Seventeen hundred." He cut the connection noisily.

Seren shivered and sealed her collar as they left the Proton dome, a short-term modular twenty years over its safe-until date. They walked out through the loading bay that took ground deliveries and into the dusty access road. Mild by Samun standards, the shadow side felt like a flash freezer to a woman from temperate Tirion y Bryniau. Damou was Mitran, so he probably felt right at home.

Among the scattered buildings of wind-blasted composites that made up Samun's freight terminal, Damou headed for one of the café-bars that scraped out a living here. The wind flapped a green awning over its one small window, but the door blinked a "closed" sign. As Seren turned away, Damou put his hand on the palm plate, and the door opened on a single room where dim natural light filtered through paper blinds onto a few tables. The room was rich in the scent of cinnamon and cloves.

A sleepy-looking man in a white apron came out of the kitchen and embraced Damou. "You found her. Another of your dead?"

Damou only lifted a shoulder.

Another of your dead. Seren saw a pattern. "I died on Claer Arian."

"Ganga." The cook looked at Damou uneasily. Ganga was a Pol world, but his voice was from Rustam or Vritra in the Neutrality.

"We need someplace quiet for three hours, Rav."

"Anything. Anytime." Rav turned toward his kitchen. "Out back is all yours."

"A table." Damou sounded embarrassed.

Seren reluctantly followed Damou down a dim corridor, then through an arch hung with lengths of some translucent filament, into another world.

Tawny plastered walls enclosed a rectangle of sand and rock no bigger than the café, warmed by concealed heat strips under the eaves and alive with gnarled and tangled plants from some sunnier place. Warm sand crunched under her boot soles. A vine heavy with blue flowers scented the warm air, and small green birds swooped and tumbled over a pool. The birds flitted freely in and out, preferring this haven to the cold desert outside. It was a pocket of beauty and longing in a drab place, an exile's garden.

She took the small blue-and-gold painted cup Damou held out and sipped the steaming black brew, thick and sweet. He pulled back a chair for her at the age-silvered wooden table and sat opposite, frowning at a wall mosaic. In the past he'd always turned the twisted side toward her like a shield, but now he turned it away. Why? She folded her arms, then recognized her own hostile body language and deliberately, neutrally, folded both hands around the small caffe cup.

Rav brought out plates of bread and fruit and set them on the weathered table. As he turned away, Damou raised a hand and told Seren, "Give me your ID."

Seren hesitated but gave it to him. She still missed being Laure Prakash.

Damou passed her new card to Rav. The cook looked at it closely, front and back and edge-on, then pulled a slate from his apron pocket and slotted the card. "Slowish response time on genetic identity, and the holomark looks blurred. Close enough for everyday, but trouble if you take it too far, Miz Hassan. A Walden customs officer would want a handful of cash cards to pass this one." He went to scatter grain for his birds.

Seren shrugged. "Local card stock, bioware, and nano."

"You did this?" Damou demanded.

"Obviously not well."

"Slate?"

Seren looked at him a long moment, but got out her slate. Damou laid his own dented slate beside it on the table. Anyone else would have spoken a password and touched palm to palm, but neither of them had data implants; she'd grown as wary as Damou of corrupted signals and being on record. Her progress light flashed for a full twelve seconds before it went dark; he'd loaded a lot of data into her memory.

"Inka's codes will give you full untraceable access to grid or archive files. You can also jack your own DNA-based identification and call a global update to point your biometrics to Tara Hassan or any new ID you create. Any questions, Rav's been through this." He intercepted her glance at the cook, feeding his birds near the sunny garden wall. "You can trust him."

Seren didn't need Damou involving anyone else, even another of his dead.

"Lock up when you leave, yes?" Rav called from the archway. "I'll be back tonight."

Seren managed not to protest his wasted diplomacy. In the awkward silence as they ate, she asked, "Why is Inka helping me now?"

"I've carried the files for a long time looking for you. Why did you disappear?"

"I was tagged." Seren described her retreat from the Alluvion archives.

The small colourful birds ventured almost under her feet for crumbs. Her glance dropped to Damou's arm on the weathered wood, sleeves rolled up as usual despite the cold. Brown hair almost invisible against brown skin, close enough to touch. It made her throat ache for no good reason, and she looked away. Damou lifted a few grains from his plate to the table, then held up a hand. *Wait.* In a few heartbeats, two birds came to forage among the crockery.

"Why didn't you contact me?"

Seren shook her head. She had tried; maybe she could have tried harder. She looked at the thick sediment in her cup, the nicks on the edge of the table, the backs of her brown hands, her blue shirt sleeve that she'd fabbed to the colour of Claer's sky, said to be darker than Earth's. Anywhere but at Damou.

"Seren. I'm on your side."

Finally, she looked up. "What side is that?"

His voice barely rose above the purl of running water and the wind-driven sand hissing across the flat roofs of Samun. "Any side you're on."

Greys didn't take sides—their side was whoever paid—and Damou was the quintessential Grey.

"We used to be one side," she said awkwardly. "Second wave. Politaya and Neutrality."

"There is only one side," he said, "there is only humanity."

Reunity. Mam had dreamed of it; so had Teak Kuhan. Seren watched Damou watching the birds. In a cold desert he'd found a small haven of warmth and grace. She wanted to touch his hand, but it would send the wrong message. Instead, she picked up her slate.

"You'll see dangerous and disturbing things in the files. Careful. Take nothing at face value."

"Delun, you said. What did you learn about Mam? Tell me."

Information too volatile for a mirror comm, hand delivered, might not be good news.

"Delun wrote a peace offer, but it never reached the Pact delegation. Globalists in the Claeran parliament and senate tried to fight the occupation. Moderates tried to negotiate. They all disappeared or died. Now the rest are in hiding."

"Take me to her."

"I can't." A long Mitran silence. "After the second attack I took her to your cousin-friend Daoud, but he died in the invasion. Now no one knows—I'm sorry."

Daoud. Seren covered her face. Daoud was her older half-cousin on her father's side, a horticulturist who'd made time to play a beggar for her in *Poison.* All dead, the woman said in the ruins of Tirion. How many other family members had she lost?

"I'm searching for her, but no leads yet. Your mother's knowledge is still critical to reunity." Damou reached into a breast pocket and lifted out a titanium bracelet, like his own but less worn.

"Knowledge of what?"

"Read the files. You can use this comm bracelet to call me, but I'll be out of range for the next six days. If you need help meanwhile, call Helli Njau, the captain of Spartí Company."

Not likely. "Where will you be?"

Silence. He clasped the bracelet onto her right wrist, tingling slightly as it aligned to her biometrics, and for a moment he took her hand between his two warm hands. Another man had done that once, in Gwernant's rainy orchard.

Seren found only the empty shell of her voice. "Meistr Damou, I need to go."

"Soon." He looked away, and back. "I have a name."

"Tas."

Her chair scraped across paving stone as she got up. He stood beside her, close enough that his warmth and his scent enfolded her. He lifted a strand of her hair and brushed it behind her neck, making her shiver. She'd felt the same small shock of live electricity that night in Izu.

She forced herself to turn away and shook crumbs from the empty plates onto the table for the birds. As she walked under the tiled arch, a whir and flutter of bright wings announced their arrival at the feast.

Damou followed her into Rav's gleaming kitchen. He leaned on the counter and pulled a flask out of his thigh pocket. Taking a long swallow, he saw Seren watching. "Water. I dehydrate easily because of the burn."

Seren shrugged, recalling Maq's warning in the Cantons. Not her business.

"I spent a year drunk. Another year on glitz. After Mitra died. And my family."

Confessions. He slid the bottle carefully back into his pocket, taking his time to think. Damou usually thought things through, just as she usually led with her mouth. He always arrived early, and she was sometimes late. Her world was a vri zone of shifting scenes and patterns, and she guessed his world rested on immutable forms and facts. No wonder they drove each other mad. Outside Rav's window, the birds flew one by one back to their sheltering vines.

"You didn't attack me on sight this time."

"Sorry. Instinct. My ancestors set the skulls of their enemies into their doorposts."

"Barbarians. All of us were, on Earth." His voice said he was smiling. "You want my head for a door knocker?"

"I don't take trophies."

"The hell you don't."

"I'd rather understand what goes on inside it." Even in the bright room it was hard to read his expression.

"Do you want me to lay it out?"

Forgetting to breathe, she forced herself to move. Ignore everything his body language was shouting. Numbly, she stacked the plates in the cleaner. *Now close the doors. Lock up. Go.*

But—what would it be like to court Tas Damou? He wasn't a Claeran, she couldn't just put her hand on his shoulder and tell him she wanted him. Claeran woman, Mitran man, it was a template for disaster. A moment's erotic heat in Izu had been easy, an accident of fear and adrenalin and rice wine, but this was impossible. She looked up. He still leaned on the counter, watching her. The good corner of his mouth quirked.

"It doesn't need to be complicated."

"All right." She took a deep breath and went to him.

His arms went around her like a closing vise, and for a long minute they held each other tightly like friends long parted. Then his warm hands lightly stroked down the back of her neck, and her consciousness narrowed to his touch. He found her hair clip and freed her hair.

Tas ran his thumb gently across her mouth until she opened to take it onto her tongue. His touch was intensely erotic. Strange but sensual. The unburned side of his face abraded her cheek. His mouth was warm on her throat, his hands tangled in her hair, and gods she wanted him—

"Taso?" A small voice said from the comm bracelet beside her ear.

Tas reached up to tap his wrist, turning off the comm.

Two seconds. It gave her long enough to regain her senses. Seren pulled free. "I can't."

It was a long time before he said, looking aside, "All right."

Seren stumbled away to rest her forehead on the cool plaster wall, still aching for his touch. Finally, she turned. Tas leaned with arms folded, watching her impassively. Maybe he thought she'd enjoyed leading him on and cutting him cold. He lifted a shutter vane and looked outside. Cloud had sailed across the sun, so that now the exile's garden looked wintry and bleak despite its flowering vines and flitting birds.

"Careless," he said at last. "Forgive me."

"Not your fault."

"About Claer Arian. I'm not asking, I'm telling you help is available. Trauma healing."

"They didn't rape me, if that's what you mean. They did a rough body search and knocked me around. I got over it."

"Tell me then." His voice was almost too low to hear.

Seren longed to go and lean on him, just lean, and be warmed by his warmth and strengthened by his strength, but it was too much to ask of a man whose nerves probably still jangled as hers did. She sat wearily at the kitchen table, head in hands.

"There was another man." It wasn't even the whole truth any more, but she couldn't say the whole truth. Not to pragmatic and unsentimental Tas.

"I know."

Leave it there, since he bristled whenever she mentioned Teak

Kuhan. "There's so much I don't understand about you, Tas. Another of your dead, Rav said. What does that mean?"

"I extract people from dangerous situations. You. Rav. Others."

"Help me understand. Tell me."

"No."

Evasion—that she had expected. Denial. Argument. Anything but simply, No.

2

Tas poured caffe with a steady hand and slid one cup across Rav's kitchen table. It was the last thing she needed, trembling from head to foot, but she clasped the warm cup.

"Why won't you tell me more?"

"I'm under oath."

Seren stared wordlessly. *Break your oath if you care.* But would she do that for Damou?

Tas offered a palmful of the red grains he was chewing, scooped from a bowl on the counter. She took a pinch from his hand—and noticed his wrist.

"You had a tattoo. A code pattern." Gone now. She'd meant to scan it, probably the one way she could ever trace his real name.

"It bothered you."

Everything about him had bothered her at first. Now she shrugged. Strange to lift a prison tattoo and leave his face twisted deep in scar tissue, but she guessed if he meant to restore his face, he would have done it by now.

"I want to tell you everything. Soon."

Soon could mean anything or nothing. Seren tasted the grains. Spicy, scented and sweet.

"Remember more about the Bight?" he asked over his cup.

Seren hesitated and let out her breath. "I discovered a file that

I uploaded to a kidgrid before I left Gandhi. It's enormous, with heavy encryption I can't jack."

Tas studied her for a moment, then pulled out his slate. "Images or database, probably. I have Pact and Mitran decryption code."

"No Pol code?"

"We sell you Mitran codes, recent but not current, tweaked into Pol languages. Second-wave cousins."

"Gods. You usually admit that?"

"No." Tas sat beside her to search his indexes and maxed his screen when he found what he wanted. "Tell me what you remember."

Seren closed her eyes and imagined herself back in Gandhi's signals office, two worktop alcoves cramped into a bare room that always smelled of heated plastic. Some predecessor had scratched into the composite wall an ancient epitaph for soldiers who held a narrow pass against a powerful enemy: *Tell them in Lakedaimon, passer-by, that obedient to our orders, here we lie.* She'd read the Thermopylai poem a thousand times, but it guided her hand that last day. There was something her people needed to know, she'd reasoned through her fear on Gandhi, even if it meant court-martial and disgrace. Report it to her fleet, then post vri to a grid site like *Singularity*, anywhere people would read it. *Tell them in Tirion.*

Memory wavered and coalesced in the mist. "A few hours after we intercepted the courier, I tried to jack the bead from a diplomatic pouch we recovered in the wreckage. My arm was broken and it hurt. We were out of painkillers and bone lattice at the end of the war, and the fracture was set with primitive metal bone pins, local anaesthetic, no regen. Someone was watching me, listening. The bead was a high-security Mitran gold oval, and I couldn't copy it, I just glimpsed a lot of indexes. I was so afraid to use voice command that I hand-keyed in the encryption to upload. I remember all of that. I still can't remember what's on this other file."

"Your pilot didn't fly you out to intercept."

"No, he'd already been recalled to Wairoa. I flew the Az myself. I only had a civilian licence, but no one cared by then. My weapons hand was—I can't remember. Maybe my signals tech.

Maybe someone else." Seren held her cooling cup with hands that wouldn't unclench.

"Your med officer on Gandhi was Mihal Villandry Biron."

Seren frowned. "I don't remember him there at the end. He must have left by then." Mihal hadn't been their best medic. Pol fleet medics topped honours and casualty lists, but Mihal was more enamoured with the glamour of being a medic than the day-to-day work. Maybe that was why he'd been sent to Gandhi, or maybe his influential family had arranged it.

"What happened after you uploaded?"

"I left my desk—I was so afraid—and someone came up beside me in the passageway. I turned to fight, but they jabbed my arm. Not a knife, maybe a needle. I suppose it was the memory block. Later I didn't recall anything that happened after we scrambled the recon ship. Not till I left Melusine with you and Maq. Now I remember most of it, but not who jabbed me . . . Why would they want the bead?"

"Subvert the treaty. Extreme globalists wanted no surrender. And the Pact wants to destroy even its weak provisions." Tas shook his head. *Never mind*. His expression and body language were easier to read now. "So you couldn't copy Louhi's bead—"

"Louhi?"

"Louhi Takahara. The courier. She was bringing me a data bead. Where is her bead?"

Seren looked miserably into her cup. "I don't know. Maybe whoever memory-blocked me took the courier's bead and left me a blank to cover their tracks."

"Seren. Look at me."

Reluctantly she did.

"You need help to open the file you downloaded. You need help to find your mother. I need Louhi's bead, and I need to know exactly what happened in the Bight."

"You don't need the data any more," she said. "The treaty is already law."

"Not valid if it's based on false information. With enough new data, we can force them to reopen it," he said. "Then we can reverse some of the harm."

"The Pact will never let go of all those rich new acquisitions."

"Not willingly," he said. "Not unless we invoke the Interworld

Accord."

"Why would the Pact agree to a new accord?"

"We don't need a new accord. Gabriel de Jong never renounced the existing accord. Nolin hasn't yet pushed the old man that far." Tas held her gaze. "We need your mother. And we need the data. There's a chance we can work this out together from your file."

Seren studied him. Not the misshapen scar tissue, but his steady gaze. *Tas.* In anyone else, she would have dismissed all this as a daydream. What did she have left to lose? She slid her slate toward him on Rav's table.

"Enter your keys."

"I don't remember," Seren confessed wretchedly.

"What was on your mind that day?"

"Staying alive."

Tas laughed, rustily as though he hadn't done it much lately.

Lt. Seren Qasri on Gandhi Base—hungry on half-rations, injured, afraid—had needed to protect the file for a few days. What keys would she have used? She tapped out her mother's name, her own birth date, Kuhan's birth date, place names, friends. *Nothing.* But when she tried an ancient poetry tag—*Long the sun's road, longer my memories*—her slate pinged, and a jagged image appeared on the small screen.

"Beautiful," Tas breathed over her shoulder.

A highly pixilated moving image occupied her screen. It ran 213 seconds in relative darkness and ended in a burst of light. But it was only a partial image, full of jagged blanks.

"Multiple encryption. You did good work on Gandhi. Do you have other keys?"

For half an hour Seren tried every possible key, even the ancient epitaph for the dead of Thermopylai. Finally, she dropped her face into her hands. "Sorry. I've tried everything. My service number, names, dates."

"Something you said at AnvilCo Melusine," Tas said. "Something about reporting to Tirion."

Tell them in Tirion. Seren keyed in the tag that had pushed at the edge of her memory. Her slate pinged, and the image came into slightly sharper resolution. Still missing some parts.

Nothing else worked. She checked her chrono. "We'll have to

try this another time."

Tas was working on her slate when it pinged again, and page after page of raw code appeared on her maxed screen. Then an image appeared in perfect detail and blossomed into a vri zone above the slate. Seren looked into a vri display of deep space, with a few distant stars and clusters scattered in her field of view.

"What was the last key?"

"Your friend Kuhan's citizen identity number divided by his Spartí serial number."

"Not my friend. I barely knew him. I wish I had." So, she'd blanked on her own painfully obvious key, and Tas had known her well enough to guess. Her virtual aide Teak could never have done that. It took a living human imagination.

Tas told the kitchen to darken and touched the slate. The sequence played again and again before she could make any sense of it.

"The Bight," she said.

Looking up from his own slate display, split-screened to an astronomical ephemeris and a space atlas, Tas froze her sequence and pointed to the small dark teardrop that was dimly starlit against the void. "Your cam tracked this. Azande AirSpace's smallest ship, an Abhaya X3. Huge converters, room for one pilot, a specialized long-range craft."

The courier. Seren's hand flew to her mouth. *Of course.* As they sped outward from Gandhi, she'd suctioned her cam to the forward viewscreen and told it to track anything on visual. It had recorded eighty-six minutes in total, but it was this segment—

The angle shifted as the recon ship darted after the courier, quickly closing the gap. She live-hailed the teardrop on emergency frequencies in Claeran Tavod and Pacter Peel, finally in Mitran Damotik. Seren watched dry-mouthed as this lost fragment re-entered her life. The courier ship hung stationary as they matched speeds and headings, so close the pilot's face was a paler blur in the darkness.

"It's a Pact scout. No surrender. Take it," a man said off-cam. "Arming—"

"Abort that," Seren snapped back. "Intruder in Politaya space, state your identity."

Louhi Takahara's voice sounded weary even through the

translator. "Neutrality diplomatic mission, urgently request escort."

Then Seren's voice. "Abort!"

"Let her go and you're a traitor!" yelled her unknown weapons hand.

A snap as the safety cap lifted on a weapons pad, and a louder click and hiss as someone released their harness. *We fought for the controls.* Her own scream was the next clear sound. Seren closed her eyes as she relived the ugly feeling of her forearm breaking on the edge of the pilot board. Then the rumble of their laser cannon.

"Neutrality diplomatic mission, urgently request escort," the pilot repeated, and added the impossible words that had frozen Seren with shock in the Bight. "Data your senator Qasri wants delivered to her and Wilm Nolin."

Now, uneasily, she asked Tas, "What does that mean? Did my mother help Nolin?"

"Preliminary peace terms. He rejected them. Delun needed more evidence."

Helplessly Seren watched as a flare of white billowed toward the teardrop. Contact. Louhi Takahara died screaming in sheets of white flame and twisted debris that hurtled toward the recon ship. Brilliance swallowed everything as the recording ended.

Seren clutched something and realized it was Tas's hand. She stared at the empty vri zone, unable to find thought or word or emotion. His arm lay across her shoulder, and she silently leaned to his warmth.

A Claeran crewman under her command had murdered an envoy seeking safe passage, an envoy bringing data to Mam. Even under memory block, Seren's urgency to deliver the data and her report had driven her from Melusine to Tirion to Izu. It drove her now.

"Reset to two ten," Tas said. "Shift point of view up and right. Stop. Restart."

Near the upper edge of the vri zone, the teardrop was a dark silhouette against a vast faintly glowing knot or anemone or tree. Within a slow rotation of immense immaterial vanes—the opening of a mirror node, it couldn't be anything else—an object flashed brilliantly and was gone. But there was no mirror node in the Bight. No charted mirror node.

"Play it back. Stop. Magnify. Stop," Tas directed until they isolated the flash. "That's an energy weapon. No tracer. An instant too late to save the courier."

"From an open mirror node? But there's no ship."

"No ship we can see. But something transited, in that second white flash."

Seren said, "Why didn't it kill us?"

"The bolt may have scattered on the debris from the courier."

"Why fire on us at all?"

"Can't say." Tas shoved his hands through his hair in his usual gesture of frustration.

"Someone needs to know," Seren said, "about all of this. Missing data. New technology. Diplomatic murder."

"We know, and we'll tell Maq. That's enough for now, while we work on it. Otherwise keep it quiet." He checked his chrono. "You'd better leave."

"Tas," Seren got to her feet, needing to say—something. She had no idea.

"What do you want?" The blunt question would sound rude from anyone but him.

Suddenly blinded by tears, Seren shook her head. What did she want? A friend. Body warmth. Someday their paths would cross again, and they'd have another unsettling conversation at another backwater spaceport—or she could tell him now. She put her hand on his shoulder. "You. I want you."

"Sometime." He looked away, showing her the scarred side. *Keep your distance.*

"Now."

Silence. Time to leave.

Then he took her hand and turned it palm outward. His fingers ran lightly from her fingertips to her inner elbow and back again, laying down a track of electricity she could see behind her closed eyelids. How did he do that?

A closed door across the corridor opened at his word, and they walked into shuttered afternoon light that fell across a chair and a bed. Tas slid her shirt off slowly, and then a warm hand cupped her breast. Her body did its own thinking, and Seren slid her hands inside his shirt to bare warm skin. He was as wonderful to touch as she remembered, muscular but lean, with coarse hair roughening his chest and belly.

Tas said into her hair, "This will transfer med nano. It's a good thing. Consent?"

Anything she'd expected him to say didn't include this. "Yes."

A long ridge of scar tissue ran down from his right shoulder through the hair on his chest to his hip. She started to ask, but then his hands stroked down gently with remembered precision.

Her need for him leaped out of her control, and she drew him down to the bed. Every movement left a wash of rich sensation across her tingling skin and a tracer of golden fire behind closed eyelids. No words. His hands spoke their own language. Wait. Slowly. Trust me. *This has to be a bad idea* . . . She warmed to his uncanny sense of how to touch her. Once he discovered what gave her pleasure, he was exact and gentle and unhurried . . . *so why does it feel so good?*

Now. But instead of giving himself to her tongue or plunging into the slick heat he'd raised between her thighs, he made her wait. They lay sweated together breast to breast and belly to belly, breathing together, faces plastered close like intent dancers. Exactly when she could no longer bear waiting, he cupped her hips and raised her so that they joined in one long exhalation. Sensation rolled and rose and broke with an intensity she'd never known as they moved together. His eyes widened and he said her name once, and gave himself to her.

Later they lay linked in the filtered daylight and birdsong. Easy. Simple. Beautiful. Better than sex could be. Most of all easy. His head was pillowed on her shoulder, a hand on her breast. Possessive? No, Damou would never be possessive. It was just sex, no illusions of romance, but it was brilliant sex. After a while he shifted position, and his fingertips gently visited her eyes, her brows, nose, chin like a sculptor taking measurements.

"What—?"

"Learning to see you."

"With your hands?"

"I was blind once. They sewed my eyes shut, trying to save them."

Her own hands flew up to his eyes like birds homing, but she would know him anyway by the set of his shoulders and chin, the straight nose and brow.

"Come with me to the Deep Outside."

"No one goes to the Deep Outside. It's sanctioned. Our drives can't even handle it."

In his soundless way, he laughed against her cheek. "I wrote the last addendum to the sanctions. It permits unarmed search and rescue operations. And your drive did handle it—you pushed into the Deep Outside chasing the courier."

"Who fired on us out there, Tas?"

Knowing how to distract her, he never answered. Later he said, "We need to go. You'll be late, and I lift in an hour."

"Where bound?"

"Three uncharted nodes out. One world is habitable, ninety-nine percent ocean, a natural high-match earthlike planet. Another is well into an old-style slow terraform. A few stops en route. You should come with me."

Uncharted nodes, unlisted worlds. Outside exploration lay in dream territory. Long ago she'd told herself stories about exploring new worlds with Kuhan . . . mercifully she hadn't thought of Kuhan when they were making love—having sex. He would always stand alone in her heart, but Tas was here now. "What about Proton?"

"Quit. Now." Tas reached down to the floor for her clothes. "All Radko cares about is his cut. Sooner or later, he'll sell you for the price of a meal."

"You know Radko?" Obviously. He didn't answer. Saying anything would be wasted breath, and Damou didn't waste much.

In Samun most sensible people took an afternoon rest. The access roads were empty when they walked back, staying near the buildings and out of the dust-stinging bitter wind. Cold seeped up from the pavement through her boot soles, but she barely noticed. In three hours, everything had changed, and even the winter desert looked beautiful.

3

Home was a secret domain of clear-cut certainties, even on a new world. Doll Sorrow loved to come and go here like brindled shadow, prowling the tangled forest paths. Only another chimera would see the infrared flash of her surveillance drones, and no chimera would sound the alarm.

This small estate sloped gently from big trees that were dropping brown and yellow leaves through a walled garden of fruit-heavy trees whose sweet scents overwhelmed Doll's senses, down to a brook tangled in smaller trees and bushes. She and Noob stayed next door in a small stone building built into the stone garden wall, still full of orchard tools, and watched the owner. Now was her best chance. The owner was here in his new house for a few days.

Earlier today he saw her near the mobile nanoform lab that was rebuilding a wall. Doll crouched in terror that he would call his predators, recognizing his chimera Baby that he had thrown away and left bleeding in a Tirion ruin many tendays ago. He hadn't reckoned on her determination to survive, far less on feral chimerai that helped other escapees to hidden dens. He also hadn't reckoned on her jacked identification bead that let her roam as she wanted. Instead of raising an alarm, he'd let his gaze travel over her body like unclean hands, and as her spine fur stiffened in fear, he turned away. He hadn't recognized his Baby. Now she was truly Doll Sorrow.

Even here among enemies, the owner needed no wires or broken glass or toxics to top his stone wall. Stealthy shadows among deeper shadows disposed of the few who tried to get in. Most were desperate people seeking their disappeared families. No one came looking for creatures like her; once they were changed, no one wanted them back.

Tonight, Doll hid among the streambank trees outside the wall to watch the grownstone rebuild itself to a new pattern. As dusk fell, the solar-powered nano slowed its work and the bot excavators in the woods stopped digging their pit. A burial pit, she'd thought at first, but it was round with sloping sides like a miniature of Tirion's sports stadium where they forced frightened chimerai to break all training and kill full humans and animals and each other in their hateful games. Noob lay curled asleep in the stone shed, and she missed him. She waited until lights glowed on in the unfamiliar house, remembering childhood discipline and rewards in a dizzying swirl of terror and longing. At full dark she re-entered the scented garden.

Her shadow slid from wall to tree, from tree to tree, until Doll had a clear view of the owner's new house. It was small compared to the government mansion, but many times bigger than the workers' houses in the Twll. Torches smoked around the back terrace, where the owner sat talking with two other men at a table littered with picked-over food. They touched hands, making some agreement, and sat back to watch six dark-mottled serpentines dance in the grass.

After a while the three humans joined in, and Doll growled unhappily as they made the chimerai hiss with pain. She sent her tiny drones out across the terrace, masked by the flaring torches. When her sampler tasted DNA, she realized the lizard-scaled man was the art man from Xanadu. The third man whirled in a frenzy among the serpentines until his glitz spin faded, then lay on a bench to let them lick and suck. The torchlight played on his milk-white hair and his pale skin, bossed with gold among swirling blue patterns.

<> Unimplanted,<> her drone reported on him. No identification possible.

An unimplanted and untraceable Grey, like Captain. Doll's ears flattened in her disappointment. Awkward with her new hand—an opposing thumb and nimble fingers were her payment for her first report on the art man—she keyed notes on his age and height and weight, the few things unaltered by his deep cosmod.

Frustrated, Doll eased back among the fruit trees. Where they tangled across the stone wall into undergrowth and wild forest, Draken lay in wait, not shadow-friendly like speckled Doll but plumed and iridescent-scaled from her small head to her beautiful wings. The bots had set her free to stalk the grounds.

"You." Draken didn't talk well. Her transgenic mods were brilliant for her fantasy subtype, but her head was wrong inside. She hissed and shot out her forked tongue. "No one needs you here. New baby."

"What kind?" Doll lowered her eyes, crouched small, and kept her words easy to understand. Submission calmed Draken's rage. Once she would have taunted Draken and fought, but Captain taught them, *Talk first. Win without fighting.*

"Sprite. Stupid. Useless. Hunt or send to body vats. Sprites never last." Draken laughed a blast of hot gas, just short of flame. She ignited mainly at the owner's command. The scales and fire-breath were for show, like her wings.

"Beautiful Draken. Smart Draken. Show me." Doll crouched lower and held out her bag of sugar balls. Draken ripped it from her still-tender new right hand.

"Come! COME!"

Doll hunched under Draken's spread wing to cross the grass to the new training kennel, shivering with the pleasurable fear of a hundred long-ago visits to her nursery. *Bad Baby. Good Baby.* Inside where it was warm, the bots stood ranked against the wall, and she breathed in the sweet remembered scent of fresh bedding and medicine.

Kennel. Doll had learned to read from signs and bot operators' manuals and a forgotten reader, her blunt animal paws carefully paging through forbidden text.

The new sprite lay in a restraint crib, much too old to be sucking his thumb. A bite marred his shoulder, and his wing stubs looked raw and ugly. Sometimes the owner was too rough with the delicate ones. Never with Draken. His high-design predator chimerai were kept to impress visitors and for his hunts.

Baby. A gold chain around the boy's neck threaded the gold letters. Claws sprang out on Doll's unrestored left paw, and her muscles tensed to rake that snot-streaked child face. Her barred tail lashed the straw. But Doll Sorrow was no longer Baby. She relaxed her claws back into their sheaths.

"Hsst, stupid." Draken's spiny foreleg grasped the child's ankle.

The boy jerked upright and cowered back in the crib, as far as the restraints would let him. Doll sat up straight and raised her human right hand to pat the furred breast beneath her black tox shreds. "I am Doll Sorrow. You?" But the child only watched warily from bruised eyes.

Draken turned her fearsome grin to Doll. "Open crib. Hunt."

"No. Owner will punish." Doll flexed her claws, and the kennel darkened as her eyes slitted in fear. Humans didn't hunt humans for sport—but if she were told to do that, Draken would only blink empty yellow eyes. The transgenics techs had left her no pity. Like the owner.

Nothing good to tell Captain and Maq this time, apart from the serpentines. Tempted to stay inside where everything was known and sure, Doll Sorrow still slid back out to make her report in the great uncertain world.

4

In the cavernous Proton transport bay, two techs lounged on the broken-backed chaise drinking chai and playing backgammon. Radko turned abruptly from the door of his cubby and vanished inside as they passed. No sign of Rozenn.

They walked out into the blinding low light flooding the apron where the old Umiak crouched wearily on its maglevs. Seren reached into the hatch for the data pad she'd tossed there in a fit of pique. She would update it for Radko, then quit.

Taking shelter from the wind, she leaned forward of the hatch and went over the revised manifest. In her absence Radko had predictably added seven items, shoving them over the weight limit. Tas came to lean beside the loading ramp, arms folded. When she finished, he clasped her shoulders, drawing her in. Seren's hands lifted of their own accord to frame his face, smooth brown side and rough discoloured side. It felt like bark on a sunwarmed tree. Friendly.

He leaned in, and something brushed her cheek, light as a moth's wing, so that only the fine hairs registered a shiver of sensation. That was as close as he would come to kissing her, she understood. Seren brushed her lips across the unscathed corner of his mouth. It was an odd one-sided kiss, without the inflexible burned side of his mouth, but it had warmth and tenderness and left her the taste of his sweet spicy taste. Tas pulled her closer, irresistibly focussing her senses. Again. All this could soon get out of hand for a spaceport lift zone.

When she glanced up, a small woman with short-cropped dark hair stood in the dome opening, duffel in hand and Claer Defence jacket hanging from one shoulder. Rozenn nodded appreciation of their performance while Lezig hopped around chirping like an unsect.

Seren hesitated, looking for the right words to say goodbye. Rozenn had been good company, and Lezig called her cousin-friend.

Rozenn spoke first. "Delivery to Claer Arian, then a meeting in Tirion. Orders."

"In a few days."

"Now. All the surviving members of Tirion city council were arrested last night. Two have died in custody."

Seren's belly clenched. Most of the Tirion councillors were family friends. "Arrested for?"

"Council was organizing food distribution. The Pact contractor in charge of food sales decided it cut into his profits and charged them with conspiracy."

"There's nothing I can do."

"Boss wants to discuss your suggestion from Marika's."

Holy fire. What had she suggested anyway? Something about remediating the treaty. At least she could search Gwernant again. But the Deep Outside . . . Stung with disappointment, Seren glanced at Tas. He nodded. *Go.* She pulled off her silk scarf and draped it around his neck. Black shirt, silver scarf. *Flash.*

"Next time," she told him.

"Next time." It became a promise.

Rozenn walked past whistling and climbed into the cockpit. Tas swung Lezig in after her, game slate and duffel clutched firmly, chortling in delight. As they powered up, Radko stumped out to order Tas off the apron before the Umiak's lifters charred him where he stood.

Seren swung aboard and put on the eyeband and glove, linking with the pilot board to augment her merely human skills and perceptions. Proton's best asset was the first-class boards on its old ships. The bracelet Tas had given her tingled to life, adding a depth of detail and sensitivity. Soon her mind would fly free through the grid of realspace with its vast complexity of time and relative motion, and the unfathomable multi-dimensional grid of mirror space. Mundane tasks first. She started her checklists.

"Sorry," Rozenn said after a while as if she meant it. One night after their third raki she'd told Seren she'd been a charts tech on *Ys,* the Claeran cruiser disabled and boarded late in the war. Her lover had died there, spaced among the dust lanes and incandescent gases that obscured a treacherous delisted node called the Dead Gate, where old wrecks still drifted and collided soundlessly in the slow currents between deadly sister stars. Rozenn understood loss.

Lezig settled into the comm chair with her game slate, a prewar model hosted by a cute lemur called Baka-chan. She'd modified the sim with green boots and a silver-buttoned green vest. It was startling to hear the virtual elf tutoring her in basic bioethics, but Claeran schooling had to be flexible. When Rozenn flew into Pact space, where rumour said children could vanish into snuff houses or body farms, Lezig stayed in her Dinan crèche.

As they rode up and out, Rozenn shook her head over her boards. "So, you're Damou's mysterious Pol flame."

"How could anyone know?"

Rozenn glanced up. "Joke? Everyone watches Damou to see what happens next—he scares the Pact spitless. And he's on the right side."

Seren bit her tongue hard and managed to say nothing. *What side is that?* she wondered for the second time today.

"All clear," Lezig sang out once they were off Samun's nav beam.

By the time Seren could spare a glance, Claer was an atmosphere-blurred gold and green curve hanging above them in the dark. The old ship started to vibrate hard and high, and they broke free of gravity singing.

5

ES2742.079

The wreckage of *Kalevala* pinged every alarm and jolted Tas awake. Orbital images showed the pieces scattered across a ridge as though the big ship had tagged the high ground coming in, then tumbled and struck hard. A spaceliner wasn't built for atmosphere, and no living thing could survive that impact. Shuttles and rafts might have cleared their bays and racks before the crash, if they'd launched low enough not to burn up in atmosphere but high enough to coast in on a long glide path. After years of tracking rumours and traces of *Kalevala's* drive signature out beyond Politaya space, Tas doubted he would find anything alive here but algae or lichen.

Closing the file on *Kalevala* would at least let the scattered Mitran survivors lay aside false hope. So he had to trust.

"*Kalevala*, Mitra Recovery Team. Do you read?" His comm board repeated the call on all traffic and emergency frequencies across the bands. Nothing. This would be a bad wreck, broken to small pieces, maybe with fragments of charred bone and possessions scattered over kilometres.

Eight years ago at Mitra San high station, *Kalevala* had crammed in double her legal passenger limit of two thousand, mostly young families with a hope of survival, then closed her boarding tubes to a screaming ten thousand others. Hours later

Mitra San space elevator fell.

Tas bracketed a landing site near the *Kalevala* impact and told his ship to descend. The world was prime habitation-zone: roughly Mitra's mass or Earth's, with a near-circular orbit around a blue-white sun, stable climate, mild seasons, a moderate magnetic field and a brew of friendly atmospheric gases including carbon dioxide and water vapor. An outer-orbit gas giant captured most comets and meteors. Centuries ago, Mitrans had sent unmanned probes to seed blue-green algae as a foundation for more complex life; in a few generations this world could be ready to settle if it didn't orbit a star in the Deep Outside, beyond the Tripline where the old Interworld Accord banned settlement.

Long ago there had been a mechanical drive limit. Craft still lost power at the old drive limit, but only because their Mitran-designed propulsion systems were carefully engineered to fail there, preventing humans from despoiling the Deep Outside as they had human space. But the brief stay of execution was over now that Pact ships pressed Outside.

Tas had worked Outside for years, and every new world quickened his interest. Inexact human eyesight, even as heavily augmented as his, could never match synchronized probes with wide-spectrum sensors. Still, he leaned through his virtual main board to look below through his viewscreen. The world was a grey rock broken by shallow grey seas, lakes, and rivers, with a few splashes of chlorophyll-producing life. Dull green belted the equator.

"*Kalevala,* do you read?" No answer, only background radiation hissing between calls as the comm unit worked through the higher frequencies.

Atmosphere wreathed the old Az in flame, then gravity snatched it. Its vat-grown skin and woven titanium skeleton, like his own, could take more punishment than any fully human passenger could tolerate. A planetbound observer would take the ship for a meteor flaring down. He dropped hard and fast, wanting to get this over with.

Tas touched down near the ridge and ran checks while the cooling ship creaked and complained around him and his samplers went to work outside. Remote-sensing surveys from

Mitra and later Rustam had long ago gathered the essential information of gravity, magnetosphere, atmospheric mix, temperature ranges, and visible light spectrum, but some things were learned only by humans going in person to deploy the samplers and sensors, filling in the details. As a boy he'd imagined exploration treks with vials and live traps, packing metrication devices cross-country to shores of exotic seas. He wasn't the only one. As a kid Seren had posted a wide-eyed poem about exploring new worlds; the memory woke a smile. *Next time.* If she didn't come to her senses.

What in hell happened in Samun? He scrubbed his hands over his cratered face. His determination to track her down, do the right thing, make sure she was safe, turn over Inka's files—all that had been self-deception. In truth he'd wanted to hear her laugh, admire the sun gloss on her silken hair. And make love to her. Once again Qasri had stolen a march.

Why? What was he overlooking? He had no illusions. Any attempt to get her to accept hideous Damou was a fool's quest. Yet her pupil dilation, body temperature, a dozen of his sensor indicators clearly said she liked and desired him. So, a Claeran beauty, a young woman of airy grace, could look past his carefully maintained mask and see something she wanted. Sex? Make it sex to remember him by. She was shyer and less certain than he'd guessed, but passionate. Friendship? Hers by right. Now he found himself wanting to give her treasures, show her wonders . . . when they were damned forever to languish in another man's shadow.

The hull samplers were reading slow old-style terraforming, no nanotechnology, with marginal atmosphere and incomplete amino acids in the organics-poor surface layers. Vegetation was primitive, which meant the seed vaults hadn't fully sprung yet, and there could be no animal life. Another few centuries, unless they accelerated the process with nanoforming.

But his biomass sensor beeped, inventing exotic life forms. Long ago on another world it had given him a bad moment, showing that plant life engulfed the ship, until he'd found an aggressive space mould inside the sensor housing. This time it sensed animal life, smaller than human, closing at six klicks. Fast. Tas tapped his screen with a forefinger. No change. He pulled on his softsuit, glad of an excuse to look around.

At the foot of the ramp, he slid the lock on his flexible helmet and started cycling air. A slope of boulder-strewn gravel, harshly overlit by the blue-white sun, dropped to a faintly green hollow that someday could be a lush valley, alive with blossoms and bright birds, like Rav's garden outside the bedroom. They had lain together there in filtered light that limned her belly and hip—

Tas dropped and rolled. A boulder the size of his head slammed the Az just forward of the hatch and rebounded past him. If he'd gone straight forward to clear the sensor, he'd have missed the blur on the ridge. His erotic fugue had saved his life.

Five shapes bounded among the jagged rocks to surround him as the rock tumbled to a halt. By then he was on his feet with his stunner levelled. One long look, and he deliberately dropped the weapon, kicked it toward the leader and clasped his hands on top of his head. *Appear nonthreatening,* he'd written in his Spartí negotiation handbook. *The most dangerous opponents are those who feel most powerless.* He hadn't thought to include feral children.

The oldest was a lanky boy in elaborate braids and assorted clothing, including parts of a MitraCorps uniform. An Clár Company's wild geese against an amber moon were embroidered on the jacket sleeve under a comm specialist's flash.

A raft had cleared *Kalevala* after all. The adults might have made the heart's cruellest error, filling it with their unattended children.

"Who fuck are you?" the boy shouted.

Tas said nothing, seeing his danger. On the ridge a catapult-like contraption was starkly skylined. They'd reloaded and trained it on him. The smallest girl came up boldly and prodded him with a broken aerial. Humans, given junk, made weapons or art. He preferred art, though he better understood weapons.

"Who fuck are you?" The child jabbed his side, pleased with her ferocity.

First contact. Tas winced silently. Unsocialized, unpredictable, marginally human, they might as well be the hostile aliens of every space adventure vri. The tall boy came close enough to read the rank on his softsuit under the Mitran double suns, and Tas saw no need to correct it. He activated his external hood speaker. "Mitra Recovery Team."

"Prove it," said the leader.

The girl prodded again. Shock troops. She was about eight, Halia's age on his last leave, and even had Halia's golden-brown hair.

The leader picked up the stunner and thumbed it off safety, but Tas swallowed his warning. *Never diminish the leader's dignity.* Another girl close to his age and a younger boy and girl came near. None of the five wore breathing gear or shoes, but the leader wore a broken wrist chrono—his own insignia of rank.

"May I open my hood?" Tas asked carefully.

The boy nodded gravely. Two leaders in parley, the one-time Spartí officer deferring to the fourteen-year-old. Tas slid the latch and let the flexible helmet fall back onto his shoulders.

The boy eyed his ruined face. "No shit. Does it hurt?"

"Not any more."

They lowered their weapons one by one when the leader whistled, and another boy ran down the rubble slope from the catapult. The girl with the aerial stood chewing her underlip, undecided now. Her spear point rested on his ribs. She hadn't the strength to hurt him much, apart from his eyes, but she was old enough to take responsibility.

"That's sharp," he told the child gently, unable not to think of Halia. "If you make a hole in my softsuit, next time I'm in vacuum I'll die."

"How?"

"Eventually I'll freeze." He spared her the full description.

She regarded him flatly as though that sounded interesting. It would be ironic justice to die at the hands of an eight-year-old refugee from a cataclysm he caused. He would have shrugged, a few years ago.

"Mei," the boy said. She lowered the spear and turned away scowling.

Another whistle. A girl appeared up the ridge and a boy downhill, revealing their flanking action. Good tactics.

"Show us your ship," the leader said. "We're taking it."

6

"Three hours. That's all I need," Seren said outside Proton Transport's dome at Tirion port. The sky was brighter in the east, and a dawn breeze stroked a green forest scent over the spaceport's weary machine smells. Three hours would give her enough time to search Mam's ruined study and still keep her unwelcome appointment.

"Can't risk it." Rozenn scowled from the Umiak's cargo hatch, hands on hips.

"I need to check something before our meeting." Seren stared down her nav, making sure her gaze didn't stray west to the low sanctuary hill beyond Tirion. On its far side lay Gwernant.

"Sorry. Orders. I'm to escort you in person."

"Priority, warrant." She hated pulling rank, especially on a friend.

"Ma'am," Rozenn snapped, turning away. "I'm taking Lezig to her crèche in Dinan. Three hours right here, or I'm razed."

Seren swung down from the maglev train in Tirion's still-sleeping high street. The Pact checkpoints stood empty, and only four troopers patrolled the citadel square. A few garish new storefronts occupied half-repaired buildings, offering Pact mediaware and hot fashions that were already outdated on Han and Walden. The shopkeepers hadn't quite gotten the hang of virtual window animage and hovertunes, and their stumbling efforts looked sad and ridiculous.

By dawn she strolled past Derw's sanctuary gates until brilliant autumn leaves screened her from casual view, then she jogged. If she was quick, later she could discreetly ask Derw clinic about lifting her memory block—though her last days on Gandhi had mostly returned now. The next turn took her through ground mist on the streambank path to Gwernant. Trees had been felled in the woods, and in a large round excavation under nano construction, steps rose to tiered seating that looked down on a round pit like an ancient outdoor theatre.

Wide shot, full sensorium. Seren told her slate to record. Outside the narrow lower gate into the orchard, she breathed in the perfume of ripe apples and falling mist. The hidden rock cairn she'd seen on her last visit looked more permanent, with flowers springing from the moist earth around it and—*gods*—small objects laid carefully on the flattest rock. A portable stage played a vri of Delun Qasri's famous "peace to the peaceful" senate speech over her cousin-friend Rhian's great anthem *Claerequiem*. Seren tensed as the vri cut to a sequence from her own satire *Poison*. She took an uncertain step closer as ground mist wreathed her knees, and zoomed her cam for a closeup. A voice breathed from her slate, "Welcome to the shrine of the Qasri dead."

Dead in name only, Seren hoped, like her. Not dead like Louhi Takahara. She put her hands to her face, ambushed by grief for Daoud and a Mitran woman she never knew.

In the brightening daylight Gwernant was a bulwark of tawny hewnstone and grey grownstone just visible through the orchard. Kneeling in the wet grass near the shrine to record, she watched the windows. No lights shone, but the garden looked less tangled and overgrown. Fallen leaves had been raked into piles for composting. An old walnut tree they'd tried to save for years now lay bucked and limbed in the orchard. Could Mam be home again? But the house looked wrong, altered somehow from its familiar shape of three centuries.

Strange growths and accretions now marred its lines. A spindly grownstone turret rose from the formal dining room, looking over the terrace and orchard from glazed lenses that caught the early light. Knobs and polyps—she could find no other description—studded the walls at irregular intervals like cancerous growths. On the terrace near the dining room doors squatted a temporary structure that looked like a portable nano construction lab and control module. Someone was regrowing Gwernant—

Motion caught her eye as she recorded. An almost human shape stooped through the orchard, silhouetted against the summer kitchen that projected from the back of the house, and moved slowly toward Seren's chamber tree. A big man wearing dark clothing—or a manlike creature with rough dark fur. Instinct pushed her closer to the ground, and she pulled up the collar of her flight jacket to cover her face.

As it walked, it cast its head from side to side, scanning the house and the terrace—then it stopped and turned toward the orchard, snuffing the morning breeze. Seren closed her eyes and choked back a scream. The face was deformed by a vicious muzzle and black on black eyes that were nothing human. It tapped its wrist and another appeared, a graceful smaller one with spotted golden fur and a long, barred tail that whipped nervously around its legs. *Chimerai.* She recorded as long as she dared.

Seren eased back into the undergrowth outside the orchard wall, making herself slow and small so as to not attract their attention. With luck they were perimeter guards on duty—why they were guarding her home was a question for later—and alone at the house. If she could slip down to the streambank path, she could get back unnoticed to the sanctuary and the road east to Tirion.

A jewelled glint beyond her slate screen made Seren flinch away, but not far enough or fast enough. Glittering claws raked down at her, and a force like a falling boulder flung her clear across the glade. She hit a willow stand hard and crumpled to the muddy grass. When she swept hair out of her eyes, her hand came back bloody—and a scream caught in her throat.

A fragment of forgotten nightmare bore down on her from the orchard gate. In a blur she saw pebbled black hide coruscating with jewels. Tiny yellow eyes in a long wedge face. Lashing tail. Arms—forelegs—raised in a stalking pace. Fangs that overlapped a heavy reptilian jaw. A forked tongue tasting the air between gouts of flame and smoke. And wings, leathery wings crusted and dazzling with subskin jewels. She was prey to some hybrid of prehistoric tyrant lizard and mythical dragon.

The beast was only metres away as Seren struggled to her knees. Then a lithe figure sprang between them. Half the jewelled dragon's height, it crouched, lashing its barred golden tail, and snarled a warning with raised claws unsheathed. An instant later a dark-maned companion joined it and flanked the attacker. Sparks flew as the lizard chimera shook its head uncertainly, then suddenly bounded away.

Now Seren could focus on the smaller pair. She eased her hand toward the stunner in her jacket pocket, but the catlike chimera was on her in a single bound. Flat on her back in the grass, with a rock or root stabbing under her shoulder blade and her right knee badly twisted, Seren could only gape up into a face that was both animal and human, and strangely beautiful in a way that was neither.

"Lie quiet," the manimal growled, and patted Seren's chest with a perfectly normal human hand. "No danger here."

Seren closed her eyes and saw, in the shadowy ruins of Tirion, a girl exotically furred and clawed who watched Maq Flett from eyes like gold coins.

"Doll Sorrow?"

"Captain's lady," the chimera said. "Come. Draken hunts."

Her larger companion, the jackal cross that had driven off the lizard, sat in the orchard gate licking a paw. Another time it would be strange and wonderful, but now it was terrifying.

"I need to—"

"Come." Doll Sorrow flowed to her feet in a single smooth motion and bounded away. At the streambank path she turned. "Now."

Seren, still dazed, got up and limped after Doll. The jackal cross offered an arm, and she gratefully clasped his thick furred shoulder to transfer some weight. He smelled of rank animal and human sweat, and he made a small whine under his breath as though he might be even more afraid than her.

They climbed slowly past the outcrop until Derw Sanctuary's silvery plank roofs came in view. The shiny green salal rustled, and a smaller creature leaped onto the path. Brindled fur, tufted grey ears, tail as splendidly striped as Doll's, whiskers as wide as the antennae they doubled for, bared diamond teeth.

Seren kneeled to put both arms around her childhood guardian. "Cedar."

"Go now, Ser? Dangers are here," Cedar said in a small raspy voice. Speaking in sentences; Delun must have upgraded her bioware.

"Love you." She turned. "Doll, thank you—" But Maq's friends had left silently.

"Safe now, Ser. I have you," Cedar said.

"Safe," Seren choked out, her face buried in warm fur and awash in hot tears. Whatever disaster had struck Gwernant could wait. Now she had family.

7

Inka dreamed of ice. Falling through frozen air, beating her hands at the whipping tornado of her descent to a dying planet's surface. Nueva Chiapas high station was infalling, and the fragile elevator pods lashed on their broken cables like seedlings in a windstorm. The gondolas floated for one long moment and sagged toward the surface.

In the chaos, other passengers scrabbled over each other like vermin to save their meaningless lives. It had been easy enough to reprogram the elevator counterweight's cable tension. All Inka had wanted was a quick death, now that her beautiful lover was lost. The Pact research team had lied about the brilliant immunity her people would gain when they released the antidote a day after she spread the virus. But then it was two days, three days, and no antidote. Who wouldn't want to die as her world died around her?

Not a dream, she realized on waking, but her worst memory. Inka had failed to die of horror or remorse. Now she had written all such weakness out of her bioware. Emotions would never again hinder her once she finished her neural adjustments, but the emotion most resistant to deletion turned out to be love. Nonhumanity drew her irresistibly—not having to feel, not having to serve others—but one human doubt lingered. Having lost her lover, was it easier to terminate love and forget him or to remember and feel loss forever?

In her tank the nutrient fluid barely trembled, and her cramped hands curled helplessly before her featureless face. Once she rebuilt her composure, she made her personal rounds. One by one, through slate pickups and surveillance cams and hovertune sensors, Inka captured her images and those satisfactions still within her reach. Information. Power. Fear.

At the specified time Renat Von arrived punctually and paced Inka's salon, seething with appetites and unformed plans, according to the metrication devices embedded in her floor and walls. Today he presented his unadorned natural appearance, light-skinned with brown eyes and auburn hair darkening in maturity, no liveware or metalling or irideco. Taller and rangier than Tas, he was also less graceful. Renat was detestable, but he could be useful now.

Inka observed him for an endless but necessary minute. With the power of eighty suns at her command, she found it increasingly tiresome to shackle herself to the human scale of petty concerns and slow time.

Left to his own devices, in one circuit of the salon Renat quickly located each of her security pickups but made no attempt to disarm them. At her old Jiao-Long abstract, he paused frowning—clearly not an admirer of Earth's last great texturalist painter—and queried his data implant about the artwork. His pulse spiked at the mention of its value, and he leaned to see how securely it was fastened to the wall. Inka smiled; she could deal with this man. Altruists made her teeth ache.

Tas had betrayed her when she needed him most. Inka had quickly amended her plan, ready to act when he tired of Qasri. Renat was one of the few people he trusted. Tas had surpassed Renat in every way years ago, but whatever Renat did, Tas still took note, and whatever Tas did, Renat wanted.

Inka's simage materialized in her vri zone, wearing a silk dress that draped softly over her breasts and belly, drawing her visitor's gaze. "You located my sensors very quickly."

Renat nodded coolly, but his pupils dilated at praise from Tas's personal daimon.

"A lucrative contract may call for your special skills," she said, tautening the silk dress over her breasts.

"Who's the client?" He liked his women voluptuous, and he'd never seen Inka's inner room or her nutrient tank. Tas would have laughed at her blatant ploy, but Renat's gaze dropped.

"Mercantile. Izu." A local prospect should raise the least suspicion. Inka named the fee. "A corporation planning a Reprise export branch needs to contact the government in exile."

"Wants them back in power?"

"Absolutely not." Inka let that sink in. "But the client needs senate documents."

Renat's face shuttered, though his biometrics betrayed keen interest. "I can't help you. You need a Reprisien. Never fear, they're easy to buy these days."

"But you've handled contracts there?" He'd also handled a removal for her some time ago in Tirion, though her nested business entities had left him thinking he worked briefly for a highly placed Waldener. As usual Tas was a step ahead. It would be a mistake to pit them directly against each other again.

Renat shrugged. The carpet under his feet roiled in shades of orange and red and brown as he suppressed his frustration at seeing a contract slip away, but he paid no attention. Tas would have muted it with alpha waves to conceal his emotional state, producing a windswept wheat field or a phosphorescence-sparked seascape of old Earth. He was better at such tricks since his reconstruction. But there was only one Tas.

Inka's vri zone persona smiled contritely. "Of course—it would expose a confidence to tell me anything further. And you would never betray a friend."

Renat turned to stare, not at the vri zone but toward the inner room as though he saw straight through a metre of solid composite. The salon carpet faded to ashen grey and froze, and Inka chilled to motionless silence.

"No." Renat turned but hesitated. "But Riordan is increasingly difficult."

"Not for long." The director-general was hardest to manage sober, but she couldn't keep him in a drugged haze forever. "Return in three days if you want the contract."

Renat palmed open the door, and Inka didn't stop him from leaving. Her nano had settled on his hair and face and hands as they talked, but he would sweep it before it entered his skin chemistry. He wouldn't so easily find the new tracking virus on his slate that would trace his movements for the next few days. Renat would either contact Tas quickly or return to accept her offer. An hour ago, she'd guessed the latter, but now she was less certain. If he accepted, he would receive a rich fee, and Inka would purge whatever useless information he turned up. Every miserable bolthole of every Politayan fugitive, every sleazy secret, every betrayal already overflowed her data banks. All she needed to know was Renat's choice.

Restless, Inka searched her archives for more challenging problems. Seconds later, skimming the Claeran feeds, she lashed out in rage.

Parvin Kerkallec, poring over a classified Pact report that Inka had nudged in her direction, demanded the location of her sister-friend. So she had no idea of Delun Qasri's whereabouts. Best to stall Parvin, prevent her from drawing the attention of the occupation forces. Kerkallec was a useful placeholder on Claer.

Last, Inka checked a transport that should have been scrapped a decade ago. Undetected she slipped through the Umiak's life support sensors, regretfully adding up risks. Too obvious. No matter. A better chance would come along, a clearer path, until Inka was done with the Qasris.

8

Moving shot, spatial wild sound. Derw Sanctuary clinic accepted Seren's vow of silence, and no one questioned the large bundle she carried when she arrived, shirt-sleeved and trying not to shiver in the cool autumn sun-mist. She walked past the house of meditation and through the healing grove to the day clinic, wishing she had time to sit by the spring and find some peace.

A white-haired doctor sterilized and nskinned the two bloody claw tracks across her cheek. He silently noted Seren's comm bracelet on an implant-free wrist and the bulk of her rolled flight jacket. Cedar was invisible to scan, but she occupied space.

"I have business at the spaceport in an hour. I'll take you. Rest till then." He glanced at Cedar bundled in her jacket and lifted an empty tote from a cupboard.

Seren hesitated. The meeting started soon; she'd explain later to Rozenn. She smiled thanks, stiffly. She scrawled on her slate, "Appt neuro tomorrow? Memory loss, may be block."

The doctor nodded and led her to a meditation cell that overlooked the healing spring in its rocky niche screened by ferns. After he left, Cedar stepped out of the tote.

Seren stroked her luxuriant fur. "Where did you live all this time, treasure?"

"Trees. Porch. Streambank. Sanctuary." Her speech fed

straight from her augmented brain to the speaker under her chin.

"How did you survive? The occupation kills augments." Hunting hadn't fed her. Cedar was a lethal fifteen kilos of woodcat backbred from old Earth's extinct *Felis silvestris,* but she was also a bonobo-transgenic, AI-enhanced cat with strong directives against killing.

Cedar nipped a burr out of her tail. "Manimals hid us."

"Doll Sorrow and her friend?"

"Others." Cedar looked up. Even her new vocabulary and enhanced Mitran speechware wouldn't run to complex explanations, and animals could be cryptic. "Download? Treat?"

Seren asked the room's food fab for a cheese wrap and a tub of fish-flavoured vat protein. Cedar crouched on her paws to await her reward for giving up her optic memory bead. Her coat looked glossy from her barred tail to the bright amber jewel of fur in her forehead M. Now that both of them were all grown up, it would be childish to roll on the floor and play—but Cedar pounced, and Seren rolled her over to scratch her belly. Finally, she put down the protein tub.

Cedar honed around her legs but wouldn't eat. "Download?"

Conditioning. She'd better go through the motions, though they hadn't loaded Cedar with memory storage beads for years. "Yes. Download now."

Seren parted the fur at the back of her neck, lifted the bead compartment door, and pretended to feel inside for the bead. But the compartment wasn't empty; her forefinger bumped across a tiny dome. Someone must have tasked Cedar to mobile security again during the war. She flipped a bead out into her palm, inserted a new bead from her bead case, and stroked down the speckled fur. "Treat now, treasure."

Unloaded, reloaded, and praised, Cedar padded off to her food. A high-density silver bead lay in Seren's palm. "Who inserted this bead?"

"Delun," Cedar answered without missing a bite.

Good. Long ago Mam had set Cedar to cycle her bead, constantly overwriting the previous record. The file would probably show hours of Cedar prowling the orchard and streambank, maybe with chimerai. Seren had viewed a full day's record once when they misplaced a nineteenth-century

Sometsuke vase, a gift from the Pact ambassador. To Mam's dismay, they watched the house bots overturn it and efficiently cycle its shards.

Cedar groomed her tail as Seren slotted the silver bead in her slate and touched play. A hand filled the screen and receded. Delun Qasri walked away across the summer kitchen tilestones barefoot in her old ruby bathrobe, hair shoved behind her ears, looking anything but senatorial.

Seren checked the date stamp. Mam had set Cedar to record last year on the day the Pact occupied Claer, ending her world's independence, long before Seren reached Claer Arian.

Mam poured caffe, then dipped a finger in the honey jar and licked it. *Caught in the act.* Seren smiled. Life as Delun's daughter had its challenges—always on view, tight schedules, long absences—but now it seemed easier to recall the laughter.

As she watched Mam take her caffe out to the terrace, Seren keyed her slate to bookmark and fast forward to each new person. The slate image blurred forward and stopped to show a man standing in the reception room. *Tas.*

A weapon hung under his arm from a shoulder strap. Alert and clearly on guard, he watched the front door. A shock shirt shimmered inside the open collar of his Spartí greys. Straight back, square shoulders, shirt sleeves rolled, brown forearms with hair sun-bleached the same colour. Even the small image in her palm made her want to feel the warmth of his fine hands.

On her small screen, he nodded at the cam pickup—at Cedar. Seren bookmarked him and let the slate search on. Mam. Her sister-friend Parvin. Parvin's son Pedr. Tas again. Daoud. No one unexpected. Yet Delun Qasri had programmed Cedar to record that awful time, expecting disaster, as the Pact took Claer city by city.

Seren fast-forwarded through the file. A green and dun blur of leaves, branches, mossy earth racing past, sunlight glittering on water. Cedar had run full out along the streambank. Fast forward again. More greenery, hours of it, through daylight and twilight into deep night shadow. Then silver static. Then nothing.

Puzzled, Seren left Cedar curled like a question mark on the windowsill and took her cheese wrap out to the quiet main garden. Outside the kitchen, in a scene from another century or another world, two novices carefully hand-sorted scraps of cloth, glass, and metal into bins.

The sun-mist had lifted. In the clear autumn light, the forest of stumps that had been a sanctuary looked like an ancient cemetery, and even sitting on a sunlit hewnstone bench, she shivered in the cool breeze.

Seren fast-forwarded through her bookmarks. In high-speed bursts Mam licked honey from her finger, Tas stood in the reception room, Cedar ran through wildwood. She reversed through a burst of static. *Again.* This time she started the sequence at normal speed. Cedar's augmented eyes saw Mam reading her slate at the table under the terrace grape arbour. Her lips moved as she talked to herself—no, talked to the comm implant in her left hand.

In a narrow band of shadow against the house wall, Tas stood with an assault weapon cradled across his chest, watching the door. He talked to his comm, checked his chrono, and nodded to Delun. It was just after midday.

Cedar followed Mam into the house and watched her change into her old fleet greens and throw other clothes into her duffel. In the summer kitchen she passed Tas, who looked up as something near the front door caught his attention. A blink of red, and a snowstorm filled the small screen. *Fast forward.* Cedar ran through woodland. *Fast reverse.* Tas looked up. Seren checked the time stamps. Ninety-four seconds of snowstorm. Ninety-four seconds were missing.

Most of Seren's cheese wrap lay on the bench beside her. It tasted like cheese-flavoured sludge and probably was; Claer was still on strict rationing. It would biodegrade if she cycled it, but thinking of the rag-pickers, she choked it down and returned to her meditation room.

On the windowsill, Cedar arched her back and yawned, showing impressive fangs. Her diamond-augmented claws could slice through bone. Delun had reinforced her programming for nonaggressive behaviour, but a Mitran-enhanced cat was not ornamental. Pol biologists had never recreated dangerous pack animals like canines, but cats had earned their keep for many years.

"Did anyone download beside Delun?"

"Delun said don't. Just Seren and Tas download."

"Did Tas download?"

"No." Cedar flowed down onto the plank floor.

"Cedar, is Tas your friend?" Seren immediately regretted her question. The cat couldn't form such judgments, even with her bonobo genes and high-level intelligence.

Cedar licked her left paw to wash an ear. "Tas took your picture and said beautiful."

Cat dreams. Tas had never taken her picture—vri or still—and no one would call her beautiful. It might be time to check Cedar's bioware. Seren reassured, "You did well, sweet."

Thoughtfully she created an index called *Return: vri doc in prog*. In Claeran Tavod the word *adre* meant not just coming back, but coming home. She dragged her sparse collection of stock shots, location shots, wild sound, and archival material into the new index, then Cedar's record and Delun's files from the station flat and chamber tree.

A good opening sequence still eluded her. A space view of Claer with a station in the foreground would be cliché. Something to capture the downworld chaos and devastation? Hungry people falling on Pact-distributed food cartons belonged later in the vri. In past vris she'd brought Pol wrongs to the attention of Pols; it would feel strangely obvious to focus on Pact wrongs against Pols and Greys. The senate committee would document war crimes; her task was to chart the emotional cost. So many of her mentors and teachers were lost, she had discovered over the past year, that if she sidestepped this, no one else might do it. *Do what you know is right.*

Seren closed her eyes long enough to hear the wind outside rushing between raw trunks and tender seedlings. The wind at Derw used to seem sheltering and friendly, but now it sounded desolate, like the torn cellusheet flapping uselessly on the ruin of Tirion's central maglev station. Quickly she found her cellusheet image, just over a hundred seconds, and dropped it into a new *Opening* subindex. Maybe. She could try it out, post a few clips to *Singularity* or another gridsite and ask for more information and advice. Claerans were never slow to offer comments.

But her vri story didn't really start with the occupation. An uneasy, insistent feeling told her it started in the Bight. The other sixteen people on the small shutdown crew could fill the blanks in her memory. She would contact them for interviews.

The spaceport's midmorning rush was in full swing when the doctor's hover dropped her at the commercial terminal. Seren ran for the lift with his borrowed tote, raising a mild warning growl from Cedar sealed inside. Rozenn might still be waiting at the Umiak. She punched for ground level and quickly straightened her shirt, which had absorbed most of the blood she'd lost. The nskin made her face feel like hardened grownstone, and the claw gashes throbbed. The last thing she needed right now was empty resistance talk from Rozenn's friends.

Her lift stopped for four techs in space traffic coveralls, three men and a woman complaining about their unpaid overtime. A man and a woman stepped in either side of her. *Too close.* Seren edged away. A man touched the pad for admin, next level down—

Once the lift started dropping, they seized Seren's arms.

9

"Your ship." The boy paused to level the stunner at Tas. "We need it to move to a warmer valley. And we need your supplies and fab and cycler. You can stay to fix stuff if you follow the rules."

Tas followed the children into deep shadow now that the distant white sun had dropped behind the ridge, tarnishing its lichen to green-black, and their breath lingered in front of their faces. The seven children—the survivors—didn't seem to feel the chill.

"What are the rules?" Tas said, buying time. His captured stunner was still off safety, blinking red, and the boy flourished it as he talked. If he touched the trigger, he might drop someone, and things could get difficult.

"Share work. Share food. Obey my orders. Don't try to make us leave, 'cause we're not going," he said, and the other six children nodded agreement.

"Why don't we kill him and take the ship?" the oldest girl asked coolly.

It was worst-case. Tas cursed silently. His palm laser lay flat in a thigh pocket of his softsuit—they hadn't checked—but he couldn't risk using it. He'd need to overpower them unarmed, and most of them were small enough to make it hard not to harm them. There had to be a better way.

Tas nodded over his shoulder at his ship, crouching on the gravel like a primitive armour-shelled creature from Earth's deep past. "It's a Spartí Company command ship."

"Suva! Your mum was Spartí," said the smallest girl.

"Don't tell him fuckall, Mei. Everyone in MitraCorps died. He's some kind of spy," the leader said. "So what if it's a command ship?"

"Heavily armed. Fail-safed. High security." Tas shrugged regret. "Do you think a Spartí pilot disembarks on an unknown world without locking down to a live eyescan? Touch the boards and you trigger the alarm. An undirected plasma blast will take out my ship and most of this ridge."

None of it was true. Mitran rescue ships travelled unarmed, moving like ghosts through Grey space and the Deep Outside with supplies as their only payload.

Uncertain now, the children looked at each other. A blast would wipe out their shelter, an easy walk from the wreck of the spaceliner *Kalevala,* even if it didn't kill them.

"Alive, I can help you." Tas worked on their uncertainty. They might be easier to sway than seasoned diplomats or soldiers, but were probably more ruthless. "You'll need to adjust slowly to new foods. Nothing too rich to start, maybe taro stew with rice and mango."

Two kids exchanged grins. Food as a bribe was definitely cheating.

"And you'll need health care, starting with plague immunization." Everyone in human space was inoculated now. In eight years, he'd met only three uninoculated people with immunity, workers in Inka's labs, and all three had taken their own lives years ago.

Mei swiped at her eyes. "My dad died in the plague."

"You don't even remember your dad," Suva said, then told Tas, "They said we'd be rescued, but no one came."

"We couldn't find you." He controlled his voice, denying himself grief.

"All right. Get the food."

Tas handed down cartons of rations, medical supplies, clothes, and bedding to the children who watched warily from the foot of his ramp. They shouldered the cartons or fitted them into back slings, not capering and yelling like most kids, but silently. When the ramp retracted and the hatch clicked shut at Tas's command, Suva braced himself to use the stunner.

Tas had nothing to gain by seizing control now. "More tomorrow."

Suva eyed him carefully and gestured his crew across the lower ridge, where they'd built up a path through the scree. In the thin grey soil they'd carried up from the valley, the first tough alpine creepers were taking root. The terraform was going well. Technically the world belonged to Mitran Exploration and Recovery, but the corporation recognized refugee settlers' rights. In another century it could self-sustain human life.

Beyond the ridge, the shuttle and the escape vehicle rested side by side on level ground. Someone had landed with professional precision, maybe the foul-mouthed comm spec who'd worn Suva's uniform. Inside a drystone wall enclosing the two craft, a drift of Earth-origin fireweed plants struggled to survive; a gentle breeze stirred their pink blossoms and scattered their silk-haired seeds. In a few years this hollow would be a mass of fireweed. The stripped shuttle was their hydroponics tank and wind-driven power plant. The raft gave them crowded but warm sleeping quarters, where they ate in a fug of unwashed bodies.

His recent searches had produced scant results: several false leads put to rest, another ship name to carve on the Mitra memorials on Claer and Rustam. Eight years after the disaster, he expected no more live recoveries. The liners *Shah-nameh* and *Isanggok* had reached Acadie in convoy after a long sublight voyage. *Mabinogion* sent a Mayday and vanished from realspace near an unstable mirror node. *Kalevala* was unaccounted for until today.

"You're our best survivors, only the second group found in the Deep Outside," Tas told them once they'd devoured their meal, sitting cross-legged on the deck plates. The first group had fallen to cannibalism and prion-induced madness, but they didn't need to know that now.

"Teo showed us how to do things," Suva said reluctantly, leaning near the hatch with arms folded. "Recode the ship comp. Start seeds in hydroponics. Care for the little ones."

"An Clár Company?" Tas asked, thinking of the comm spec.

Suva nodded stiffly, still holding the stunner off safety.

"How did you get here?"

"Teo got twenty-four of us into the shuttle when *Kalevala* started to break up."

In eight years, they'd lost seventeen; Tas had seen the cairns on his way to their base. Even with all the dietary supplements he could cram into them to supply missing amino acids, they couldn't last much longer.

"You're well organized."

Suva described a textbook survival plan with food, shelter, work parties, guard duty, lessons, and celebrations. Expeditions had explored several days' walk in every direction. Their favourite discovery was a cliff studded with flower-shaped quartz crystals; they proudly showed him their best samples. At the scattered wreckage they'd eventually gathered and buried the few charred bones. Somehow, they'd kept the little ones alive. Mei must have been an infant. *Impressive.*

"You did everything right."

"If the plague's ended, can we—?" The youngest boy didn't know quite how to ask.

"Mitra is still under quarantine."

Then the floodgates opened, and all of them wanted to know everything at once. Tas fielded any questions he could, but he had no answers about their lost families and friends.

"Can we go back to school in Bolivar?" they wanted to know. Even their speech had improved over an hour's talk with an outsider. "In Zheng He? In Iqaluit?"

"All the places you remember have changed." He held back the rest for now.

"My cousins?" Everyone asked questions at once. "My school? My lemur?"

"No humans survive on Mitra. Some people escaped and resettled on other worlds."

Finally, the truth sank in. In the silence Tas heard the hydroponic pump cycle on, run for three minutes, and groan to a halt. It might last another year. Probably not.

"Kalevala is our world. Our parents and sibs died here. We won't leave." Suva's declaration was as eloquent as anything Tas had heard at interworld summits.

Six heads nodded. Tas hadn't ordered them to pack, but they still expected it. Two were dying each year from sickness or malnourishment or accident, and if the girls survived past puberty, one or more would die in childbirth. But Tas wouldn't order. He wouldn't even ask.

"All right." Tas slipped into his calm mediation voice and began his work. He'd kept his distance from the children. They were self-reliant, they didn't need anything from him, and they might yet cut his throat. Mostly he tried not to remember his daughter Halia. "I'll leave rations and supplies, but I'll need the ship to notify search headquarters. We'll try to check on you within twenty years, but I can't promise."

"We need a full medical fabricator and supplies," Suva said.

"Sorry. I'll leave you what I can, but our resources are strained." Steadily he shifted his role from prisoner toward emissary.

"And tutor slates," a girl said. "And building materials. And fab stock for clothes."

"Don't let him go!" The oldest girl leaped up. "Suva, we need the ship!"

"Maybe we should go with him," the youngest boy said.

Tas lifted a shoulder. "If you leave, you'll have family. You'll never go to bed hungry. You'll have teachers and rec time and useful work. And you'll be heroes." He didn't add that being a hero was a tiresome task, in his experience. The year Spartí negotiated a peace on Alma and fought down the Churinga conflict, they'd survived a newsgrid frenzy. The true heroes were his ratings and noncoms and juniors who'd endured a firestorm at his command, but that truth wasn't glamorous enough for the grids.

"But we can't go back to Mitra," Suva challenged. He was a good leader, maybe officer material, if MitraCorps survived.

"Your children might see Mitra rebuilt. A fast nanoform is underway." He found ways not to think of Xeniteia as he'd last seen it, a charnel house overhung with black smoke and a complex stench of death.

"Where will we go then?" For the first time Suva sounded uncertain. He set the stunner on a worktop and sat down among the others.

"Claer and Anansi in the Politaya. Rustam and Vritra, other Neutrality worlds."

"What are they like?" Mei grudged her curiosity.

Tas lowered his voice, drawing them closer, and told them about Claer's towering silent forests and tawny grasslands, and Rustam's shallow seas. By the end Mei leaned on him, her head growing heavy against his arm, so that he unthinkingly reached to steady her, and she snuggled close. Two others found ways to edge nearer to him, unwisely deciding he could be trusted.

Overpower them now and capture all seven? Possible. But even the miracle of their survival paled beside their shining exploits and their pride. *Heroes.*

Later, half-asleep, Mei rambled through a story about blue trees that had told her secrets near the wreckage.

"How many trees?" he had to ask. "Are they friendly?"

"A thousand trees." Mei eyed him speculatively. "They came a thousand times."

"Can you count to a thousand?"

"I showed them my slate was broken," Mei evaded, checking to see if he was angry. "They gave me tree stones."

This world supported lichen and a few sedge analogues, but no trees. Some story had captured her imagination. A tenday after he'd told Halia a story about mythical centaurs, she'd seen six-legged flying horses everywhere. It still made him smile.

Mei poked his ribs with a stubby finger. "You can see my trees."

"Tomorrow."

Later, with Mei propped asleep against his leg, he found strength to ask Suva and the oldest girl about Lira and Halia.

"Not on *Kalevala*," Suva said after they'd exhausted their memories, though two children could easily have missed one woman and one child among four thousand unlisted passengers. Someday Tas would know their end and close his own file. Lira's death he'd accepted long ago; they'd parted as friends, and Lira had lived a full life. But Halia . . .

Mei snuggled closer, and his hand automatically dropped to support her head, spiked with many small braids like his daughter's. One afternoon when Lira had meetings in town, he'd rashly agreed to braid and bead Halia's wonderful hair. Eighty-four braids. It took six sunny hours when he'd planned to cut hay. On his next leave, he'd given her one hundred beads of Paraiso turquoise. *Sixteen extra beads to grow into, sweet.*

In the morning, Suva asked him to bring his ship to their base. When he dropped the ramp, they waited in their drystone forecourt between the shuttle and the life raft. Fireweed silk drifted over them, lighting on their braids and ragged clothes. He told his comm to record, still unable to guess what came next.

Suva handed back his stunner and said simply, "We'll leave."

Tas nodded, matching the boy's gravity, and hid his relief by unloading his extra med supplies, readers, inflatable shelters, and comms that he'd carried for years against this remote possibility of finding survivors. A rescue transport with a trauma team could be here in days, once he reported contact to MitraCorps search HQ. But he would report in person, not risk a message mirrored in from the Deep Outside. After losing ships recently where they had no business mining and surveying, the Pact was twitchy enough to nuke seven kids on a bare planet.

"Come now." Mei tugged at his shirt sleeve.

Suva grinned over her head as Tas let himself be commandeered. Together they rambled along the gravel ridge and descended a long algae-tinted slope under Kalevala's pale grey sky. Mei jogged down into a sheltered pocket that held a lens of surface water. Nothing here remotely resembled a tree. Mei probably didn't know what a tree was. She looked across the water, silent for the first time in two days, and he slowed to the profound stillness of this place.

It was a barren spot, but to a child of this world it might be beautiful. No sound carried from the survivors' base, and his sensors picked up no motion or scent. The cold stabbed between his brows as though he'd gulped ice water. Air stirred against his face, sunlight shimmered above the clear water and a great lightness swept his mind.

"No trees." Mei walked away.

"No." Tas followed her, smiling. Last night at the shuttle he'd half expected to face his reckoning. Today he realized these children knew nothing of his wrongs and cared less. He was just a bringer of food and equipment, a messenger, and Mei's new friend.

"We can look for your slate. Maybe it's still here." She might have dropped it somewhere on the path or in the water.

"Gone. It was just my sister's boring schoolwork. And it was broken. They wanted it anyway." Mei picked her way back up the slope, singing to herself. "Taro stew, taro stew . . . Come on!"

Tas admired the group's scant treasures after they ate. He gave inoculations, tried and failed to repair their second protein vat, implanted a contraceptive behind the oldest girl's knee and answered several hundred questions. Then he prepared to lift, and they gathered silently at the ramp. Most children would have shouted to leave instantly, but these were survivors. In twenty years, he'd bet they were still together somehow, somewhere.

Suva clasped his hand, blinking and looking for a moment like a kid, and Tas drew himself up to give a crisp parade salute.

A tap on his ankle stopped him halfway up the ramp. Mei stood on tiptoe to hold up a grubby ration container. He didn't need food, he started to say, but a glance at her expectant face saved him. In the end her scrappy courage reminded him less of Halia than of Seren. He touched her braided head and ducked inside.

Hours after he cleared the gravity well, Tas pulled a meal from the heating unit and remembered Mei's gift. It wasn't food. Inside the carton lay two perfect crystal flowers and one flat blue-grey stone carved with a leafy plant. *Tree stone.* A treasure from home, far beyond an eight-year-old's fine motor skills. He put the stone in his pocket and silently wished Suva's band the luck they needed.

The smaller crystal he held in his palm, turning it slightly to catch the cockpit's faint light. The children called them flowers, but they looked more like stars. Opal from old Earth looked like this, with points of iridescence burning deep in mist. *Seren glaer.* Radiant star—or Seren from Claer. Probably there were other meanings, too, knowing Claerans and their Tavod. The larger crystal he would take to Inka's geolabs for analysis. This one was for Seren.

Tas shook his head at the message now repeating on his board. Wilm Nolin wanted him in Havre, now that he'd levered himself up to defence secretary. Havre was a quick stop en route, but every hour counted. Nolin could have one last half-hour before

Inka spiked any further contracts. After that he'd report the *Kalevala* survivors.

Then he would tell Seren everything that Inka's files omitted. They had the beginnings of trust and friendship, but what they shared was fragile and too preliminal to name. Right now, she would be deep in the files, and she would hate him. If nothing hindered her, Tas trusted her to follow his path to the truth.

The ancients had briefly believed that an invisible shadow matter shaped the visible world. If she saw the visible outcome of his invisible hand, maybe she could forgive him.

V
FAMILY

1

ES2742.080

"Walk normally or we stun you," one of the men said in a rich Ayiti lilt. *Claerans?*

"Peace, Cedar," Seren warned. It was no time to fight, with a hand laser nudged under her chin. She let them empty her pockets and take the bag holding Cedar. The lift door opened, and her four captors steered her out into the admin corridor.

In postwar Tirion they might work for the puppet regime, a crime ring, an interworld corporation—anyone with a private army. Openly bearing illegal weapons, they passed two nervous clerks outside the spaceport main office and turned into a narrower hallway. When the woman palmed open an unmarked door, Seren shuddered. Anything could happen out of sight, just like a year ago on Claer Arian, and no one would know.

Now. Seren twisted away from the stocky blond man on her right, but the other man only tightened his grip. She spun away as much as she could and jabbed her free hand at the blond's eyes. He snapped backward, avoiding the blow, but it put him off balance. In that instant Seren twisted her left arm hard and was free. Heel of her right hand to the blond's chin, and when he staggered, left elbow at his cheekbone. One down.

The dark man on her left grabbed her arm again. Instead of fighting him, she hooked her foot behind his knee and threw her own weight back. They went down together like a falling gantry, and she felt a rib crack. But she couldn't pin him, and he bounced back up. She lashed out hard with both feet, ready to kick him across the hallway, when the woman charged back at her. A dark glint in her raised hand, a red spark—

Seren woke with her face gummed onto cold tiles by tears and mucus. Her hands were cuffed behind her back, too tightly to twist her wrists, and urine soaked her front. *Dirty stun.* She rolled onto her side and gasped as her rib shifted.

In silence they freed her wrists and handed her wetpacs and a brown prison coverall. Once she'd cleaned up, they took her to a room marked Immigration 2 and stood at ease inside the door.

Cedar sprawled motionless in a corner. Seren's laser and slate lay neatly centred on a dingy plastic table. Her ID was in the hand of a small woman with round shoulders and tired brown curls, the image of a minor civil servant—until Seren met her cold grey eyes.

"Call the Taupan consul," Seren tried.

"Don't waste my time, Lieutenant," said Mam's sister-friend, her own second-mother Parvin Kerkallec. "You have one minute to account for your actions or face summary conviction for treason. No jury. No counsel. I judge. They execute."

So, her four captors weren't hired thugs but Pol special forces. *Has Parvin lost her mind?*

It took fifty seconds for Seren to tell her about the courier, the dwindling memory block, AnvilCo, Alluvion. Parvin didn't need to know about Tas. She ended, "At home an hour ago I was attacked by a chimera." Would Parvin believe any of this? It sounded like a vri thriller.

Parvin weighed her without expression. Seren ached to embrace her and be welcomed home. *So happy to see you. Glad you're alive.* But Parvin would only brush that aside as an attempt to curry favour. All Seren's worst fears confronted her now.

"Where's the courier's data? Quickly."

Seren heaved in a deep breath and winced involuntarily. Parvin was the first familiar face she'd seen in a year, apart from her son Pedr, but instead of a second-mother's warm greeting she got interrogation and threats. And how did she know about the courier? "Commander Kerkallec—"

"No ranks. We're not fleet or ground forces."

"Ma'am." *What are you, then?* Not fleet, perhaps, but still in authority. Was Parvin working for the Pact? Unlikely. Parvin had shocked Delun by transferring to the regular fleet after they spent the last war as reserve officers called to active duty. In the last battle of this war, her destroyer was battered to scrap around her off the Wairoa Cloud. Some people still thought she'd died with her ship.

Cedar moaned and her tail flopped feebly. She would wake ready to kill anyone who threatened Seren. "Permission to stand down my guardian?"

Parvin nodded once. Seren went to kneel by Cedar, straightening her head and stroking her until her eyes opened.

"Alert. Armed. Take cover, Seren." Cedar tried to get up.

"Peace, Cedar. Friends."

Tail lashing, Cedar wobbled to her feet and gave the four specials a golden stare that should have frozen their blood. Fools, stunning a guard animal. Gods knew what they'd done to her bioware.

"You're lucky we intercepted you," Parvin said, eyeing the nskin on her throbbing face. "The Pact station troops scan for enhanced animals, fry their augments, and toss them to their manimals for sport. What got you at Gwernant?"

"Reptile cross." Seren's knees shook, and even in the small stuffy room, cold sweat ran down her back. Fighting the specials had been a mistake. If she'd known they worked for Parvin . . . Now between stun and long accumulated dread, she could barely talk. The specials stood poised, and the tallest hefted his weapon as though he wanted to use it soon. She couldn't fight her way out of this. Win without fighting, Tas would say; or was that Kuhan?

"Where's the courier's bead? Consider your words. You're on the record." Parvin folded her hands on the table.

"The bead I brought from Gandhi was empty. Someone either wiped it or stole the original and gave me a blank." The confession was bitter on her tongue. Seren shifted weight carefully. Cedar crouched by her foot, quietly growling.

"I need the image file you uploaded to an entertainment site."

How . . . ? Seren stared, forgetting even to answer.

"Stun." Parvin ran a hand through her hair, making a worse tangle. "You talked."

The image file was multiple-encrypted again and hidden in her stock footage indexes. "First there are things I need to know, Parvin."

Parvin would rip off her head for insubordination—but she only opened the table drawer, found a loop of string, and wound it around her thumbs and forefingers. Good. A woman who made cat's cradles probably didn't plan an immediate execution.

Seren clasped her Spartí comm bracelet, wishing she'd gone Outside. Tas was too distant for casual rescues, but the cool metal was reassuringly real. Rescue by intent. The thought steadied her.

Parvin tracked her gesture. "Rozenn Milosz tried to cover for you. A loyal friend."

Resistance. Parvin made sense now. "Ma'am. I didn't plan to be late."

"We thought you'd bolted until Milosz flagged you on the landing pad. Derw Sanctuary carries patient privacy to extremes." Parvin shook her head. She never took her feelings into her work, but she seemed to struggle with them now. "I'm sorry about Gwernant. The Pacters rushed in to grab properties and resources. Anyone with connections can assemble a personal empire. Wilm Nolin has a personal grudge against Delun; she blocked him at every move through the war and surrender. He seized your home and started nanoforming it to some bizarre fantasy—turrets, towers, private arena, predator manimals patrolling the perimeter—and for all I know, he plans a moat and drawbridge."

Arena, not theatre. She shivered. "I saw some of the construction."

"You're lucky to be alive."

"Cedar came for me." *Among others.* Against all reason Doll Sorrow had defended her from one of her own kind.

"And Doll Sorrow and her lover Anubis. There's a lot you're not telling me."

Anubis might be the terrifying jackal cross. What else did Parvin know? Clearly more than Seren. Cedar rose growling to lean at her knee, sensing her fear.

"I've told you the truth." *But why would I tell you everything?* The sheer weight of working alone, running alone, all this time crashed down onto her shoulders.

Parvin brushed that away. "Why did you attack my escort?"

"Escort? Four illegally armed thugs stinking of death squad grabbed me in a lift."

"I said discreetly." Parvin's reprimand to the specials sounded deceptively mild.

"Ma'am." The blond would explode if he stood any straighter. His nose was a deep blue bruise. Broken. A nose for a rib, close enough to an eye for an eye. It should feel satisfying, but it only drove home her failure to deal with this peaceably.

Parvin nodded to the chastened specials, who filed out silently. Then she steepled her hands to think, making Seren uneasy. As a Pol commander, she'd had created fast Mitran-style mobile squadrons that alarmed the Pact into deploying two full fleets at Wairoa. "We can't find anyone who saw your abduction on Claer Arian, and we have no way to corroborate that a Pact mining operation bought your work contract."

Tas could speak for her, but Tas wouldn't welcome Parvin's scrutiny.

"Here's how it sounds to me. You doubled for the Greys right through the war. You intercepted the Mitran bead and stole it for your employers. One thing I need to know before we deal with you. Why?"

"I intercepted the courier by accident. If you think otherwise, remember your damned fleet sent me to Gandhi Base to get me out of the way. And Mam backed that decision."

Parvin was on her feet faster than should be possible, right in Seren's face if she were twenty centimetres taller. "Never fault Delun to me. You were her dearest love and hope. She trusted you as few others. Absolutely. And may the gods help you if you've betrayed that trust."

Seren stood her ground under the verbal assault, barely. "So you say. I'll ask her."

Parvin turned away too quickly.

It stole Seren's breath. All her fears escaped her frozen heart. "Where is she, Parvin?"

"Missing for the last year." Parvin turned to her reluctantly.

"Sit."

Mam. Seren pulled out a plastic chair and sat numbly.

"We're searching. We need her. Your cousin-friend Daoud was taking her to safety, but a Pact patrol fired on his hover. When we found the wreckage, Daoud was dead and Delun had disappeared."

Parvin sat and pushed a slate across the table.

A spaceport scene filled the maxed screen. Ships, prefabs, domes, space traffic control tower. A man and a woman embraced at the cargo ramp of an Umiak transport, and from the woman's neck a silver-grey scarf flew in the dust-laden wind. A deeply private affair—and half of Claer probably knew by now. She dropped her head into her hands.

Seren was spared explanation when a medic came in and had her strip to the waist. The woman checked the nskin on her face, sprayed in bone regen agents to speed the rib's healing, and ordered no heavy lifting for a tenday. Then she packed up and left, trying not to hurry too obviously. The interview room stank of fear and anger.

"Milosz says you're involved with Damou. Dangerous man."

"Not to me. Not to Claer. Mam told me to trust him with my life."

"Damou works for Pols one day and for the Pact the next. Right now, he's in Havre with Nolin. Another overpriced Mitran freelance with unknown ethics and far too much power."

Nolin? That can't be true. "He's the most ethical man I know."

"You don't know him," Parvin said. "Seren, I speak as your second-mother. He's using you. You're deep in high-risk Mitran survivor politics. Get out now while you can."

"No." Seren fought tears. *So Parvin has finally remembered we're family.*

"Think. The Mitran Grey companies are a worldless mercenary force with formidable strength and expertise, no accountability and no allegiance. Their director-general is corrupt, and their advisor Inka Loukanos is treacherous. Five people hold a veto on the focal, their council—representing the sciences, arts, military, philosophy, and commerce—but one alone now controls balance of power, thus the final decision on Mitran policy. The military delegate. Damou."

Tas? No. Tas held no authority. *A passable dangerous-cargo pilot. One of the people. Everyman.* "Damou can be anyone. It's a working name they use in MitraCorps."

"Only in Spartí. And as long as this man claims the name, no one else will touch it."

Seren studied the slate. Parvin was wrong. Had to be wrong. "Why did Mam trust him?"

"Damou told Delun that the Senate hired him as her aide. He told the Senate that Delun hired him. As if she could afford to hire a Grey adviser." Parvin shook her head. "One day no one's heard of Damou, the next day he's all over Claeran affairs."

"Tas said they were friends."

"A story. When she disappeared, important Senate materials vanished."

"Mam may have them, wherever she is."

"Or Damou may have them, if he hasn't already sold them to the Pact. If so, we're teetering on the edge of a disaster."

"A disaster worse than the occupation?"

"The invasion forces didn't take prisoners, they butchered fleet officers and used ratings as forced labour. A young cadet recorded the killing grounds and mass graves and managed to transmit the files before they killed him. Delun loaded the files onto a titanium high-security bead. We had them cold."

"Has anything leaked?"

That only irritated Parvin. "No."

"No copies?"

"All lost."

"Damou doesn't have your files." Seren would stake her life on it.

"Prove it."

The female special brought in Seren's cleaned clothes. Seren pulled them on, kicked into her boots, and strapped on her chrono. Then she walked to the door. Locked. She leaned beside it, waiting. "Let me go, Parvin. You've heard everything I can tell you. I have work to do."

Cedar yawned fiercely, decided to ignore this family quarrel, and went back to sleep with her black-barred tail over her nose.

"What work?"

"Vri doc, now that you've had your report. How the war ended and why it ended so badly, including what happened in the Bight. People need to know that a Pol spacer killed an unarmed diplomatic courier requesting our help."

"Classified information. Out of the question." Parvin frowned at her hands, where a complicated cat's cradle grew between her fingers. "Do you know who fired on the courier?"

"No."

"We do." Parvin took in her daughter-friend's shock. "Comm specialist Pawel Lebel demobilized last year with other Gandhi crew. He died in a food riot a few tendays ago."

"Lebel?" Seren remembered a quiet kid with primitive ink tattoos of Tariqa scrollwork. They'd trained together on the gym track—he won every sprint, she won every thousand-metres— and joked about the bad food and boredom. In haste, with no one else available, she might have taken him to check out a screen blip. "Why would Lebel fire on a diplomatic courier? Why would he memory-block me and take the bead?"

"Extreme globalist patriot. He may also have bombed the Pact data centre in Reprise." Parvin lifted her shoulders. "Seren, we need you to reclaim your own identity."

Seren shook her head. Her pursuer had been alive less than a few tendays ago, but this wasn't Parvin's business. Most of her memory had returned, but there were gaps. "First, I need to get the memory block lifted. Mihal Biron can help me, or maybe Tas."

That stung Parvin's head up. "I told you—" But she stopped herself and said, "We can't have a fleet intelligence officer working openly for Greys. You answer to me now."

"It doesn't work on me, Parvin. I'm not in your command. The war's over. Play soldiers if you want, but leave me alone."

Parvin considered her coolly; that was far more alarming than her anger. "We need your skills to help us get the treaty reopened—your suggestion to Danek Arwyn and Rozenn Milosz in Dinan was good."

"I'm not political." *Any more.* Damou's hard Mitran politics made more sense than Claerans' endless convolutions.

"You volunteered."

"I was press-ganged straight from prison. We lost. End of file."

"You're back on active service now."

"No." She managed not to laugh. That was one thing she didn't worry about. "I've been out for a year. And I was shoved into Claer Defence, not into an unsanctioned resistance against an all-powerful occupying enemy."

Parvin carefully removed her cat's cradle from her hands to lay it on the table. It looked like Claeran interlace in a ribbon of eternity pattern, with no beginning and no end. "We answer to the Claeran government in exile and the Politaya shadow council. Our mandate is to end the Pact occupation. Peaceably."

"Good luck." Seren would say nothing harder to Mam's sister-friend.

"We'd like your consent. Otherwise—" Parvin let it hang for a few seconds. "You're officially missing, you never demobilized. If we produce you, we gain the image coup of Seren Qasri back from the dead to aid the resistance. We need heroes."

"I was attacked at Gandhi by my own crewman and spent a year running like a rat. That's not heroism, it's black comedy."

Parvin said, "You always did underestimate your worth. Delun was so proud of you."

It was a gut blow. Seren's eyes stung. "Fuck you, Parvin."

"Say that tomorrow, Lieutenant, and you're on report."

"I'm not your lieutenant. I'm your prisoner."

"You have an hour to consider that. Danek Arwyn is on his way to talk with you. Then we'll need your images from the Bight." Tugging at her ill-fitting clothes, always too long unless she custom-fabbed, Parvin pushed past Seren at the door. In the corridor she turned. "The Politaya can recover. Maybe we can save ourselves and the Greys and even the damned Pact."

Since when did Pols worry about saving Greys or the Pact?

Parvin left, and Seren stared blankly at the closed door. Got up and tried the door handle. Locked. Asked the room for an offworld link. Nothing.

2

Over the shoulder, hover. Seren opened her slate. At least she could check Mam's records. Her Mitran security had worked; a quick diagnostic showed no missing or altered files.

Elbows propped on the table's ingrained stains, she skimmed the indexes copied from Mam's senate card. Reports. Minutes. Household accounts; they'd been shockingly poor but they'd never gone hungry. Mam's speeches. Reviews of *Poison*. Orchard records on tree grafts, plantings, and yields. Records from house security cams, upgraded on the advice of her aide.

Cedar curled at her feet like a house pet, not a fearless guardian who'd survived the wild.

"Did you miss us, Cedar?" As soon as she said it, she knew it was foolish. An animal mainly lived in her own senses and the eternal present. The past was a different place no longer visited.

The cat's brow furrowed with effort. "Always miss you, Seren. Home soon."

Gwernant. Closing her eyes, Seren saw it in late summer as it was on Cedar's forgotten bead. Mam read under the grape arbour, Tas stood at the summer kitchen door . . .

What if a house cam had caught something Cedar missed? Quickly she loaded the record from her chamber tree and fast-forwarded till she saw Tas walk through the reception room. She told her slate, "Follow."

Jump cut. Now Tas was in Mam's study, kneeling near her desk. He looked over his shoulder at Cedar, crouching at Mam's foot, and Seren followed his gaze to a blue-corded white streak down one leg of the old carved deadwood desk. Ntex explosive. A small metallic shape glinted in his hand.

Zoom. Tas held a titanium bead between thumb and forefinger. Mam's missing files?

A blink of red. That was where Cedar's silver bead went into ninety-four seconds of static snowstorm. But this recording showed Tas standing in the lounge, weapon levelled toward the study door. Its tracer eye blinked red on the stubby barrel. He'd just fired. That was the red—

Then she saw Mam sprawled in a spreading dark pool on the old silk carpet just inside the study doorway. Tas turned at a hissing roar that could be a heavy laser or a hover and took one step toward it. Then he kneeled and lifted Mam's head, reaching for a wound at her throat.

Frozen, Seren stared at her mother. *So much blood.* Delun tried to talk, and her mouth shaped one word. *Seren.* Seren folded over her grief, face in hands, but forced herself to watch.

Jump cut. Mam and Tas were gone. She heard a crash of falling stone, and bright fingers of fire caressed the slate's screen. Cedar ran back and forth calling for Delun, and finally bolted through the summer kitchen, obeying her fail-safe directive to protect herself and her data.

Seren sat in the hard plastic chair, how long she didn't know, watching flames leap through billows of smoke till the final silver static. Numbly, she touched the off pad and invoked her aide on her slate screen, wishing Tas were there to ask instead.

<> Teak, what does it mean? <>

<> An unknown person jammed your guardian animal's surveillance bioware and attacked Delun Qasri. <> He looked up at her from the maxed screen, his expression sombre.

<> How? Cedar is tamperproof. <>

<> Someone used current Mitran control codes. <>

<> Who gets control codes? <>

<> MitraCorps senior personnel. <>

Tas. If Parvin was right, Tas was a senior officer in Spartí.

Grasping at straws, she asked, <> Why would my friend and Delun's friend, Tas Damou, set explosives in her study? <>

<> You didn't see anyone set explosives, Seren. You saw someone examine explosives. Another unknown person could have applied and armed Ntex. <>

<> So where is Mam? <>

<> Delun Qasri remains untraceable. I search for her at five-minute intervals. <>

<> Thanks, Tas. Stand by. <>

A long moment's silence.

<> Teak, Seren. You coded me for initiative as an autonomous AI answering to the name Teak. Do you now wish to call me Tas? <>

Seren stared in shock. <> No! <>

<> Steady, Seren. Courage under fire. <>

<> That was you, not me—courage under fire. <> Seren felt hot tears spill from her eyes. *Mam. Daoud. Pawel. Claer.* So many people to mourn, yet still she had tears for Teak Kuhan.

<> Take heart. Pay attention. Keep talking. <> Then he blinked out.

Seren sat, head in hands. *Impossible.* Tas was Delun's trusted friend. Seren's friend and lover. He'd given her Inka's files to aid her research. Tas hadn't stolen Mam's Senate records of Pact atrocities. No one needed them outside the Pol anyway . . . except to destroy them as evidence. *Nolin?*

Inka's files might hold answers. Her hands shook badly as she loaded the files Tas had given her at Samun. Her screen listed index after index, but first she tapped *Readme Seren*. It was empty. She tried other files, other indexes. All of them were blank and silent.

It all started to make cruel sense, if she believed her eyes. This could be why Tas wanted her to stay away from Tirion. Maybe no one had pursued her at Arian or Tirion port or Alluvion, it had just been Tas finding ways to keep her distracted and on the run.

Whatever side you're on, he'd said. A clever operative would divert suspicion, then strike again. Every element was in place.

Opportunity? No one was better positioned than Delun's security adviser.

Motive? A stack of cash cards could be the only motive a Grey needed.

Means? The man was a loaded weapon.
All questions had one devastating answer. *Tas.*

3

Two graceful blue-upholstered Saarinen chairs, mid twentieth-century originals, flanked an arched window in Wilm Nolin's office high in a Walden tower. First-wave cultures had transported antique furniture offworld and left living humans to starve and drown and choke in Earth's poisoned atmosphere.

Finding Wilm Nolin alone was never a good sign; he usually travelled in a swarm of courtiers and aides. Tas got most briefings from the chief of defence, Anton Rethel. Uneasily he wondered what had changed. Walden's Secretary of Peace and Reconstruction, as he currently styled himself, took a chair and gestured to the other. Tas glanced at his chrono and sat.

Damn Inka. This contract was her price for aiding Qasri, and he grudged every minute. He should be at search headquarters right now reporting the new survivors—but even to think of *Kalevala* here was dangerous.

"Pol resistance. We need to put it down before the occupations bleed us dry." Nolin propped his chin on a fist. "President de Jong wants a presence for ten years, but corruption is so high on these Pol worlds that we put in more than we take out."

"If you let capital accrue on Anansi and Claer, their economies will prime recovery," Tas said, thinking of the significant percentage that went straight into Nolin's personal funds and investments on Xanadu. "The more you take out, the less remains to generate wealth."

A server brought coffee and pastries and set the silver tray on a twenty-second-century Noguchi glass table. Precious and rare things gravitated to Nolin's sumptuous office.

"We need that capital," Nolin said in his flat inner-worlds Peel.

"War is costly."

Nolin grinned engagingly around a cream bun. "Spare me the philosophy. I get enough from de Jong. I don't need pacifist crap from my fucking assassin."

"I'm not your fucking assassin." Tas wondered how far he could push without dying. Nolin was more intelligent and vastly more dangerous than he seemed.

"You don't fuck. Got it shot off at Tanna. Must give you a steadier hand." Nolin barked out the laughter he reserved for his own witticisms.

He debased every conversation in this way, pissing around the perimeter like any predator to mark his territory. It was the coarseness of an ambitious sixty-year-old adolescent with unlimited power and wealth since marrying into one of Walden's six great family cartels.

Tas rested his elbows on the upholstered wings of the priceless chair, trying to look at ease in this trophy room. Sculptured hands caught in a dozen gestures, some holding mementos or tools, were wall-mounted on the fine wood panelling behind Nolin's vast desk. Most were bronze or titanium or carbon composites; one was solid gold. Tas had delivered each of Inka's sculptures, hoping Nolin would never fully appreciate its humour.

Nolin took a call and gestured for a privacy cone, and Tas turned to the window. As Walden's administrative capital, Havre also effectively governed the Pact. Sprawling as far as he could see, it was a landscape of many-storeyed buildings on terraced levels, punctuated with vastly taller spires despite Walden's higher gravity. The Barrier Sea gleamed sullenly to the northeast beyond the spectacular Treaty Towers. Every Pact world had its own tower, sheathed in irradiated titanium film to reflect a different phase of the visible spectrum. New Politaya towers were rising in Anansi limestone, carved with scenes of happy

Politayans at work and play; there were no blockade-starved children or disappeared artists or shallow mass graves. Mitra and Maq's dead homeworld of Sitkum had no towers. No Pact record acknowledged that those worlds had ever existed.

Tapping off his palm implant, Nolin glanced at the window. "How does it feel to sit at the heart of an empire?"

Tas didn't answer. Around Nolin there was a good deal he didn't say.

Nolin got back to business. "Another ship vanished, no trace, but a Mitran ship in the same sector wasn't touched. How do we stop this shit?"

"Don't send ships Outside."

"Who said it was Outside? But we can go where we want. Ever since we broke the Tripline drive limit, the treaty boundary is meaningless Grey crap."

Tas felt a hot rush of anger. For years Mitran intelligence had tracked Pact ships Outside, but the Pact had always denied it. Now Nolin openly admitted Pact travel beyond the Tripline.

"New job for you," Nolin said. "Go find out why these ships go missing—unstable nodes or Pol pirates or whatever damn thing— and blow them to hell. Fast. Specially any bases or hab sites. I want you on exclusive contract."

"Committed elsewhere," Tas risked. Nolin usually found that irresistible.

"Get uncommitted. You Mitran dicks can't keep on playing every side."

"Why?" The real question was, Why now?

"Nothing stands in our way now. We need to expand."

Tas nodded. He would bill Nolin at his top rate for what he'd done for five years anyway, apart from blowing anyone to hell. Logs and charts and records would take special care, but he needed to keep Nolin's hands off this for a while longer.

"First another removal." Removal was Nolin's favourite euphemism for assassination.

Tas preferred plain talk. "Who do you want killed?"

"You like taking down politicals."

"Yes." Better him than another, and prisoners of conscience were pathetically easy to handle compared to gangsters like Duri Balint.

Nolin spoke a command into his hand around a meringue, and a list of names shimmered and steadied in a vri zone beside the silver coffee service.

All six were names that MitraCorps intelligence had flagged. Mihal Biron headed the list, predictably; his well-known hatred of the Pact was an open provocation. An outspoken artist from Ojin over in the Broken Cluster. And at the bottom, Seren Qasri.

Tas drained his Delft coffee cup. *Steady.* His mind raced but his pulse stayed even and slow, a minor benefit from many tendays of surgery in his prison on Mesa.

"Usual proof. Give me a hand with this," Nolin licked a finger, beaming at his own joke.

How would Nolin have him removed if he missed a step? Poison, Tas guessed, or a tailored virus. He needed to distance himself from Nolin with extreme delicacy. To hell with Inka's schemes. This was becoming a different game. And he urgently needed to leave. Now.

"Not Biron. If you kill him, you'll make a martyr."

"Why?" Nolin took another pastry.

"Politayans will smoulder and conspire if you take their listed metals and spaceworthy craft, but they'll strike back hard if you mess with their family ties. And Biron's family has the power to drag you through the courts for years."

"Bad. Drop him." Nolin hated anything that bounced back at him. They all did, the opportunists who infested de Jong's government, hiring others to do their in-close work.

"I'll start on Ojin." It condemned others to a worse death, but one at a time was the best he could do now. Tas set down his cup and stood.

"Know Qasri?" Nolin asked, watching closely. His round pink tongue found sugar crumbs at the corner of his mouth.

"Claeran vri artist." Tas knew that Nolin watched him for secret flaws. He liked to find leverage on men he feared; unwisely he didn't fear women.

Nolin smiled slowly. It had been a test. "Any good?"

"Qasri's been dead for a year." Sweat prickled under his arms and down his spine.

"Investigate. Make sure. Or someone else will."

Tas said nothing. Nolin was sending him a message: *We*

know. But what did he know? He should know that Seren died on Arian, with no trace of her since.

"Report to me on Claer. I'll be there overseeing my construction project."

Nolin spoke to his implant, and a grainy hovercam image floated above the glass tabletop—he'd defaced the Noguchi with an inset vri stage—of a Bryniau Claer stone house with sweeping rain eaves and verandahs. *Gwernant.* One of Nolin's fantasy monsters stalked from the orchard down to the stream with clawed forearms raised, ready to strike. The image faded to sequence readouts and a twisting ladder of DNA. Gwernant, a chimera, and someone's geneprint: it took a while to solve Nolin's riddles.

A few minutes later Tas idled across the kilometre-wide ceremonial square in front of the Ministry of Peace and Reconstruction, purveyors of war and devastation. Knowing he was under close observation, he took time to admire the artificial waterfall and backbred gingko plantings. Eventually he stepped onto a maglev train.

At the spaceport he quickly swept the old Az for surveillance, killed four intruders with his own nano hunters, neutralized the nanobots teeming on his clothes and hair, and lifted to orbit on an easy trajectory to avoid any suggestion of haste.

4

Head in hands, Seren barely noticed when Parvin returned, followed by Rozenn Milosz and the man who'd questioned her in Dinan.

"All right?" Parvin leaned close. She had probably asked two or three times.

Unable to speak, Seren nodded. Rozenn stood by the door, looking uncomfortable with a Pol fleet hand laser. Yesterday they would have joked about accidentally shooting out the light panels, but now no one was smiling.

"We're pleased that you're with us," Danek Arwyn told Seren as they sat.

"I'm here under coercion, *yr athro.*"

"Why do you call me teacher?" He had an nskinned gash across his knuckles, a professor doing rough labour.

"Grid search. Your global cultures department seems to have entered the building trades."

"Our families still eat, even if the occupation closed the colleges."

"Danek is our political strategist," Parvin said.

And you're the military strategist? Seren didn't need to ask.

"'Strategy succeeds only with benevolent intent,'" Arwyn said.

"Don't bother quoting Kuhan. I've read his *Consent to Peace.*"

Seren gave Parvin a hard look; she'd clearly told Arwyn some personal history. "You don't have Kuhan. You don't have a Grey company on contract. You don't have a Claeran armed force. You don't have a government to mandate it. I won't bomb Pact offices or garrotte draftees in alleys. I'm no use to you."

"Wrong." Parvin wore a cat smile that Seren distrusted. "We're not hotheads with homemade bombs. Violent protests damage our efforts, and we weed them out. We hold the high ground."

"Claer is our home," Rozenn said. "We can't let them destroy our only place to live."

"Tirion city council defied occupation demands a few days ago, and the councillors are dead or in custody," Arwyn put in. "Rumi, Dinan, what's next? We need to pursue other measures as you suggested. If we compile enough evidence, we can force the Pact to reopen an illegal treaty."

"How? Delun Qasri headed the peace committee, and her files are missing. No one else has her knowledge, experience, or public respect."

"Except her daughter." Arwyn nodded at her. So Parvin had blown her cover.

"Certainly not," Seren snapped. "I have none of her resources."

"You have Damou," Arwyn said.

Seren saw where this led. "According to Parvin, he's a dangerous unknown."

"Mirror transit is a dangerous unknown, but we manage it," Arwyn said. "*Poison* warned about the war and the Pact resource grab years in advance."

"*Poison* was heavy-handed student work. Satirical allegory about an imaginary society."

"We work with what we have," Parvin said. "As you did with *Rain*."

Seren looked up sharply.

"Delun had me view *Rain* before she decided to take it to Walden. It was detailed, analytical, passionate, and absolutely damning of Pact covert operations on Tanna. You showed that Kuhan made a costly error based on bad intelligence, but he was no war criminal. Even now, if you cleaned up a few scenes, *Rain* would be a powerful document."

Bad edits, clumsy transitions, overlength sequences, redundant shots. Seren shrugged. She'd ducked school to work nonstop for an afternoon, shuttled up to Claer Arian, and stolen the first long-range ship she could fly—the prime minister's, she learned later—trying to take *Rain* to the Justice Department on Walden to prevent the execution of a man she barely knew. She'd almost outrun Claer Defence in the rock belt, and if the yacht were armed, she'd have fired instead of trying to ram. But it worked. Mam took the vri to Walden under diplomatic protection, and Kuhan lived. At least another few tendays.

"*Rain* must be the best-known vri that no one's ever seen," Arwyn said. "I teach it in a senior ethics seminar. 'Compare and contrast Qasri's and Kuhan's belief structures and tactics.' You have enormous respect."

"Only since I died." Seren pushed back her chair, having heard enough of this. "Let's be real. I made obscure, zero-budget art vris."

"*Poison* was an art vri before the war. Now it's a prophecy."

"Enjoy your cultural circle." Seren got up. *Where were you when theatres refused to show my work? When protesters hurled garbage? When I was arrested for treason?* Someday she'd laugh about this. Right now, she needed to remember every detail about the Bight, find Mam, get Tas to explain.

Rozenn answered a knock and slipped back inside the room. "Ma'am. Urgent call."

"Not now."

"Emergency, ma'am."

Parvin answered her call and quickly signed off. "Dinan. The city's burning."

"All those wood-frame houses and flats after a dry summer," Arwyn said. "There'll be a firestorm in heritage districts like Kumun Arvorek."

Rozenn took a half-step closer, wide-eyed. Lezig's crèche was in Kumun Arvorek.

Seren headed for the door. "The Umiak." Radko would flay them, but no matter.

"Nothing you can do," Parvin said. "My son's in Dinan, but I can't run off to his rescue."

Pedr. "All the more reason."

"Go," said Danek Arwyn.

Parvin glared at him, but her eyes betrayed her.

Seren ran. She ignored the lift, flew down six flights of stairs, and reached the Umiak a second behind Cedar. The actuators engaged and the converters groaned to full power as Rozenn climbed aboard gasping. Parvin turned up last. One glance at Rozenn's white face, and Seren hurried her preflights. While her nav filed an emergency flight plan, she lifted slowly, climbed an extra thousand metres for safety, rolled the Umiak onto its port stabilizer, and burned harder than she'd ever tried in atmosphere. The old ship shot up through the morning cloud cover like a hawk.

Flying low over the seacoast, they spotted Dinan on the northeastern horizon ominously early by the smoke roiling up from the old town.

Parvin pointed toward Kumun Arvorek. "Put down in that park."

Air traffic control would ream her for landing here. Too bad. Emergency vehicles were gridlocked around an area of several blocks that were engulfed, and a great crowd of people stood nearby watching the fire devour their homes and businesses.

Seren was out of her chair before the engines moaned to a stop. "Three softsuits in the aft locker. Cedar, guard the ship."

"On guard." Cedar crouched on her paws, a watchful sphinx.

Parvin was already out and running, making good speed for a chunky middle-aged woman, but Seren overtook her with long, powerful strides. The injured were being packed out of the park, crowded with dazed people and disabled service vehicles. As they ran in, Parvin yelled the names of her children. And miraculously, in a sea of screaming children and adults, two young women forced their way through to embrace Seren and their mother.

"Pedr?"

Yasmin's face was a mask of tear-streaked soot. "We heard about the bombs so we came to help. Pedr got some children out, but no one can find him now."

Rozenn searched among the children and shouted Lezig's name, but there was no answer.

Seren ran after Parvin, out through the north side of the park. The boulevard trees burned standing, and farther east more trees flared like torches. Firefighters were dragging out their gear to dig firebreaks. Someone shouted as they passed that the mist engines were blown and the tanks were dry, making their equipment useless. Water fountained out of broken mains while the old city burned.

This had been a shady avenue lined with intimate sidewalk cafés. Parvin ran for one of the smaller islands that had burned for a long time. Seren's suit comm picked up an inhuman sound, a sobbing moan, that had to come from her second-mam or Rozenn.

Softsuits weren't designed for fire protection, but they blocked the worst heat. Half an island away from the blaze, the carbonglass fittings at her cuffs and helmet scorched her flinching skin. As others fell back from the heat, they passed alone through a sea of fire and crossed a boulevard littered with smouldering rubble. The buildings ahead had no floors, only billows of flame barely contained by the remaining walls. No living person could remain inside.

Seren stopped on the grownstone pavement as her skin bubbled up on her forehead and wrists. It was suicide to go closer. Parvin finally stopped, but Rozenn ran on toward another building. Seren plunged after her, blistering inside the helmet. She wrestled Rozenn back from the fire, fighting her adrenaline-fed strength, and dragged her back a metre at a time. Parvin came to help.

As they retreated into the park, Rozenn staggered against Seren's shoulder. The park was almost empty now as people fled before the encroaching flames.

"I'll stay here to organize the withdrawal," Parvin said.

"No. You're needed in Tirion," Seren told her, without a shred of authority to back it—someone had to keep Parvin on task. "They know enough to run."

Yasmin and Janin still waited on the ship's ramp, and Cedar watched anxiously through the viewscreen.

"Friends, Cedar." Two glowing eyes winked out as the cabin lights came up.

"Emergency override," Cedar told her. "Passengers."

The cargo hold was full of people, soot-tarnished or bloody or shocked pale, sobbing or silent. Rozenn was already among them, searching the faces. But none of the children was Lezig.

"Good work, sweet." Seren knew the ship's payload to the gram, thanks to Radko's endless efforts to squeeze in one last package. "Take in three more parents with kids."

Six more people stumbled in to huddle on the floor. Below, others stood quietly waiting: children and adults, a robed imam, even animals driven out of hiding, all painted in ruddy light as the fire crowned around them in the park trees. As she lifted, they still looked up in hope.

The ship rose staggering out of the flames. The last thing she saw through the smoke below was a ground convoy of heavy logging equipment rolling toward the town centre. If they could blast firebreaks and spray retardant mist, they might save part of the city.

Southwest along the grey coast, Seren flew half-blinded by stinging sweat and tears. Dinan clinics would soon fill. She asked Parvin, "Derw? Or will occupation troops shoot us down?"

"Manimals can hold them off," Parvin said from the nav chair.

Seren didn't even ask. Rozenn was aft, trying to help their casualties. It might buffer her own pain a while longer.

Outside Tirion the transport wallowed down onto Derw Sanctuary's hover pad and settled hard, and thirty-seven Dinan survivors dragged themselves out to the waiting staff. Someone tossed Seren a burnskin tube for her face and wrists, then hurried on to serious cases. She lay on a bench in the clinic garden, clutching a galette someone gave her, to catch her breath.

It was a bright, cool autumn morning when Parvin shook her roughly awake. Both their hands and faces glistened with burnskin. Seren got to her feet, blinking grainily. The Umiak still sat on a hover pad, breaking countless airspace regs, and another three small spacecraft and several hovers rested nearby.

"I'm taking Milosz back to Dinan. There are bodies to identify from the fire. She needs to know." Parvin couldn't bring herself to say that she also needed to know. "We'll talk again here tomorrow."

Watching them away, Seren ached for both of them—but by tonight she'd be far from here. She could reach Grey space before

Radko realized she'd hijacked the Umiak, leave it at Vritra Ek or another transfer station, and disappear. But then she'd still have no way to find Mam and no answers from Tas.

Seren tapped on the comm bracelet on her wrist and for a moment heard faint static. "Come in." But there was only silence. Finger poised to tap it off, she hesitated. The comm bracelet contained nanoprocessors and a small memory bank. "Data query. Location request."

"Access denied."

Try again. This time Seren gave her Politaya Fleet number and password.

"Outdated password." A long pause. "Biometrics scan to 99.5 percent, 0.5 percent error factor. Acknowledged, Lieutenant Qasri."

Seren recoiled as though the wrist comm had hit her with live current. Tas must have programmed it to recognize her.

"Location of Tas Damou?"

"Leaving Havre for Mitran search and rescue headquarters on Claer."

"Why?"

"Herra Damou has an urgent report to make now that he has briefed Secretary Nolin." The red light winked out.

Tas briefed Wilm Nolin, the Pact deputy defence secretary? Seren scrubbed her face in her hands—a Tas gesture—and wondered if she really wanted to know.

A novice overtook her halfway to the ship. "Doctor says you're next up. Come."

Seren hesitated, but making her break now would draw attention. She called Cedar toward the low timber clinic behind a swaying screen of green-plumed native grasses. Even in chaos, the sanctuary preserved a measure of peace and privacy.

The novice stumbled with weariness, and probably hadn't rested since the first survivors came in. In a better time Seren would offer assistance. Growing up, she'd spent many hours in Derw Sanctuary, attended services, poured out her heart to a priestess after Kuhan died. Now she had to break free of this nightmare and be her own person again. Claerans didn't thrive on self-obsession and solitude.

"Can't stay away?" The white-haired doctor who'd treated her clawed face less than a day ago looked over her burnskin patches. "Sorry, I forgot your vow of silence."

"Ended now," Seren said.

This time he looked too tired to ask questions as he cleaned the burns. "You'll want to refresh your cosmod. New skin grows in your natural skin tone."

"I was thinking of woodcat stripes anyway."

It got a creaky laugh. He probably needed one. "We saw you on grid news, landing casualties outside. I'm surprised your ship got off the ground with that crowd."

"We were between freight runs." Grid news? *Trouble.* Seren remembered, and waved a hand at Cedar, guarding the door. "Your tote that I borrowed—"

"Next time. It's a spare."

At his simple kindness, Seren was dismayed to feel hot tears sliding down her cheeks between nskin and burnskin. She must be a mess.

"Let it out, sweet, we all feel that way." He patted her shoulder and lifted her left wrist. "I thought you didn't have implants."

"I don't." Seren glanced down. Above her comm bracelet, near the faint incision where Tas had removed her data and comm implants, a welt reddened the inside of her forearm.

The doctor swiped a hand scanner over her arm and turned the scanner screen. It showed the two bones in Seren's left forearm, and a small blur against the longer curved bone. "You have an object just inside the ulna. It seems the burn has made it visible."

"A bone pin probably came loose. My arm was broken, and we had no medical resupply late in the war. No bone lattice, no regen."

"Wrong shape. It's not a standard implant either." He magnified until the screen showed a pierced oval with a rounded top.

Seren stared and took a deep breath. Derw Sanctuary respected privacy; there would be no better place to do this. "Can you remove it?"

A list scrolled above his palm, and he nodded. "Only one patient after you, not urgent."

The anaesthetic spray made her shiver, or maybe it was fear.

The doctor pulled over a robot arm and put his hand into the servo glove, and in seconds a small metallic shape lay on a sterile tray. Seren rubbed blood off it one-handed as he nskinned the small incision. A gold oval data bead lay in her palm, a high-yield secure Mitran type, and she closed her fingers over it. The old doctor had the unClaeran courtesy not to ask, only handed her the comm bracelet she'd pulled off. She followed his gaze. *Mitran comm. Mitran cat. Mitran bead.*

"Pol fleet intelligence," she said, before he joined Parvin in thinking she was a Mitran spy. "Classified." And then she remembered Pedr's joke.

Pedr. And Lezig. More tears slid down.

"All right?" he asked as she pulled on her flight jacket.

Nodding, Seren wiped her face and walked out into the leafy colonnade. Outside the chapel she ducked into a coatroom and pulled on a deep-hooded mourning cloak. Instantly, she was invisible. People made way for her in the corridor but averted their eyes as she passed. In the chapel a few people sat or kneeled between the small trees and the pool, but no one paid any attention to her or even the banned animal leaning at her knee.

Seren sat in the darkest corner and slotted the Mitran gold bead into her slate with shaking hands. It would self-wipe if she jacked it, if she knew anything about Mitran encryption. When she keyed, she got only a short line of alphanumeric symbols.

"In Tavod," she keyed a command.

Louhi Takahara, Lieut., MitraCorps/Spartí.

That was all; she could call up nothing else. Maybe only a secure standalone Mitran system could open it. As more people filed into the chapel, she kneeled for a moment and left.

Seren walked blindly away from the building complex and was halfway to the healing grove before she realized where she'd instinctively turned. A few old-growth trees towered over the seedlings even now, spurned by the Pact loggers for a broken top or a double trunk. She went to the nearest oak and leaned, pressing her face against its dry scented bark. Across the grove near the healing cells a priest stood quietly, and she longed to lay down her burdens and take a dream. But she turned and stumbled from the cool shade back to the landing pad.

The Umiak was a mess, even after the nano cleaners absorbed

the blood and soot. Putting the ship in order, she wondered if she were too hard on Parvin. Her second-mam and Rozenn should be back from Dinan soon. Maybe she should wait. Undecided, she sat on the ramp as Cedar chased seed fluff across the grass like an overgrown kitten.

One thing tugged at her memory. Pawel's lover Yan was an Anansi boy; on Gandhi they'd endlessly planned to tour Anansi after the war, travelling oasis to oasis until they settled. Had Pawel returned to Claer alone?

A grid search of Claeran stats drew a blank. An Anansi search made her shake her head in regret. Specialist Pawel Lebel had died with his lover in a widely covered murder-suicide. Poor Pawel, poor Yan. They deserved more. Then the date sank in. Lebel hadn't died in a food riot a few tendays ago; he'd died nearly a year ago.

Parvin lied.

Seren dropped her slate in her pocket, pulled her duffel out of a crew locker, and called Cedar. Taking the Umiak to Vritra Ek was far too obvious. Leave it here and walk away, lay down no trail for Parvin to follow. Right now, she needed somewhere safe to work this out.

Seren tapped the comm bracelet. "How do I contact Tas Damou?"

A few answers, that was all she wanted. No matter how she tried, she couldn't see Tas harming Mam or Claer. Wait and see, keep an open mind until he explained.

"Next mirror relay in seventeen minutes, forty seconds," advised the comm's small Mitran-accented voice. "Leave your message."

5

ES2742.081

By moonlight Doll Sorrow kept to the thickest woods near the old stone house. She slid from dappled shadow to shadow, nearly invisible in the woodland.

Damp soil caressed her bare pads, and leaves stroked her fur, murmuring how easy it was for a manimal to revert to the wild. Sometimes she met feral chimerai on streambank paths or in the deep wildwood. If they bristled or growled, she quickly retreated. Born human, Doll would live human. Another tenday of watching her old owner, Maq promised, meant she would earn another hand.

Crouched in a willow thicket outside the old orchard wall, screened among narrow grey-green leaves, she watched the house. Its walls were transparent to the device Maq brought last night, a handheld monitor that displayed the output of nano cams that hovered from room to room. Captain's tech, always better than Pact tech, winged unseen through the owner's elaborate security net.

The Mitran who tormented armless serpentines and laughed about sculpture with the owner brought a new guest, a Claeran, a younger man whose yellow hair brushed his shoulders. His biometrics throbbed purple and red across her small screen, more like a tortured manimal than a human. Fear. Uncertainty.

Maybe he meant to hurt the owner. Doll Sorrow would save him, and he would love her forever . . . no. Not any more.

The Mitran paced the salon, but the Claeran waited, tensely quiet. His name meant nothing to her, but he acted important. Doll keyed careful notes when the owner's favourite guest came down to meet them, scrubbing his hands. The art man invited the Claeran to play, but that made him so angry and afraid that he walked out rudely without touching hands—foolish man, said the art man's thinking stare at his back.

Doll crossed the grass to the kennel once the Claeran left. The kennel door opened to Doll's human palm as her comm mimicked a keeper's DNA, and she slid into the straw-scented dim light. The sprite was gone. Late at night, hiding from the monitors, he'd chewed his wrist like a small animal escaping a trap. In the morning he was white and still. Draken sulked over her missed hunt. Noob was afraid. When the owner returned from Walden tonight, he would yell and break bots.

A new girl Baby curled in the restraint bed. She'd come back from the lab white-haired and white-skinned and white-winged, too drugged to properly open her pale blue eyes. The bot was on standby, with a yellow light blinking on its thorax, so Doll padded to the bed and looked in. The new Baby looked at her sleepily and reached through the mesh as far as her hand restraints let her.

"Beautiful cat girl."

On a gold chain around the brat's skinny neck hung gold letters. *Baby.* Doll pulled back with a silent hiss and showed her claws.

"Don't be mad," the girl said.

This Baby wasn't afraid. A trick? The owner liked tricks. Doll sheathed her claws, but her spine fur stood out. She growled, "Who do you work for?"

"Mam. She'll come and get me."

"No, she won't. Mamas don't come for you after you change," Doll said.

"Then my cousin-friends will come." The new Baby settled back on her quilt. "Or you can help me go find Mam."

"I might eat you." It was a nasty idea, but Baby might not know that.

"I'll run and run."

"I run faster."

"Baka-chan says it's bad to scare people." Baby blinked, and Doll blinked involuntarily in reply.

"I forgot." Doll's ears flattened and her tail tucked. Maq and Captain had taught her too.

"It's all right. You didn't mean to." Baby yawned.

"Tell me how to find your mama," Doll said in a rush of generosity. "Baby?"

When she looked the girl curled on her quilt, fast asleep. Her small ruffled wings were perfect, so she hadn't played with the owner yet.

6

Hover 360-shot. Overlooking the Gwynfa glacier, Hafoty was a barren place of bare stone and high meadows wisped in cloud.

A buzz from Seren's comm woke her on the last leg of her journey up, nodding half-asleep on the empty pod she'd taken at the Gwynfa maglev terminus. Over the pod's hum of well-kept antique equipment, her comm's mirror link clicked with several relays. Then the familiar ruined face appeared on visual, showing the Az cockpit behind him.

Tas noticed the mourning cloak. He averted his eyes in silence until she unsealed it and let it slip from her shoulders. Then he said, "I heard about Dinan. All right?"

Seren nodded, unable to speak again, and fought down a temptation to say, *I missed you. Let's go far away, put all this behind us* . . . First, she had to know. "We need to talk. About Gwernant."

His long silence had nothing to do with the relay. "I'll tell you all I can."

"Now."

Tas glanced across his boards, probably checking his schedule. "If I burn hard, I'll get there before an urgent meeting. Coordinates?"

"Send," she told her slate, and his eyebrow rose at her deep south location.

"Five hours." He signed off looking as though he badly wanted to say more.

The narrow old trail to the Hafoty way hut rose in steep switchbacks from the main Gwynfa path; in the migration period, it had led to a manned forestry tower on the summit. The pod paused at the junction long enough for her to climb out, and then it hummed back down to the maglev. At the first switchback, Seren let Cedar out of the duffel to run free.

"Good work, treasure. Not much fun to ride in the dark."

"Strangers hunt us, Ser. Death is a long ride in the dark."

Not for the first time, Seren was unnerved by her guardian's words. "Do you ever make poems?"

"I breathe."

Served her right for asking. "Who hunts us?"

"A man."

After that, Seren saved her own breath for the climb. Her rib twinged if she moved too abruptly, and her face throbbed with heat under the healing skin. By the time she reached the slate-roofed stone way hut, she was weak-kneed and gasping in the thinner air.

Three hours to wait. She slotted a cash card in the food fab and punched for biscuits, but could only choke down a few bites. Cedar shook a paw at her cheese protein and stalked off to hunt seed cones.

Heartsick, Seren tried to remember her last words to Pedr and Lezig. Early in the war, Mam had come to see her board her transport among the flowers and banners and promises of an early return. Mam had been wasp-tongued and witty, and they'd argued and laughed as usual, but at the five-minute signal all talk fell away, and Seren saw her mother's eyes were blue-black in a sickly pale face. She felt the same way now. Shocked bloodless.

Calling up her research notes, she counted off key points.

One. She'd been memory-blocked after the courier died, then planted with a gold data bead—perhaps Damou's missing bead.

Two. Mam was attacked in her own home, where her adviser and supposed friend Damou stood over her holding a titanium data bead—her missing senate files—and a newly fired laser.

Three. Hours later, two men seized Seren on Claer Arian only to turn her over to Damou.

Always Damou.

Another two hours. Tas should arrive before dawn, if customs remote-scanned his ship in orbit to clear it for a surface landing. Seren walked to keep warm, forced herself to eat, and finally lay on the stone bench outside the hut, hands clasped behind her head, to watch the stars wheel overhead. *Please* . . . Her thought remained formless. She didn't even know what to want.

When she woke, she realized that she'd dozed. Half an hour left—but lights moved steadily above the eastern mountain wall, growing as they approached. A small craft's nav lights.

Seren got up stiffly. At her side Cedar stretched herself and sat up to wait. The nav lights descended, framing the black outline of the old MitraCorps command ship as a deeper darkness in the night sky. Tas hovered for a moment, cut the power a metre off the small landing pad, let the ship sink with a hiss of pressurized air, and jumped down before the ramp dropped. *Show-off.* Despite everything, she almost smiled. Maybe somehow, she'd misread the signs.

"Seren. I brought you something from the Deep Outside." In the near dark his voice was warm and alive, marvellously good to hear.

"I have questions." She wanted to lean to his warmth, forget all this trouble, but she couldn't let herself be seduced by his presence.

Tas Damou stepped closer to search her face, expressionless. Then she knew she hadn't misread the signs, and she was afraid.

"Ask your questions." He stood with arms folded, dark against his dark ship.

Start with a neutral question, Kuhan's mediation handbook said. Seren asked carefully, "The day I returned to Arian, did someone break into Gwernant?"

"Not a break-in. A man walked in using current security codes. The monitors sensed the entry, but he reached Delun before I did. You missed that in my notes?"

"What notes?"

"Long files in Inka's index. Come aboard. We can check."

Inka's index was empty. Seren would trust him to a point, but still put Cedar on guard. In the familiar cockpit, lights came up at Tas's command, and the pilot and nav chairs unlocked and swivelled to face each other as the hatch closed.

"Tell me about that day. I can't put it together." Seren kept her voice level.

"Your mother took a call on the terrace an hour before the scheduled Senate evacuation. It was a man saying you were held hostage on Arian. She offered a ransom, tried to negotiate, but the call ended. I traced it. He was lying. It came from your inbound transport from Gandhi Base, still hours away from Arian." He seemed calm as always—yet he had set explosives in Delun's study and kneeled in Delun's blood.

"Who made the call?" It didn't make sense.

"A Claeran. Delun thought he was Ayitien from a hint of Kreyol. Inka traced further and said his name was Pawel Lebel. You knew him?"

Seren nodded. Had Parvin told the truth after all? Pawel wasn't from Ayiti, but Kreyol was the easiest Claeran dialect to mimic.

"The call came from Lebel's slate, but he'd just reported to Claernet that it was stolen," Tas said. "A decoy call. Delun asked me to take her to the senate ship, then intercept you on Arian before you came to harm."

"But Mam never made the evacuation." Seren fought to stay calm.

"I don't know." Tas met her gaze steadily. "The man who entered the house shot your mother with a primitive laser-guided ballistic device like some we saw on Tanna. A killer's weapon. Fortunately, it was a superficial wound."

You expect me to believe she survived that? "Then what?"

"I stabilized her and took her to the first person we could locate, your cousin-friend Daoud. When they headed for the Senate ship, I lifted for Arian. The station was in chaos, and Pact guards detained me in breach of treaty. It took me an hour to call in favours and get to you."

Seren felt the skin walk across her shoulder blades. Damou had his hand on every element of Claeran political life and her own family. He was far more than a senator's security adviser, but what did that make him?

"Seren, why don't you know this? It's in my notes." He seemed perplexed, not evasive.

"Mam said there were attempts on her life."

"We worked to draw out the assassin, but he got to Delun first. I failed her, as I failed you." He glanced away as though the memory caused him distress. "It's in my security report."

Seren tried to hide her rising panic. *Hang on to trust by a thread, and the thread frays strand by strand.* "There is no security report in Inka's index. Or anything else."

"You didn't read the file? None of the files?" Tas looked up, and the nav board underlit his face to a demon mask from some ancient theatre.

"There are no files."

"I checked each one. I wrote you readmes and chained note files to intro the reports." His slight frown said he didn't know why she would lie.

Convincing. Almost. "One file said 'Seren read first' but it was empty. I couldn't even view the code." Inka's code had more traps and deceptions than anything she'd ever seen; she'd tried hard enough to unlock it. It would take a powerful artificial intelligence with unlimited time to crack such a complex structure. Inka clearly lived in a realm of extended memory and augmented computation—another Grey freak.

His frown deepened. "Everything was there. You couldn't miss it."

"You told me none of this for a year." Seren's eyes stung. "All you had to do was trust me enough to tell me."

"I trusted you enough to let you find out for yourself."

"You expect me to believe that? I saw the house security record. You stole her Senate files, followed her in, fired into her study. Then—" She steadied her voice. "She lay bleeding."

Tas looked up. "When I came through the lounge, Delun was down and a man was running for the front entrance. I fired but I missed, and he ran outside to a hover. My choice was to take him or help your mother." He closed his eyes. *Not bad acting.*

"Where is she now? And her titanium bead with the senate files?"

"I don't know."

Seren scrubbed tears off her cheeks with the heel of her hand. "You betrayed her. You betrayed Claer."

"No. Delun was my good friend, she was crucial to treaty negotiations, and she was under my protection. I staked my life on Claer. Remember, I warned you not to take this at face value."

"You had no contract to guard my mother. She could never afford to hire an—someone like you." She struggled to keep her language neutral. "Claer was bankrupt, and you Greys wouldn't take our scrip. We melted down half our maglevs to build ships."

Damou shook his head. "Delun thought the Claeran Senate hired me, and the Senate thought she hired me. No one needed to know otherwise."

"A Grey gave away his time?"

"Debt of honour." A shadow of his twisted smile.

"Why?" It came out as a strangled whisper. Damou had to be the only man in a cynical century to soberly invoke a debt of honour.

"You know why." He looked like a hurt friend, not an assassin.

Seren closed her eyes tightly enough to see sparks. Damou said things like that, as though she knew things she couldn't possibly know. She had a sensation of time and space falling away like the walls of a badly made set, leaving their words tumbling in darkness. What would Teak Kuhan do now? His ideal was always to bridge gulfs, find common ground, create calm out of chaos. *Keep talking.*

"What does 'good friend' mean? Were you Mam's lover?"

Damou laughed, damn him. "No."

"I need to know." Her face heated, and he could probably see that right through her ruined cosmod. Why not? He seemed to see through everything else.

"Let's make it easy. I had a difficult affair with an older woman. I was happily married for eight years and separated. Since then, I've had passing encounters and one affair that ended badly. And you." Now he was angry. "I like women, and they used to like me. I hang left. Anything else you need to know?"

Seren was angrier. "No. I didn't need a rundown of your sex life either."

"So, let's talk about yours instead."

Don't do this. Seren sat frozen, helpless to look away.

"When you were very young you fell in love with someone wildly unsuitable, and your mother dreaded you would do something rash. Then he died."

"She told you everything?" *Mam, Mam.* It was unbearable that Damou knew.

"Not his name, though I checked vri stars and artists who'd

died. Later you had an affair in art college. Your fleet pilot probably never knew what hit him. Biron still carries a torch for you. You took a run at me. Miss any?"

Not your business. Vri stars, for gods' sakes. "Why did you check who died?"

"I cared." Damou looked away, giving her the scarred side. He'd developed a new vocabulary of gesture. That one said as clearly as words, *Not any more.*

Seren shoved herself to her feet, and the nav chair slapped her legs as it turned. Leaning at the port screen, she blinked away tears.

"Seren. We're friends. We don't have to do this." He held out his hand.

Unable to speak, she shook her head. If he clasped her hand, she was lost. But he let his hand drop to his knee and got up.

"Stay where you are." In her pocket she released the safety on her palm laser.

His eyes tracked the motion. "Not many people have the balls to hunt a hunter."

Seren held his gaze, chilled by his admission. "I'm under obligation. Admit that you stole Claeran state secrets."

"No sane obligation requires you to kill a friend. At least let's get the right man."

"I have no intention of killing you. I mean to bring you to justice."

"I can't risk sensitive data and take years to be acquitted of a crime I didn't commit." Now he was serious.

Seren drew her laser from her pocket. "Empty your pockets onto the galley counter."

"Seren, this has gone far enough." But he laid out his palm stunner, slate, data fold, and a few smaller items, and backed away with open hands raised.

Seren picked up his stunner and slid it off safety. "Laser?"

"Clipped under the pilot board."

"Sit in the nav chair." She edged toward the pilot chair.

Too quickly even for her to react, he seized her wrist. Seren fired the stunner blind. He convulsed and fell forward against her, driving her back against the bulkhead, and for one drawn breath her arms rose automatically to enclose his remembered warmth. Then she let him drop. He slid down, rolled onto his face on the deck, and lay still.

7

Seren numbly pocketed the weapons and kneeled beside Damou, half expecting him to leap for her throat. Limp. She rolled him over and gasped. His shirt was soaked in blood.

Dead? Tas lay twisted half onto his back with his left arm outflung, eyes open but sightless. Seren straightened him onto his back, closed his eyes, and opened his shirt to feel his chest. Blood seeped from a puncture wound on his chest where a small object still protruded. A shard of bloody glass; something in his pocket had broken and pierced his skin. She pulled it free and found a slow, strong pulse.

Her own heartbeat finally slowed to normal. All she wanted was to lie beside him, hold him close one last time until he woke. Seren checked her chrono; he should stay stunned another quarter-hour, but he would come out of stun raging, and she didn't want to be in reach.

Typically, his bladder had emptied, an indignity Seren recalled all too clearly. She pulled off his boots and rolled him again to strip down the wet clothes and his shorts. A chest pocket held shards of glass or crystal and a palm-sized painting in a clasped frame. Opening it, she looked into the untroubled smile of a younger Seren Qasri with long dark hair curling over her shoulders. She'd been in art college when cousin-friend Griff painted this for Mam.

Tas took your picture, Cedar had told her. Naturally—he'd needed to find her on Arian.

Seren wadded his clothes into the cleaner and found spares in a locker. Unconscious, Damou looked slighter than he did awake, and in repose his fine bone structure showed more clearly. He had the emergent Mitran look, not just his broad brow and straight nose but something about his high cheekbones. A mat of brown hair on his brown chest tapered down to his belly and groin, and through it a puckered ridge ran diagonally from his right shoulder to reappear on his left thigh. There her fingertips found the dimples of old sutures, and the skin looked different on either side. Dark and smooth with glossy body hair on the right, lighter and rougher on the left. Why? Seren pulled out her slate to scan.

On his right side, her slate analyzed titanium-ceramic compounds and carbonglass in Damou's hip and ribs and skull. It identified regenerated bone in his right leg and arm and his left leg below the thigh. Only his left arm and chest scanned as normal bone. Tas Damou was mostly a brilliant, unimaginably detailed reconstruction—or revival. With those injuries, he had probably died and been forced back to life. Lying on a battlefield or in a hospital bed—a multiple amputee, blind, terribly disfigured, sterile—he must have preferred death. Yet he'd kept his sanity and compassion. A tear splashed off her hand onto his arm. Damn him, he got around her defences even unconscious.

Cedar stood on guard, eyes glowing red, as Seren checked his dented slate and equally old data fold. It held unmarked cash cards and a smiling still portrait of a blonde woman and a young girl with golden hair in many small braids. A trespasser there, Seren put aside the fold.

Seren washed him with wetpacs. Nskinned his cut chest. Pulled on clean clothes and boots. Then she rolled him to bind his wrists behind his back with cuffs from his arms locker. She shoved the used wetpacs in the cycler as he started to stir.

"Seren. We need to talk." He sounded quite normal, though his eyes stayed shut. Trust an augmented Grey to stay alert through stun.

"Talk." Seren leaned on the bulkhead and set her slate to

record. "Cedar, guard."

Damou opened his eyes and blinked as though they felt grainy or unfocussed. Golden hazel made an impossibly beautiful colour for the long almond eyes of his ancestry, pale next to his brown skin and red-streaked burn tissue.

"Talk but don't think I'll give anything away, did this in training so many times we swore we'd set on Muda some dark night and drop him in the river till we found out the bastard could swim, just because it stimulates the brain's speech centre I could talk for four minutes, a hundred and forty words a minute, five hundred and sixty words, four hundred to go, should have started counting sooner, can't think about you or I'm fucked, glorious fuck, gorgeous ass—"

Seren nudged him with a foot. So much for the myth that stunned Greys only talked politics. Libido wins every time. Was she this gormless under stun? Unnervingly, he looked completely rational while spouting nonsense. "Talk sense, Damou. Talk about what matters."

"What matters a kid with a handful of wet apples I loved no way to return."

Wet apples? Where did he get that? Then she recalled talking with Maq en route to Walden. Amazing what the unconscious threw together. In the hypnopompic post-stun state, people would say anything that crossed their minds. Love, sex, and apples—it sounded like a senior school play. *Stun talk.* So even Damou took flights of fancy.

"Damou, who are you?"

He said nothing for a while, then resumed in Damotik. *Return a debt a promise.* It flowed past her ear in a sensual stream, but it made no more sense in her slate's translation. *Children die near a mountain of stars and the youngest brings a spear and tree stone and all that she says is music and my heart burns to ash and my words.*

Poem? Song? Then he swore—no mistaking that in any language—and surfaced.

"Seren." Damou focussed on her, tried to sit up, and fell over. She couldn't bear to watch. Cedar growled quietly as Seren knelt to pull him upright. For once he was cold to her touch, and his unscarred cheekbone was bruised. She dragged a cover from his pulldown and wrapped it around his shoulders. If he went into some Grey-augment shock reaction, he could die.

"Seren. Nolin's death list. He wants me to kill you. Run."

Another stun fantasy? Seren had other things to fear than Pact mandarins. "I can't run. I need to find Mam and bring Parvin her atrocities data. And Parvin's son died in the Dinan fire with Rozenn's daughter. Pedr's my brother-friend, Lezig's my cousin-friend."

Damou was silent a moment, eyes closed. "Fools. They just started the next war." His eyes opened on Seren. "What work have you done for Parvin?"

"Nothing." This was the time to say she'd found a bead, a gold Mitran high-security oval, but she now had no good reason to trust Damou any more than she trusted Parvin.

"Leave now. Come with me to a safe place."

"No more rescues." Still trying to protect her—he claimed. Seren stood up. "Meistr Damou, you are under investigation for the theft of Claeran state secrets."

Damou lay still, contained. If she freed him, he would go for her throat. A dangerous man. Crazy to have ever gotten involved with him, and worse to take him captive here, with no backup and no way out. Probably she should stun him again. Instead—what would he do if she agreed? *Let's run for Grey space, disappear together.* She clenched her hands safely behind her back.

Seren got him on his feet, leaning heavily on her, and restrained him in the nav chair before she dropped into the pilot's chair. The main board came to life at her palmprint, so he'd left her ID active. She gestured for her restraints. "Cedar, take hold for lift."

The Az hovered straight up for two thousand metres and burned. In a few minutes the aft cams showed her an arc of the Claeran atmosphere glowing above her planet's clouded curve. She would set a heading for Tirion port, call on Parvin to have him taken into custody.

"Not Tirion. I can explain," Damou said. "Go to stealth. Pact defence will target us without my override."

At last, an explanation. "Tell me the override code."

"Not with humanity's survival at stake." He looked calm for a man making a wild claim.

Seren studied him a long time and, risking everything on his word, told the Az, "Stealth."

Somewhere quiet to talk . . . she burned higher into low orbit and slipstreamed a communications satellite swarm. The ship approached at a velocity that felt like a slow drift until it backburned for braking. In visual range the displays showed comm arrays on stark carbonglass platforms, almost invisible against the night until Claer's distant sun silhouetted their skeletal shapes. There was even a new platform in nanoconstruction waiting for elevator cable and gondolas. Not weapons. Mitran tech. Claer had been building new orbitals with Mitran help, probably late in the war.

"Free my hands."

Seren flipped his stunner off safety. Was she crazy to do it? She couldn't ask Teak; the avatar glitched out when Tas was present. His augments must jam the signal. "Do I have your parole?"

"Yes."

Somehow, she still trusted him that much. She pulled Damou forward and opened his cuffs. He didn't go for her throat, only rubbed his wrists where she'd been careful not to abrade the skin. She kept an eye on him as he felt his empty pocket for his slate. Seren fetched the small heap of his possessions from the galley counter.

While he searched his slate, she scrolled her own slate back through his stun transcript. Even under stun he was evasive.

Damou turned his slate to show her an index. He told it, "Open 'Seren readme first.'"

The note that scrolled up listed files and suggested a reading order. One by one he opened files and closed them. Then he said, "Play images from Gwernant entrance security cam."

A high view from the dining room showed Mam walking toward her study. Something moved ahead of her, and a laser's red tracer streak sparked near her desk. Mam put her hands to her throat, leaking bright blood. As she fell to her knees, Damou ran in, firing through the open front doorway at a pale green blur across the cam's peripheral pickup. The assassin.

Seren covered her mouth, sick. Damou was still running across the summer kitchen when Mam was shot. He didn't shoot her. He couldn't have shot her. Seren had stunned and captured an innocent man.

"Who was he?"

"Professional job. Only your mother entered the house that day, according to the security log. My own entries and my backup's were stealthed. The real question is why. Delun made enemies—she wrote tough Mitran restitution terms that tangled the Pact in legal claims, and her peace offer enraged the globalists. One of the factions may have put a price on her head."

"Why did you set the explosive and blow the house?"

"The Ntex was already in place. I didn't take time to disable it. I got Delun out."

Seren tapped his screen. "How can these files show on your slate and not mine?"

Damou held out a hand for her slate. Could she have screwed up her commands? Children could access data files before they could walk. But when he called up an index, he found no more than she had. The "Seren readme first" file was empty. Not a screw-up. Not her imagination. They looked up together, close enough that his breath warmed her cheek.

"Bitch," she said. "Sorry. I know she's your friend."

Damou gave her one of his unreadable looks and spoke a comm code.

Inka appeared within seconds on the virtual nav screen, a lovely dark woman in a dress that perfectly matched her blue eyes. She sat in the barred shade of a grape arbour near a house with amber clay walls. The countryside beyond the gate was subtly different from Izu's. Mitra? In a warm voice, Inka said something Seren couldn't understand.

"Your files give us trouble," Damou said in his blunt Damotik, slowly enough for Seren to follow. "Do what you know is right. It's all that I have asked of you all these years. What locks the files, an invisible-archive routine keyed to her ID? Qasri needs to know."

"Taso, she's dangerous."

"We are lovers," Tas said. "If you cut her, I bleed."

Seren met Inka's gaze on the screen. Beautiful eyes, cruel mouth.

"So, he told you." Inka smiled slowly. "Not what you wanted

after all this time?"

"Everything I wanted."

Inka studied her for a long second, no doubt analyzing her pulse and irises for the truth.

"Code book 2742 process 19 inverted. Fleet ID, thumbprint, and eyescan in sequence. Harm him and you answer to me."

"No! You answer to me!" Seren flung back. "You have a world's power at your command, but you have no wisdom or kindness or even an animal's good sense. Your evil game nearly got him killed. Without those files, to all appearances he was a murderer. Mess with our lives again and I'll burn you to the ground."

She'd lost her mind, threatening Inka. To prove it, her slate gave her hand a shocking jolt, and Seren dropped it on the board. Damou moved inside cam pickup range to stand behind her with a hand resting lightly on her shoulder, and her heart leaped to his touch. Inka looked at them for a moment, and the screen swirled and blinked out.

Seren dropped her face into her hands and managed to hold back the flood. Tas held her shoulders lightly between his two hands as though she might shatter, but she shrank away into her own solitude.

"Your files should open now," he said after a long silence, and settled into the nav chair. "I'll take us down."

Tas flew the Az westward in a long curve over Tariqa, passing over the hemisphere of daylight and back into Bryniau's night. He set them down gently in a Hafn meadow in sight of Derw Sanctuary. Two overarmed Pact troopers jogged over from their post, recognized the ship, and retreated. He ran his checks methodically despite the hard tremor in his hands, shut down the systems one by one, and opened the hatch.

Seren couldn't look at him. "Tas—" Words fled her. "—I could have killed you."

"Yes."

"I betrayed your trust. I betrayed my honour." By choosing violence she'd even betrayed her memory of Teak Kuhan. She watched his profile reflected in the side viewscreen. Their eyes met in the reflection and moved on.

"Worry about things you can change. Who am I to condemn one mistake? Every life that I cost, I carry forever." Tas offered a hand. "Seren, come Outside with me."

"No." There was no going back, and she didn't know the way forward. Loving a dead man half her lifetime, she'd never had to think what to say to a living man. She closed her eyes, wrestled with her regret, and finally mustered the strength to say what she needed. Reached blindly for his hand. "You know I want to go with you. But I can't leave till I make this right."

No answer, and he didn't take her hand. She was alone in the empty Az, and cold fresh air blew in through the hatch.

Seren went out into the night. Cedar sat waiting on the grass, but there was no sign of Damou. She slung her duffel over her shoulder and started toward the trees.

8

ES2742.086

Abandoning sleep as a lost cause, Tas paced Claer Arian's high ringway, pausing at a spin-corrected viewport from long habit to look for Mitra's yellow prime star. Farther around the ring, the high-hub docks clattered into third shift.

His station clearance was on hold again, so he'd unlatched his pulldown bunk in the Az to rest. Memory ambushed him as soon as he closed his eyes. *Seren.* It used to be Tanna that stood mutely between him and sleep—mutely because his eardrums split as he went down in Piñar's fire and ruin, leaving him with images of hell as a strangely silent place.

Now she'd gone invisible again. Reporting the Kalevala survivors at search HQ, planning their recovery mission, dealing with Inka and Riordan, he'd checked her location every hour. Her comm bracelet showed Derw, but she was off-grid.

Arian had been on the skids for years, and now it was a place where sensible people took armed backup. Tas walked the station, walked the perimeter. Eventually he walked into a low-hub sector that Seren Qasri would never have seen, perhaps never knew existed. Once he knew it well. He passed grimy spacer bars and tired hostels that glared raw colours and blared raucous music all the wearier for its blatancy.

In a noisy, fight-prone pit he'd avoided for the last year, he punched in his order. A woman whose name he almost remembered came to lean beside him, giving him the full view of perfect breasts and a flawless new face.

"Company, Taso?"

"Spoken for," he told her, which was a damned pathetic lie.

"Another time." She gave him a wise look and left.

Akvavit topped by a few clouds of glitz would solve all his problems, and scoring glitz on Arian was so easy it should be a proverb. But he'd lost his gift of self-destruction. He gazed into the oily-looking clear liquid and cursed his delusions.

Tas cycled his akvavit and turned off his comm, knowing Seren wouldn't call. Then he turned it on again, just in case. *Fool.* Damou was the last man she'd listen to now. Pity he couldn't bring back Kuhan, an even bigger fool. It was unsettling how often she quoted a man everyone else had mercifully forgotten.

In Tirion he'd wrapped himself in his rejection when he should have stayed and talked her through her shock. By the time he'd found the courage to go back, she was gone. In postwar Tirion she could easily come to harm, even with her cat on guard, so he'd hovered the Az at the horizon until she reached her sanctuary. When she walked under Derw's livewood gates without a backward glance, loss shook him to his bones.

Tas checked his chrono—mid-morning in Bryniau—and activated a privacy cone to call Parvin Kerkallec.

"What do you want, Damou?" Parvin's small image scowled from his slate screen; her head was shaved in mourning for her son.

"Seren Qasri. Her life's in danger."

"Less danger if you leave her alone." These days Parvin had no time for Greys.

"I'm under obligation."

"Tell whoever hired you that she's ours. I know your game, Damou. Stay out of Pol space."

His screen blanked. Parvin had grasped his lesson on concise communication when he trained her years ago—not that she would know him now—but she'd forgotten his advice to keep talking.

Time to move on. No transport jobs here worth the trouble—even hazmat runs drew ex-Pol fleet pilots willing to work for meals and a futon in the hangar dome. He had no reason to stay, every reason to leave. Soon.

Long after midnight, walking alone and grittily sober on the high-hub deep space docks, Tas abandoned his resolve not to call Seren. Cupping her miniature in his palm, he tapped her locator code. *Careful.* He often spoke too bluntly, but now he desperately wanted to tell her . . . Once again, he had failed in wisdom and justice, in all the virtues. At Derw he could have waited to hear her out, not walked away in anger. But no familiar lilt of Tavod answered her comm.

Inka called as he retracted the Az boarding tube for drift, but he couldn't face her now. Tas let her message record, then listened. "Maq Flett relayed a message from Qasri. Please leave her alone." Inka couldn't be trusted; was she meddling again? He'd find out after he finished Nolin's removal on Ojin. At least he'd have time to find the right words.

Two days later, as the Az dropped from orbit, Tas saw a world that bled fire from every crater. This had to be humanity's least welcoming landfall; only a performance artist could love Ojin. Nolin's contract gave him an excuse to visit the Politaya's most extreme environment.

Domed green Ojin City floated, mould in a petri dish, on a relatively stable landmass near the south pole. It was a luxury to be a passenger, looking over the shoulders of Kai in the pilot chair and Sunny on nav.

Ojin people and their architectures were equally dramatic. But Tas didn't wear the gaudy wings and trains and capes that floated across the concourse and walkways. In the spaceport he drew stares in his rarely worn uniform. *Good. Take note. Remember it.*

The relocation centre occupied a former civic art gallery, a typical Pact efficiency: use the waste space to house suspected subversives on their way to unspecified destinations. Many of Ojin's supposed subversives came from the rich and influential arts community, but the irony of their prison probably escaped their jailers.

Ojin's most famous sculptor greeted him at the door of her improvised workshop in the gallery kitchen. Her big hands were splashed and caked from shaping a maquette, and she wore a blue apron with pockets full of her clay and stone tools. Tas had viewed her planned new piece as he burned insystem, a twisted multi-focal tableau of Politayan agony. In a century the small clay model would probably be a cherished museum piece. He nodded dismissal to the guard.

"Neiti Akiko Sigridsdottir? I've come to take you offworld." He handed her a data card that flashed the logo of the Pact of Human Worlds ministry of relocation.

Unexpectedly she found a faint smile. "I always wondered what death looked like. Now I know. You are an extremely ugly Valkyrie."

"Neiti Sigridsdottir, I need to scan your hands and your three favourite sculpting tools. Then we will leave quickly."

"No." She stood her ground calmly, a big-shouldered woman past her physical prime and trembling with illness or hunger. "Do what you have to do here. I've said everything I can say, and your presence here tells me I've been heard. I'm ready."

"Neiti, your hands and your tools. Your future depends on it. I can't promise you immortality, only a productive life."

"No one told me death was a joker." She sounded uncertain now. "Or a Mikkeli-Mitra star man. Your accent is deeply archaic, captain."

"Neiti. We have seven minutes." Tas set his slate to record.

Akiko Sigridsdottir searched her assassin's face for nearly one of those minutes, then slowly reached into her pocket and held up a handful of her sculpting tools.

9

ES2742.103

Wide shot, pan. Beyond the dry ridges of Tariqa in blazing afternoon sunlight, Seren's maglev pod dropped its last passengers in the scattered eastern villages of the Rumi flatlands. She rode alone to the end of the line and walked on through irrigated fields to find another farm, another place where she could work without an identity, then eat and sleep. She spent her nights searching her files or making short vris that she posted to *Singularity*. There must be some way to find Mam and her missing data.

Seren was not the only fugitive from the occupation, she discovered in hidden camps and unlisted hostels. On warm nights she slept out on streambanks or field margins while Cedar sat on watch, never staying in one place more than a few days, always moving on. Farmers paid in food and shelter or unmarked cash cards; she pitched hay outside Rumi and picked strawberries near Tel. Twice she suspected someone followed her, but she kept to herself and guarded her slate with her Mitran security code.

One day walking to the fields she invoked her aide, almost invisible in the sunshine.

<> Teak, how do I compile a vri doc from a few fragments? <>
<> Other people will give you their ideas and images if you

304

ask, Seren. <>

Sometimes she recorded people in the northern-hemisphere towns, asking them about the war and the occupation. Her clips were full of people looking over her shoulder and offering ideas, then ending up on cam to act out their suggestions for her vri doc *Return*. A working title only; it didn't convey the desolation of coming home to ruins and empty streets, fearful old people and children who watched from hard eyes. Seren experimented with her opening sequence of tattered cellusheet, chosen that day at Derw—she'd never kept her Derw neuro appointment, having spilled far too much to Parvin. At two Tariqa sanctuaries, hoping for a meal as much as a neuro clinic to dispel the last of her memory block, she'd found ash and charred timbers and broken doors creaking in a dryland wind.

Twice she heard rumours about Mam, but nothing new; most people thought she'd died in the invasion. She reread Inka's files, trying to make sense of year-old events. Damou could explain the files, but Damou wasn't answering her calls. Inka's doing? She would give it a while longer, then try to reach him another way.

Hedgerows and streambank willows bordered the shimmering wheat fields that she passed after the berry harvest. Released from the duffel, Cedar bounded off into the cornflowers and tall grass, always happiest outdoors. Seren played ambush with her, both of them instinctively also watching and listening for real trouble. Soon she'd find work offworld, but for now it was good to walk among green growing things and breathe air that smelled of grass and trees and the slow-flowing stream—air that hadn't passed through a cycler a thousand times.

Claer's soil showed rich brown on the fused-earth path and between the rows of rust-resistant, nutrient-adapted durum wheat, bright tender green at the last-leaf stage. Walking south along the field margins, Seren retracted her pants to shorts, absorbed her shirt sleeves and told her new UV slow-release implant to protect her skin. Cedar leaped after an unsect gliding on its leathery leg-frills, but gave it up and loped back. In the nearest field, an autosprayer hovered at the end of a row, nozzles still dripping, then turned with a hush of compressed air and started down the next row. That was the only sound, apart from the light breeze stirring the willows and poplars.

Seren raised her palm cam to fill more gaps in her stock. Panned a few seconds across the green farm fields and went wide on the vast bowl of cloud-streaked deep blue sky. Pulled back to the distant skyline. She sat on a disused wellhead to file the sequences in her *Return* index; soon she'd have enough for her vri doc. It would be patchy, but she needed to post it and keep working on it as material came in. Download a few more public records, select some Bight sequences, narrate over her images, speculate to-camera on their significance. Then she needed to book a vri production studio for a tenday. Somehow.

Information was scarce. Pawel and Yan were dead, like her pilot and one of the ratings; they could give her no information. But the rest? In the warm afternoon light that made everything seem real and reasonable, with Cedar patiently curled at her feet, she listed everyone she could remember from Gandhi Base and grid-searched the small shutdown crew. By the time the autosprayer had finished another three rows, she'd traced almost everyone.

Unnerved, Seren checked again. Since they intercepted the Mitran courier in the Bight, fifteen of seventeen people on Gandhi had died. Suicide. Natural causes. Accidents—far too many accidents. She was the sixteenth. Who was the seventeenth? Mihal might know, if he'd kept his Gandhi sickbay records. Damou could probably tell her, too, if he ever returned her calls.

On higher ground something glittered among the poplars. As she walked closer, she saw a small private spacecraft, a rare sight these days; not many people could afford Claer's exorbitant surface landing permit.

A small brown man leaned on the ramp, and a restless creature ran across his shoulders and jumped down to greet her. Seren searched the hatch behind Maq Flett, but there was no sign of his Grey shadow.

"Happy Seren!" The mongoose ran back and forth, chirring.

"Hasi!"

Cedar growled and bared her diamond fangs. Her spine fur spiked and her tufted ears lay flat. Seren stroked her guardian. "Friends, sweet. Don't be scary."

Hasi bounded to Cedar's feet, sniffed and leaped back at her dry hiss. Seren found a grassy patch and sat cross-legged for Hasi to climb onto her shoulder and nuzzle her ear. Cedar's guard programs kicked in, and she crouched to keep a close watch on them both.

"What in hell are you doing out here?" Maq crouched beside her with a grunt. "I haven't had to squat on the ground in a hundred years."

Seren shook cat hair off her folded jacket and told it to inflate. "Take it or leave it."

"Thanks, Green. Want a ride?"

"Don't get into the rescue business, it's overcrowded."

"What's to eat?" Maq settled himself gingerly.

Seren rummaged in her thigh pocket for a fruit bar and Cedar's protein tub.

Maq eyed them with distrust. "Let's go zap a steak."

"Barbaric."

A few minutes later she chewed a rib at the pull-down table in his luxurious new ship while Cedar ate grilled lobster at her feet. Hasi crouched on the cat's back nibbling a nut bar. Best friends.

"Ready to come back to Melusine?"

Seren shook her head. "I need to find Mam. My cousin-friend was taking her to safety when he was shot down and killed. She disappeared, and so did her crucial Senate files on Pact war crimes. Her sister-friend in the resistance took me prisoner, partly to drag in Damou."

Maq made a silent whistle. "But they didn't get either of you."

"I ran, made myself invisible. Now I record all I can, talk to people, make vri, post it for comment. Maybe Mam will see it and call me."

"They'll track you. Better stick with me."

"No. Thanks. I need to put together my vri. Are you en route from AnvilCo?"

Maq gave her a bluff smile, warning her to expect evasion. "As it happens, AnvilCo's now in high orbit around Rustam."

"Grey space?"

"Pol's a mess, and the Pact's looking dicey, Green. Protest movements are getting noisy even on Walden. Students, tox, religious groups, human rights people, labour, manimals. Soon there'll be hell to pay."

Seren shivered, recalling her manimal encounters at Gwernant. "How soon?"

Maq flipped a blue lahal stick end over end before he decided to tell her. "Not that long. Four days ago, the tox nanoglopped the new Pamir Treaty Tower."

"It's easier to spray glop than retake a world."

"Damou trains them between other jobs."

"Dangerous." Her pulse leaped, and she wanted to seize Maq's arm and demand news. *Is he all right? Is he angry? Did he mention me?* Instead, she managed to breathe steadily.

"Ayuh, dangerous in all the right ways." Maq held the stick between two fingertips and gazed into its clear blue light. "But I don't like him working for Nolin. Inka blackjacked him."

Seren looked closer at the lahal stick. Gem-grade bevel-cut Matane blue beryl. These days someone would cut his throat for that if he flashed it in a Tirion bar.

"The Pact's holding all the sticks this time, Maq." She'd failed to convince Parvin of it, but Maq was a realist.

"Ayuh. But let me tell you some history, kid. History is about predators. The peaceable and civilized and poor get cut out of the pack and eaten alive. I saw it on Sitkum and Vanuatu and Mitra. You wouldn't like to see it on Claer. That's why you need to fight the bastards."

Unexpected. Now even the realists foresaw a new conflict.

Maq pulled more sticks from a drawer: iridium, ivory, gold, and emerald, a handful more.

Seren shook her head. "No lahal. Not this time. I'm broke. On the run. Dead."

"You look all right." Maq's small brown eyes held steady on her. "Better than Damou."

Seren kept her eyes on the sticks, wavering as her vision blurred. "How did you hear?"

"Hell, I hear everything. You two are a matched set. Not many people need a daily novena in duplicate to Saint Jude."

"You could have told me more." Seren gathered herself to leave.

"Tas asks me to keep quiet, I take a vow of silence. Tas asks me to walk on water, which he does ask pretty often, I step right out. Love the man. Too bad you don't—" he finished awkwardly,

"—know a good thing when you see it."

"Stay away from him, you said." A lump was forming in her throat. If Tas had cared enough, he'd have told her everything—but then no one could predict Inka.

"Standard disclaimer. I kind of hoped you'd tangle him in your pretty hair, keep him off his crazy jobs for Nolin. He's used up more lives than a cat on glitz. Sorry, Cedar." The cat twined purring around his legs. *Traitor.*

Seren kept quiet, too heartsick to hear any more. Cedar jumped in her lap to lick her face.

"Ah hell." Maq handed her a linen napkin.

A small fortune in lahal sticks still lay on the table among the plates. She picked up two sapphire sticks and shuffled them under the table till the plain stick was in her right hand. When she nodded, he pointed left.

"You cheat, Maq." She held up the banded stick.

"Never." He fished in a shirt pocket. "Guess you need cash cards more than sapphires."

Seren took the cards without argument; twenty low-denomination cards would keep her alive a few tendays. Then—she didn't mean to say anything, it just slipped out. "I miss him."

Maq folded his hands, deadpan. "Did I ever tell you how I met Damou?"

"No." She leaned forward, ready to hear anything about Tas.

"Few years ago, I was bored crazy, obscenely rich, tired of the ladies, refusing rejuv, and I hired in a new bodyguard. The Mitrans sent a disgraced officer with detox shakes. Being Tas, he was drying himself out instead of taking an antox spray. Three times I asked him, 'You always do things the hard way?' Finally, I got an answer. 'The hard way works. Take hold and make yourself useful. Do what needs to be done.' I guess we rescued each other."

"I don't need to be rescued."

"So you say. That's what he does. Besides, you rescued him first."

What did he mean? Maybe her stunt to divert pheromone sniffers. "It was all I could do."

"Ayuh." Maq looked satisfied.

Seren studied him, waiting for the payload.

"Here's what I told him a couple days back. *Halo tumtum.* Life hurts. Put it behind you and go do some good."

Seren wiped her face and stood up as Cedar bolted down a last chunk of lobster.

"Not so fast, Green. Save humanity tomorrow. Damou asked me to show you a place." Maq tossed the meal remnants into his cycler and told the table to fold. "Want to fly?"

Maq's newest SenAer runabout was as heavily automated as a drone probe, so flying mostly meant admiring the view. Their heading took them nowhere near Tirion, the destination she expected, but all the way south into a glowing celestial night that would not lighten till spring when Claer's sun swung south again. The small ice pack glittered in the distance when she descended to a thousand metres to overfly a long narrow archipelago of reefs and islands.

"What's that?" Seren pointed below at the largest island, where snow or hoarfrost dusted a series of dark rectangular shapes.

"Research base, abandoned during the war." Maq didn't bother to look, tapping coordinates into his nav board.

Not the pole, but close. Seren's pilot board showed S87 as they began their descent. Height above ground was hard to judge visually, but soon the maglev strut pads deployed and the ship touched down gently. Maq pulled two thermal coats from a locker and dropped the ramp. Cedar took one look outside at frost sparkling on rock and gravel, sniffed the cold air carefully, and curled up under a chair with Hasi. Off duty.

"Bring your cam, Green." Maq walked down the ramp.

Seren walked down onto the surface and swayed dizzily when she looked up into the great bowl of Claeran night. The familiar southern constellations spanned horizon to horizon, and starlight cast the ship's shadow dark across the frosted ground. She pulled out her palm cam and panned great sweeping starscapes. Wonderful. But had they come all the way to the polar region for a beautiful sky?

Maq nudged her elbow to turn her east. "Close your eyes. Let them adjust. Now look."

A line of stones led away from the ship, picked out by a light dusting of snow. Not stones. Stone. Claer's bedrock rose here to pierce the fine gravel in sinuous ridges a handspan high that curved and twisted as far as she could see, moulded like soft clay. In places the ridges came within a few metres of each other, but there were also open spaces many metres across. It looked like traces of some gigantic creature's shell casing, a cross-section through one of old Earth's primordial sea creatures, an ammonite or trilobite. Starlight picked out ridges that stretched a hundred metres or more in great waves and arabesques that never joined and never ended. An installation artwork at the end of the world.

"It's wonderful. What is it? Who made it?"

"I brought you here to ask that exact same thing."

Seren turned to see the joke, but he watched her carefully. "It's too big to tell."

Maq spoke a command and rotated a vri image above his open palm, a delicate tracery of silver on deep green for contrast. It still looked exotically ancient and marine, perhaps because of the flowing lines that fanned out and branched both upward and downward from a central stalk.

"Ganglia in the human nervous system?" she suggested.

Maq shook his head. "Not a close match."

"Some substance secreted by animals."

"Same composition as the bedrock."

"An electrical circuit? A tree of spreading branches and roots. Coral. Shattered glass." She kept trying. "Watersheds divided by a mountain ridge. Static electricity. Fork lightning."

"Heya. No one else suggested glass." He spoke to his hand in an unknown language.

"I give up," she shrugged, though other images nagged at her awareness. Something she'd seen recently. "Natural or created? You can tell me that at least."

"Nope. Sorry."

Seren turned to look at him. A small wind rose from nowhere and wandered over the barren landscape. Nothing for hundreds of kilometres but the pattern of ridges. The air was cool, clear and absolutely silent, and she felt a lightness of time and absence. "Why not?"

"No one knows. There's another near your north pole."

"Identical?"

"Similar. Different climate, different erosion pattern."

"Veins in the eye of heaven."

"Good one. Damou was right. We never thought to bring a poet."

"Who else knows about this?" Seren sat cross-legged between ridges, and got up again quickly as the cold burned her calves. Cold pried inside the heated coat, and her bare hand felt like glass that would snap if she touched anything solid.

"Damou. Scientists. A couple heads of state. Early survey crews. In the settlement era they covered up the images for a century or so. It's still heavy-duty classified."

"What do you think it is?"

"Biologists think it's a natural formation created by some force we don't understand."

"But if it's not natural?"

"Settlement-era antiquarians liked to copy old Earth monuments."

Why build a replica and cover it up? Seren studied the pattern. "It's not like a living tree. Real trees lose branches or grow toward sunlight. They never grow in perfect fractal patterns."

"Not bad." He turned to the ship. "Want a job? Comes with a vri studio."

Tempting. She opened her mouth to accept, but it would take her away from her research, and she was doing all right producing vri in pickers' sheds and hostels. "Sorry, I'm booked."

Shoving her hands inside her sleeves, she followed Maq back to the ship.

10

At closing time Mihal's nightmare sauntered down the ringway into Claer Arian's best medical clinic. Mihal ducked back inside his private door, but there was no safety.

Reception called moments later. "A man to see you. Not a patient."

A curse and a punishment, rather. Mihal leaned against his closed door and found his voice. "Send him in, Lise."

"You know better than to come here," he said when Revo lounged in his office doorway. He wore clothes that should look more elegant, given the amount they must cost. Today his black bioleather had silver facings and silver clasps, a combination that jarred with his pale freckled skin and auburn hair. Last time he'd been blond. "This is not—"

"Rest it, Mihal. Mind if I call you Mihal?" He smirked over his folded arms.

"Yes."

"Watch your step, Mihal. Pretty lady out there wouldn't like your secrets." Revo conducted his sordid business like a schoolyard bully.

"Don't threaten me. There are others who can keep you in line." Another Grey might help him break free. The hideous security specialist he'd met last year, vexing as he was, came from a different mould than this coarse brute.

"Careful. You might hire a skin-walker. What we buried on Tanna didn't stay buried."

What nonsense was that? Mihal turned to his desk, and to hide his trembling hands, picked up a transtylus he didn't need. "Tell me what you want. Then go."

"What you want is the question."

"Quickly. I have people waiting."

"No, you don't." Revo handed him a graphic tearoff. Clammy hands; of course, the man was a spinner. A grainy still showed a dark-skinned woman and man in workers' clothing embracing near the ramp of a small spacecraft. The wind streamed the woman's long, straight dark hair. The camera angle obscured the man's face, but he wore a narrow metal bracelet on his wrist. Mihal shrugged and dropped it on his desk.

"Sad. After all that effort to trace your sweetheart."

Mihal grabbed the tearoff again and stared. Seren Qasri? This woman was darker than Seren and thinner—but she had the height, and there was something about the way she carried her head. Anger flickered up, and a sting of envy. She had spurned Mihal but seduced some common spaceport worker.

"A long time ago, yes." No need to let Revo know how much he still wanted her.

Revo smiled and stood away from the door frame, balancing on his feet like a wrestler looking for his hold. "Leave a cash card for ten thousand with the pretty lady out front this time tomorrow." Revo smiled slowly. "Or we'll have no further need of your data, Mihal, and no Pact fleet movements to tell you in return."

Then the doorway was empty, and tuneless whistling floated faintly back through the clinic. Mihal stared numbly at a blank wall for an unknown time until he stumbled to a chair. *Seren.* Outside his spin-corrected window, the home stars of Claer silently sailed past. There was no help to be found in a cold universe.

All he'd ever wanted, once defeat became inevitable, was an honourable peace. Instead, the Politaya was cruelly enslaved, and his efforts brought only destruction. For the past year, as Revo came and went with chilling demands and insinuations, his life had been in ruins.

Driving off the Pact would take more than the illegal arms depots in Arian's abandoned lower ring and the downworld supply caches in desert or barren tundra. But the family merchanters and decommissioned fleet ships, secretly rearmed and travelling dark orbits, those held a certain promise.

Mihal called up a space atlas, and when the vri rotated slowly above his desk, he studied his fleet. Cruisers and dreadnoughts, mostly working in Pact space now the Pol fleet was no longer a threat. Frigates and destroyers and transports, scattered through Claer system's rock belt. Small craft, working in Claer orbit or from the three stations.

Downworld, the occupation troops were slack and careless, now that fool Kerkallec had forbidden direct action, and the Pact fleet was even slacker. A few Pact ships clustered at Czarne Station, orbiting the smallest moon of an outer gas giant, but one might send them on a false alarm. It would be poetic justice to fabricate a threat in the Wairoa Cloud's flattened ring of primordial planetesimals. If he gave the word now, his ships could be ready in two tendays.

An incoming craft drew his attention back to the window. A scarred old Azande burned in steep and hard. A few Az conversions were in service around Claer system, but their small holds and powerful drives didn't adapt well. This one still carried faded military colours: MitraCorps/Spartí. It was bound not for the military docks but for this level's emergency bay.

His slate buzzed as he leaned for a closer look. Lise said, "Incoming priority."

Serious. MitraCorps usually handled its own sick and injured. Mihal was out the door at a run, cursing secretive Mitrans who didn't see fit to advise whether they had disaster survivors or amputations or plague. Even now the Greys went where they chose and did what they wanted.

By the time he got to the emergency bay, the stubby Az was nosed in. At the membrane the Pact guard stood red-faced with fists on hips, bristling as a Spartí officer gave him orders. A tall man with severe facial damage; he had turned up like a summoned demon. *Damou.*

Lise had a patient strapped on a gurney and was scanning vital signs. The woman looked unconscious, but she opened bright blue eyes and made an effort to smile at Mihal when he took her rawboned wrist. Middle-aged, fair-skinned, and blonde, but by the way her skin hung loose she had once been more substantial.

To Mihal's annoyance the three armed Mitrans stayed close. The woman with spiked brown hair briefed Lise, the dark man took notes, and the man with a blond braid stood guard. Damou finished telling the Pacter his business and turned to Mihal.

The woman's liver infection resisted standard antibiotics, Damou said as they floated the gurney into the surgery. The bacteria hadn't matched any grid scan, so they'd brought her here instead of waiting till Rustam.

Good judgment, Mihal reluctantly admitted. "We'll fab a spray that could neutralize a plague lab and observe her for a shift. Where has she been, this woman?"

Damou hesitated only an instant. "Ojin."

Mihal masked his reaction. The Pact had recently tightened its occupation on Ojin and imprisoned the renowned sculptor Akiko Sigridsdottir as a dissident. He'd bought three of her monumental pieces a few years ago and met her at a gallery opening. "Her name?"

"Maria Schmidt." Damou looked him in the eye, daring him to say otherwise.

Mihal repeated it to his implant. If Damou wanted to draw Pact fire for some deception, it was his affair. He gridded *Xenobacteriology, hostile, Ojin* and loaded the codes into the surgery's fabricator. Lise filled a hypospray with the antibiotic cocktail and triple-dosed the woman. Then he told Lise to put her on a nutrient pac and went to zap his hands. When he returned, Damou leaned against the emergency bay wall, arms folded, listening thoughtfully to the Reprisien chamber group Mihal favoured. Portrait of a primitive encountering culture.

Damou's three subordinates reboarded to move their ship to the hub docks, working smoothly and needing no orders. Closer than family, survivors of the Mitran diaspora. Mihal turned to Damou, who had been studying him impassively. The man gave him a chill, with his watchful air and the sickening damage to his face.

"Dinner? The market has fresh prawns." The Mitran could eat

energy tabs on his ship for all Mihal cared, but this might be an opportunity.

"No," Damou said. "Thanks."

"I have Anansi rice and fresh shiitake mushrooms at my flat," Mihal tried again.

Damou gave him a long glacial frown as though he'd proposed a wild evening of glitz and virtual senselink. "Why?"

Subtlety was wasted on this man. Let him taste the unvarnished truth. "So, I can ask you everything you know about Ojin, MitraCorps, and any Pact news, and you can tell me what I already know."

Surprisingly it made the Mitran laugh. "Thanks."

"My pleasure," Mihal said, though it would be anything but. "Melyn 412 in an hour."

An hour later, cuisine still occupied his thoughts. Shiitake from the Claer Arian farms were rubbery, something to do with the artificial soils, but Mihal coaxed them to succulence in a light curry, saffroned the rice, and sautéed a macédoine of fresh vegetables. His professional-quality food fab could do this superbly, but he enjoyed the slow demands of natural food.

Recognizing the sculptor gave him leverage on Damou, Mihal realized with a small frisson, so the evening would not be a complete waste. Mihal set out two wine glasses. This was not an occasion for Lise's company, and he could not invite a second woman to meet such a questionable man. Then Damou palmed his door, still damp-haired from a shower.

Over dinner Mihal wondered how to broach his subject. *Seen Seren Qasri lately?* wouldn't get him far. He needn't have worried. Damou talked easily over his meal and thanked him courteously afterward. The man was sombre, but washed and combed and wearing well-made daywear—the jacket was handloomed linen in the grey-green of West Sea storm waters— he made an acceptable guest. Easy to forget what he was, if his ruined face was turned away. Damou would have fascinated Seren, always irresistibly drawn to the dangerous and outlandish.

Finally, their conversation stumbled. Damou looked silently out through the apartment's big spin-corrected window, out beyond the glow of Arian's nav beacons toward the shimmering galactic core. Somewhere in that direction lay Mitra.

As the bots cleared the table, Damou spoke quietly without turning. "I need your medical advice."

"Certainly." *Good.* Mihal could ask his own questions soon. He fetched glasses and poured his second oldest calvados. So, at last Damou wanted advice on his face. It's quick and painless, Mihal could honestly say, and you can stop frightening strangers. He'd tried not to stare, but it made his hands restless to think how easily one could laser out the scar tissue and lay in a cultured graft.

"A colleague is in trouble," Damou said.

"How can I help?" Mihal thought, a colleague with half a face? But Damou startled him.

"She was badly injured in an accident."

An invisible hand squeezed the breath from Mihal's chest, and he set down his glass hard enough to spill the calva. *Seren.* He'd never imagined her maimed, disfigured, clinging to life.

Damou took in his shocked face. "It happened years ago on Mitra."

Not Seren. Mihal listened dazedly to his story of the woman's terrible injuries when a pod crashed from the Nueva Chiapas elevator in Mitra's last days. "Impossible. No one could survive that damage. Or want to survive."

Damou coldly itemized the treatments. Vat-grown skin, hand-laid silk-lattice bone regeneration, many transplants, brain reconstruction. Desperate to save a brilliant scientist, Mitran surgeons had used incomplete experimental techniques, ancient remedies, anything they could muster. Some had taken, some had failed. Now an important leader of Mitra in exile survived with life support and a powerful neural link.

"Is she failing?"

"Her judgment fails."

A brilliant scientist with a powerful neural link—Mihal froze. This could be the client Revo mentioned. Why did Damou trust him with this? Maybe he knew everything and this was a warning. Seren would know—she understood Mitrans—but Seren was far away.

"Can—your colleague discuss this?"

Damou gave his one-sided Mitran shrug. "Won't acknowledge."

"Can you delegate her responsibilities?" Mihal poured both glasses full.

"No. If we disconnect her from external sources, it only deepens her obsession. Hers are built layer on layer. Her nanotech effectively makes her a self-replicating machine. If we remove her physically, say outsystem, she'll develop new messenger nano and remotes." Damou held his gaze, challenging his disbelief. "We need her consent to power her down."

"Would she ever give consent?"

"If I asked."

Not if anyone else asked. Interesting, and alarming. "Launch her into the heart of a sun?"

"Murder."

"You kill. It's your work." Mihal winced at his own raw statement. Unwise to insult the man if he wanted to ask his help with Revo.

"Is it?"

Staring at him, Mihal wondered how far he could plumb an old rumour. "One hears that you won't take hits on common criminals."

"Let the courts handle criminals. No one has a right to act as judge and executioner."

"But you do judge, by taking certain tasks and refusing others."

"Yes. It is a flawed system. I have to guess at the consequences of each action."

"Surely there's great injustice in assassinating political prisoners whose only crime is divergent opinion." Too far. He would lash back.

"No doubt. Some contracts I convince the clients to drop." Damou looked amused. "Yours, for example. That integral dart-thrower in your right hand is difficult to aim effectively, by the way, and won't protect you from a competent assassin."

Mihal froze, shocked sober. "Pact contract?"

Damou didn't answer, only held up his glass of clear amber liquid. "What is this?"

"Calvados. Apple brandy. Innocent to the last, like a beautiful woman." It was a bad sign, straying into caprice.

Damou smiled and drained his glass. *God,* Mihal thought

through a blur as Damou poured this time, *I'll regret this tomorrow. Better spray an antox.* He reached for something to say. "You said your invalid was obsessive."

Damou looked into his glass. "She thinks another woman will steal me away."

"But your colleague is scarcely human now, let alone a woman."

"She lives in illusion." Damou sounded terse and blunt. Mitran.

"And has another woman stolen you away?"

Damou didn't speak, but for once his face was eloquent.

"Love is like that," Mihal said lightly. Mistake. Damou looked too troubled for levity. But the Mitran only turned his glass between two hands. Monstrous. No woman he knew would go near that inhuman mask. He knew he was too deep in drink when he heard himself demand, "What about your face?"

"Says she doesn't care." He leaned back in Mihal's chaise, eyes closed. "Maybe she likes the notoriety. She would never admit that. Or anything else."

"Remarkable woman." Lise or Seren would care intensely. Claerans loved beauty above all. Improbably he envied Damou and his woman. They had each other; Mihal had only regret.

At the bottom of their last calvados, still with no sign of intoxication, Damou got to his feet and stood with arms folded, looking immeasurably weary. When had he last slept? He was all right in his stiff-necked way, even if he unnerved Mihal.

"No need to return to your ship. I can put you up here," Mihal said on impulse. Then he could ease into his unasked question: how to extricate himself from Revo's trap.

Damou shook his head. "I sleep lightly."

"Flashbacks," Mihal guessed from first-hand knowledge. He closed his eyes, and a young woman's auburn hair flowed with light that expanded to fill a small screen. "You probably shouldn't be so much alone." *God.* It sounded like a bad pickup line.

Damou didn't notice, looking past him at the spin-corrected stars and beacons. "You'd better know something. About Seren Qasri."

"Alive, I heard. Involved with another man." Mihal shrugged and gripped the arms of his chair. Revo's image from some backwater spaceport could easily be a fake.

"Not—" Damou started to say something but changed direction. "I have vital information she needs. If you have a way to reach her, tell her."

"Certainly," Mihal said. *Revo told the truth.* Seren Qasri lived. So much for signing her death certificate; as he'd suspected, that was a sham. The thought flew from his mind as Damou raised a hand to the door palm plate.

"What is that?" Mihal looked at the metal bracelet on his exposed wrist.

"A MitraCorps officer's command communications band. Linked to my biometrics like a data implant. Easy to replace in the field without surgery or repair."

"Is this band readily available? Perhaps as surplus?"

"No. It's costly personalized tech. Tell Qasri to call me. And forget Gandhi Base. What happened there is done. Let it go." The Mitran spoke so quietly that the door sighed open and he walked out before Mihal felt the chill.

Mihal lurched to his feet and walked with Damou to the core lifts through a maze of small passageways designed to give the station human scale. Clearly, he knew the station well. This late in the second shift, few people were out, and they crossed Melyn into Glas in deep silence.

Claer Arian had been lavishly furnished two centuries ago when it was built, but its rich fittings now looked worn and dated. The luxurious smart carpet had frozen in spots where its nano died, and fittings hung from bare walls where Pact crews had looted artworks.

In a residential square, Damou walked into the station's immense kinetichron. The constantly shifting sculpture of light metallic glass turned on slow maglevs set to randomize, stirred by passing movement. Standing among the iridescent vanes, the Mitran studied their changes with obvious appreciation. His interest made Mihal unhappily aware that he'd barely glanced at the installation in tendays, lost in his work and his tasks for Revo.

"It will probably go to a Pact museum eventually," he said as they walked on. "Pity. Art is wasted on barbarians."

Damou only shook his head and looked back into the moving sculpture, which threw dreamlike spears of light up and down its broad corridor.

In the core lobby, before Mihal could fully absorb all this new information, a lift had carried the Mitran off to his ship. Mihal stood long seconds staring blankly at the lift door, then carefully retraced his steps with his palmshot off safety.

Back in his flat he loaded the data from his doorplate into his powerful desk system to run some of Revo's code. Nothing. Damou had somehow wiped his geneprint from the palm plate. The tableware was already cleaned and sterilized, so what else could he use? The calva glasses sat forgotten on a table, and Mihal quickly scanned Damou's. Soon a DNA sequence coiled neatly through his vri sphere. Damou was a nameless man, and predictably his DNA keyed to no known personal file. MitraCorps databases came up blank year after year for fifty years. So did Mitran sports records, scholarships, court documents. Nothing. In the end it was a Pact criminal file that rocked Mihal back in his chair.

An hour later he still paced his flat, failing to outdistance his anxiety. How fortunate that he hadn't asked the Grey for help. Revo was a minor threat compared to Damou.

VI
NAVIGATOR

1

ES2742.113

Aerial shot. All afternoon and into a pastel spring evening, the West Sea islands and the western shore of Bryniau Claer slipped astern a thousand metres below the freight dirigible.

Seren stretched and scrubbed her face, buzzing with her third strong caffe. A navigation shift on the TransGwynfa airship was closer to offshore sailing than to spaceflight, but with a better view. The crew had put her to work when they discovered she could navigate and helm. Fair skies and light winds for three days had let her record hours of aerial footage.

Running again, running away. Her memory might be as good as it was going to get, and she had no leads on Mam. Now it was time to work.

Cedar curled asleep at her feet under the bridge's nav board, weary of the slow trip out to the West Sea. The clannish airship crew—a full three live watches, as required by transport union regs—welcomed an animal in the forward gondola in defiance of the Pact ban; once the Pact patrols discovered the freight dirigibles were vulnerable to laser fire, many crews had suffered terrible deaths. To Cedar's satisfaction, all three watches competed to feed her treats and groom her brindled coat to a gloss.

When Seren left the airship at Westport, the captain paid her in fresh food. Barter and a black market flourished now; an unlisted, unofficial half of the dirigible cargo was Bryniau cheese and Tariqa produce for the West Sea settlements. It was another quiet way to thwart the Pact, she'd learned in her farmland travels, and a highly Claeran attitude to oppression: helping each other hurts our enemy. More than any resistance talk she heard, it gave her hope for Claer's survival.

Westport's dirigible towers stood inland, kilometres from the surf-pounded cliffs and strands, but a greenway led to a network of trails and paths. A morning's walk with her duffel in backpack mode, full of Nevez smoked bacon and calvados, Gwynfa hard cheese, and Tariqa fruit, took Seren south along the wild shore. Cedar bounded ahead through tall bracken and misty groves of tree ferns until they emerged half a kilometre up a small west-coast river in a salt meadow shadowed by first-growth cedars and firs.

Settlement-era miners had prospected rare metals here before Mitran nanotech enabled Pols to fabricate composites for almost any need. Claerans had arrived onworld determined to create a paradise, and they loved their forests and woodlands, orchards and gardens. The result was Claer y Coed, Claer of the trees, though the old-growth forest seeded by Earth-born emigrants was now as commercially redundant as the silver and zinc mines.

The salt meadow hadn't changed since Seren had camped here years ago with Mam and cousin-friend Rhian. The miners' long-abandoned equipment shed had more moss on its roof and more tangled vines climbing its log walls, but its plank door still shut tightly, and it was hidden from casual view. After days of shift-on, shift-off navigation, she rolled into her nanosilk sheet and slept ten hours.

In the morning sun-mist, Seren sat on a down log on the bright side of the meadow and shared a mango-and-brie galette with Cedar. Then she opened her slate, trusting the Mitran comm bracelet's stealth capability to cloak her from orbitals. She'd forgotten to return Damou's wrist comm and stunner, and he was still refusing her calls. *Damou.* Where was he now? In his ship's cockpit with feet propped on the main board, no doubt, reading some antique book and listening to his strange music that she'd never again hear . . . Damou gave no second chances. Once he'd walked away, he was gone.

"Record voice-over only." Seren gestured over the pause sigil. She'd already roughed out a sim-production script and recorded a first-take intro and extro; now she needed to work out transitions between main sections. "Why this war started is a question for future historians. Right now, we need to ask what happened as the war ended, and why."

Weak, but that's what second drafts are for. Seren was feeling her way, experimenting; she was getting steadily better feedback by posting to *Singularity* and another arts gridsite. Next add an image sequence of the invasion of Tirion that she'd downloaded from a pirate grid . . . but it was hard to keep her mind on vri production. If only she could call Tas to Hafoty again. Ask him what happened, instead of making stupid accusations fed by Inka's deceit. Keep talking, keep listening, until she understood. Her reconstruction of what happened at Gwernant still gaped with blanks she couldn't fill.

Seren minimized her Bight files for a moment to call up Inka's index, and entered the passwords. The override still worked. The first file opened.

One by one she opened Gwernant's house records, starting with Tas's messages, all recorded before he found her in Samun. The first message was classic Damou, cold and concise, directing her to newsgrid clips on the occupation that he'd downloaded into Inka's indexes. In his second message he forgot a citation and backed up, swearing under his breath more audibly than he probably knew. After the fourth he loosened up, even joked about excessive Claeran bureaucracy. This had been a great burden for him, she realized now, a lengthy task that he'd done for someone he'd once called a friend and lover.

Damou. His face was frozen on her maxed slate screen, burned side and whole side together; he'd forgotten or refused to keep the damage in shadow. That lifted corner of his mouth was a cautious smile. It had pleased him to steer her through this tangle. If Inka hadn't hidden his files, if Seren hadn't stunned him in Hafoty, where would she be today?

Soon Seren's head swam with Tas's reports, Gwernant security cam footage, and Mam's treaty work, viewed over and over, but she ploughed on as if Mam stood at her shoulder urging her on. Finally, bone-weary, she slept her slate and stared at its blank screen.

Cedar came to crouch on the down log at her elbow. Seren scratched her lightly behind her ears, and the cat lifted her chin in a show of trust, exposing her throat to be stroked.

"What do you want now, treasure? Hungry?"

"What does Seren want?"

"Everyone asks me what I want. Maq. Parvin. Damou. Tell them and they walk away." She yawned. "I want to know who attacked Mam."

"A man."

"What man?"

"A man wore a green coat."

"Dark green?" That would make him Pol fleet. Not good news.

"Light green."

That pale blur across the security footage. Seren sat up sharply, and Cedar watched her with an anxious crease on her forehead that folded her tabby M into a vertical bar.

"How did he get into the house?"

"A door opened."

Seren's hand flew to her mouth. Someone got in with current security codes, Tas had claimed. Cedar hadn't elaborated before—enhanced animals answered narrow-focus questions, not generalities—and she hadn't asked the obvious next question. It was far too long ago for her cat to recall, but she had to try. "What happened next, Cedar?"

"Delun said never you don't know you're the second." Cedar blinked unhappily.

Hopeless. It could mean anything. "Did he say anything?"

"Never fear Damou dies next." Cedar's tail lashed nervously. "Go now, Seren? Hurts."

Damou dies next? The intruder knew Damou? But Seren had to ask, "What hurts, love?"

"My remembering." Her eyes held a human depth of sadness.

"Go now. You did well. Love you." Seren smiled to make it clear. Another dozen questions pressed on her, but before she asked again, the cat needed time to forget her distress.

Cedar walked along the down log and sat to watch unsects feed on the rotting Claer-adapted heartwood. She didn't hunt the crawlers but found them endlessly fascinating. After a minute, she curled up to sleep with her black-barred tail over her grey paws and nose.

A man in a green coat. Who was he? How did he know Damou? Seren closed her eyes a moment to recreate the sequence. A man walked into their house. Mam's Grey security adviser realized the house was breached, ran through the summer kitchen, took one fast shot—and missed. Or did he miss? The tall blond man who'd seized her on Claer Arian wore black— he could easily have dumped a green coat—and had a streak of badly matched nskin on one cheek.

Seren called up Inka's index with unsteady hands to play the security cam sequence. A peripheral flash across the cam's field of vision was too brief to permit identification, but this time she thought she saw a blurred dark shape in the intruder's raised hand. A primitive weapon, Tas had said. Seren called up the sequence again. There and gone, about half a second. She ran it in hundredths of a second, but it was still a blur. *Useless.* The man wasn't visible long enough for her to use an image editor.

Her sightlines ghost, the code she'd written years ago to interpret the nightmare Piñar footage, was her last resort. She called it up and reloaded the sequence. Damou ran from Gwernant's summer kitchen and fired through the door. In the ghost's small silvery screen within a screen, his tracer was invisible.

"Bring up infrared."

This time the laser trace showed clearly for an instant before the snowstorm of missing data. It rose at about 1:10, rising about half a metre over five metres from his position across the lounge. Damou had fired on the run, aiming for the head in case the man wore a shock shirt. Seren told her ghost to insert a default male form in Gwernant's front doorway and project the tracer beam. Then she ran the sequence. The beam passed above his head.

"Make the man five centimetres taller."

This time it was at eye level, but passed through the open doorway before the man did. Damou had fired ahead of the intruder, anticipating his arrival. It was a good shot, a smart shot, but the man moved more slowly than he expected.

So, a man above average height, light-haired, and wearing a

pale green jacket, had fired a primitive weapon at Senator Delun Qasri with intent to kill.

A few million men in human space could fit that description. No problem, if she had a century to check their whereabouts on the chaotic first day of Claer's occupation. *Hopeless.*

"End program." Seren laid her slate beside her on the log and took a shaky breath. All over Claer other people were living real lives, but in this sunlit meadow she felt like a collection of digital impulses, like her own sightlines ghost.

Tas needed to know what she'd learned. *Damou dies next.* Never mind her pride, never mind his anger. Seren spoke his locators to her slate, trying yet again.

A Mitran recording told her crisply, "Herra Damou declines contact with this caller."

A request to the comm bracelet produced the same message. Seren sat quite still, slate in her hands. Till now she hadn't fully believed she might never see him again, never hear his voice. What had she done? Slowly she called up her virtual aide.

<> Teak, what can I do? <> she asked for the first time in many tendays. <> I've hurt a friend, and he won't take my calls. Now I need to tell him something important. <>

Keep talking, he would say, governed by his code, but instead his small-screen image turned and smiled.

<> If he's a true friend, he'll find you. <>

Seren shook her head and shut down. Teak didn't look at all like Tas, not even like the reconstruction she'd tried on her night walk south from Alluvion, but his voice was eerily close. The young man who'd illuminated her life would always lie near her heart, but Damou was probably right that Kuhan had been naive, an idealist in an age of cynics. It was blunt Damou that she wanted now.

A distant sound overhead came closer, and a shadow crawled across the meadow, spilled over the down log, fell on her feet . . . Seren forced herself to sit absolutely still, trusting the Mitran stealth to hide her presence.

"Cedar, lie still and make no sound."

The cat watched her motionless from round golden eyes.

Seren didn't look up, but she heard a large hover; its crew knew enough to scour this area. The craft searched back and forth for long minutes before drifting slowly away.

Hikers looking for a campsite? Few people took wilderness trips now, and it was a chilly spring. Tas would have made himself known. Parvin's people? Parvin would have her shot on sight for desertion. Pacters? Manhunters might be on her trail at Nolin's order. Or it might be an unknown man who'd shot Mam, threatened Tas, and grabbed her on Arian.

Seren shivered in the bright sunlight until the craft disappeared over the wooded ridge, and waited another twenty minutes. Then she gathered her things, waited for the slight advantage of darkness, and headed down the forest trail to Westport.

Running again, running toward—what?

A message pinged her slate, and she paused under a tree fern to read it through tears of relief. *Talk? Arian high hub 2230. Damou.*

2

Nolin's new Claeran office occupied the former madrasa school of Tirion's oldest mosque, today offering a view of a low grey sky. A settee in carved black wood, no doubt as rare and costly as it was hideous, occupied the place of honour at the window. Next tenday it would be some other treasure. Nolin constantly reassessed his favourite things.

Tas sat reluctantly on the settee's green silk cushion. His attaché held the new specimen from the cloning vat, oozing at the severed wrist. Tas lifted the clawlike hand from its chest of inlaid wood. Inka's bots might have overplayed their artistry this time. The lightly charred hand held a sculptor's hardwood clay-modelling tool, complete with trace isotopes and minerals from Ojin's volcanic eastern archipelago. Akiko Sigridsdottir would never miss her unknown extra hand.

Nolin admired the scorched hand but immediately passed its case to Anton Rethel. It was the impeccably created vri sequence of the Ojin sculptor's blasted body that he lingered over.

"You really don't give a shit, do you, Damou?" Nolin leaned forward in his matching chair, a fellow conspirator. "Hunt them, kill them, butcher them. Not that I don't value your services. A regime needs men like you. Evil in the service of good."

"It's a contract." Leave the pulp-grid sentiment to Nolin. All

331

Tas wanted was to survive long enough to detach himself carefully, permanently.

Over his shoulder, Anton Rethel frowned at Tas for a second too long. They'd met long ago, when Nolin was still making his way up in the Pact's vast public service with strategic alliances and marriages. As chief of staff, Rethel was the last of Gabe de Jong's old guard, too well-informed to leave at loose ends and too powerful to remove. He kept Nolin in the dark on many things, including whatever he knew or guessed of Tas Damou's history.

"And the other terrorists? What about Seren Qasri?"

"Still dead."

Nolin failed to see the humour in that. "I have a new job for you. Our lifetime president finds his island residence tiresome. He's moving back to Havre for a while. You can oversee security."

"No. I lift in an hour." The tox thought Gabriel de Jong had already gone virtual. Nolin had every interest in knowing his status, so if Nolin said it, Gabe probably was alive.

Nolin studied him, not pleased by his refusal. Tas had no illusion that he'd be allowed to sign off and walk away. He knew too much, like Rethel. One day the game would end. Even now Nolin had his assassin under observation on assignments. The solution was to know more, just enough to make Nolin reluctant to terminate him. The new-generation nanodrones Tas deployed at every hit routinely disinformed Nolin's last-generation spytech.

Tas caught Rethel studying his own hands—surprisingly slender and shapely for a heavyset Outlooker—as though measuring them for Nolin's trophy wall.

"Heading for Rustam? Vritra?" Nolin didn't wait for his answer. "Relocate, Damou. We're going to slap down those Grey assholes. They shelter Pol terrorists."

"Ship upgrade on Han One."

Nolin wasn't diverted. "And I don't want you taking any jobs for the fucking Pols. We don't need a bunch of Green zombies wandering around that haven't noticed they're dead."

Tas chilled his voice to indifference. "I work where I get paid."

Nolin leaned forward in his ugly chair, grinning. Decency confused him, but he understood the callous and mercenary. "Stay. An hour. I've got an entertainment."

"No." Tas got to his feet and stood over Nolin, who recoiled in fear. His entertainments were whispered around the precinct. He wrestled down a temptation as intense as glitz craving to seize the man's bland face and twist once, sharply, sideways. But he had failed at nonattachment. Love of life bound him as surely as the silver scarf Seren Qasri once cast around his neck.

Seren. All his messages and calls to her still bounced. Inka's work, probably, but Tas had no time to sort her now. Once he found Seren, he would do whatever it took to keep talking.

Nolin called up a palm scroll. "Delay your ship upgrade. Here's a good one for you. Kasumi. Rescue job, double your standard fee plus danger. A mob of Pact guest workers and Pol relocatees have the regulator under siege. Don't contact our sector command—they screwed this up. Let them watch the pros do it."

Hiring in MitraCorps to humiliate his own regulars was typical Nolin. Tas weighed it: one-day turnaround, cash out and disappear. Pols and Pacters together in rebellion were worth a look. But quick acceptance would rouse Nolin's suspicion. He shook his head. "You have your hand. Pay now. I'm not waiting out another six-families coup."

"The coup's over. Several conspirators volunteered for reconstruction worlds. Others were unable to live with their guilt. Regrettably my late wife trusted them unwisely." Nolin managed to look pensive for a few seconds.

Rethel stumped across the priceless carpet to touch palms and transfer funds, then remembered and touched Tas's slate instead.

"You need new implants." Nolin was improbably jolly again. "What about Kasumi?"

"Send me the briefing notes."

Tas turned for the door. He didn't need new implants. Not when his destroyed and rebuilt body still contained the molten lumps of his old implants along with the charred ruin of all his old certainty. Every day he knew more and understood less. Even so he understood that he could never again face Nolin as a free man.

3

On his way up to Claeran low orbit after three days well spent in entertaining the Bryniau environment ministry, Maq folded into his pilot chair and spoke a mirror code.

"Damou," Tas answered on the first pulse. "How did you get through?"

"Must be that skookum comm equipment you told me to buy for half my GWP. Where in hell are you?"

Smoke drifted against a dripping wall of variegated green above Damou's head. Armed and light-armoured, he lay on his back among dead branches with mud on his face and leaves in his hair. Steam rose around him. Tropical rainforest, by the size of the trees. Maq heard two neat *thwacks* as laser bolts struck a massive trunk above Damou's head. *Jesus wept.* Live-bodies ground war. It brought back bad memories of Maq's last ground war a hundred-odd years ago.

Damou snapped, "What do you want?"

Maq got to the point. "You heartless son of a bitch, what have you done to my girl?"

"Stay out of it." Tas cut the connection.

Progress. Now they were both pissed off at him instead of each other.

"Location of Tas Damou?" he asked his ship.

"Herra Damou is on Kasumi," the ship's tinny voice told him. Maq liked his machines to sound like machines. "Next request, tyee?"

"Full report for Spartí ops on Kasumi, text only," he ordered.

Maq read the scroll above his comm board, faster than he could listen to it, with growing discontent. The usual Pact resource-world mess. Pol slaves and Pact criminals, rising together in outrage at their brutal handling, had broken through force-field barriers around their burned-out industrial site and swarmed across the hills toward the Pact regulator's enclave. Spartí had already declined the job; they didn't fight other worlds' civil wars. Now Damou had taken it on personally. *Mahsh siah.*

Maq thoughtfully flipped his favourite emerald lahal sticks from hand to hand, checked Spartí day rates, winced, and made his call to Teak Kuhan's hotshot successor. Kuhan beat her hollow at strategy, but Helli Njau was a better tactical soldier.

An hour later he shuffled his sticks and hid them.

The ship AI called, "Left!"

His left hand held the unbanded stick, of course. No matter how he hid them or pointed, he never could fool his ship. He gave it up and commed his Xanadu banker. These days he was aggressively trading arms and military tech, selling as selectively as a Sitkum trout eyeing a naked hook. The last thing he wanted to do was arm fanatics and splinter groups. Yet.

Maq pocketed his gems and burned for one of Damou's uncharted mirror nodes, outbound to join his fleet. AnvilCo mostly cruised the Grey Tripline these days. Five hundred people fit without a bulge into his new ore hauler *Sedna,* and all his small craft easily rode her racks. The ore hauler and four freighters—a carrier, a cruiser, and three frigates to any educated eye—made up the small but growing nomadic Democratic Republic of New Sitkum.

4

Tas lay in a pool of sweat beside Kai Rivera, keeping his head down. The tangled understory of a Kasumi forest offered shade but no relief from the heat, and there was an overpowering stench of rotten vegetation. He tried to be grateful that Amity Industrial, which processed this world's rare native alloys, lay in the northern temperate zone. Kasumi's equatorial regions were a steaming, bubbling hell where humans needed softsuits and breathers.

A grey overcast held in enough heat and humidity to torment him. His shock shirt abraded his sweating chest and back even with its cooling system maxed. His boots couldn't stretch enough to fit his swollen feet, his exo legs chafed, and he felt as if a native slime mould analogue had colonized his head. The Pact paid double-time and danger for a reason.

"Cover!"

Sunny's drone exploded another crude spyhover in a puff of acrid smoke. Spartí countermeasures were overkill for primitive visual surveillance devices sighted by naked eye, and it made tiresome work.

A dimensional blueprint of the regulator's residence turned slowly in the air above Kai's slate, propped between two leafy purple-flowered vines on Kasumi's red jungle soil. His second's braid was ravelling into blond spikes; his patience remained intact.

Escort regulator to safety on Havre, read their orders, then let his guard round up the rebels. Easy—until the angry slave workers occupied the rocky height overlooking the government mansion, beautifully but indefensibly located in a gentle valley. Waiting on the regulator's whim, Tas and the other three held the wooded opposite slope against surprisingly well-organized irregulars who appeared and disappeared in classic guerilla style. Now his quad needed a better approach.

"Boss planned all this," Mitros muttered to Sunny.

Untrue, but let it pass. Tas had other concerns.

Kai shoved a blunt finger deep into his virtual blueprint. "The insurgents have captured energy weapons. They're shooting selectively and hitting the mark." The regulator's barely-trained Pact guards, on the other hand, were running down their charge packs by spraying laser fire at every wind-stirred leaf.

Sunny reported, not lifting her head above a fragrant flowering vine, "Pact sector command on comm. Clean slate ordered in one hour. Want to reply?"

Clean slate meant a ground sweep, maybe a plasma bomb. Why was sector command calling him, when the plan was to keep this quiet? So, Nolin had changed his mind. Not the first time.

"Acknowledge only. Try the regulator again."

Playing his virtual game with live gamesmen, Nolin was bored with the realtime moves. He craved excitement—lasers, artillery, and blood. A one-hour ultimatum speeded the play, pushing Tas to fire on the rioters and grab the regulator. He studied the mansion blueprint, hating this.

"Still in his strong room, sir."

Tas had given up telling them, no ranks. Kai and Sunny and Mitros complied for an hour, then it was back to boss and sir.

Regulator Bailey-Ramirez answered his comm this time. "What a pleasure, captain, and will you join us for the opera tonight?" Then he disconnected. His slack mouth and glazed eyes suggested a recent hit of glitz. If they did get him out, he would babble until he plunged into quivering paranoia.

"Insurgents have climbed to a hollow between the standing rock and the neodar grove," Mitros reported from his drone cam readout. "Hundred and forty-one adults, seven possibly wounded, four children. Six lasers, twenty-two handmade projectile weapons."

The regulator's guard had taken shelter behind the mansion. Tas commed their sergeant to hold fire and clear off now that Spartí had arrived. No need to say four Spartí; let him think it was a full thema. The guard retreated to their compound, leaving the residence wide open.

First a personal matter. Tas called up a standard will and testament on his slate, keyed in a few words, and transmitted it for Kai to witness.

Kai read the names. "Haven't seen that lately. She knows?"

"Not that she admits it." Tas checked his chrono, avoiding Kai's gaze. *Fifty minutes.*

"No message?"

"I told her." At least he'd tried to tell her, fighting stun up near the Gwynfa glacier, struggling to stay coherent. Seren knew everything that she wanted to know. Tas pressed his thumb on Kai's screen to sign his will.

"You could always tell her again." Kai read his expression and left it alone.

Tas dropped his weapons and goggles and descended the narrow hillside trail with his hands clasped on his head. As he crossed the government house landing pad, a savanna starred with white asters, a laser bolt furrowed the ground at his feet and sprayed him with sandy red soil. His cochlear relay buzzed.

"Who in hell are you, man?" a man demanded in a hoarse Pact backworld accent.

"Negotiator. MitraCorps/Spartí. I've come to hear your grievances."

Tas counted to fifteen before he got an answer, long enough for sweat to stream down his face and back, long enough to wish he'd had a better idea. His contract didn't cover negotiating a damned thing, only getting the regulator out, and that meant these people would be left to die alone. Screw that. There was always a way.

"Grievances? Start with murder, torture, rape, enslavement, labour infractions."

Standard procedure in forced labour camps. *Damn the Pact.*

"Your immediate needs?"

"Food. A medic."

"Done."

Then a woman's broken whisper chilled him in the steaming afternoon sunlight. "None of us will leave alive, Spartí. Run while you can." Her accent was Peqin Claer.

Tas glanced up uneasily at the outcrop, thinking of snipers, thinking of Piñar.

"Live one at three o'clock, sir." Sunny's steady voice became his lifeline.

"Scoped." Tas's arms ached from his prisoner stance. Pols and Pacters taking up arms together—maybe this was the first stirring of Maq's new social experiment. *Forty minutes.*

His hands and face throbbed in the merciless heat, and even with his heavy UV treatment, he would blister soon. A small man in mud-caked work trousers and a once-white shirt, richly embroidered in Paraiso leaf and vine motif, walked onto the pad's margin. He'd stepped from a blur of stealth wrap, and he carried a recent-issue Pact energy weapon. Not so low-tech after all. Assassin? People should know a last hope when they saw one. If the runaways harmed Tas, their fate was sealed as surely as his own.

"Other demands?" Safe passage, amnesty, cash cards: Tas could probably write his list. In an hour he could know this man better than his own lost brother, every want and weakness he could exploit, every virtue he could build on—but they no longer had an hour.

The small man turned to face the high ground and raised his arm.

"Sir!" Sunny yelled in his ear, making him wince.

Tas tracked the dark tide sweeping down from the outcrop. *Throw hard and win,* Maq always said over his stick game, but sometimes you throw hard and lose.

Kai this time, calm as ever. "We can drop a sandman on them."

It was too late to deploy a stun net, and anyway, people could fall unconscious to their deaths on the steep slope. The first insurgents reached the level ground in a ragged mass.

"Hold your fire. Prepare to retreat. Call sector command for backup." Tas kept his voice level, not to raise alarm. *Thirty-five minutes.*

Not calling down laser fire, not running for cover, was the hardest thing he'd done in years. Seren Qasri would be a modestly wealthy woman within a tenday. But now who would keep her from harm? Not Biron, he'd been useless on Gandhi—The last piece of Seren's puzzle clicked into place. Biron. How had they missed it?

"Pact ship on descent," Sunny said too steadily, not giving in to panic. "Visual in twenty, nineteen, eighteen—" The rest was lost in cross-signal static.

An hour was a lie. He had no time at all.

The small man led the others forward in a dark ragged line, knee-deep in grass and asters. Kasumi's harsh light flared and dazzled on primitive metal and wood firearms, curved cutlasses, hand axes, daggers. This was what the front line saw at Thermopylai and Shang-jao. Tas let his hands fall to his sides, but despite his exo legs, he couldn't stop the trembling in his knees. Renat was right: he was afraid. He had the vanity to hope Kai would tell Seren that he hadn't turned and run.

The armed mob stopped abruptly a few paces away, and he remembered to breathe.

"Tas Damou. I welcome you," he said formally.

"Marek Cabral. I greet you, captain," the man said. "No time for talk. We intercepted this."

A woman came forward—the owner of the Peqin Claer voice, by her narrow face under a head wrap—and held up a slate even older than Tas's. A Pact voice spoke from it. "They're all in place. Drop the ship and proceed with clean slate."

Tas looked up. A handful of diamonds glittered against the high cloud cover and became brilliant lights. Ship landing lights. Probably a destroyer in orbit, transports for landing troops. The Pacters would wipe out every trace of life for kilometres, including runaways, a glitzed regulator, and the Spartí quad hired to get him out.

Sunny's voice crackled in his ear. "Sir. Their CO advises you as a professional courtesy that contracting services to terrorists in rebellion against the Pact of Human Worlds removes you from all Pact conventions and safeguards. Secretary Nolin has ordered him to put down the rebellion and let nothing and no one stand in the way. Clear off before he sweeps."

Tas stared up at the ship for long seconds as the exact nature of Nolin's betrayal sank in.

"They'll kill every one of us," Marek Cabral said. "Why did they bother to send you?"

Tas had no answer. Nolin knew, but Nolin was safe on Claer. All the haste and secrecy made sense now. So, it wouldn't be poison or a tailored virus, just a minor operation gone wrong. Nothing remained to discuss here. He stepped from his unplanned negotiator role and beyond the bounds of law.

"We can fight them together."

"Why side with us?" Cabral demanded.

Good man, to challenge it. "It's a trap. We're in it too."

Cabral turned. "Ewa?"

The Claeran woman nodded assent. "We want to live our lives. We fight."

Respect, restraint—not the bloodthirsty mob of his briefing notes—and no hope of survival. It wasn't a bad way to go. Tas consented, as he had not consented at Piñar.

"Relay my orders," he told Cabral, already on comm. "Kai, get noncombatants and wounded into the regulator's strong room, fast. Alert the regulator. Attack is imminent. Prepare to defend the valley." Against an attack force ordered to wipe out every trace of life, he had four specials and a few runaways armed with knives and moral outrage.

This was what he'd wanted to do at Piñar, God knew, gather the villagers and lead their defence. It raised memories of his last thoughts: terror, light pulsing from the moulder object, going back to an orchard bright with sun mist. He'd fought many years and worked down a vast debt to earn his return.

His quad mates broke cover low on the wooded slope, running full out for the landing pad, and Sunny tossed him weapons and goggles as she passed. By then a third of the rebels were stumbling into the compound, and Mitros was giving orders to the protesting guard sergeant.

Tas scanned the outcrop that the runaways had swarmed down. No cover, no advantage. He pointed his rabble toward the wooded slope where his quad had been pinned, and they bounded through the grass and asters, God help them, laughing like kids on a field trip. When the last stragglers passed him and climbed to midslope under the tree canopy with Kai, Tas ran to join them. Sunny and Mitros arrived seconds later, and Tas told them to spread the insurgents up and across the slope.

"Hold your fire." Cabral and Ewa relayed his order, and he heard it echo among the trees.

Most of the battle-hardened Pact troops had been sent to swagger and thieve on the occupied worlds, so they might be lucky enough to face untried recruits. He'd know soon.

Tas felt alone and present in the breath pumping his chest, the smooth stride of his legs as he climbed. The tawny grass and white asters and lush green forest might be the last he saw, and he felt a great love for it all. Would he really kill now, even to save life? Lying flat among the vines, the rebels raised lasers and primitive projectile weapons like the one that killed him at Piñar. Tas settled behind a down-log.

The tree canopy whipped, showering them with small flyers and crawlers that burrowed into the leaf mould or fled, and a roar built to thunder as a Pact ship descended in the narrow upper valley, cutting off one avenue of escape. A mid-range craft, not a full-sized transport. Tas saw ten ten-squads jog out after a lieutenant and five noncoms, five field lasers, and the usual launchers. They stood too long, looking for orders. *Recruits.* Finally, they dropped into the long grass and set up their equipment. *Slow.* A MitraCorps thema could wrap them like gift packages.

"High stun only." Tas settled his goggles.

Cabral snapped back, "They didn't stun us in the camps, they shot us to rags."

"Blood on your hands won't look good in court." As if they would get near a court. "Drop the noncoms."

Tas set his long-range stunner and aimed carefully at the Pact lieutenant. His augmented vision and goggles painted her close enough to touch. He fired, and she sprawled bonelessly as two of the noncoms went down, then a third, fourth, fifth. Some good shots among the runaways.

This was the dangerous time. The recruits did nothing at all for a long moment, then returned fire. High-energy laser shots struck the trees upslope. Branches dropped, and someone screamed, but the dripping humidity contained the flames. Mitros reported injuries.

They might have a chance—then the transport disgorged another four squads that took cover quickly and readied their launchers. Tas spotted their heat signatures in the long grass, spreading out quickly. They'd kept the seasoned troops in reserve. Fire raked the upper slope again. A handful of trees burst into flame, and nearby trees steamed and smoked. If they got the rainforest to ignite, they'd force the rebels onto the flat or burn them alive. His skin tightened in remembered dread.

"Wait."

Another wash of flame above, and Cabral shot him a hard look. Tas had to act now. "Kai, drop a stun net on the regulars." It wouldn't extend as far as the new recruits, but they worried him less. Slightly. A terrified teenager with a deadly weapon was not a negligible threat.

"Sir."

The valley went quiet for nearly a minute as the stun net stilled the core positions. Then another four squads of heavy-armoured troops emerged from the transport, and their robotic exoskeletons brought them halfway to the trees in seconds. Their suits were stun-proof and fearsomely armed. The game was up. Tas eased his laser off safety.

"Live charges," Tas told Cabral. His next choice was no longer tactical, it was a legal choice. There would be no record of Nolin's contract to extract the regulator. No rules of engagement that he knew could excuse a Pact-hired Spartí quad firing on a Pact force.

"Ready—" Tas glanced up as new lights penetrated the overcast, dropping out of stealth.

"Ships on descent," Sunny reported through a crackle of static.

Taking no chances on this situation, they must have sent down reinforcements. All over.

A blinding flash penetrated the clouds.

"Cover!"

Tas threw himself beside the down-log and covered his head an instant before the roar. Cabral relayed the order a second later, but the explosion knocked others to the ground and uprooted trees around them, flattening them back to the slope. Then there was silence. Tas lay still for a moment as the last sandy red soil showered down.

Four shuttles settled with a great hiss and groan near the landing pad, and through the cloud of red dust he saw their Spartí markings. He rolled onto his side to see Spartí troops fanning out, and a dozen stun nets fell over the Pact squads among the long grass.

"You're taking the wrong contracts, boss."

Tas looked up at a grinning Helli Njau standing with one boot on his down-log and her partner and second Amalie beside her on comm to someone below. Helli gave him a hand up.

"Captain Njau." Tas respected the protocols with Helli.

"Herra Flett says you owe him one." Her expression suggested that Maq Flett had said a few choicer things as well.

"Captain Njau, I must advise that you have committed an act of war against the Pact of Human Worlds."

"Not a chance. Just fulfilling your contract. We have the regulator in protective custody, spun to the eyeballs and moaning about an opera he's missing in Havre."

"Take him there. He'll miss the first act."

"Sir."

Helli wouldn't let him forget this rescue—he'd saved her skin too many times and lessons-learned her over it. She called the medics and jogged back downslope to the regulator's residence, where the guard sergeant was turning over a gaggle of kids and a handful of stretcher cases to Mitros. Kai and Sunny were already leading their insurgents to the Spartí shuttles.

Tas followed, keeping a weather eye on the cloud cover, but there were no more ships.

"Captain." Cabral held out his hand at the foot of the slope where the trees opened out. A scatter of white aster petals fluttered past them from the savanna, dislodged by the lasers.

Tas touched his palm, recognizing Cabral's gesture as important. Ewa silently came to do the same. Tas told them, "You did well."

"Thousands more are prisoners in the camps. We could free them."

Tas knew where this led—the man's first taste of victory, the first triumph of their lives for some of his people—and headed it off sharply. "I'm not leading your revolt. The best thing I can do for all of you is put these human rights abuses before an interworld court."

Cabral nodded, more relieved than disappointed, and turned with Ewa to their people.

Tas slung his laser and started across the savanna. His work was done for now. Helli could take the regulator to Havre and the quad back to the Cantons. He'd found another hundred and forty-one citizens for Maq's nomad republic. A rescue transport was on its way to the children on Kalevala. And for now, he was alive.

Everything else sprang from that simple fact. No time for pride and distrust. Time for only what mattered. *Seren.* He summoned his Az from its stealth zone back near the ruined processing plant, and as it dropped onto the savanna, he tapped his comm. "Where's Qasri?"

A long silence, then Inka replied sullenly. "Near Tirion on Claer."

Tas brushed off leaf mould and headed for his ship.

5

ES2742.114

Moving shot, aerial, hover. Head down inside the hood of her borrowed mourning cloak, Seren was ignored by the few people around her in the shuttle cabin until they docked at a low-hub berth on Claer Arian. She walked out of the gate between crowds of people waiting to board. Shift change? A few thousand Claerans still worked and lived on Arian, and it looked as if most of them were on the hub trying to get downworld. Cedar stirred cautiously in her duffel, under Seren's order to lie still.

Seren checked Damou's text message on her slate. *Talk? Arian high hub 2230. Damou.* He'd blanked the sending address, but the locator code was Mitran, and it read like a Tas message. Raw hope pushed her through the crowd, searching faces from under her cowl. No sign of Tas in the hub concourse, but being Tas, he would meet her exactly where and when he said. It was still only 2140; for once she was early. As she crossed the defaced hub lobby to the core lifts, her neck prickled.

Near here the two thugs had grabbed her on her return from Gandhi. A call had come in, not from Mam as she'd expected, but from a man who claimed to have new orders for her. Pawel and Yan and the rest of the Gandhi shutdown crew took the lift without her. All dead now, all but her and one other, the one she hadn't yet traced.

Her steps echoed on bare grey composite. Service tubing hung from the stripped walls, and even the low-relief images on the lift doors had been pried off and taken away.

A man waited at the core lifts, and her heart stumbled. But it wasn't Tas. A stocky man with dead-pale skin and light hair brushing his shoulders. Mihal Villandry Biron. Wonderful clothes, as always, typical Mihal. Not the beautiful boy she'd known; his eyes looked bruised and wary.

Mihal gave her a cursory glance and looked past her, scanning the lobby for someone else. Most people respected the privacy of a New Grove mourner, but she was the only one not rushing onward, and he glanced again. Seren hesitated, unaccountably reluctant to make herself known. Everything would change. Cedar growled quietly in the duffel under her elbow. But this was a friend. They'd had their misunderstandings, but what was there to fear now? Seren pushed back her hood.

"Mihal."

His expression exploded through shock into wonder, and he whispered her name. One person at least cared that she was alive. Seren walked into his arms. His kiss tasted of vanilla—Mihal always had a sweet tooth—and that made her smile. Finally, Seren caught her breath and pulled away to arm's length, holding back a hundred questions.

"Come. I have something of yours I want to give you."

Tempting—she could ask him the questions she'd puzzled over for tendays—but Seren shook her head. "Another time. I'm meeting a friend."

"Ten minutes."

Seren hoisted her duffel and turned to the lift. "Quickly then."

Mihal clearly didn't want to be seen. He led her through back corridors she remembered from years ago, shortcuts and odd corners where she'd ducked Mam's watchful eye, into small service alleys behind the hanging gardens and sunny piazzas of Melyn. The station's prime residential district looked almost untouched by the war and economic crash. Carpets and tiles remained in place, and water splashed and swirled in the fountains. Fine arts ornamented the walls and open spaces. Small animals, not augmented as far as she could see, frisked through the lush trees and vines.

On an outer-ring corridor, Mihal palmed a door plate and led into a large flat impeccably decorated in cream and gold, all natural fibres and natural woods, no wall scenes or projections. It looked uninhabited, as though he spent little time here. Seren dropped her mourner's cloak over the nearest chair and went to the spin-corrected outside window, five times larger than the one in Mam's tiny senate flat. She walked into its outward bulge and looked out, and the beauty and grandeur of Claer's starfield stole her breath.

Mihal closed the door, dimmed the lights, and straightened a table, as though he didn't know what to do with his hands. He looked up at her and aside. "You must tell me everything—including how you are alive. I thought you died a year ago on Arian."

"New identity," she gave the simplest answer. "I couldn't contact anyone."

"Gods, look at you." Mihal came from the food fab with two glasses of white wine. "I'd never have known you if you hadn't spoken. You're very—brown. And dressed like a mercenary from the adventure vris."

Seren glanced down, startled. Comfortable shirt and pants with enough pockets, flying jacket, ankle boots of soft vat suede, long silk scarf to replace the one she'd given Tas. She shrugged as he set the wine glass beside her on a table. "Work clothes."

"Tell me what you've been doing." He sank into a buttercream armchair with his wine.

"Later." Now that she'd caught her breath, there was no time to waste. "We may both be in danger. Have you been pursued or attacked? Has any data disappeared?"

Mihal's laughter stopped her cold. "You realize how paranoid that sounds, Ser? If a patient said that, I'd admit him for observation."

Mockery was so Mihal, dismissive and infuriating. This was a bad idea. Try a different tack. "There were seventeen of us on Gandhi at the end, after they pulled the patrol ships and pilots. Have you checked on those seventeen lately?"

"Should I?" Mihal was still smiling. "Let me guess, they declared themselves cousin-friends, started a native grassland preserve, and now breed unsects together in an ecocommune."

Seren wanted to shake him. "Mihal, they're all dead."

"I'm sorry to hear that. And happy that we're alive." He folded his square hands around his wine glass. His old family ring, gold with an emerald intaglio, scattered sparks of green fire that colour-coordinated perfectly with a fine landscape painting over his butter-cream chaise.

Wake up! How could she say this so Mihal could hear? "My signals tech died first. Then the others. Mostly they died one by one, but Pawel and Yan died together. The occupation enforcers called that one murder-suicide. Most didn't even get investigated by the provisional governments. Fifteen deaths. All but me and one other person on the shutdown crew."

His attention sharpened. "Who?"

"Exactly my question." Seren chose her words carefully; mentioning her memory block or her suspicions would clearly only draw more laughter. "My memory is shaky. You left ahead of the shutdown crew?"

Mihal looked relieved, so maybe she sounded less scatty. "Yes."

"That other person may be on my track. Do you still have your clinic records?"

"Let's think this through, Ser." Mihal's patronizing tone annoyed her, but at least he was paying attention. "Why would anyone kill the Gandhi crew?"

"Do you remember the courier ship we intercepted in the Bight?" Seren left it there. Let Mihal come up with his own theory.

"Ser, there were fifty-four of us on Gandhi at the end, and postwar death rates are high among Pol veterans. Sad. God knows we need them all to wrestle Claer out of the Pact's grip." As always Mihal raged at the Pact from a black hatred she could never fathom.

"Fifty-four was our full complement on Gandhi, not our shutdown crew." Why would he say otherwise? Having laughed off her fears, he now had a thoughtful inward look. Thinking it over. Maybe that was all she could really ask.

"Forget the war. It's over." Mihal sipped his wine. "How's the esteemed senator?"

Missing and presumed dead. His question was not amusing.

On supposedly class-free Claer, he'd always scorned Delun Qasri as a populist.

Seren lifted her wine glass. A small vri zone unfurled above her left wrist, exactly where the Mitran command comm lay inside her jacket sleeve. The image, stealth-angled so only she could see it, was a formula for some substance that seemed to have a strong alkaline component. Below that scrolled, DANGER. DO NOT TOUCH.

Seren set down the drugged wine glass. Its smell was cloyingly, unpleasantly sweet. A distraction, quickly. "Mihal, I haven't eaten today."

"Forgive me. I was so delighted to see you," he said, his manners flawless as always. Seconds later he was opening storage shelves and tapping pads on the food fab. Toast with pear jelly and brie. Too bad she couldn't risk tasting it. He'd left a shelf open above the food fab. A small familiar object rested near one side—the art glass ovoid that Mam had given her, stolen more than a year ago on this station. *I have something of yours.* Why did Mihal have it?

When he turned his back, Seren poured the entire glass of wine into the pretty cream carpet out of Mihal's sight. It would cycle by the time he returned, with luck. *Knockout drug? Psychedelic? Poison?* Letting her eyes close sleepily, she leaned her head back and slid her hand into her jacket pocket. Empty. No stunner.

Under her eyelashes she watched Mihal set a plate beside her empty glass. Then he was behind her, breathing on her hair. She managed not to shudder, but she couldn't stomach that for long. Wait for the best moment. Where was her stunner?

Then Seren's gut wrenched, and she thought she might be sick. Not at the skin-crawling attempt at chemical coercion, but at the image now taking shape in the mist of her memory: Mihal leaning over her berth . . . There were still blanks in her memory of the last day on Gandhi. Whoever hid a memory bead in her arm. Whoever blocked her with a primitive needle jab in a dim passageway. Whoever punched the ship's firing pad with a fiery blink of green—but a firing pad would flash red.

Her command comm buzzed and announced in a small Mitran voice, "Alert. Band one. Danger. Tirion y Bryniau." *Tas.*

Not on Arian, but in Tirion. *In trouble.*

Mihal's fingers gripped her shoulders painfully hard. "Where did you get that bracelet?"

"No." *Not your business.* The mourning cloak, maybe that was where she left the stunner.

"So. It was him all along. Always."

Seren let her head loll forward as though half-conscious. Keep Mihal talking. She'd said too much already. Something hard and flat slid up and down her right forearm, then her left forearm. A handheld scanner.

"Where's the bead? You gave it to him, didn't you?"

No, but good idea. So Mihal knew about the gold bead in her arm. Seren let herself be pulled upright in the chair. She half-opened her eyes to see his face pale with anger.

"You never learn. He's a world-killer, a murderer, a brute. He would have picked you clean of information and killed you like the rest."

Seren let her eyes shut and slumped. Unwisely Mihal leaned closer to check. She drove her elbow at his nose and kicked him halfway across the room with both feet. He staggered up again, making a fist, and a dart shot across the room to thump into the wall behind her. She leaped for the mourning cloak and clawed the stunner out of the pocket. As Mihal raised his hand to shoot another dart, she fired. He fell heavily.

Twenty minutes—then he would wake and come after her. Before then she needed to get back down to the Tirion shuttle. *Tas.* Seren swept up the duffel where Cedar had waited as ordered, flung the mourning cloak over her shoulders, and bolted for the door—then turned back to seize her glass egg from the shelf and drop it in a thigh pocket.

In the hallway she forced herself to walk normally. Another bridge burned. Heading for the core lifts, she entered Tas's locators on her slate. No answer. Tried again on the command comm. Nothing. If it wasn't Tas who'd called her to Arian, who was it? Someone with a Mitran locator code who'd told Mihal. What had Mihal gotten himself mixed up in?

Even in alleys and residential byways, people still crowded toward the core with bags and hover trunks. Something had happened. Seren checked a wallscreen for the station newsgrid but saw nothing unusual.

Her alley opened into a corridor where a seething crowd slowed her to a shuffle. People in Melyn didn't queue, they pushed to the front demanding explanation. These ones looked angry and frightened, jittering toward panic. Her mourning cloak made her socially invisible, and that was now a disadvantage. No one noticed when she dropped the cloak into an alcove.

A roar parted the crowd behind her, and a rowdier mob shoved through, some in Pact uniforms or station workers' coveralls. Incredibly, among them strode fantastical chimerai, and animals rode their shoulders or loped at their heels. Neither kind supposedly existed on Arian.

"What's wrong?" she demanded until people tossed her hasty answers.

"Station workers' strike."

"Manimal breakout."

"Pact mutiny."

Clearly no one knew what was going on. People fled in every direction. Outsystem and downworld transport would be packed; Seren would be trapped in a place that still gave her flashback terrors. Cedar would die, betrayed and alone—the whole nightmare spun away like a broken wheel. *Damn Mihal.* It was hard to believe they'd been friends once, but they'd all been friends on Gandhi, until the surrender.

Seren took a back-alley to Glas and found her own familiar corridors less crowded. Cedar's weight dragged on her shoulder strap, and she felt dizzy and light-headed. She should have grabbed Mihal's food after all. *Pay attention. Core lifts. Shuttle dock. Tas.* So many things she wanted to say if she saw him again . . . *Focus.* Time stretched and broke and washed over her in waves, and she was adrift.

The old kinetichron loomed in the corridor ahead, and she steadied herself for a moment against the wall. Her fingers tingled, and a delicious warmth flushed her. Impossible. She'd poured out Mihal's wine. Hours ago. She checked her chrono. Fifteen minutes ago. What had been in the wine glass? Or on it?

Seren drifted toward the kinetichron's turning timevane panels, drawn closer to their seductive beauty and sweet wordless song. Today a full A-major chord played out in transient waves of violet and deep blue flashed with silver. She watched herself coming and going in its changeable truth. Tas was there too. Maybe they could stay there forever, shadow images glimpsed together in transit to some other reality where they finally lived in peace.

But the vanes shifted toward shadow in A-minor, and she was back on Gandhi, destroying files as Mihal packed their few remaining medical supplies into hexlock crates; they'd raced to shut down the station as the Pact transport docked. The vanes swirled on, and she stood stunned at the new memory splinter.

Mihal was on the shutdown crew.

Tas was in danger downworld, and Seren would be in danger the instant Mihal woke from stun. She needed to reach Tas, but first she had to save herself and Cedar. *Run. Now.*

A man stepped out of the sculpture into her path. Null-masked, tall, thin; his hands glittered with gems and writhed with liveware. "A word with you, Lieutenant."

6

In the soft blue dusk at Derw Sanctuary, a novice who barely topped his shoulder intercepted Tas outside the meditation wing. He described a Claeran friend who might be here, but the woman blocked him from the fragrant spring garden until a white-haired doctor emerged from the clinic.

"You are?" The doctor sized him up, deep UV tan and command comm and offworld clothes, and folded his arms.

"A friend." Words didn't say enough, but maybe his eyes did.

"Security clearance?"

Odd question for a sanctuary medic, but Tas touched his comm to the man's wrist and spoke a command. The Claeran Senate seal and his clearances rotated between their hands in the twilit garden. The man raised a brow but carefully checked his virtual clipboard before he said, "No patient or guest matches her description."

Dead end. Tas turned away, but the doctor silently walked him out to the gate and the Tirion road. For an instant he turned his hand to reveal a handwritten scrawl on his clipboard.

others asked for her
avoid Gwernant
danger

Tas nodded thanks and turned toward Tirion. Now he needed

to move quickly and unseen; good thing he'd left the Az on Arian.

It took him a few minutes to double back toward Gwernant. He'd gotten to know the area as Delun's advisor; when Ren relieved him long enough, he relaxed by running cross-country. But the network of trails tangled and crossed, and when he jogged past the same outcrop twice, he stopped to check his position, wasting seconds. In the woodland he ran on past a new sunken courtyard the size of a ball court, ringed by seating, but he didn't pause. Finally, he reached the streambank below Gwernant's orchards.

Evening deepened the shadows among the immense firs and cedars the Claerans had adapted to their world's grassland soils, but his augmented eyes picked out every nuance of colour and temperature and texture. Soon he crouched on the spongy streambank outside the lower orchard with a clear view of the old Claeran house. Tas had always found Gwernant homelike and familiar, a farm like his own where many generations had worked with soil and sun and rain, sometimes in ways that startled a Mitran. Now Wilm Nolin had made it a monstrosity.

Dark figures passed the windows several times, chimerai of different sizes and fantastically altered shapes. Tas watched the manimals patrol the house and gardens and home orchard. Jackal crosses, big cat crosses like his best student Doll Sorrow, and one huge reptile cross. Too many, too dangerous. But Nolin savoured his pleasures like a spider with silk-wrapped prey, and if she were here, Seren might still be alive.

Tas circled widely to enter at the gate and cross the flagstone landing pad. He walked openly to the front verandah. The big wooden door swung open as he stepped up, and Nolin himself stood framed in a reddish light.

"You're late," Nolin grinned.

Two massive augments stepped from shadow behind him to tower over Tas. Either one could break him in half like a dry stick. One showed a laser and nodded toward the house. Any hope of quietly retrieving Seren and drifting from Nolin's sphere now guttered and died.

"Personal report from the Deep Outside." Tas knew Nolin's appetite for the exotic, and there was a chance he'd been wrong about the trap on Kasumi.

"As I said—too late." Nolin laughed merrily and walked away.

The two huge enforcers searched him but didn't take his slate or comm, a clear message that he could do nothing to make a difference. They led him to an overlit windowless room down two flights of stairs. Tas sat cross-legged and slowed his heart, trying to guess Seren's location, trying not to dread interrogation. A memory surfaced: a prison doctor on Mesa weeping with anger as she reset recently healed bones after an interrogator's visit. But no one came. His devices were jammed, so he couldn't call the Az down from Arian. A meal arrived through a wall hatch; he left it untouched.

Four hours after his arrival the two huge guards hooded him and led him back up the stairs. Hard floor gave way to carpet, then to something like grass or moss, and he felt warm, moist air on his hands. Outdoors.

"You betrayed me," an androgynous voice said softly. Nolin.

It had always been an easy choice: betray Nolin or betray the rest of humanity. It astonished him that his deception had gone unchallenged so long.

"Who told you?" Tas asked to gauge Nolin's direction from his voice.

"You're not the only one to romance a lonely AI that can't accept it died years ago." Nolin stood about two metres to his right, out of arm's reach.

Inka. Even now, after every other loss, her treachery was a blow to the heart.

"You never figured out she'd been playing you for years." Nolin couldn't resist gloating. "You screwed us up on Tanna, flagging our little arms deal, but that didn't kill Mitra. Loukanos killed Mitra. She sold you all out, spread the plague virus for us so she could take credit for a mod to save the world, but the mod was delayed. You should have heard her bleating that we'd killed her. As if she hadn't killed twelve million."

Tas stood frozen, trying to comprehend: Tanna hadn't provoked the Mitran plague? Ten years ago, Nolin said the virus was payback for Tanna and a check to Mitra's growing power. But Nolin never told the truth when a lie would do.

The hood lifted from his head. He blinked and squinted into a mild Bryniau evening; he stood on grass a few steps from the terrace where Delun took her morning coffee, looking out among blossoming fruit trees that stirred in a small perfumed breeze. Another man stood silently in the shadows to watch, showing jewelled teeth in a serpent's scaled face. Duri Balint.

Nolin watched him with curiosity but no trace of his usual fear. Not a good sign. He wore an embroidered red silk robe and carried a fan, and his face was encrusted with irideco. He wouldn't know or care that he looked like an old Earth emperor. Nolin lived wholly in the here and now. Once he killed his assassin, he would complain that he had no assassin.

"You'll get to start my new minimalist art collection. We'll strip your right hand to the bone—or titanium." Nolin was relaxed; his usual histrionics would be more reassuring. "Like some kind of commentary on evolution. Human flesh to clone to titanium."

Tas managed not to look at his own hands, as he'd seen Anton Rethel do. A flight of small dun birds wheeled over the orchard and settled in the big plum tree, then lifted again as a man-sized dark shape rose from a lower branch.

"Too many hands." Nolin seemed disappointed at his lack of reaction. "A man called Rav helped us figure that out. A cloned hand of his somehow ended up on my trophy wall, but now I've got all three. Rav got careless and talked to someone who looked a lot like you, thanks to our AI friend. Those hands you brought me are real artworks. Cloned, aged, carefully damaged. You've gone to a lot of trouble—so I've gone to the same trouble to show exactly how much I appreciate your efforts." He waited for Tas to say something.

"Rav was a trained chef," Tas said. "It's not a crime to work for a Politayan head of state. There was no reason to harm him."

"But he's cooking now. Mesa's fifty degrees in the shade. As you know." Nolin laughed. "Once you're finished, I'll deal with your Claeran piece before she stirs up the tox again. You'll both survive one way at least. Draken sharpened her claws once on Qasri. I have her DNA, and soon I'll have yours. You two won't be around to make babies, so I'll crossbreed you in a fantasy chimera. Basilisk or gorgon, I think." Nolin waited for a reaction again and finally shrugged. "Now you're the opening act in my new private arena—if you can find your way there. I like my entertainments to last. Run hard."

In the blossoming orchard, a black man-sized shape flowed down from a tree, and Tas knew his last task from Wilm Nolin.

His hands rose of their own volition. He could snap Nolin's neck before an alarm sounded, but he threw all his will into resisting that temptation. Since Piñar he'd taken no life, least of all the targets of Nolin's hits who now lived under new identities. On Kasumi he'd done everything possible not to kill. Now he refused to become the cold-blooded assassin Nolin had once delighted in. He forced his hands down.

Beneath the tree the black shape crouched like a long-limbed panther. Then it stood almost upright, manlike but for the ears set high on its head and its lashing tail. It dropped to all fours to run, a solitary hunter from Nolin's menagerie of mythical beasts. Tas stood his ground as the creature bounded close, and he met its powerful leap in mid-air with a fist to the lightly boned side of its man-shaped skull.

The chimera dropped like a stone, rolled, and ran hissing for the trees that clustered around a small grownstone building in the next orchard. In the air above Tas's head, fading a little toward twilight, a hovercam sparkled in the last twilight, recording the hunt.

When he was halfway down the gentle slope into the orchard, he saw the pack among the trees, heads up to snuff the breeze, waiting.

Tas gathered his strength to run.

7

Barred shadow slanted from the dark trees into the tangled undergrowth, giving enough cover for a human form. Doll Sorrow silently tracked Draken on her hunting rounds, twenty paces behind her for safety. Other manimals mostly left each other alone, unless they had prey. Draken hunted everything, and the owner laughed. Draken's eyes and brain were dim, but at a stealthy rustle she struck quickly and brutally.

Doll whimpered at the terrified screams and pleading words of a small animal, one of the lemurs or cats that the feral chimerai defiantly sheltered in these woods. The small one's protests sank to bubbling squeals as Draken slowly tore it apart and ate it. Doll swallowed her sickness and miserably imagined ways that Draken might die before she struck again; this morning the monster had learned how to open the latch on new Baby's crib. Her taste for terror grew with each kill.

When Draken stalked on toward Derw through the gathering dark, Doll turned back to the old stone house. A branch heavy with scented red fruit hung low across the orchard wall. Her new slate told her they were apples, and she paused to snuff deeply. Still no sign of the danger Maq's message warned of, and she was ready to sleep.

Noob met her at the unmarked gap between the stone wall and

the kennel. Before she could speak, he grabbed her forearm with his one human hand.

"Come. Help," he growled.

"Help what?"

But Noob was gone, loping at a crouch through the kennel grove where a horrible baying and shrieking racket started up. The beasts had prey.

Doll crept along the kennel wall and slid inside, where new Baby curled silent in her bed. Outside the prey would be down soon, and if Doll stayed outside the pack might fall on her too. Draken was worst, waiting in the streambank thickets for the pack to drive her meat closer.

Doll's new implant buzzed, and she slapped her wrist in irritation. *"Fuck sabat?"* she snarled, then belatedly remembered comm protocol. "Doll Sorrow. Come in."

"Heya, kid. Tagged the captain yet?" It was hard to hear over the shrieks outside.

Captain? She ignored Maq's voice from her wrist and opened the door.

8

Tas ran with a wind that carried his stink of fear. The pack loped out to meet him, and a few split off to flank his approach. The leader, a dire-wolf cross, ran on two legs but stopped to think on four, a nightmare shape of patchwork fur and a human head with a snarling blunt beast muzzle. Tas pounded straight toward him, and as the chimera leaped, he drove an elbow at his face.

A flash of yellow fangs and misshapen hands. Claws raked his shoulder, and powerful jaws snapped air near his wrist. He ran straight through the screaming melee and beyond it—he didn't climb as they expected—before they understood his ploy. His hundred-metre pace put him far ahead as he ran through the orchard and reached the first trees of the wildland. He slowed to a marathon pace on the streambank path through forest and open woodland, around an outcrop of grey bedrock, on into long pale grass. Glittering sparks of glass and composite that flitted under the tree canopy gave away Nolin's hovercams, recording images of his hunt.

Nolin had his chimerai created in his own image, less clever than they thought, vicious without courage, slower over any distance than a heavily augmented human like Tas. If the leader was smart, he would order half his squad to rest before Tas ran them into the ground. But in the end, he would tire, and they would pull him down. It was a matter of time.

Think. He risked looking over his shoulder and saw his pursuers crouched at the edge of the longer grass, hesitating to follow. The sweet evening breeze ruffled the grass like a child's hair—but the ripples ran across the wind, not with the wind. He leaped for the rock face, and the manimals scattered before him in seeming fear.

A glance backward. The grass was alive with serpents or lizards that he couldn't see clearly. As he turned to run, a chimera swiped him with a powerful forearm. Tas fell headlong onto the lowest rock shelf, and dazed, rolled to look into a madman's hell. He lay between beasts with tormented human eyes and a wall of knotting and twisting serpents with many heads on a single body. The heads spat venom that smoked and charred the grass around the creature's nest.

His hip ached from the fall, and he bled steadily from his clawed shoulder. If they saw him weaken, they would tear him down. Tas levered himself to his feet and stumbled away from the now rested pack. The leader hadn't needed to be smart, he'd only needed his quarry to be stupid.

Tas dragged in a lungful of air and ran on heavily, deeper into the streambank woodland, with the pack in steady pursuit. Ahead to his left lay Nolin's new arena, and the chimerai were herding him in that direction. Every time his path branched, he bore right, until he halted teetering back again on the edge of the arena with the pack suddenly baying at his heels and the huge reptile cross rearing ahead. He vaulted the outer wall and leaped down the steps onto the arena's gritty sand, knowing he might never leave it.

At the rail Nolin lounged in a thronelike seat. He'd cast off his emperor's silk robe to reveal a tunic of studded leather. The archaic weapons in his hands revealed small laser apertures to Tas's augmented vision. Nolin had senselinked too many adventure dramas.

The pack jostled through an arena-level door and crossed the sand toward Tas, but this time he'd had a minute to catch his breath as they circled. The dire-wolf and two hyena crosses were wary, but the huge reptile cross closed on him, hissing smoke and flame. The only safe place was behind it, even with its spiked club tail. Three times he leaped over it as it lashed, but finally the reptile worked it out and turned thunderously to pour fire from its fearsome jaws.

Soon the others would corner him and the reptile would char him where he stood. In the small arena he had no room to manoeuvre. Tas danced beyond their snapping jaws, catching his breath, trying to buy himself time and distance, just enough to survive and find Seren.

Two new chimerai bounded onto the arena sand, a spotted serval cross and a hulking jackal cross. The cat leaped around her slower partner, taunting him with slashing claws and bared fangs, but he closed in steadily with his powerful jaws ready to grasp and tear. Their performance gave Tas a minute to catch his breath.

Faster than even he could brace for it, the spotted smaller one leaped and knocked him flat on his back. Now it would raise its hind legs to disembowel—but it crouched, snarling, on his chest and pawed at his face, strangely with sheathed claws. One of its small paws was furless—a hand. He was still processing that when the chimera leaned close to his head on the sand.

"Be dead now, Captain." Doll delivered an open-handed clout to his head, pulling it short, but leaped to her feet snarling her triumph.

Doll Sorrow and Anubis. Tas closed his eyes. Under his eyelashes he watched their shadow play, Doll crouching over him to defend her prey from Noob, both of them snarling and slashing at each other and then at the other chimerai. The reptile cross stalked outside, deprived of its triumph. It wouldn't fool anyone for long, even with all the blood he was losing, but for now they'd convinced the one essential onlooker. Nolin hooted and cheered from his throne.

Yapping and howling hideously, Noob grabbed his ankle, and Tas let his arms and head flop lifelessly as he was dragged across the sand into the portal. Through a dim, rank passageway he was dragged on his back out onto a mossy forest floor, where Noob helped him up. Tas followed them at a foundered jog between riverbank alders, heaving in lungfuls of air, somehow alive. As the first chimera topped the wall behind him, he stumbled into a run.

Tas staggered on till he saw a slate roof through the branches. His wrist comm buzzed insistently, and he slowed to hear the message. *Alert, band two. Claer Arian, Melyn 4.*

Inka had lied again. Seren wasn't here, she was on Claer Arian. In trouble.

9

Doll looked back from the kennel door, but Captain was no longer at her heels. Winded and bloody, he stood his ground out between the orchard trees.

The pack leader leaped at his throat, all crazed eyes and snapping teeth, but Captain kicked high and drove him back—for now. Doll raised her fist, cocked her new hand dart and shot the dire-wolf cross in mid-air as he leaped again. He hit the ground stunned, but Draken leaped from her thicket and flamed the others to a distance. She made a sickening noise opening the dire-wolf's belly and dragging out his entrails.

"Captain!" Doll yelled through the door.

Draken was distracted for now, but even with a fresh kill, she might attack again. Noob loped out and snarled his threat at Draken and the others until Captain staggered inside and fell against the wall. Noob leaped inside, laughing in a way that wouldn't reassure most humans, but Captain grinned. Then he slid to the floor.

"Doll? Doll? Come in," her comm was yelling again.

"You owe me another hand, boss, and one for Noob," she growled back.

"Got him? Hands all around."

Noob already had the first aid pack open as Maq and Captain

had taught them. Doll wiped off blood and sprayed antibiotics. Then a window shattered inward, and glass hung on the nanowire mesh. That should keep out the pack for now. Later they might have to run, but Captain was looking shaky, and new Baby—

Baby's bed was empty, and she was nowhere in the nursery. Draken roared outside, and the monsters snapped and shrieked over their fresh meat. Let the beasts have her. Bad new Baby. But Captain said stick together and help each other, that's what humans do.

Ears back and tail down in misery, Doll Sorrow wearily opened the door and slid out into the twilit orchard. A gutted and torn chimera body lay under a nearby tree, and Draken crouched over it, growling as she gorged on its wreckage. The leaderless pack was gone for the moment. *Where?* Doll snuffed the blood wind, gazed from the pretty orchard and gardens to the tall forest beyond, and listened attentively. Nothing. Then a shrill scream ripped the stillness deep in the streambank woods. A child's scream.

Doll loped half-upright among the trees in silence until she saw the milling pack, jostling and snarling for dominance. The brindled wild dog cross looked like the new pack leader. Their prey was treed. One small pale leg slipped down from a branch and drew up quickly as two chimerai leaped for it and missed. *Baby.*

Now. Doll had to move, before they decided on a single purpose. She dropped to all fours for speed, raced down the gentle slope between the fruit trees and leaped in to scatter the pack. Claws extended, screaming defiance, she lashed out with her gene-ancestors' natural weapons until she remembered the stun dart in her new hand and sprayed the last two charges around her. Two chimerai fell, and the others ran, all but the brindled wild dog and his sleek black mate. They turned together to attack.

"Baby! Stay high!"

A black shape cartwheeled past Doll and fell heavily. The brindled dog crouched to protect his injured mate. Towering over them on her scythe-clawed hind legs, Draken swayed her head from side to side with small spurts of smoke and dark flame.

"Mine," Draken hissed. "My Baby now."

"Owner will punish you!" Doll shouted. "Bad Draken! Shame!"

Draken cringed back uncertainly. It was Doll's only chance. She leaped, raked her claws across Draken's nose and eyes, and shoved hard. Draken snapped at her, and bone splintered horribly in Doll's new human hand. Then Draken fell, roaring and rolling on the grass, crushing the pretty blue flowers. Doll leaped straight onto the tree's lowest branch, below where Baby crouched weeping and shaking with fear.

"Come now. Friend," Doll pleaded.

The child hid her face in her hands. If she held back, they would both die.

"Come, good Baby. Come and find your mama," Doll lied desperately.

"Pretty cat girl." Baby edged along the branch far enough to reach down and clutch Doll's neck.

One leap dropped them on the far side from Draken, who still shrieked and rolled in pain. Doll tightened her strong arms around Baby and ran. Noob guarded the open door and slammed it on her heels, and blood sprayed across the nursery from the ruin of Doll's hard-earned new human hand. She choked back a whimper, but Noob made a grievous sound that frightened humans would hear as an animal whine. Noob wept.

Bad air. Doll snuffed the room, and her mouth pulled back in a rictus of terror. *Smoke.*

10

ES2742.115

Hovering in stealth, Maq called Tas as the Tirion sky faded through a deep blue twilight. Not answering. Maq's eyes and ears said Nolin was en route to Claer Arian station. So where was Damou?

His trace still flashed silver on Maq's hand vri, but mercifully he wasn't in the old stone house. Instead, he was in a small building deep in the trees, and Doll and Noob were close by; he owed them plenty for sticking with their hated former owner.

Maq never dealt head-on with Nolin if he could avoid it. Year by year he'd watched the man launder himself with seed money from his latest six-families wife and Balint, buying up leverage, but the relentless flattery that won Gabe de Jong's ear was all his own. Gabe was like Tas, he wanted to think the best of fools and sinners. Maq sadly knew better.

"New plan. Drop the stealth, use one of our local registrations and nano our paint to a Claeran corporate." He gave his crew coordinates.

His tox pilot took it calmly, but Maq was relieved to see that her hand shook as she keyed the change. Nothing was worse than fearlessness, Tas and he agreed on that one.

Trees everywhere, big trees, more trees than even his homeworld Sitkum. The first time he visited Claer it was mostly grassland and seedlings, but now it was farms and towering forest where the Pact hadn't razed it. The pilot kept the runabout high for air security to paint, sent a scan decoy to the landing pad to confuse ground security, and dropped like a brick into a grassy clearing between the house and Tas's trace. His crew hit the ground running, and Maq followed. Nolin's current freak show seemed to have the stone building under siege, but by the time he reached it, the others had stunned the chimerai and put out a fire. Maq arrived as his people opened the door.

Dark inside, and no sound. A light seep showed one big room, and another unlit room lay beyond it. He stepped in slowly, quietly, and judged he was halfway across the main room when something hit him fast and hard.

Face-down on cold tile with his arm pinned back to breaking point, it didn't take any guesswork about whose warm palm was flattened across his mouth. Tas breathed next to his ear, "Say a word and I'll break your neck."

Maq slurred against the tile, "Damn it, I knew you'd do that. I hate this ninja crap."

Tas lifted his hand. "Seren's on Arian. Let's go."

"Runabout's outside."

"Wait." In the blackness he moved away silently, guided by his infrared sensors.

Tas came back carrying a bundle in his arms. "How many can you take?"

"How many what?" In the dimness behind Tas, pairs of eyes glowed iridescent red and green, raising all the hair on Maq's neck in a primal instinct. Then someone told the room lights to brighten. "Oh no. Not a chance."

The bundle in his arms whimpered, and the blanket fell away. *God almighty.* Maq said, "Go."

They pulled hard Gs lifting in the runabout, and a Claeran police craft paced them and peppered them with comm warnings. Tas talked to them in Qasri's mother tongue, and the Claeran craft pulled ahead. No tracers streaked past, no bolts rocked the runabout and no stasis net deployed to stop them at whiplash velocity. Instead of a tail they now had an escort. It might be sweet and righteous to die for a just cause, but surviving was a whole lot sweeter.

Airspace traffic control helpfully cleared them to the inner beacons, then onward to station approach. The Pact ships standing off in orbit stayed put. Maq realized he'd been holding his breath and heaved a great gusty sigh as they left atmosphere. There was a vertiginous instant of micro-G before artificial gravity kicked in. He asked Tas, "Champagne?"

"No. Thanks. Gets up my nose."

That struck Maq's funny bone, and Tas laughed too, reluctantly as though he hadn't done it much lately. Maq poured two glasses of akvavit instead. "How the hell are you, kid?"

Tas shook his head and belted his drink in one shot, staring out the port beyond Maq. "A ship's running off our beam. Looks familiar."

Maq folded his hands across his belly, reminded that he hadn't eaten in most of a day. "So it does. My new freighter. Used to be PSS *Gwenllian*. Now it's named after you. *Phoenix.*"

"Good."

"Good?" For years Damou advised him to bury the weapons, scrap the surplus warships like *Phoenix* aka *Gwenllian,* put the transports into freight service, dismantle the intelligence networks, break up the military tech consortium, and learn peaceable ways—and now he saw a major military retrofit and said only, *Good.*

"Endgame," Tas said by way of explanation. Then he slid into the comm chair and scrambled a call in rapid-fire military Damotik. Maq caught stray words like security and plans. Tas came back looking happier.

"Champagne. I never tried that," said a small husky voice from the crew compartment passageway. One of Doll Sorrow's hands was bandaged and the other shepherded a small weary hunchback shivering in a blanket.

Maq forced himself not to flinch. An angel. Merciful mother of God, another hard case for Saint Jude. Nolin was running a high tab. Someday soon Maq was going to escort the shitheel to hell, personally. He fished the fat bottle out of a locker. If he owed Doll and Noob new hands, he could throw in champagne. "Go easy, it's strong." He asked the small girl, "And what's your name, young lady?"

But the angel walked straight to Tas, never mind all the blood and a face that should scare a kid into nightmares, and threw her arms around him. Maq knew enough Tavod to guess she called him cousin-friend and said she wanted her mam.

VII
FREE

1

ES2742.115

Montage, overexpose. Huge time-shifted probability vanes turned slowly outward as the old kinetichron keyed down to a booming F-major, and Seren stood awash in the corridor's reflected ambient light. The null-masked man who stepped to block her way held up a glittering hand.

"So, we have you again." An almost Mitran voice, sharp-edged with fretful energy.

"No." Seren watched his hand. Every motion of the artwork's three-storey panels left shimmering tracks in the air, and the multi-dimensional beauty of mirror space drew her in. Somehow Mihal had drugged her anyway, maybe when she touched the glass . . . *Fight it.* What would Teak not Teak but Tas say now? *Keep talking. Keep moving.* But it was a bad dream of running in deep water.

Sudden brilliance shattered outward as though two centuries of trapped light exploded from the kinetichron, and a great soundless force slapped her staggering backward. The duffel strap slid from her shoulder, and Cedar yelped as the bag hit the ground. A hissing gout of plastic from the ceiling smoked down onto the writhing carpet, which cried out in pain.

Vanes parted. A second man crouched among the moving sculpture's panels—now hidden, now mirrored a hundred times, now insubstantial as clear water—and raised his clasped hands to sight at her. She wrestled her stunner out and sprayed tight-beam across the man. But the panels pivoted closed, and she faced only her own image, white-eyed in shock, stunner braced in shaking hands.

Time folded. The nulled Mitran stood behind her. A ruby eye spat tracer fire across her as someone shouted, "No!"

Seren twisted to fire again into the moving sculpture. But the man was gone, another illusion. Then a blow to the back of her head, and darkness swallowed everything.

In a grey mist she felt a hypospray on her arm, and beauty came riding a cloud of fire. Seren lay under the kinetichron and gazed up into a world of smoke and flame. *Swirls of dust and pulsar flares of incandescent radiance turn and turn within its own knowing. A live cosmos wheels around us, births and dies in great swathes of power. In us the seeds of a new heaven and a new earth. Bodies charge with life, and the terrible beauty of the mother of time lays liquid gold into our veins and gilds us in brilliance* . . . A familiar voice, her own voice, spoke.

"Shut up," the Mitran voice said. "Call him on her slate. Tell him we've got Qasri."

Tas. Something she needed to do, more important even than this cosmic perfection and pattern. But the time-shifted reflections turned again in a breath of moving air, and creation fractured into many dimensions—*Pay attention.* It took an aeon to drag herself up down out of the brilliant cosmos.

Seren lay in the heart of the kinetichron, her senses alive as never once ever, a thousand times more real. *Chemical reality, all life in a molecule, beautiful beyond words and images* Some distant part of her mind noted the drug hallucination. *Focus. Tas.*

"No answer," said a Claeran voice. Razor spiked velvet. *Mihal?*

"Spun up somewhere. No one ever quits. He'd kill you for a cloud. Look at her."

Two brown boots stood near her face, wonderful boots of fine vatskin polished to a rich shine. Love filled her for their perfection, and she reached out. A brown blur ended at her cheek, and bright flowers of pain exploded in her mist. She savoured the rich sensation of seeping warmth and raised a hand. *Crimson. Lovely. Life.* Blood filled her mouth, warm salt and metal.

"What are you doing?" Mihal—maybe—said. "We won't hurt her, you said, I just need to talk to Damou."

"Contract changed when the boss realized the chimerai didn't finish him. Now the offer's double, dead or alive."

"Let her go, Revo. This wasn't our deal."

"You believe everything you're told?"

Maybe-Mihal didn't answer, but brilliant green light flashed from his hand.

Mihal. It was Mihal. Swearing the courier was a Pact scout. Unlatching the weapons pad, his emerald ring glinting green. Breaking her arm on the pilot board when she tried to stop him. Blocking her memory, hiding a bead in her arm, hunting her for a year—or knowing Mihal, hiring this dreg to hunt.

The man crouched to grip her wrist. A finger tapped her comm. "Talk to him."

"Can't." It was hard to talk. "Blocks my calls."

"Inka?" the Mitran said. "Fix it now. Playtime's over."

"Barely begun," Inka's contralto purred from the kinetichron.

"Talk." His voice tasted familiar. Angry. Keyed up. Bitter.

"Seren? All right?" Tas said from her wrist. A tidal surge of happiness swept her, greeting the sound of his voice.

"Tell him to come here, you need him," someone hissed.

No don't come they'll The kinetichron shifted, and Inka's cruel smile turned toward her and away. *Think what would offend most* In a cold high-Tirion voice, "Please. Do not intrude."

A long silence. Tas said, "Forgive me."

A double tap on her wrist, and her arm fell. She told him, "Anything. Always."

But he didn't answer. *Never answered never returned so long ago now.* Lost to sorrow, she rejoined the cantata of light and shadow over her head. Fell forever into its complexity, more real than ever. The kinetichron vanes turned in a minor key, and in their reflections were all worlds, all suns, all faces living and lost. Seren drifted into the pattern and became one with its splendour.

A great many-branching tree of song spreads massive trunk and branch and twig and worlds and suns flower among the leaves immeasurable tree ageless real. Mirror deep and root to root, branch to branch, galaxies and universes of leaves. All time, all matter, all motion, all space, all worlds in a mirror

"Shut up."

Tas the mirror tree

"Leave her alone," Mihal said, but his words ended in a gasp.

Tas needed the mirror tree, but Tas didn't answer. *Mist and starlight. I know this place in music labyrinths in moulded rock in fractal fire in Kuhan's long sleep in shimmering not water of the deep of the Outside*

"Comm him again," the Mitran muttered. "And keep her quiet."

"No one cares. Arian's gone crazy with this tox rising. Manimals everywhere."

Time flows and freezes and vanishes. Evil struts the pivoting planes and branes in irideco and a speckled animal fur long-limbed unnatural its tufted head pulled over his own like a monstrous child's doll. His mouth a card slit in a flushed pale face. Pain his shadow stalks beside cradles assault against a blood-smeared chest. Their steps melt into the dying carpet and fires spring up across the half-lit hall. Greed grows in a great turning vane of light and triumph destructs to microscopic machines of death

"God, she talks." A tendril of fire lashed across her forearm, raising a rich scent of burning textile and skin. *Laser burn.*

Seren shuddered, fighting the flood of sensation. *Thought speaks. How long does this last? Never end. Beautiful erotic real. Tas. They hate. Don't try*

"Make her shut up." A hand over her mouth. "Here he comes. Get out of sight."

Tas Tas Tas Joy illuminated every bone and every cell of blood that pounded her veins and arteries. Tas stood with hands on his head in the corridor.

"Take me. Release her."

Seren rolled onto an elbow. Blood gummed her mouth and throbbed across her cheek. *I know you honour strength beauty I can show you the way you show all I want forever*

"Glitz?" Tas asked the nulled Mitran, who crouched behind Seren touching something cool and hard to her cheek. "Kerkallec's offered ransom."

"Not yet. She wants me again, don't you?" Now the Mitran was disguising his voice with an old theatre trick, running it through a translator to give it Xanadu's narrow vowels, and he'd put on a long, billowing surcoat.

Tas Her hair was roughly dragged back. Pain spiked tears into her eyes. *Focus.* The drug had begun to wear off, and she wept also for its loss.

Tas said, "A hundred thousand."

"Five hundred thousand."

"Not for a woman who tried to kill me for another's crime."

"Not for your lover?" Inka challenged lazily.

"Not now."

Not betrayal to love Teak Tas one the other Tas Teak to love both

"Far too late," Inka murmured. "You had your chance."

Not too late Seren focussed. Bone by bone she tested her strength, muscle by muscle. Nothing was broken, and her head was clearing. The nulled man was tall and slight like the Gwernant intruder. Darker. Cosmod. His real appearance could be anything.

The Mitran said, "What about your crime? You're just like me except I don't play hero."

"So, we can deal."

Something important to say. Something to tell Tas— Remember Her attention strayed back. His glance sent a tingling warmth through her. *Tas Teak Tas.* He shook his head fractionally, and she was desolate.

"Two hundred thousand," the Mitran demanded.

Crazy talk Parvin has no money A thousand could buy a human life or death in Tirion's back streets—Tas would know.

"Done."

Something important a leafless tree mirrored in the starry blue waters of a vast sea a voice of crystal and death is regrowth now the long sleep ends Seren turned her head and saw Cedar's duffel crumpled flat on the floor. Dead? Near it lay the familiar whorl of her stunner.

"Now. No tricks."

"All right," Tas said easily. "Seren, get up and go now."

Something important Now she remembered and yelled, "Teak. Kinetichron. Inside it. Killer." *Nolin Inka Von Mihal power pain death revenge want*

Tas went down, either diving out of range or shot. Seren lurched to her feet, legs shaking badly, and everything hurt, but she stumbled to a stop. Wouldn't leave him while she lived. Walk through fire. She scooped up the stunner through a wall of pain, and as her fingers closed on its cool shape, the glitz spun her off into another hallucination.

Cedar strides tall and terrible as moonlight diamond claws glitter crystal blue time shifts Doll Sorrow Cedar bounded beside the chimera, barred shadow beside dappled light.

Then the small cat leaped at the man Mihal called Revo, and Doll Sorrow plunged between turning kinetichron blades to bring down the screaming watcher. The corridor flickered with tracer and smoke and silence.

"Come." Tas had her arm.

Another rescue.

2

Guarding a glitzed Seren Qasri from residential Glas up to the high hub fell somewhere between rash and suicidal.

"Keep moving," Tas said when she stopped to gaze through a viewport at a Pact military shuttle on approach. He wanted to be far away by the time it docked.

"Tas Tas Teak Tas."

Easier if he carried her. Then she wouldn't have a restless hand on his hip and tell him every three paces how much she loved him. In ten years maybe he could laugh about it. Now she'd spin up a while longer, then plummet into paranoia. He needed her aboard the Az before she decided he was the enemy and tried to run or fight.

A low-level machine voice stuttered from overhead speakers. "Warning. Military action in progress to secure station. Humans, clear hub docks and return to residential levels. Transgenic and augmented animals in violation of custody regulations, report to administration level."

Anarchy, all according to Maq's plan. Chimerai and animals running loose, Pact troops panicking—Screams and laser flash promised trouble ahead in the core lobby. Cedar stayed at Seren's knee, but where was Doll Sorrow? Run the wrong way, and Pact troops would shoot her on sight. Maq's locator buzzed without any response. Helli Njau had left Havre for the Broken Cluster. Maybe Renat was still here on his surveillance contract. His wrist comm blinked no-signal for long seconds, but finally told him, "Lieutenant Von is presently on Claer Arian's high-hub docks."

Relief swept him, though he felt increasingly light-headed. Maybe he needed something stronger than the antibiotic spray Doll gave him at Gwernant to counter the damage from Nolin's toxic pets.

The crowd slowed and congealed as they neared the station core. People jammed the emergency stair that stretched kilometres in each direction to the high and low hub docks. Some might not make it, the old and young and injured, even if the shaft maintained its atmosphere.

Tas tapped his comm. "Inka, what's wrong with the lifts?"

"I'm holding centre crimson for you."

Why? Inka always built debt collection into her favours. Tas steered Seren past a wallscreen that showed Inka reclining in her old garden on Mitra. In life she'd never been so beautiful or seductive, but now she constantly rewrote her simage. Inka, whatever Inka was now, had come unmoored from reality.

"Don't trust." Seren gripped his arm too tightly.

"Stay close. She won't hurt me." Tas led her to the crimson doors in the central lift group, hoping he was right. When he invoked her old obsessions, Inka complied—so far.

Then the core lobby plunged into blackness. Station gravity shuddered, and people screamed. His infrared sensors kicked in, and in the dark he pulled Seren between lift doors that half-opened and quickly closed. The pod rose rapidly—and stopped with a jolt.

Tas tried the keypad, but Inka had seized its functions. "Take us to the high hub, Inka."

Soft laughter insinuated itself into the lift pod. "Why would I do that, Taso? To watch you waste your life? I need you."

Remember it. "And sent me to Gwernant for Nolin's hunters to drag down?"

"Never any real danger, augment against chimerai. Or was there?" Inka seemed lost in some internal debate. Then she moaned, "How could I know he meant to harm you? Nolin is nothing. I'll make him pay."

"Leave Nolin to me." Tas fought to keep his voice neutral. Inka lacked subtlety, and Nolin's death at her hands would be a diplomatic disaster.

"You deserve your revenge, of course. But get rid of Qasri."

"No. Take us up."

"Let me help you, Taso. I can give you everything you want." The lift screen blinked on and showed Inka in a flowering garden, far younger and lovelier than Tas had known her. But her simage broke apart and partially reformed, leaving her slashed in greyscale.

"Restore the lift power now. We have work to do," Tas said calmly, hoping desperately that Inka could still hear an appeal to ethics or mercy or even good sense.

"AI not human machine mind," Seren murmured.

"Let it all go, Taso. I've set up a link. Put your hand on the palm plate and you can upload to my vats. Then I'll let the lift drop."

Tas didn't answer but edged away from the hand plate, and Inka's voice sank to a velvet promise, perhaps taking his silence for indecision. "None of it matters. You've done all one man can do. Let others carry on. Live for an aeon. Enjoy pleasure and power. Watch Mitra's rebirth."

"Not that way. I answer only to the Mitran focal."

Inka laughed. "And Jaime Riordan, when you feel like it."

"Riordan's no part of this. He's been a walking shadow since Piñar."

"You won't need to worry about Jaime again, Taso. Jaime is very ill." Inka managed to sound improbably regretful, so she might have engineered his illness. "Come with me now."

"I'm not throwing away the life Seren gave back to me. Or her own life."

"Of course. I understand. I'll take care of her for you."

"Harm Qasri and you kill Politayan reunity. Harm me and you kill Mitran survival," Tas said wearily.

Inka laughed and turned away into her imaginary garden. "Then I'll have to help you."

The lift pod jerked down, knocking Seren off her feet, but Tas grabbed an emergency handhold and caught her. In his narrow infrared spectrum of greys and blacks, he saw the lift door open a centimetre on the void between the station rings. It snapped shut again on a puff of vapor. The lift shaft was enclosed to protect it from orbital debris, but it was cold as space with no atmosphere. The pod swayed lightly, then harder, and Seren fought him in panic. Every time the pod rocked up, the doors opened facing down the kilometres-long shaft, releasing a cloud of breathable atmosphere.

"Now?" Inka's voice came from the lift speaker. The lift pod dropped again, hard. Tas fell, and Seren flew from his grasp across the floor, but he caught her lasered arm and held on so hard that she gasped in pain. "No. I might lose you again," Inka said. "Not yet."

"On the authority of the focal of Mitra in exile, I invoke emergency powers," Tas said. If she hadn't gone beyond their command, it might limit her power. "Stand down and await diagnostic intervention in your bioware routines. This is an order."

Then the ceiling panels glowed on and the pod climbed. The lift doors opened on the high hub: not on the brilliant honeycomb lights that normally lit the busy deep-space docks, but on a humming rusty darkness that flickered with flames like the shores of an alien hell.

His slate's light showed the lift plaza in chaos. Hexes, freight floaters, equipment, clothes, and artworks lay tangled in heaps as though a tornado had dropped them. No bodies, no stench of death. That at least was different from his return to Mitra San—

"Tas. Teak. Oh no no no." Seren fell to one knee.

A man's hand and outflung arm lay between two broken hexes of glassware. No older than Pedr, he wore the black uniform of a Claer Arian station guard. No pulse, and his wrist was cool.

Tas pulled Seren to her feet and picked a route across the commercial departure hall through drifts of abandoned goods, deeper here as though people had dropped everything to run. They stepped carefully around the last debris and out through the dockside portal.

The dock itself looked undamaged, and the atmosphere membrane was intact, but he saw no station crew. Dim emergency lights outlined the motionless grapples and gantries, neat ranks of bots and unused boarding tubes retracted high above the docking level. They passed a sleek new SenAer nano'd to Claeran green and silver leaves—Maq's runabout—and walked upspin around the dock toward his own ship, still nosed into its boarding tube and service hookups.

Tas's comm buzzed, and a text scroll appeared above his wrist. It was from Maq. "Got my people to stir things up. Strikers freed prisoners and chimerai from cells. Prisoners rousted bars and glitz pits. There soon. Time to drift."

A man strolled toward them down the dock, tall with a shock of spiked red hair, in MitraCorps jungle camouflage and a loaded weapons belt. Thank God.

"Taso." Renat stopped at the wall display of commercial arrivals and departures, now mostly blank, and gave Seren a speculative glance. It had been nearly two years since they'd met in Izu, of course, and she didn't look much like Laure Prakash, especially draped on his shoulder and murmuring his name. Ren tucked his thumbs into his belt and nodded. "Trouble?"

"We need clearance. Nolin's on me."

"Burned out another identity? You live wrong, Taso." He eyed Seren. "Glitz?"

"Maybe." *Explain later.* Caution had become his natural state. "We need to drift unnoticed. Static on the traffic control channels and a dockside distraction should do it."

"Never fear." Renat weighed him carefully, sizing up this new advantage.

Let Ren have the leverage. Tas's years as CO shouldn't stand between two old friends. *Why you and not me?* Ren asked once years ago at the bottom of a bottle. *Luck*, Tas said, *not good luck.* But Ren didn't laugh, just said, *Luck can end.* He was right. Luck and everything else ended at Piñar.

Ren delicately lifted a shining coil of unshielded nanowire from a pouch and walked behind them. Tas felt the wire kiss his wrists, a millimetre too tight, and saw Ren cuff Seren too. Raw nanowire was an assassin's device, highly illegal and never meant for use as a restraint. Any struggle would slice the strand right through human flesh and bone. He could stop a hemorrhage, but Seren's med nano might not yet be at full strength; she could bleed dry in minutes. She was pale and trembling with fear—she hid it well, but he read her heat pattern. Good. Fear was her best reaction so far. The nanowire was a dangerous mistake, but he didn't challenge the plan. He needed Ren's help too badly.

A hand on his shoulder steered him along the dock—downspin, away from the Az.

"Other way," Tas said, but Ren's hand tightened.

An arrivals-departures wallscreen behind Ren shivered, and the text swirled into an image of Inka lounging in her courtyard. Her hair was loose, gilded in late sunlight, and her draped robe revealed one perfect golden breast. "Renat, Wilm needs you. He's deployed a fleet off Acadie and wants to move on Grey space. Leave these two to me."

Renat hesitated, ready to refuse her—he'd always begrudged the resources her survival demanded—but his hand lifted. Since when did he obey Inka?

On the wallscreen, three quasi-human figures in extreme cosmods separated from shadow in a wrecked corporate lounge upspin on the docks. A fantastical jewelled creature in studded leather strutted between two giants, dragging a smear of blood from some dismembered small animal like a crazed celebrant from an ancient story. An extreme avian mod reluctantly trailed the other three. Interesting: they didn't want to look human, as though they knew they'd failed any test of humanity.

The jewelled creature smirked from the wallscreen through a mask of blood. "Good. You got them. Your Pol tit let the woman stun him and run off," it said in a flat Walden accent that lifted the hair on Tas's neck. Wilm Nolin with his bodyguards and Duri Balint, playing predator among Arian's frightened animals and chimerai. It was exactly his kind of sick self-indulgence. He'd lost all caution and restraint, coming here to play his twisted game.

"Inka, keep them here," Ren said and headed upspin.

But Inka had no way to hold them. Seren tensed at his shoulder. Now, while Ren was distracted and before she fought the unshielded nanowire and sliced an artery, Tas snapped his nanowire cuffs. The filament cut the top of his wrists to the titanium bone, then parted and fell to the deck. His cuts were already self-healing when he murmured to Seren in Tavod, "Stand completely still. I'll free your hands." She nodded fractionally. He snapped the nanowire, wincing as it sliced his fingers.

The wallscreen's field of view broadened to show a score of other figures stealthily closing on Nolin. Most walked upright, or nearly so. A throaty growl made Nolin turn in irritation, then terror. A spotted cat chimera and two jackal crosses circled nearer, and behind them, Tas glimpsed Maq Flett cradling an assault laser. Nolin hadn't seen him yet. Tas had to hope Doll Sorrow and Anubis remembered their training.

Far downspin, a knot of men and women appeared around the curved hub dock. Even in dim light at this distance, between the gaunt gantries and loaders, their subskin irideco and fantastical costumes gave them the festive air of travelling players. Some advanced in a dreamlike drift; others leaped and ricocheted from tube housings to service nodes, shouting and carolling like carnival gone wrong. They travelled to a cacophony of broken glass and mad song.

Spun, drunk, or mindshot in some new and exotic way? Arian was not only awash in glitz, it offered a Pandora's box of designer stimulants and synthopiates. Tas didn't want to find out. A grey streak passed them—Cedar—as he grabbed Seren's elbow and ran for the Az.

3

Full sensorium. Light bored through her eyes like a parasite eating its way to her brain. After some time Seren saw it was only a faint glow from dimmed cockpit boards. When she sat up quickly, restraints threw her back in the nav chair. *Prisoner.*

"Seren, I need you to stay calm. No needless movement."

Seren recoiled from the shape that loomed over her. *Tas Teak Tas.* In the Az, in flight. *Words flirt away like silver fish in a sea of stars in the viewscreen stars beautiful stars beacons nothing how can you see in the dark*

"Infrared," Tas said, and gestured so that light glimmered over the boards. "Someone glitzed you. If you come down naturally, I'll have to restrain you for hours till you're through the paranoia and psychosis. I'd rather spray antox into you. It'll reduce glitz craving, but you'll crash hard. Permission?"

Only you would ask that's why I love you don't keep me trapped freefall I want to touch you your voice tastes of cloves your skin breathes sandalwood I know you your wrath is a pillar of fire and your love is a sacrament

"Qasri, rest it. Right now, you're in love with anything you see. It's the glitz."

No you'll never know A small sting spat onto her wrist. *The cockpit spins turns to stone iron earth fall all the way*

Seren vomited into the sickpac he held to her mouth, and retched again dry. She rinsed her mouth from a water foil he handed her. No silver fish glittered through the cockpit now, and he'd lost his dark beauty.

"Better?" He opened her restraints.

"Alive. You were supposed to stay away."

Tas shook his head. Seren put her arms around his neck and leaned to his warmth. Warmer than usual, and he suppressed a wince when she ran her hands down his arms. He held her carefully for a moment, long enough for her to guess he'd forgiven her, then reached for a softsuit. His own suit hung by his chair. Not reassuring. Cedar was asleep in a locker under the pulldown. Seren went to scrub her face, wincing at nskinned abrasions, and her bandaged arm hurt. Tried to remember. Something about the kinetichron and fire and mist.

"Where are we?"

"Running for Czarne Station."

"No pursuit?"

"Not yet." Tas took the pilot chair again and lit his board.

But their escape was pointless. The nav board showed her their power reserves would carry them far short of Claer's three transit nodes that lay out past the sun's gravitational limit.

Aft cam and a drone probe cam Tas had released near Claer Arian showed nothing. They ran dark, slow but secure, as the Az's stealth nanoskin deflected sensor scans at the cost of increased drag. Tas's hands glided surely over his board, checking position and velocity and acceleration, the tug of gravity and the brutal sweep of solar radiation.

"All secure, prepare to transit." Tas spoke coordinates as though they were millions of kilometres farther out.

"Here?"

"Uncharted mirror node in the rock belt. I used it last time I got you off Arian," Tas said. "Take hold."

Transit inside Claer system? But the board zeroed, and she felt a familiar wrench as mirror space inverted. Deep strangeness rippled from the crown of her head to her feet and back again, and realspace shifted in slow parallax outside the viewscreens. *Where. In the cosmos.* Galactic coordinates flashed across the nav board. When she opened her eyes and breathed again, Tas was on comm, they were through the inner rock belt, and Czarne Station's multiple rings hung in the forward viewscreen.

"I need to show you something," she said. Maybe he would trust her, if he'd really forgiven her for stunning him at Hafoty. "Urgently. Now."

Tas nodded, no questions asked, and commed the station again with a request to stand off. Once he engaged the Az's maneuvering engines to hold their position out of the roads, he powered down and called for a freestanding sim to give the Az the squat lines of an insystem station tug. The ship had returned to zero g, but he glanced at her and mercifully brought up the artificial gravity. And waited, still not asking.

Three outbound transports drifted from Czarne and crossed their viewscreen in the distance before Seren took a deep breath and pulled her slate from a pocket. Maybe she could ask Teak if this was wise . . . but Teak would only say, *Do what you know is right.* Carefully she lifted out the backslotted gold oval of Louhi Takahara's bead.

"I can't open her files."

Now Tas gave her a hard stare. "Where did you get this?"

"Someone hid it near a bone pin in my arm. The sanctuary doctor removed it."

Carefully he took the bead. "I have code to open the files."

But it took some time. Seren lost count of his attempts to open the heavily encrypted files on his slate. Lives and worlds depended on the bead's security, and they were meant to be opened on a secure system at MitraCorps HQ.

"Got it," he said finally.

In the vri zone above the boards a woman turned to her cam pickup. Her hair was braided and beaded close to her head, and she wore Spartí greys. Louhi Takahara was finally delivering the report she'd compiled before human space changed beyond recognition. Seren keyed her slate's translator to follow the rapid Damotik.

"This is the only compilation," Louhi said.

Then she heard her own younger voice. "—in a desert where no rain falls. A drylander priest told the Mitran captain, 'On this world tears are the only rain.'"

Rain. Seren knew this archival footage better than her own heartbeat. "This can't exist. I destroyed the last copy."

"A copy went into Spartí files."

Seren covered her face, but at the smell of lemons and heat, she had to look.

Swirling dust. A man walked out of it with an easy athletic stride, and an elder beckoned him to join a religious procession. Teak Kuhan. Relentlessly *Rain* illuminated his last day on Tanna, and again Seren silently thanked his dead cam op Zari Lind. Seren herself was also there in each image and narrated word, unsparingly lit by a passion that still burned clear and bright.

Tas watched the vri impassively, but he had to be living it all again, the choking smoke and flame, the insurgents with their illegal tech, his friends' and officers' deaths, his own death— everything he could never say and she would never ask.

Silently, he reached across their armrests to take her hand. *Friends.* She closed her eyes to hide the flood of emotion and held on to his warm steady hand, waiting for this to end.

In the vri zone Louhi Takahara paused and looked directly at the cam. "You need to see this file we acquired from Pact military archives, sir. Now we know where Zari's vripac disappeared after she mirrored the earlier footage offworld. I'm sorry." She wanted to say more, but lifted a shoulder and quickly turned away.

A new and unknown sequence unfolded in the zone. Seren leaned forward to absorb every detail. Zari's first shot panned from the burning buildings around Piñar's village square to the stone wall where Kuhan crouched. Still untouched by tragedy, he was barely a year older than when Seren had met him in her orchard. Zari followed his gaze to the Dipper insurgents with their illegal Pact field lasers inside the east gate.

"Hold back the thema," Kuhan ordered.

"Sir." His lieutenant Renat Von had red hair braided down his back and irideco swirls on his face. Seren saw—as Zari saw—that Von watched his captain with a chilling flat stare and didn't repeat his order to the Spartí troops.

Kuhan looked north across the square to a small dryland garden where a straggling neodar tree shaded a chair-sized rock. The armed insurgents swarmed in from the east gate. He got to his feet, giving a comm order to Von, and walked out into the square with his empty hands raised. The square erupted in laser fire, aimed not at the captain but at the hover roaring in low from the east. Taking direct fire, it exploded into clouds of flame and slid bucking sideways down toward the square.

Zari turned back to Renat Von and saw the weapon he trained on his captain. Not his Mitran service sidearm, but a primitive laser-sighted projectile weapon he might have taken from a Dry villager.

"Drop it," Zari told him, and a tremor in the vri suggested she'd raised her own sidearm.

Von ignored her, took careful aim at Kuhan, and fired.

The captain went down, vanishing in the crashed hover's billowing flame. Von turned to face the cam op with his crude weapon still levelled and fired again. Zari Lind's last seconds of footage showed his face, devoid of expression, until it jerked upward from view. Then smoke and a flame-shot sky. To black.

Seren gripped Tas's hand so tightly that under his warm skin she felt his strange titanium bones lock. Barely human, but more human than Renat Von. Relief washed through her to see the clear record of Von's guilt. "Now he can face justice."

"I doubt that he fired the killing shot."

Seren opened her mouth to protest and clamped it shut. He wouldn't hear her. Show him Piñar through murdered Zari's eyes, and he still refused to see his friend as a traitor.

Louhi resumed her report. "Once Nolin had you in prison and Riordan pulled MitraCorps off Tanna, the Pact disabled our orbitals to help Inka spread a mutated plague virus."

Tas froze her there, with her hand outstretched as though entreating her Spartí captain to avenge her death and set the human worlds to rights. If only it were that easy.

Seren struggled to absorb her words. "Inka conspired with Pacters to spread the plague?"

"A Pact faction convinced Inka that Mitrans would benefit from her new virally delivered mod. The plague would quickly spread a mild illness, and they would send the antidote sequence in two days. They lied. The plague was deadly, and the antidote never came," Tas said. "We developed it ourselves days too late."

"Your director-general collaborated, aided by traitors in Spartí, and the Pact started a war that killed millions," Seren guessed. Once Kuhan was out of the way, they made sure he took the blame.

"War would have broken out anyway. They wanted all the human worlds under Pact control and started the war as a way to seize it."

Tas skimmed Louhi's files. Delun Qasri's Claeran peace proposal was among them—Seren was beyond shock to see it there—along with images of gross human rights violations: executions on Pamir, mass graves on Claer, detainment and torture on Tolm and Tesla. Seren recoiled from the overwhelming brutality. It was more than enough to reopen the Politaya treaty.

As she paused the sequence, Tas copied Louhi's gold bead and Seren's copper bead with her Bight sequence and locked them into a drone capsule directed to Helli Njau by way of Maq Flett.

In the dimmed cockpit Tas spoke a word, and Louhi resumed her report to her captain. "You were never meant to see what they had in Piñar, sir. You were never meant to go into Piñar." She gestured over her slate, and the vri zone blanked.

"Why did you go into Piñar?" Seren asked. "It was outside the intervention zone."

Tas, still gazing blindly into the empty zone, didn't answer.

4

Mihal stumbled dazed toward the lifts—stunned twice in an hour. When he woke under the kinetichron, there was no sign of Seren or Revo. He still couldn't believe she'd stunned him. *Run with killers, act like a killer.*

"Let me through! Medic!"

Screams and lasers pierced the darkness, and a stench of fear and scorched plastic gave him a sick reminder of Gandhi Base's last days.

A joke that got out of hand, that's all it was. He had to find Seren, explain, reason with her—she would accept his apology with that glacial Qasri courtesy. Her imaginary extra person on the Gandhi shutdown crew had thrown him off. Revo said everyone was dead—accidents, suicide, sickness—but that didn't mean someone deliberately eliminated them one by one. Did it? Would Revo gain from those deaths? If not, who did?

"Help my father! He fell and hit his head," a woman pleaded as he passed.

"Station admin is sending a team." Mihal shook off her clutching hand. It was almost certainly true.

Lise and the surgery bots could handle emergencies till he returned—but maybe he wouldn't return. Not once he recovered Seren. If Revo delivered the Pact fleet movements as promised,

Mihal could call in his ships. Soon.

Seren. Where was she now? Damou had died at the kinetichron, Revo said, but maybe she didn't know that and would still head for the deep space dock on the high hub.

"Medical emergency." He shoved onto a crowded lift and unlocked the override pad. "Extreme danger. Everyone out." They didn't move till he raised his bloodied fist.

On the high hub, Mihal threaded through a shambles of broken equipment and discarded household goods lit by eerie twilight. Looters were busy, by the screams. A red sigil flashed a threat warning over a tumbled stack of industrial bioware hexes, but Mihal didn't waste time calling in the hazard.

At the dockside he emerged near a scarred ship of dark metal. Its needle nose and angled stern had the familiar Pacter freight-drone look of Revo's ship. His Villandry Biron yacht lay two berths beyond it. A man stepped from the black ship's boarding tube, and Mihal ducked behind a gantry housing. Spiked red hair and facial metalling and jungle camo made him anonymous, but he stood braced with his legs apart and arms folded over an assault weapon that looked like MitraCorps standard issue. Revo was an expert at quick self-cosmod, but he somehow changed more than his skin colour and hair and clothes; it was as though he screened through some nightmare catalogue of his own and with each change became a different man.

Staying low, Mihal followed him. A distance downspin, Seren Qasri leaned heavily on the Grey assassin who'd thumbprinted her death certificate, and his arm circled her waist. Revo hadn't lied for once; Damou wasn't dead. The monster was still alive, holding Seren like a lover.

Words passed between them, too low for Mihal to hear, as the man who looked like Revo watched Seren with predatory interest. She and Damou didn't protest as he cuffed them. Then they all turned to a nearby wallscreen and briefly talked with a beautiful woman *en déshabillé* who stretched seductively on a garden bench.

Mihal kept down, desperate to work out what was happening. The wallscreen view shifted to a jewelled freak who postured between two augmented hulks and an avian mod. It was Wilm Nolin, the Pact degenerate who'd threatened him in the ruin of

Gwernant, trailed by his Xanadu gangster.

Revo, if it was Revo, strode off upspin and left Seren and the Grey cuffed on the empty dock. Mihal agonized between following Revo and liberating Seren. He needed her, needed his data, but the cuffs would restrain her and Damou for a while. Carefully he picked his way through the debris to follow Revo. Just another few metres upspin—

Then a blow from nowhere slammed him forward onto the cold, filthy dock plates, and the world spun away into darkness.

Song and a wanton music of breaking glass eventually filtered through his dizzy stupor. A new wave of looters had reached the high hub. He needed to leave—But powerful hands dragged him onto his back, and he blinked up at Nolin's two huge augments. They lifted him like a child and propped him on his feet.

"You. The Claeran tit. Decide to take my offer?" Wilm Nolin swayed on his feet, looking glassy-eyed and completely deranged, with blood on his hands and face.

No. Mihal shuddered, recalling Nolin's threat at weirdly altered Gwernant.

"Villandry Biron provides important information." The redhead appeared at Nolin's shoulder. Revo, definitely. His lazy Pact drawl never quite masked his own raw Mitran accent.

Mihal nodded weakly. Revo could hold off Nolin and help him seize Seren.

"Claeran traitors are in oversupply. Get rid of him."

Claeran traitors? Claeran traitors didn't amass ships and wait their chance to strike Landfall, Prospect, Seneca, finally Walden. *Soon.*

But Revo stepped forward. "Done."

"Wait!" Mihal cried. "I can tell you who—"

"Shut the fuck up!" Revo yelled in his face, but added in quiet Tavod, "Fall down."

Mihal felt a weapon shoved at his back and heard a laser discharge nearby as he folded to the cold dock plating.

Revo seized his wrist and said, "Dead."

"Your turn, Von. You're not going to sell me like you sold your last boss."

Nolin wasn't as spun as he looked, Mihal saw between closed eyelashes. Von? Kuhan's second at Piñar was Renat Von.

Revo only laughed. "Still want him, don't you? And I can still deliver him. Then you put me on retainer, and MitraCorps never troubles you again."

"Dead men don't bargain, asshole." Nolin lifted a jewelled hand to command his two huge augments, but before he could speak, they both silently slumped to the dock.

When Revo lowered his left fist, blood trickled between the knuckles where two darts had fired. The Xanadu gangster turned and ran. Nolin looked around wildly and stumbled back toward the departure hall as a mob of chimerai and animals flooded from a service corridor, led by a little brown man. Spotting Nolin, the beasts broke into a hair-raising chorus of howls and screams as they gave pursuit.

Revo toed Mihal. "Get up. Stun won't knock out these two for long. You'd better be worth the trouble."

Mihal levered himself upright, staring blankly at the man's insolence. "Biron Villandry EntreMondiale takes no orders from a Grey criminal."

"Call it a request." Revo smiled horribly, creasing the metal on his face. "First request—teach the Pact a lesson. Comm your captains."

"We're not ready. A tenday."

"Now." Revo drew a MitraCorps sidearm and motioned downspin.

Mihal stared at the laser in Revo's hand, off safety and slowly blinking red, and he turned downspin. Far ahead, Seren and the Grey eased out of sight behind an old Az patrol ship. Why tell Revo? He would do the man's bidding only until he could get free, then go after Seren and his data. It eluded him yet again, when he'd been so close . . .

His fleet waited among the ice rainbows and rocks of Claer's dim outer asteroid belt. For a year the smaller ships had crossed and recrossed Politaya space and Neutrality space as surveyors and freighters and private yachts, and dreaming or dead in untravelled space, the larger ships had hung derelict.

One by one the ships answered Mihal's call. Captains stripped away double bulkheads and flooring, retrieved their arms caches, deposited families on the nearest station or drifted and burned with their cargo still netted down. Dropping their stealth, they

cleared the rock belt and ran at fast sublight speeds out through
Claer system.

5

ES2742.116

Pan 360° on y axis, found sound. Commercial ore haulers and Pact military traffic came and went around Czarne Station. So, he wasn't going to answer her question about Piñar.

Seren got up to pull galettes and strong coffee from the food fab, and by the time she brought them back, Tas was on comm getting cleared to leave the station roads.

"No shortcut via uncharted node?" Seren asked as they ran outsystem at sublight speed.

"Out past your ice world." Tas set auto and unlatched his chair to prop his boots on the board, looking weary and the worse for wear, much as she'd seen him first on Arian. He'd had to fight to save her skin that time too.

"How? Only rare special conditions enable the opening of a mirror node."

"True," Tas said between swallows of coffee, "three centuries ago. Since then, we've refined the technology. We'd have listed more coordinates recently if the Pact hadn't defied the Interworld Accord. Now—why make it any easier for them to travel Outside?" He checked his chrono, set an alarm on the board, and closed his eyes.

Cedar flowed down to the deck, yawned and stretched mightily, and went to get food. Tas had adapted the galley food fab so she could operate the controls, and the cockpit smelled like a West Sea fish plant.

Tas didn't sleep. Instead, he shifted and turned as though unable to get comfortable. Then he sat up, scrubbing his face, and finally answered her question. "Spartí went into Piñar at the Dry elders' request. The village was threatened, and they asked us to protect a treasured monument."

Seren closed her eyes, visualizing the sequence she'd viewed so many times. "The rock under the neodar tree in the square?"

Tas nodded. "You noticed that. No one else did."

No one else cared as much. But Seren kept the thought to herself.

As though he'd heard it anyway, Tas took her hand. "Their founders had brought the object back from the deep south in settlement times. They wouldn't let me record images, and it disappeared after the Piñar massacre, but before that I saw it several times." He hesitated. "It was covered in ridged patterns. Like the polar site Maq showed you on Claer."

Seren frowned, puzzled. "The rock under the neodar looked smooth."

"They protected the patterns by coating the object in clay. No one saw the light pulse until some of the clay coating cracked under fire."

"But I thought antiquarians made the polar pattern to duplicate an old Earth monument."

Tas shrugged. "So we believed at first. Our surveys charted extensive patterns, but the information is lost. Most of the Mitran scientists who worked on them died in the plague."

"So, what are the patterns?"

"Unknown." Then reluctantly he said, "It is possible that we just missed meeting some galactic neighbours, another sentient race that explored this galaxy's life-generating belt, by a few million years. No time at all in cosmic terms."

Seren waited for a joke about ETs, but Tas looked sombre and sane as always.

"And the pattern on Claer?"

"Once we knew to look in the polar regions, we found sites on a handful of worlds. Mitran scientists guessed they could be habitation traces from a spacefaring race now long vanished from human space. We call them moulders because of the patterns. The Pacters call them moles after an old Earth rodent. They could be artworks or attempts to communicate."

"Hello?"

Tas smiled then. "A highly complex hello. I ran a schematic of the largest site—at Mitra's south pole—through pattern-generator programs as math, music, dance, visual art, architecture. Interesting, but not especially communicative. It could be an invitation. Or a warning."

"There's been no contact." Seren couldn't believe she was speaking these lines from a vri drama.

Tas studied her face. "Soon I'll tell you everything."

"Soon? You said that in Samun. It's been a year."

"All right."

Now, after this long evasion? Seren forced herself to breathe.

"Pact and Pol warships disappeared in the Deep Outside for years, but Grey rescue and exploration missions come and go freely beyond the Tripline."

"Why?"

"Our rescue and survey ships travel unarmed." Tas weighed her expression, which had to be a study in perplexity, and nodded. "An ancient network may still function—to destroy armed ships but let unarmed ships move freely. Whoever made them must be long gone. We've found no sign of life, no organic matter, no remains."

"But artifacts—that's wonderful!"

"Gabriel de Jong learned of the object on Tanna. Wilm Nolin told him it posed a threat, and he agreed humanity might need to fight for human space."

"Fight ghosts? So, they destroyed the Pol to train for a war with an ancient system? And you move freely, while the rest of us cower inside the Tripline or get mistaken for an enemy that disappeared a million years ago. Or do you just lead a charmed life?"

"I thought so once." Tas delved in his pocket and handed her a small flat stone that fit into her palm. It was dull grey-blue, incised with a polished labyrinthine design that could be two West Sea corals laid root to root or maybe a watershed. He closed her fingers over it. "I found Mitran diaspora survivors—safe now on Claer—on a barren world in the Deep Outside. One of the children gave me her tree stone."

Seren smiled as he described the small barbarian who prodded him with a broken antenna, told him fantastical stories, took him to her special place, and sent him away with gifts. His rescue venture in the Deep Outside captivated her, especially his warmth for Mei and the other young castaways. A year ago, she'd have guessed children only irritated Damou.

Tas touched his slate, and in a moment a small vri blossomed above the pilot board. An unknown world of the Deep Outside— she could have walked its dun gravel hills and algae-streaked plains if Parvin hadn't dragged her back to Tirion. Tas fast-forwarded to show a barefoot girl in ragged clothes trotting down a long incline of gravel to a small lake. The path wound sinuously across a slope where faint ridges were just visible in the slanting light.

"Did you locate the moulder pattern from orbit or did you see it only when Mei took you there?" The girl skipped along the outer margin of a small pattern, partially overbuilt with gravel and sand to make a path. Much of it seemed to lie hidden under the glassy lake that reflected Kalevala's pale grey sky.

Tas frowned his incomprehension and glanced back into the vri—and his face lit with wonder and understanding. He hadn't known. "Write up your observation for the Astrobiology Institute on Rustam."

"You write it. You know what to say."

"We'll coauthor it then. The honorarium should almost cover a meal."

"What do you think they were like?"

"Maybe they were like us, driven from their planet of origin and looking for new worlds. Maybe they were completely different in ways we can't even imagine. Maybe we misinterpreted the data, and they never existed."

"Maybe they wanted our worlds," Seren said, knowing how phobic that sounded.

"If they'd wanted our worlds, they'd have them now. Their tech was more advanced."

"We could share," Seren said. "They only wanted the polar regions."

Tas gave her a bemused look. "Good idea, if they weren't long gone." An alarm sounded on the nav board. They were beyond the ice world's orbit and approaching their mirror node. "Now we run for Grey space."

"But we're three nodes away from Grey space," Seren said.

"Not by the old Claer-Mitra node."

The Dead Gate, where Rozenn's lover had died. And many others. The wrecked Pol cruiser *Ys* probably still drifted in its deadly currents. No one sane risked a dangerous delisted node—but she'd never known anyone as sane as Tas. Long before anything came up on visual, the Az shuddered, and perturbations flashed the boards. Seren struggled with nav calculations she hadn't done since flight training, and Tas was busy with hands-on manual.

No beacons marked the approaches to the old node, but on his pilot board image, Tas pointed to a ragged darkness veiling the starfield they would enter. "Dust band around Las Hermanas."

In his archival image, two planetless binary suns stepped a complex dance within the dark swathe as the white dwarf Bella dragged a river of gas from its bloated, dull red companion Gorda. The dust band faded to invisibility at their approach; its molecules were scattered almost vacuum-thin. Seren called up a sim, touched it to fast-forward, and watched the giant's matter pour into the smaller but hotter and denser white star over the next few million years. Finally, Bella slammed into Gorda and both exploded into a fiery globe of released energy.

Tas looked up from his scrolling ephemeris file. "Remarkable, isn't it? Dust rings doing figure-eights around unstable binaries. They probably absorbed or ejected any planets long ago."

"Is that why the old Interworld Accord closed the node? The instability?" A dozen adventure vris claimed the Dead Gate dismembered ships in transit.

"The dust is highly magnetized, but the charge fluctuates. It can be harmless or it can trigger a mirror flaw that fries sensors and boards. Centuries of human use may have altered it in quantum-mechanical ways. Someday it may self-destruct."

"So, our passage could touch off total destruction?" Seren glanced out through the faint dust ring and cleared her nav board to locate the node by his coordinates. Close now. "You won't really transit into that."

"No." Tas cycled his board back to a status display. "You will."

A small delight lit somewhere deep inside her to see his smile crease his ruined face. Warmth curled her mouth and softened her shoulders, and she recognized it as simple happiness. She asked, mostly to hear his beautiful voice, "Why do ships still use the Dead Gate?"

"No one's lost a ship in a century. Greys use it as a fast route from Claer to Mitra, Rustam to Vritra, Xanadu to Han, and a good place to sit out trouble. Match radiation signatures and you fade into the background, unless someone mirrors right onto you."

"Isn't it clogged with wreckage from ships that failed in transit?" Seren said, remembering Rozenn's stories. "How do we get through without a collision?"

"The wrecks are mostly in vri dramas. There were no more wrecks at the Dead Gate than any other node in the trial-and-error days. A few well-marked hulks that are thousands of kilometres apart pose no serious hazard. We tow them into solar orbits, and eventually they infall."

"So why isn't the node charted as safe with a warning?"

"Hard radiation. Spend too long there, and it ravels your DNA. I've set you up for transit."

No one else had ever heard Seren Qasri say this: "I'm afraid."

"Good. Fear tells you to be cautious," Tas said. Teak Kuhan had said the same thing a lifetime ago. "You need to learn this. I'm here if you need more hands. Go."

Seren checked his board setup—flawless, with engineering centred and nav reports neatly ranked above—and touched the transit pad before she could lose her nerve.

A moment of dislocation, an unknowable subjective span inside a black pearl of timeless nonspace, and they wavered into a new realspace. Their cams showed the red giant and white dwarf arm-in-arm in their dust and gas ring, looking innocently beautiful on their background of night and glittering stars. Seren checked their converter reserves, confirmed their coordinates—

A vast power seized the small ship and shook it. Space twisted, flared with brilliance, and darkened again.

"Tas!" she gasped out, clutching her chair arms.

"Mirror flaw. Happens. You can handle it."

Alarms blared, cockpit lights dimmed to power-save, and gravity tugged spitefully at the Az. In the viewscreen, space swung a dizzy retrograde until the ship righted itself in jolts like a carnival ride. Too shocked to do anything at first but hang on, Seren found the green pad and burned away from the sister stars' grasp. Still shaking minutes later, she touched the onscreen symbol for Grey space, and as they travelled onward, the pilot board came alive in virtuality. They had made their transit.

A spur of the Neutrality separated inner-worlds Pact from outer-worlds Politaya. Ahead in a jagged path outward lay Rustam, Vritra, Xanadu, dead Gandhi Base, the distant Tripline, and the Deep Outside, guarded by deadly ancients.

Seren rotated the sector in virtuality on the nav board. Shipping routes blinked in blue dashes; nav beacons flashed red and green and white. Ships were sparks of Pact gold, Politaya green, Neutrality silver, unIDed amber. Two silver sparks approached on the blinking blue route from Xanadu. She zoomed out to their own position, showing their mirror nodes. Their engine output slid steadily toward the redline as the Az vibrated with contained power.

Now. Seren folded her hands and leaned back. "Renat said your identity's dead."

Tas lifted one shoulder. "I'll build another. Get a new cosmod. Do other work."

"I thought you never planned to get a cosmod," she got out, when she desperately wanted to say something quite different. *Now I understand. Or maybe I knew all along.*

Tas looked at her sharply. "Not until I was dead without it."

And a dead man can't keep a promise to return, or pay down a debt of honour. But he still didn't admit anything openly. Seren studied her linked hands. "Blank slates, new names. Tas, we can do anything we want. Run for the Tripline."

Tas hesitated. Now he would say, *I'm needed. No one else can steer Mitran recovery and renegotiate the ruinous Pol terms of peace.* But instead, he said, "All right. Go."

Seren turned uncertainly.

"Choose a heading. I can't do any more good here."

Wrong. Seren touched the nav board. It couldn't be true. Soon he would give her some Grey-space vector . . . But he checked power reserves and waited for her choice. If they travelled without major burns, they could charge the converters at any Neutrality station.

<> What's the nearest, Teak? <>

No answer.

"You don't need the avatar," Tas said. "You have me to answer questions."

"You jam it," she realized.

"Not deliberately. Biometric interference. Go."

Any direction would do. Unmarked and unpatrolled, the Tripline enclosed all of human space like the skin on an apple. They could retrace their back trail to Claer, run out to Gandhi and the old drive-limit boundary, or follow any other route they chose.

"What about your ordnance if we run the 'Line for Outside?" Seren asked. *Our ships travel unarmed.* It was one thing to hear it, but a less comfortable thing to strip out all munitions and point a small unarmed ship into an unknown that suddenly teemed with ETs—she smiled at her own fears.

"We'll launch a freight capsule to the nearest MitraCorps depot."

Seren punched in a course for Vritra and wild Xanadu in Grey space. The Az slowly swung across the brilliant galactic core and steadied on its new heading.

6

A blood red ship floating against a silver-beaded black velvet curtain: for the first time in a century, Maq thought of his Illahie Sitkum school getting ready for the winter dances. One year he'd carved a ship in cedar, painted its bow with large white and black eyes, and made the pupil of each eye an open green hand. His teacher hung from it the hall rafters among a wooden fleet. It didn't seem all that long ago.

Outside his forward viewscreens, space was a shifting pattern of silver beads as *Phoenix* ran outsystem. Maq called up a chart on his implant. In his small vri zone the green dot of Claer turned within its blinking shell of stations and nav beacons. Beyond the inner rock belt near Czarne Station, beyond the outer rock belt, beyond the star's gravitational pull, the Dead Gate blinked a slow grey near the thin veil of neutral space. A virtual silver shimmer marked the Neutrality's inward boundary with the globe of Pact space and its outward boundary with the larger shell of Politaya space.

On the far side—the Grey side—of the delisted node, Tas's old command ship travelled alone in the vastness of an empty star system. A drone probe relayed an image of the Azande bathed in Gorda's rusty light, and Maq turned it like a jewel on the palm of his hand. The blinking green dots of Pol ships showed Biron's passage outbound through Claer system from Czarne. Still far behind despite their greater speed, Maq's neutral ships blinked silver as they slowly closed the gap. Both groups were hours from the Dead Gate.

Maq flicked off his vri when Parvin Kerkallec returned from tactical ops. "Bet I could make a bundle skimming the rock belt. Those planetesimals scan rich in heavy metals."

Parvin usually snapped at such provocation, but this time she resisted the temptation. "Status report?"

"On your screen." A Claeran commander asking a Pacter for help—but now he was a Grey again, so maybe that was easier. He'd put *Phoenix* at Kerkallec's disposal, since she was too dangerous to leave downworld as foreign powers quarrelled over Claer's bones. The other Claeran refugees he'd brought from Melusine, and as far as he could see, all they did was sing and screw and argue. If they didn't make him smile, they'd be driving him crazy.

"Current conditions at the node?"

Comms three, report to captain. Maq had somehow slipped a few centuries. He touched through his probe images. "Bella doesn't look good."

Parvin's curse was beyond his grasp of Tavod, but whatever she'd said, Maq agreed.

The vri zone over his nav board rotated the distant binary system where the node mirrored out. Graphs beside the vri scrolled radiation levels and instability probabilities at near-lethal levels around the cannibal star. The white dwarf pulled a long skein of glowing red dust from its red giant companion, and a single twisted hoop of dust and ice circled the angry sisters.

The Dead Gate now looked scatty as hell, and he mistrusted it. Tas had already triggered a mirror flaw. If Biron transited, he might collapse the node. Then he'd vanish into mirror space, Maq would be stuck on the Pol side with Wilm Nolin and that asshole Balint in his lock-up threatening mayhem, and Damou and Qasri would be stuck on the Grey side with a possible solar event they couldn't outrun. *Halo mesachie.* Hell of a mess.

Parvin clamped her jaw and called Rozenn Milosz to the bridge. An intense little dark-haired woman arrived smartly with Nolin's pet angel in tow, dark and wingless now that an emergency cosmod had kick-started her regeneration process.

Maq handed off, and Milosz started work with the kid attached to her like a limpet mine.

At first his crew had balked at Claeran kids roaming the bridge, but they behaved. Kerkallec said her own kids had nursed in watch chairs and played under the feet of weapons hands and comm specs in peacetime, but a warship on task wouldn't normally carry children. No one really knew what *Phoenix* was now, though, with her heavy military retrofit and Grey registration and crazily mixed crew. Ex-Pol fleet officers and ratings were all over his ships, but he wasn't that upset. Parvin's people knew their tech.

Milosz saw Maq watching and told him over her shoulder, "Charts two on the cruiser *Ys*."

"Call Biron," Parvin ordered her comm tech. A coil of cord lay invitingly before her, but she sat at the nav board with hands clasped, motionless. No cat's cradle. Must be serious.

"Mihal Villandry Biron on *Marianne*."

The vri zone cameo'd a young man whose elegance shouted Reprise citadel. He wore his blond hair long; his eyes were dark water-iris blue in a flawless face and his arrogance outshone even Kerkallec's by orders of magnitude. Mihal Villandry Biron made an unlikely revolutionary, but then so did Maq Flett. What happened to Sitkum wasn't going to happen to Claer or any other world, not on Maq's watch. As Damou said, some things you need to do over and over till you get them right.

"Why are you in contravention, Biron?" Parvin demanded.

"Go home, Parvin. Run and hide." Biron wore a flash Claer Defence uniform, but he looked pale as though he walked with ghosts. *Marianne* must be a family freighter, since his bridge watch wore company livery.

"If you engage, you'll last only minutes against a Pact battle group, and the blowback will kill us all," Parvin barked. "We can't survive another war."

Maq winced. He'd followed the newsgrids during the war. Parvin Kerkallec had no patience for negotiation or compromise, but she would defend her ground to the death even if she had to do it with rocks and sticks. It was pure accident that she hadn't died at Wairoa in the wreckage of her ship. And once she scented blood, any subtlety fell away like a null mask.

SHADOW MATTER

Biron didn't sound as supercilious as he looked. "You prefer to watch our worlds despoiled one by one? At least we'll go down fighting. Join us. And in reality, how can you stop us?"

Doll Sorrow appeared at Maq's armrest, crouching in the bridge's dim light with Hasi and Anubis at her heels. A delegation. "Important, boss. Report on Claer surveillance and what Herra Nolin told Herra Biron."

Biron's eyes hardened when he saw her, and Maq shook his head. *Later.* Manimals had their own agendas and sometimes screwed up their timing. *But—Nolin told Biron something?* He muttered to Doll, "Record it and send it to me."

"We'll stop you. Board your ships and disarm you forcibly— though the Pacters would like nothing better than to see Pols in open conflict." Kerkallec's anger failed to mask an undercurrent of fear.

Maq groaned inwardly. She wasn't asking any of the right questions. *Why are you doing this? What do you want? What are your plans?* Threats and lectures wouldn't work on a madman with fire in his eye. What had gotten into Biron, anyway?

Biron's answer was to lean forward in the zone. His image blinked out.

Kerkallec swore. "Freighters and pleasure craft and travelling scrap."

"A rebel fleet, to the Pact," Maq said soberly, recalling Sitkum's death. "Call Damou." He hated to say it. He'd rather Damou and Qasri escaped and had a life.

"Damou can fry. Another overpaid Mitran thug with too much power. He abducted my second-daughter." Parvin got up to head aft.

"Sure she didn't abduct him?" Maq minimized his space images and called up the new image sequence Tas had sent. He could put it to good use before he couriered it on to Helli Njau.

Parvin turned away angrily.

Tanna unfolded in the vri zone like a desert flower, ochre and tan and white as Piñar village was once. "Sit down, commander. It's story time."

Parvin said from the hatchway, "I've seen it. I know about Piñar and *Rain*."

"Not this part."

Closeup. Seren cleared the boards and rechecked the probe images from Politaya space, but the ships reappeared in a Pol fleet cruising formation. All had Pol or Neutrality registrations—but no Politaya fleet had existed since the war. *Scan ghosts.* She asked Tas uneasily, "Thirty-two ships in two groups, two and five hours from the node. Who are they?"

"Unknown. They scan weapons-rich."

Tas had positioned the Az between Bella and Gorda, the unstable binary stars on the Grey side of the node, and launched drones. Now he rotated images of the largest freighter under Grey registration, outbound through Claer system. No colours or corporate logo, registration numbers only, so it could be a backworld hauler risking the fast Dead Gate route. New comm arrays and housings—in a warship they would conceal lasers and particle beam cannon—didn't hide its distinctively Claeran backswept lines.

When the comm buzzed, Tas nodded Seren to answer. The heavily encrypted and frequency-spread call carried Maq's locator signature, but it was Parvin Kerkallec who scowled out from the vri zone. She had sleepless purple bruises under her eyes and hair like a brown stubble field, sheared in mourning. Behind her lay a dimly lit bridge designed like a Claeran warship's but retrofitted with more attention to efficiency than aesthetics.

"Get me Damou. I'll deal with you later, Lieutenant."

Tas greeted Parvin soberly, though beyond visual pickup he put a hand on Seren's arm, and she leaned to his touch. Reflected in the viewscreen's glittering starfield, the reddish light from his board gave him on one side a human face, on the other a demon mask.

"Situation, Captain," Parvin snapped as though he was one of her juniors. "A fleet is heading your way—armed merchant ships and warships that were supposedly scrapped two years ago. They belong to Villandry Biron EntreMondiale."

"Unwise," Tas said mildly. "A Pact fleet's on exercises near Acadie. Nolin ordered it out before leaving Arian."

But Villandry Biron ships armed and en masse? Mihal had lost his mind. Cedar emerged from her hidey-hole, saw Parvin, and crouched with ears back and tail lashing the deck plates.

"If he launches a rebellion, he'll destroy any hope of reopening treaty talks. Meistr Flett says negotiation is your strength. Stand him down before the Pact does. You're on contract."

Seren caught her breath. Mihal had already tried to kill her once, maybe twice, and she and Tas were outbound from this mess.

"No," Tas said. "Let them come to their senses and go home."

"Can't risk it. Payment up front. What's your fee?" Parvin demanded.

"Two billion to negotiate end of hostilities."

A minor backworld's gross world product, enough to buy a small moon and a nanoform. But Claer Defence didn't exist, as Tas must know, and the Claeran shadow parliament was bankrupt.

"Start now."

"No."

A compact peat-brown man stepped into cam pickup range. Maq wore a laser that belonged in a museum and a Mitran shock shirt that gleamed under his bush gear as if he were prospecting in brigand territory. Hasi's sleek head peered over his shoulder, dispelling the sombre effect.

"Why not?" Maq demanded.

"Other plans."

"They can wait."

"No."

Parvin and Maq acting together? And Maq taking a hand in Claeran affairs? Seren didn't have time for outrage. She touched the symbol for Parvin's ship, and details marched across the display. *Phoenix* was registered on Rustam in Grey space, but a search showed its specs and hull scan matched Claeran ships decommissioned soon after the war. Full rider racks shadowed its flank. Last time she saw this ship, in a Claer Arian deep-space berth beside its sister ship *Heledd*, its bow plates read *Gwenllian*. What had Maq said on Melusine? *New station. I bought a decommissioned Pol cruiser.* But this was no longer an orbital station, if it ever had been one. It was an operational warship.

"The Pacters will cinder any Pol fleet they encounter near Pact space," Maq said.

Tas agreed. "Biron's ships are no real threat, but this is an act of aggression. Here's my best advice, freely given. Go home. Don't escalate this into another war. An open exchange of fire would be a bloodbath."

"We have no choice." Parvin folded her arms.

"You always have a choice."

"MitraCorps could neutralize the threat. It might take several companies."

"Noted and declined."

Seren listened uneasily. Tas, speaking for MitraCorps? On whose authority? But she recalled Parvin's claim that one man had veto power in the Mitran focal: Damou.

Over her shoulder, Parvin asked Maq, "How many ships can you lift?"

"Carrier, cruisers, destroyers, frigates, bunch of small stuff. More every day."

"You have a carrier?" Tas asked.

"*Sedna,* used to be *Cité Soleil.* Pol surplus. It made a skookum ore hauler."

Seren barely registered their words. On the bridge of *Phoenix,* where Maq's crew monitored their boards, Rozenn Milosz had nav one. A woman in old Pol Fleet greens at the next worktop watched Parvin closely. Blonde hair pulled back from a round face, nearly Seren's height, about Parvin's age: a stranger who somehow looked familiar. Seren touched the woman's image on her display, and her name scrolled: Nur Davi, AnvilCo. One of Maq's people.

Parvin fixed her gaze on Seren. "Lieutenant, you're charged with desertion. A launch will come for you once we transit. I strongly suggest you cooperate."

"No," Tas said.

Parvin glared from Tas to Seren and blanked her screen.

Tas stretched carefully and captured Seren's hand from the nav chair armrest. He gently unclenched her fingers one by one. "Vritra and Xanadu. Let's go."

Seren dropped her chin onto her fists and studied the starfield beyond the viewscreen as Tas moodily considered his node charts and ephemeris. Cruising the Tripline, she could finish her vri *Return*, release it on the grids. But first—What could she say that he could hear? *Mihal's deadlier than you know, not a starry-eyed patriot trying to save his world.* But Tas needed to leave Pol space, and she needed Tas—unsettling to need a man without a name or a past or even his own face. All that really bound them was a fragile trust. But she still had to try.

"Tas, we can't let millions die for one man's political naïveté. We can stop Mihal."

"High risk." He didn't sound especially surprised.

"Once we're done, we'll run for the Tripline."

Tas touched his comm pad, and Parvin reappeared in the vri zone.

"Pardon for Qasri. She's done no wrong, only followed her original orders."

"I can't rewrite regulations, Captain." As though she were still Pol fleet.

Tas waited while she weighed the alternatives. Then he added, "And secondment to MitraCorps."

Finally, Parvin nodded stiffly as if it might break her neck.

"I'll send my contract."

The vri blanked.

Seren studied her hands. Steady. The Az might take down an armed merchant but not a battle group built around a Pol carrier and fast cruisers. Finally, she asked, "What if we need to fight?"

"We won't."

Tas had positioned them between unstable binary stars, which could be great courage or suicidal madness. But she still trusted him with her life.

Now he was screening through data files at AI speed. Someday Seren would ask the full extent of his regeneration and mods, if she really wanted to know. Sweat shone on his forehead and trickled down the furrowed scar tissue. His fear at least was fully human—or maybe it wasn't fear. He'd been shifting uncomfortably in his chair and held his right arm immobile. Seren touched his hand but recoiled from the fever heat. "All right?"

"A chimera clawed me on Claer."

"I'll spray antibiotic."

"Med nano can deal with it."

Finally, Tas took a deep breath and spoke locators to his comm board. In seconds Mihal gazed from the vri display, and Seren wondered if she'd been overconfident about stopping him. Mihal Villandry Biron, merchant prince and admiral of a non-existent fleet, wouldn't easily let anyone turn him aside from his grand quest.

"Seren's unharmed," Tas said calmly.

Leave me out of this. Seren swivelled to see Tas leaning easily in his chair, chin on hand, probing the raw nerve. She checked the cockpit cams. *Recording.*

Mihal's expression changed. "I'll talk with her."

"Certainly," Tas said and, as Seren opened her mouth to protest, added, "after we discuss an offer of amnesty for you and your captains."

"Amnesty for what?" Mihal looked surprised. Did he actually think the worlds would applaud his mad crusade?

"All charges will be dropped if you return insystem and disarm. No one wants to harass a Claer Defence reservist who overlooked an interworld boundary."

"Who hired you?" Mihal demanded.

"Parvin Kerkallec for the Claeran shadow parliament."

Mihal's eyes slid left, to a point just outside cam pickup. "What does she want?"

"What you want is the point." Tas lowered his voice enough to make Mihal lean forward. "It's the same thing I want. Justice."

Seren found she'd nodded approval like a director in rehearsal. Straight from Kuhan's negotiation handbook. Justice would be a keyword now, a device to create common cause and a personal bond.

"Spare me that 'enemy of my enemy is my friend' line." Mihal turned slightly toward his unseen companion. Who was it that he minded so closely? Someone who advised him dangerously. "I know your history. Seren might want to know it too."

Blackmail. Seren could slap him, but Tas looked amused. "She knows everything."

"Remember she was mine first."

"No." Tas paused, and Mihal sharpened. "Not yours. Not mine. Her own person, always."

Text scrolled across Seren's small comm screen as Tas keyed, *"Brief me. Was he your lover on Gandhi?"*

"Turned him down once," she wrote, but the lurch in her belly said there was more. *"Memory block. Can't remember later."*

"Everything you know."

"Villandry Biron EntreMondiale heir. Brilliant student. Dismayed his family by studying medicine. Later joined family corporation. Arts patron. Vain, self-absorbed—" Seren entered everything she could recall about Mihal. None of it seemed likely to help.

"Why are you doing this, Mihal?" he asked mildly.

"Not your concern, Damou—are you still calling yourself Damou?"

"No."

Beyond the viewscreen, sparks flared red as an asteroid or debris plunged toward Gorda's ruddy furnace. In the sisters' glowing halo, Seren saw a great flower of light open and slowly close fractal arms that must span thousands of kilometres. It pulsed brighter within that blinding brightness, shifted, turned, and was gone. Spacers told tales of strange lights that strayed in from mirror space. So many mysteries and so much beauty filled their own vast home galaxy. All she wanted was time to explore it with Tas.

Tas folded his hands in his lap—good body language, neither belligerent nor impatient—and waited. Mihal's sneer faded and he glanced up, probably through his bridge viewscreen. His expression for one unguarded instant laid bare uncertainty and something like terror. So Mihal knew he'd set deadly forces in motion, and he feared the outcome. For the first time Seren felt a tremor of reluctant empathy.

"What would you know about love of a world that you would die to defend?" He looked away, maybe realizing that a Mitran survivor would know all too well. "If you knew the whole story—" He shrugged.

"Tell me," Tas suggested gently. "Your actions mean nothing if no one knows."

Seren heard him reach toward eloquence, lost with everything else in a dry land where the only water was tears.

Mihal returned a long considering gaze, looked sharply to his left, and shook his head abruptly. "No. You have no authority from any recognized state to act as an intermediary. I have nothing to say to Parvin or her assassin."

Tas smiled as though the insult were a gift, but before he could answer, Mihal's face clenched in surprise and the comm blinked out. Someone else had signed him off.

"Good."

Anything but good. What had happened to the cultured Claeran loyalist she'd known? The fleet medic who saved lives?

In the vri zone, the drone probe back in Claer system showed the green sparks of Mihal's ghost fleet drifting nearer to the Dead Gate's slow grey blink. Seren counted two, three, green sparks that veered from the node on headings that would send them back insystem to Claer. It seemed some of Mihal's captains had second thoughts—but far too many held their course.

8

Gorda brightened outside the viewscreen. *Keep a safe distance.* No ship could completely shield the human body, and the radiation alert bar on the ship status board was still climbing.

Tas willed Biron to come to his senses and comm back so they could all finish this and leave. He set autopilot to maintain position near a deactivated marker at the node approach and mirrored an all-points advisory: "Las Hermanas decommissioned Claer-Mitra node has been mined by order of the Mitran focal in exile. Transit is prohibited."

"Is that true?" Seren asked.

"Yes. And completely meaningless. The focal has no enforcement power."

"Mihal knows his interworld law," Seren said. "It won't stop him from transiting."

"A glorious death quickly loses its charm. Give him time to work it out."

"Mihal may not be making his own decisions. He kept checking with someone at his left, outside cam range, who signed off at the end."

Tas nodded; he'd noted it too. "Crew?"

"A superior or an equal. Mihal would politely dismiss advice from hired crew."

"So, we apply pressure and watch for cracks."

"Cynical."

"It works."

Tas dimmed the cockpit. Next, he needed to get Seren away to Maq, who had the firepower to keep her safe. Biron looked deranged enough to fire on the Az as he'd fired on Louhi Takahara. It was always easier the next time.

9

Red bars flashed on Seren's navigation board. A ship was attempting to transit the Dead Gate into Las Hermanas system, and it had all the signs of an imminent mirror flaw. Many nanoscale quantum events over the years could eventually build to a cumulative macroscale event. In conditions of rising instability, it could explode the node, the binary stars, the dust rings, and the ship itself out into the complexity of mirror space.

The laws of physics didn't fit Mihal's plans; he'd always acted on the belief that inconvenient laws were for other people. If he transited, his ship's greater mass could kick the Az into mirror space with fatal results. Seren gestured for her seat restraints, trying to read their position. The Az bucked and shimmied, and her nav board blurred and morphed as though it couldn't choose a universe.

"Mihal will steal right-of-way. We need to stop him."

"We already have. Steady," Tas said, though the only steady thing here was his voice.

A blur in the node portal wavered into the sweeping lines of a Claeran freight liner—and blinked out. Seren searched the starfield and the binaries' orbits on her boards, even looked as closely as she dared toward Gorda through the darkened viewscreen, but there was no sign of another ship. Mihal was in position to transit.

An emergency comm alert shrilled. Mihal ordered, "Disarm your mines. Clear the node. We'll make transit."

"No need," Tas said. "Nothing here calls for conflict."

"What's your price? Quickly. I have nothing to lose." His high-citadel voice allowed for no refusal. Everything was for sale in Mihal's cosmos.

"How will sacrificing yourself, and probably thousands of others, help Claer?"

"Not Claer alone. The Politaya. The Neutrality. We may fail. But we win nothing at all by slinking home."

Seren glanced at Tas and opened her comm. "There's another way, Mihal. We have new information to reopen the treaty."

"Years from now. We don't have years." He eyed her dully.

His expression, or lack of it, chilled Seren. Mihal could be charming, she'd learned on Gandhi Base, but now he would kill them if they stood in his way.

Tas remained patient. "Nothing happens instantly. But if you do this, you won't be available to speak for Claer and the Politaya."

"I'm no diplomat." He added sullenly, "The Qasris can run that show."

True. Others build, you destroy. But Seren bit down on the words.

"You have your own gifts," Tas said. "You plan, you travel, you represent one of Claer's surviving mercantile houses—and you care enough to act."

"And?" Mihal leaned forward as though he wanted to be convinced.

"We need people to imagine a livable future. How should the Politaya look in ten years?"

Mihal considered it, improbably. Tas reached him in ways she never could, even when he'd probably rather knock Mihal down and drag him home in irons.

"Free of greed and predation and fear," Mihal said finally. "We can make our worlds a peaceful haven for technology and the arts."

Even sounding like an election campaign speech, his dream Politaya stung salt into Seren's eyes. It was a wonderful notion.

In truth Mihal would detest such a Politaya.

"The Pact is hostage to its own predation and fears." Tas said. "Our real enemy is the fear, and we can fight that better working with the Pact, not against it."

"Impossible."

"This will change soon. Why do you feel it's impossible?" Tas had subtly moved the discussion from armed threat to philosophy.

"In this century the Pact is built for conquest, not cooperation."

Seren glanced down at flashing insets on her board—a radiation warning, the next level up from a radiation alert. Mihal's presence had deepened the instability.

"Why mobilize now?" Tas was finding ways to keep Mihal talking.

Mihal looked subdued now, no longer haughty. "Nolin threatened me."

Tas nodded and waited. His patience was rewarded.

"He turned the old Qasri house into an armed fortress, with rooms for—" Mihal visibly paled. "He likes to hurt people. And chimerai. He likes his creatures afraid and obedient. But he offers—rewards." He shuddered at some memory.

"So, you gave him information?"

A long pause, and Mihal's gaze slid offcam. "Not—exactly."

"Disinformation," Tas surmised. "And he found out."

Mihal put his face in his hands and deliberately dropped them. "He called me there one evening. He had a small hermaphrodite with fins and gills, major mods, heavily drugged. I wouldn't—but he said it didn't matter, his AI could sim anything and release images on the newsgrids. My family would be ruined, and Villandry Biron EntreMondiale, unless—"

"What did he want?"

"Treasury codes. And the last government fugitives before the planned takeover."

Mam, and the other missing senators and members of parliament. Seren shivered.

"Tell me about the takeover."

"Nolin sold Claer to the highest bidder—Duri Balint's Xanadu cartel." Mihal raised his head, gathering the tatters of his arrogance. "This fleet is my answer."

"So, you need to protect Claer. You need to protect your family. You'd rather live than die, but to do this you're willing to die."

"Yes."

Mihal, willing to give his life for Claer? Willing to give his life for anything?

"Will you accept help?"

Mihal weighed him for a long time. "How—"

Seren stared into a blank vri zone. Someone had cut Mihal off again.

A comm alert buzzed. Mihal again, audio only, with anxiety roughening his voice. "Parley. In person."

Tas hesitated at the unexpected request. Seeking refuge? Private talk? Kuhan had always believed mediation depended on trust. "Come alone in a small craft. You're free to transit."

Seren zoomed her display on their drone probe's view of a yacht drifting from the Villandry Biron ship. The sky-blue Daimler-Alenia had to be Mihal's personal craft, built for beauty as much as for speed and mobility. The graceful dart looked like a manufacturer's promo against the spangled black of Claer system's comet belt. Seren's nav board gridded Mihal's position. At his current speed, he should transit to Grey space in twenty-three minutes.

Seren pushed back her hair and twisted it into a quick knot. She kicked out of her chair and went to wash her face, trying not to flinch as she eased fresh nskin onto her abraded cheekbone. Her arm throbbed with the raw laser wound. She felt sore and grimy, and she still wore the same work clothes Mihal had sneered at. There was time to shower and clean up—but Mihal had tried to kill her, and she refused to play to his aesthetics.

As she reactivated her restraints, Tas drifted out of his chair to unlock the lower airlock latch. In addition to its main hatch, the Az had a rarely used universal ring lock beneath its cockpit so it could join belly to belly with another ship. Bad idea to bring Mihal aboard; Tas was too ready to trust people. Sometimes people changed and grew to merit his trust. She didn't think Mihal could change enough for anyone to trust.

A message from Maq scrolled as text across her display: *"Doll*

Sorrow report from Gwernant. Von and Loukanos sold Tas to Nolin. Von owns Biron. Tell Tas."

Renat Von was a walking horror. She keyed back, *"Agreed."*

"Soonest, Green. Pact fleet en route to Dead Gate from Acadie via Grey realspace."

Seren handed over her slate, but Tas only glanced at Maq's text and shook his head. Why couldn't he hear anyone fault his friend? Loyalty was wasted on a man like Von.

Then the Az lurched and coasted to a crawl, and manual controls caused only a sluggish yaw that Seren hastily corrected to prevent a spin. Gravity vanished. They were powerless in the faint but strengthening grip of the binaries that ruled the Dead Gate. Mihal's yacht was still minutes away. What caused their power loss? An incoming call flashed on the comm panel.

Inka—of course. Tas glanced at Seren and kicked a foot into a deck hold-down to answer.

"It's not too late, Taso," Inka breathed.

"Stand down and await diagnostics, Inka, by order of the focal."

"Taso, Taso. I'll always—"

"Stand down." Tas cut the connection. The Az emergency lights died, and swirling patterns lashed across the boards and vri zones as Inka seized their system. Grotesquely underlit by his slate screen, he ordered, "Ship systems default. Block access to all systems by previous caller."

Nothing happened for a long minute. Then the small ship shuddered to life on emergency power with all the boards flashing as the data bank sought lost files and wiped commands. It steadied to full power, and a neutrally pleasant voice asked in Mitran Damotik for the captain's orders. The ship had defaulted to its original settings.

"Maintain position." Tas gave a heading, and the starfield in the viewports swung and steadied.

Seren had tensed, ready to act, but now she let out her breath and slumped in her chair.

"Default your slate."

No! All her personal files. Old vris of home, new vri sequences she hadn't yet uploaded to her storage site, her friends, her Teak avatar—and all she had of Kuhan. She couldn't bear to lose it.

Seren took her slate from her pocket and held it between her hands.

"I know. But your files are corrupted. They're already lost."

Numbly she gave the command, and her slate blinked dark. Her life vanished, everything she'd clung to through the years. Tas silently wiped his own slate. Drifting near his chair, he closed his eyes for a moment, and sweat beaded on his forehead.

The probe image of Mihal's pretty little yacht vanished as it passed from Claer system in Green space into the momentary visual dislocation of the node—and emerged simultaneously in Grey space, so that Seren briefly watched two ships traverse her display. But for one instant they were two different ships.

The sky-blue Daimler-Alenia yacht flashed the telltale acid green halo of a fading sim and vanished from her vri zone. For one heartbeat she saw a leaner and darker ship enter Grey space—then her display shivered and once again showed the yacht.

"A simage. A deception," Tas said. He shadowed her shoulder, intent on the boards.

"Who is it? We'd better prepare to fight."

"No."

Seren slid her hand into the pilot glove and pulled down her full-vri eyeband. At once she flew inside the display, one with the ship, another moving spark in space. She gestured from their silver spark to the green spark, creating a vector in blinking blue dashes.

Staring into the darkness of space that had become her greater self and her surround, Seren tried not to tense her glove or stick hand. Nothing. She was so frightened that her field of vision narrowed to a black funnel.

A waver in the vri zone was Tas joining her in virtuality. He'd put on the weapons glove and eyeband, and she sensed his presence. Steady eye movements, shallow breathing, quickened heartbeat, pain in his injured arm and shoulder. It was as close as she could get to being inside his head. Last time they'd linked in virtuality, outbound from Melusine, she'd hated everything about the man. Now she considered what she'd rather be doing with him in virtuality, making no attempt to suppress her physical reaction, and felt his ready response and his breath of laughter.

"Run. Let's see what he does." His words sounded inside her brain.

Coming in fast, the other ship appeared as a narrow dark blur at extreme visual range on the aft cam display. Her heart jolted and she slammed the throttle in. The Az leaped forward like a startled cat, and gravity squeezed Seren back in the chair as the ship took off steeply upward from the ecliptic, to a zone where space was sparsely starred and dark. Through the link she felt Tas take gravity hard, labouring for breath through a searing pain. Stupid, she hadn't realized—should have sprayed him with painkiller. *Hang on.* The aft cam tracked their pursuer, but when she touched the vri, the readout said the ship had fallen back.

"Now drop speed. Let him close." Tas touched his board to override the simage.

"He'll be in range."

A silent nod, his usual way of answering the obvious. Seren eased back the throttle, watching the other ship get larger. She lifted her gloved hand, pulled a position vector in the vri zone, and asked for intercept data. Thirty seconds till he could cinder the Az.

"Shields." He told the Az, "Cancel incoming ship's sim."

"Shields will slow us." But she slapped the pad, trusting his judgment even now.

Unsimmed, the black ship looked familiar—slender, needle-nosed, raked at the stern like a Gwynfa racing yacht—and her shoulders prickled with a fragment of her glitz dream. It looked like the Landfaller that attacked en route from Melusine to Arian. No registration, running dark.

"Dive. Then dump speed."

Oldest trick in the book; they'd probably used it on old Earth war galleys. Seren shoved in the throttle, pushed the Az's nose down, and throttled back. A nano later a slender black ship scorched overhead close enough to make the Az shiver to its frame, and she looked up at missile launchers on the other ship's belly. Then the backwash caught the Az in opposite and equal reaction, and the ship staggered in that airless place.

Tas fired a single laser bolt, and its tracer seared out to glow on the other ship's starboard stabilizer. It disappeared in a shower of debris—it must be an antique with solid metals annealed in some backworld hand fab shop—and the other ship spun away in a tightening spiral driven hard by its own forward momentum. Another bolt sent fragments tumbling outward in a globe.

Seren lit her positioners in delicate backburns as the black ship, drifting in visual range, slowed its spin and steadied. A single burst of its port positioner turned it one-eighty around its vertical axis like a sailboat coming upwind. *Good pilot.*

Tas hit his comm pad. "You are detained for attempted piracy. Proceed to Vritra Ek and report to Neutrality port authorities."

A sullen voice on the comm. "Pan pan. Pan pan. Pan pan. Man hurt. Request assistance."

"Assistance granted." Tas freed his restraints and kicked down to the lower hatch.

Seren gestured to focus the Az's forward cam on the other ship's viewscreen, then enlarged and enhanced the image. The pilot's face glittered with subskin jewels. Not Mihal. "Tas, he's going to fire."

Even as her mind formed intent, her hand reached for their high-energy laser—too late.

A wave of brilliance swallowed them and swept away as the shock wave blasted through, but it lived on in afterimage long after the bioware screamed and the Az shuddered into darkness.

10

Light bloomed in Maq's vri display, white to gold to deep red shot with the black geometry of scattering debris, and the assigned-sound system gave out a torn shriek that rose to a roaring totality of static.

Then Maq ordered replay, and his vri zone showed the Landfall needle ship and the Az hanging in the void. A shower of fiery crimson rain drifted forward gracefully from the amber spark to the silver spark. How come they let the Landfaller get in range? A gold and scarlet burst illuminated the Az in sharp outline for an instant before it spun away from its attacker. The explosion printed itself on his eyelids like great yellow flowers in a centuries-vanished garden.

Someone was crying. Nur, the blonde Claeran refugee, sat frozen on comms. Even Parvin was shocked silent.

"Man was born lucky. Bet that one rattled their teeth," Maq said, willing the impossible into existence. That blast had to have disintegrated the Az even with Tas's heavy upgrades.

Parvin leaned over his shoulder to stare into the vri zone.

Maq looked again.

Magnified in the vri zone, the amber and silver sparks became ships bathed in the red giant's rusty light. Impossibly, the Az sat intact against the night. Smeared along its flank was a sooty flower, the negative image of the bright chrysanthemum still tingling Maq's optic nerve. The Landfaller hung near Tas's old ship. No one was answering his comm.

"At least you win the image war," he said.

"Who gives a damn?" Parvin stood hands on hips, bristling with belligerence. *Claeran women.*

"You do. If those two die out there, you're up two martyrs and decades of vri dramas about your Green artist and her Grey captain. Too bad famous lovers always come to a bad end."

Before Parvin could curse him, Milosz reported shakily from nav, "The node's stable, for now. No mirror flaw."

Parvin shot Maq a thoughtful look and gave orders, managing to make them a request in her Claeran lilt. "Prepare to transit."

"Don't try anything stupid." When it came to war, Maq had been there and back too many times. Nur nodded agreement from the shadows behind Parvin. Time to move out—the Az sat disabled in Grey space, on the far side of the node, in need of rescue—but it wasn't time to fight.

Parvin snapped, "Let Biron take down our family ships, our transports, our old fleet ships, thousands of our best surviving crew? We lost too many in the war."

"Biron doesn't scare me." Maq didn't add that Parvin Kerkallec and the evil fuck in the Landfaller scared the crap out of him. "Think another war will help? I don't." He almost smiled. Qasri and Damou would be proud of him—an old shit-disturber turning into a pacifist. "Transit. Go help the Az. And keep talking."

VIII
DEAD GATE

1

ES2742.116

Hand-held shot, ambient light. In the dark Seren manually released the protective foam buffers that her chair had thrown around her at the moment of impact.

Cedar reported in, muttering that she was all right. No word from Tas. How long had they sat dazed in a dead ship? She fumbled her slate out of a thigh pocket and shone its light across the cockpit. Debris tumbled around Tas's empty chair.

A red glow appeared on her board when emergency power came online. Seren unbuckled and swam carefully through an eddy of unseen drifting objects. Some felt like broken glass against her reaching hands. If their artificial gravity or acceleration kicked in, or another blast hit the Az, the fragments would become a volley of flying daggers.

Her small light didn't find Tas anywhere. Not in a chair, not flung under the boards by the blast. She overhanded aft through the galley passage to the cargo hold, but he wasn't there. His softsuit floated from his chair back, so he hadn't EVA'd.

Forward again, she found him by touch, lying wedged between a locker and the side viewscreen. Soaked in blood, by the faint red glow and her slate's light. Whatever he'd slammed into had shattered on impact, slashing fragments of composite or glass into his arm and chest and face. No heartbeat. Seren heard herself keening. *Stop. Check again.* She tried his throat—nothing—until after a terrifying minute, his slow but steady pulse restarted. When she freed him and drifted him across the cockpit, shards and blood globules swam after them. She restrained him in the nav chair where she could work on him.

"Systems status?" she asked. Miraculously, a control light glowed on the boards.

"Restoring available power," the Az said in its default machine voice.

Seren told it to assign cockpit bots to clear any jagged debris, activated a hull bot to assess and start repairs on exterior damage—repair estimate, forty hours that they didn't have—and tapped the control pads one by one. Displays came up in green-on-black monochrome on a virtual screen. Weapons systems were offline, and the navigation and maneuvering functions ran only at minimal levels.

An emergency med kit was clamped under the board. Seren worked quickly while Tas was still unconscious. His right side had taken the worst, and his face bled heavily from cuts in the fragile scar tissue. Still fever-hot from the chimera attack, he needed a surgery, but all she had was first aid. She tweezed out shards and nskinned the lacerations.

Seren brought up her probe images on her slate. In Grey space, Mihal's ships now ranged out beyond the gravitational ballet of Las Hermanas. They must have transited as soon as the Landfaller disabled the Az and knocked it off-station. In Green space Maq's handful of ships now ran for the node.

When she checked Tas, he stirred. Seren pinched the inside of his left forearm. His eyes flew open and he cut off a ragged sound. Shaken, she forced herself to continue her checks. Normal pupils, probably no serious head injury.

Tas frowned in her direction and said too loudly, as if he couldn't hear, "Take us to *Phoenix.* Sitkum will pay ransom."

Blind? Deaf? Seren tapped his palm, then lifted his less-damaged left hand to her face. He controlled a wince; with all her nskinned cuts and abrasions, he didn't know her. Seren felt the tension in his arm and sensed his quicker breathing. She couldn't leave him alone in the dark, not knowing if he faced death or torture. The med kit manual didn't cover everything. She unsealed her shirt and drew his hand inside to her breast.

"Seren. Leave now." Still trying to rescue her.

Movement drew her gaze to the board, where radiation lights leaped up the gauge in yellows and reds. She should try to move the Az. But if she burned farther out, Mihal's people might take it as a threat, and if she held her orbit, their DNA—hers and Tas's and Cedar's—would come apart like a broken ladder.

Sparks that would normally be silver or green moved across the monochrome display. A whirl of dust, gas, and planetesimals that had never materialized into a planet orbited the centre of gravity of the far-flung binary stars. Mihal's ships clustered beyond their ring.

An alarm flashed silently on the margin of the useless weapons board, then on the defaulted nav board. A more distant probe cam showed her Pact warships in close formation, travelling insystem. All through the war she'd expected to see that sight as she died. But they were just ships, drab carbon-grey composite hulls with a dully efficient look, blotting darker holes in a sparse starfield with a faraway dim red giant.

A solitary Pact military shuttle approached the Az from the direction of the node. How could that be? Seren desperately wanted to ask Tas, but his eyes were closed again. She reached across to take his wrist, reassured by his steady pulse.

At her touch he stirred, and she lifted his left hand to her mouth. At least he would know she was speaking. "Tas."

"Can't hear you. I can see only in infrared."

Infrared. Partial vision in his augmented eye; the blast had only seared away his normal human-range vision and hearing. She asked, "Cedar, can you talk with Tas? Higher frequencies?"

"Trying," Cedar said, and soon after, "He doesn't answer."

Their proximity alert sounded, but Tas didn't move. Seren quickly magnified to see Maq's *Phoenix* had transited the node and re-entered realspace. Silver starlight from the brilliant galactic core haloed its port side, and the russet glow of Gorda washed its starboard flank. The Pact shuttle had taken position out near the gravitational limit.

"Maq's ship transited," she said before she remembered Tas couldn't hear, couldn't even see her speak. There had to be a way. She quickly keyed his name to appear on the display in high contrast, black on white in the dim cockpit.

Tas remained silent.

"Ship, the captain has blast injuries and sees only in infrared. Can you display images in the infrared range with a visible light overlay?"

"No." The ship's androgynous Mitran voice produced a blunt negative. "Double-image display requires factory reset."

"Emergency priority. Life and death." Her words brought home the reality.

"Scanning technical data." A long silence later, by bioware standards, yellow Damotik letters appeared on the nav display and slowly scrolled left: "Satisfactory?"

"Yes," Tas's answer startled her. "I can read it. Now I need to talk with Biron."

Seren set her slate to text conversion and said, "Not a chance. You may have internal injuries. I'm taking you to *Phoenix* as soon as we can move." Yellow text marched across the nav screen as she spoke.

Tas said, "Another century of war if Biron engages Pact ships."

"Let Maq talk with Gabriel de Jong."

Tas shook his head. "No time. I need to do this now."

"You need a medic now," she said aloud, forgetting to use her slate, but cockpit comm picked it up, and words scrolled on the display anyway. *Good, that's easier.*

But his answer was to right his chair and fumble for his controls. Seren got up and edged between him and the board. Anyone but Tas, deaf and essentially blind, would be incapable of flying. Tas would try.

"Life capsule's next to the hatch," he said. "Go."

"Don't do that Mitran thing: 'I don't need anyone's help.'" Her eyes stung. "All that stands in the way is your damned pride. I can handle Mihal."

Tas looked through and beyond her, a billion kilometres past the red giant. Sweat stood out on his face, and heat rolled off his body. Work alone and die. Work together and maybe live. It should be an easy choice.

"Good." But his eyes closed, and he said nothing else.

"Pact of Human Worlds ship *Seneca*. Confirm your position, *MC/So9*," a man's voice demanded on the comm in Peel.

Seren swivelled. No time to hesitate. "*MC/So9* off Las

Hermanas node, *Seneca.*"

"Equipment failure, *MC/So9?*" the comm specialist asked mildly in the broad vowels of Stamford or another late first-wave backworld. "You're too close to the prime. Need assistance?"

"Negative. Thanks. Destination of your insystem shuttle?" As she described the Pact vessel she'd seen approaching from the node, their words scrolled across the screen.

After a pause he said, "No such craft, *MC/So9.* Clear the area."

Another sim? But when she checked the board, there was no sign of the shuttle.

"Tell him," Tas said. "Anything. Buy us time."

Tell him what? Seren took a deep breath. "Stand by, *Seneca.* This is a diplomatic mission operating under protocols supported by the Politaya and the Neutrality. We are in negotiation with Captain Villandry Biron."

"Designation?" asked the *Seneca* comm spec, bewildered.

"Interworld Accord task force." Seren plunged into pure invention and signed off.

Not our craft? So the shuttle probably was a sim. She had no way to scan it now; the bots had barely started their repairs. With all surviving systems lit, she risked a short burn to ease the damaged Az farther from Gorda. She monitored the images on her boards for movement among the Pol ships. Motionless. Waiting. Which would break first, Mihal's nerve or Parvin's patience? No sign of the black ship that had attacked them.

Tas was asleep or unconscious. Cedar lay curled in her hidey-hole. Seren envied them both. A great lassitude dragged at her, slowing her thoughts till they crystallized like winter honey. Dead controls, stale air, emergency backups failing. She needed to know why Mihal hadn't reached the Az, who had fired on them . . .

Seren realized that she'd fallen asleep only when she woke. How long? Only half an hour since the black ship approached, her slate said. They'd drifted closer to Gorda again, taking another step in a deadly dance with the sister suns. She unbuckled and floated to the nav chair. Tas was hot with a rapid pulse. Fresh blood on his face. At her touch on his throat, he stirred.

"Good work," he said. "Anything new?"

A muffled clank below her feet, and the ship vibrated. Another ship was grappling the Az's universal lock almost underfoot, and partial gravity suddenly turned their overhead panels into deck. A few pieces of debris still unabsorbed by the nano drifted downward. Boarding party—and anyone who fired a missile at them wasn't here for a friendly talk. Tas gimballed his chair upright, and the comm buzzed on his left wrist. He fumbled for it and tapped.

"Taso. Thought I was too late," said a Mitran voice from his comm.

"Renat. Come aboard."

The lock panels irised open. Warmer air swept in, and light filtered through from the other ship as Renat Von vaulted neatly down into the Az. Seren sucked in sweet air and blinked up at colourful swirls of encrusted 'Line deco in another ship's cockpit— definitely not Mihal's Daimler-Alenia. Tas unbuckled and pushed to his feet, one hand on the chair back. Seren swallowed her protest. At least he knew not to show weakness to Von.

"You looked better dead, Taso."

Renat glanced around the Az cockpit. His appearance was more bizarre every time she saw him. His clothes were a wild mix of blue silk trousers, worn boots, shock shirt, assault weapon on a shoulder strap. An irideco labyrinth pattern on his face had subskin bosses and ridges between the swirls, and he had irideco'd his teeth and eyes so that he looked like a man-sized bot skinned in iridescent metals. He freed his sidearm and touched it off safety, and Seren looked into its narrow aperture and gently blinking tracer light.

Piñar. Everything came back with terrible clarity. *Renat Von. Zari Lind. Teak Kuhan.* In her pocket Seren touched her slate to record.

"Bad?" Renat eyed the nskin on Tas's face and his bloody clothes.

Tas hesitated, reading Renat's question on the comm screen. "No."

Liar. Seren stood forward from the pilot chair she'd clung to, drawing Renat's metal stare. She breathed deeply to drive out the poisonous fog. Cedar crept partway out of the cubbyhole under the pulldown, but Seren shook her head minimally. *Stay hidden.*

"Can you take us off, Ren?" Tas spoke in his direction. *Don't let him see you're deaf and blind.*

Renat said softly, "You won't need off, Taso."

2

This was going to end badly, Maq finally had to admit. The disabled Az drifted near the node, and out at the gravitational limit of Las Hermanas system in Grey space hung a threatening array of Pact ships. The Pol couldn't win, any more than Sitkum or Mitra had won. *Principles fold every time to brutality.*

The Pacters started insystem dead slow. When *Seneca* hailed the Az, Parvin watched carefully, as edgy as Qasri's magic cat. Then, like a hot lahal pointer with a million-copper stake, Seren nailed them. Greens and Greys still followed the Interworld Accord, and the Pact had never formally renounced it. Appeals to interworld law had as much effect on the Pact as one balky skin cell had on *Seneca's* maneuvering speed, but it set a precedent.

Finished with the repair, his Mitran tech stepped back from the main pilot board. It now displayed the craziest malf Maq had ever seen, bright yellow images on top of infrared images.

"That's how they reset it." The tech lifted one shoulder.

Why? Maq studied the attack replay in his vri zone. Again, the black Landfaller closed on the old Az, two falling sequins against the night curtain, and again he felt a shock of grief that no human person should feel this many times in one life.

"Two fighters have unracked from Pact cruiser *Seneca*," the scan officer said.

"Ready two of our fighters," Parvin said into her hand comm.

"Frequency-spread mirror call for you and Meistr Flett, ma'am," comm one said. "Decrypted to your board."

Parvin slapped her comm pad, and Anton Rethel appeared in the big nav vri. About time the old reptile got worried.

Maq nodded. "What in hell is Gabe's chief of staff doing out in Grey nowhere?"

"Exercises."

"Lot of exercises around here these days."

"We've lifted two fighters," Rethel said to Parvin. "Surveillance only. No hostile intent."

Parvin leaned to the comm board before Maq could curb her. These two had squared off at the Wairoa Cloud, and the result was history. "Shall we lend you a scout, general? We rarely do our spying in fighters."

Rethel didn't smile. "We need to clear that node. Your patrol craft is in our line of fire."

"Fire on an Interworld Accord task force at your peril," Parvin said coolly, as though she could actually back her threat. "My officer and a MitraCorps negotiator are in the disabled Azande. I'm lifting a response team. No hostile intent."

"Extreme volatility. Request you stand by."

Long silence. *Blow it out your valves*, Parvin would snap back. Maq knew exactly how this part went. A Pol would defy any Pact order with Greens under threat in Grey space. *Family*.

But Parvin had learned something from the Mitrans after all. She stared at Rethel's image so long his expression hardened a notch. Then she ground out, "Standing by."

Maq breathed again.

Scan one sent a drone cam display to Parvin's board, pulling in an image streaked and broken by extreme range, crackling with short-wave radiation. The needle-nosed black Landfall ship and the Az were now locked together hatch to hatch, drifting slowly toward the Pact fleet, and the two Pact fighters flanked them just outside visual. If Rethel broke his word and threw them in, Maq would personally dismember the man.

Then Parvin cursed as the display greyed out. The tech jumped to reset it, with no effect.

"Dreamer." A voice like the red solar wind breathed through

the board, a beautiful Mitran whisper across the face of the deep. *Inka.*

It raised the hair on Maq's neck. He'd never seen ghosts, only heard their voices crying through his time-swept memories of home and the sighing green shores of Illahie. A billion years of ocean swells had polished Sitkum's boulders to sand, and as he'd watched from orbit, one blinding instant had fused the sand to glass.

For the first time in many years, he said aloud, "Hail, Mary, full of grace, be with us now and in the hour of our need."

"Same," said a crewman behind him.

Nothing yet in Maq's three centuries bore witness to the power of prayer. Faith and kindness might be dead in space somewhere between Sitkum and Vanuatu, but a gambler always hangs onto hope. Maq reckoned some AI subroutine was still around to hear him say, "Looks like you get one more chance, Inka. This time do the right thing."

3

Freeze focus. Tas gripped the chair too tightly, and Seren didn't move—couldn't move.

"You should have played Loukanos better." Renat looked around the Az cockpit. "'Yes, my love, I'll tank my brain and join you in virtual paradise.'"

Seren's gorge rose. So, it hadn't been her glitzed imagination. In her lethal obsession, Inka had wanted Tas to die so she could possess him in virtuality.

"Careful, Ren. She never gave more than she took."

Renat scanned them with his slate. "How touching. Unarmed to meet an old friend."

Tas had his eyes closed again, barely there.

"You work for Mihal Villandry Biron," Seren guessed. Anything to keep him from studying Tas too closely.

"Mihal gets things mixed up. Truth is, he works for me."

"If you can't take us off, call *Phoenix*. They'll pay." Seren's head was clearer now.

"That an order, Qasri? Remember what I said last year when you begged for your life?"

Seren frowned at his ridged irideco and remembered the overclocked man who'd threatened her. Twice. Once in old memory, and once just hours ago when Mihal called him Revo.

Fear and rage seized her then and shook her. No bluffing their way out of this. No escape. Her slate was recording in her pocket, so eventually someone might learn what happened.

"I'm waiting." Renat planted his feet wider. The shallow glitter of his eyes said he'd recently spun up on glitz. "Last year. On Arian. What did I say?"

"'Kneel,' you said. 'Beg.'" Seren's mouth froze so she could barely form words, and colour surged into her face at her remembered humiliation.

"What is this?" Tas said quietly.

"Go on. What was the rest?" Renat waved his hand laser far too freely.

Anger swept the last mist from Seren's brain. "You said, 'Couldn't leave it alone, could you? Kuhan. Takahara.'"

All that time ago, when they'd grabbed her on Claer Arian, it hadn't made sense. Now it was already too late. Renat's thumb caressed his laser's fire pad. As the glitz took him deeper into psychosis, he would relish every second of their suffering.

"Couldn't leave it alone. Till you started meddling, it would have been easy, never fear—our onetime hero found drifting with a hole in his head, ten empty pods of akvavit, and a note that said, 'I can't bear the guilt.'"

Seren had nothing left to lose. "Zari Lind recorded right to the end. Everyone saw you ignore a direct order to hold Spartí back. You shot your captain, then you killed Zari. MitraCorps has her images, and its lawyers have you cold. Take us off, and we'll plead for clemency."

Tas bent over the chair as though Renat's betrayal had finally struck to his heart. His fist clenched the nav chair back, and sweat ran down his face.

"Shut it, Qasri." Renat raised his laser.

Seren held his glittering stare. She couldn't take him, and if she tried, he'd kill them both now. Delay gave them the slightest chance. Renat moved closer to Tas, staring. Her hand eased into her pocket and palmed the familiar plastic whorl of the stunner.

The cockpit lights brightened slightly, and repair status flashed on the nav board. *Positioners operational.* They could maneuver again, but it was too late to escape Von.

"You taught me to always finish a contract, Taso. You screwed up my chances with Wilm, but I can still make it right." Renat rose into his glitz spin, all expansive talk and sudden violence. "You've been dead since you outran Nolin's zoo, in fact you've been dead since Piñar. You just didn't notice. I missed by centimetres on Duri's freighter. I thought I had you at Kai's moon hut, but you ran. And again, on Arian. Nowhere to run this time. Now I'll need your head, and Qasri's. Wilm didn't like her stirring up the tox."

"What about Delun?" Tas asked. So he did know, or he was working it out now.

"Contract hit. Every way Nolin turned, Qasri tangled him up in interworld law—Mitra, moulders, investments, treaty terms. You screwed me there too. That asshole Flett spirited her away."

Maq Flett rescued Mam? Another of your dead? Where is she now?

Tas wouldn't give up. "Ren. You're better than this. It doesn't have to end this way."

"It never did, if you had the balls to fight instead of talk. Alma. Kuantan. Piñar."

"Fighting isn't what takes balls. It's preventing a fight."

"One word and I'd have done Riordan for you." Renat grimaced as tears fell out of his eyes. He was losing his spin. Now was the dangerous time. "You could have been director, and I could have had Spartí. We could have taken the corps back to the glory days. Now you're out of places to run and hide."

Keep up the glitz talk, buy us time. Tas flexed his right hand and glanced in her direction for an instant. What did he plan?

Renat raised his laser toward her with a rictus grin. "You first."

In her pocket Seren squeezed her right thumb onto the stunner. Renat jolted in midstride, gave her an incredulous look and folded to one knee. Then he jerked and fell near the bulkhead, wide-eyed, clutching his chest. Tas stood with his fist still braced, blood streaming from his right knuckle and tears on the wreck of his ruined face.

Seren pulled out her palm laser and crouched to check Von; he was only stunned. "We can take him to Parvin. *Sarhaad.* I can charge him with the Arian abduction and trying to kill Mam. And you can lay murder charges."

"Leave him to Spartí for now." Tas fell into the nav chair and closed his eyes.

"Let him go, and he'll hunt you everywhere you turn."

Tas, unconscious again, didn't answer.

In the light gravity she dragged Renat into his garishly encrusted ship. Some of his trophies looked like human hands in metal or ceramic. She restrained him in a chair, dropped back into the Az, and sealed the hatch to disengage.

Now to try the positioners—but before she could activate the boards, the actuators engaged and the converters shuddered to life, and the repair status report showed full power. The cockpit boards lit one by one, then the vri stage. Impossible. Seren checked the engineering screen. The ship's nanobots had replicated and worked at extreme speed, much faster than they could replicate, sacrificing many. Something—or someone—had accelerated the process.

"Goodbye, Tas," murmured a voice as dim as the ruddy night around them. *Inka.*

Seren nodded, acknowledging her help. Inka's one virtue, her loyalty to the man she'd lost, had twisted and fossilized into desire for his destruction, heedless of the living man. This was a farewell gift from the woman she had been long ago.

Tas didn't stir. Seren scanned him with her slate and found recently healed bone breaks but no internal bleeding. Blood had soaked through his shirt again faster than the fabric could absorb it, and she opened it to see four oozing claw tracks. She couldn't even guess how to aid a regenerated and augmented body like this. She sprayed antibiotic from the med kit and trusted his strength.

Cedar crawled out of her locker and clung to the pulldown with ears down and tail tucked, looking her age. This wasn't her kind of fight.

At the controls Seren burned away from the red giant's insistent gravity and growing electron storm, still grappling Renat's ship. Then she released the black Landfall ship and uneasily watched it drift outward. No simmed image made it resemble Mihal's yacht or a Pact shuttle now.

4

A bright speck in the viewscreen grew and took on detail to become the heavy cruiser *Seneca*. Lights glowed distantly from the bridge, and its weapons housings and racked riders bulked it to the threatening grace of a primitive Earth predator. The Pact ship outmassed ten thousand small craft like the Az, and a single shot from its energy weapons or short-range projectiles would break them to debris the size of apple seeds. *Seneca* slowly approached their last known position.

Seren programmed the Az's skin nano, raised its shields, set visual deception to make the ship read like a planetesimal rock of their mass, and created minor movement with the positioning engines. Now, unless someone jacked in override codes for the nanoflage, the Az was detectable only at visual close range. Tas was asleep, so she loaded the three remaining drones to observe Mihal's ships, the Sitkum ships, and the Pacters. A touch sent them skimming across lonely space.

"Listen." Tas sat up, startling her.

"You can hear?"

"Barely."

A faint signal already came from the first drone in position, noisy with interference from the binaries. She gestured to bring up its relayed images of the Pact fleet.

Tas put his hand into the nav position weapons glove, squinting at the munitions panel on the board. "We have ten decks of ten scatter missiles and five plasma devices."

"You're not taking on a Pact cruiser," she said. He always talked first.

"Peacemaking is as powerful as the threat that backs it."

It was a distinctly Mitran interpretation of pacifism. Seren froze in fascination as *Seneca* backburned to a stop.

"Steady."

"Until they open fire or jack our systems?"

"They won't risk firing near an unstable node."

The comm board flashed, but the call wasn't from *Seneca*, it was from *Sedna*.

Maq hit the display talking. "—need you to fix this mess, not play shadow hand. Riordan died twenty hours ago. You know what to do. Destealth. I don't mean the Az."

Seren held her breath. Maq was right, but Tas was immovable.

Tas thumbed the comm pad, cutting off Maq, and leaned back in his chair. Sweat ran rivulets down his face, glistening on the nskin.

"You understand what Maq wants?" Tas asked finally.

"Yes."

"Can you sim me?"

All her old files were gone. Seren recorded a still image and pulled up an editing tool on her slate. She slashed dark misshapen scar tissue down the right side, then patched on his nskin. A fine sensitive mouth, at least on one side. Beautiful eyes inlaid in gold.

"It's a cosmod. I needed it when I was dead—in deep cover," he said, anticipating her question. "Normalize it."

Swallowing a joke about unTaslike vanity, she smoothed away the damage. The simage that rotated in her slate's small vri zone portrayed a mild-looking man with conventional looks and a direct gaze. It was this face she'd seen when she simmed his image one desert night south of Alluvion.

"Tas." She hesitated, but he needed to know. "This is not what's needed here."

Tas took a deep breath and floated his slate to her. "Load the backslotted steel bead and look for a sun sigil. Your eyescan opens my personal index."

Seren maxed his screen and followed directions to a list of cosmod templates, knowing long before they opened that the images and schematics were not for a man she knew as Damou. Damou no longer existed. Instead, she gazed at a striking young man with light hazel eyes and tan skin darkened by UV treatment. His face was so familiar that she could model it blindfolded, yet he was a stranger.

"I have your templates."

"Sim me as I looked at Piñar, and age me to the present. We don't need studio-level work. A fast retouch." Tas creased a smile. "Forgive me for asking a routine task of an artist."

The artist felt honoured, Seren wanted to say, but tears gripped her throat.

"Why tell you what you always knew?" His warm hand rested on hers for a moment. "We'll head for the Tripline after we finish here. Go out with flash. No one will ever know for certain what became of us."

"We'll do that." Seren reckoned they wouldn't be running for the Tripline anytime soon, but she kept her voice as steady as his. "What else do I know that you don't tell me?"

"You know that too."

"So many years."

"Don't look back." Tas sounded half asleep. "We might turn to shadow again."

"Is that a proverb?"

"Old story. You know it—you told Maq. A poet called Orpheus rescues his lover Eurydike from the land of the dead, but he looks back, and she slips from his hand into shadow."

"Hold tight, and we'll never look back."

Adrift off the Dead Gate might not be the ideal place to reclaim a life. Tas could go on forever as a man like Damou, buy a new name and face, find work on the Tripline, travel the outer spaceways with his lover, rescue his lost souls one by one. But he had said long ago that some things you need to do over and over till you get them right.

All the times she'd dreamed of Teak Kuhan coming back from the dead, she'd thought it would be a shining hour. Instead, it was a bitter loss. The worlds would regain a good man, but she would lose his stubborn shadow. Damou.

"Tas—Teak." She didn't even know what to call him, but he didn't stir anyway. Let him rest until it was time to make his comm call.

As Seren called up her slate's image tools and started work, tuning colour values and texture and detail, she laid aside her complicity in long silence. Her fingers danced over the pad, restoring life to a face she knew better than her own.

5

Alone in an absence of place, Tas saw the Dead Gate as a heat image on his display. A handful of ships stood off just beyond visual range, unregistered and running dark. Tripline runners, some in MitraCorps configuration. Some companies would come to their aid with Riordan gone. Others that had scorned Spartí's shift to mediation might hold back, waiting like scavengers.

Tas moved cautiously, trying not to shift the shards still embedded in his face and arm. Seren had nskinned only the lacerations that she could see. For hours he'd slept and woken, healed, gathered strength—but not enough. Sweat ran down his back and sides, plastering his shirt to his skin and stinging into cuts, making it hard to concentrate.

In infrared his scan board targets were cool blue dots, and the binaries were two globular swirls of incandescent haze. Odd, but better than nothing. Seren was a burning yellow-white-orange human shape. Cedar's smaller form also radiated life before she retreated to her cubby.

"Now?" Seren watched his new simage rotating in the vri zone and glanced away. Years ago, she'd done that in her orchard— glanced away, shy with his unwanted fame—but she'd learned to look past Damou's hideous face and she would learn to look past this one. So he trusted.

"Now we stay in the Dead Gate. No one passes."

"Capital offense in the Pact to block a mirror node. Lifetime rehab in the Pol." Seren sounded anxious, and for good reason.

If a ship exited nonspace into another mass, both objects disintegrated with the force of colliding asteroids; if a ship wedged in an unstable node like a pearl in an oyster, it could evert a whole system. Mass proximity sensors made mirror transit safer than the early days, but a mirror flaw or sloppy navigation or tech failure could still cause disaster.

Giving him a long look, she gestured over the positioner pads to keep the ship in place. An uncharted node was easy to lose on manual, let alone an unstable uncharted node, but she'd handled it so far. If she failed—he didn't need to tell her that radiation would char the ship or gravity would pull it into the nearest sun's hydrogen furnace.

No panic, no complaint. Tas wanted to reassure her, but his raw face had stiffened into a mask and his heart stumbled. He swam down into in a bloodshot dark. Seren leaned over him, but her words drifted unheeded around him like bright fallen leaves. Gwernant in autumn. Tas dreamed of apple harvest, children laughing in the orchard, and Seren singing beneath a russet tree with a green bird perched on each raised hand.

Seren stirred him to greet Mihal, now free of Renat's terror. On the nav screen his ship *Marianne* wavered and resolved.

"Anastasios Kuhan, acting director-general of MitraCorps, on service to the Parliament and Senate of Claer, operating under Interworld Accord protocols." Tas sounded calm, as even dying at Piñar he was calm. "Captain Biron, it's time to end this peaceably."

It was done. Dragged back to life was worse than dying, Maq said, but as his deceptions fell away from him, Tas felt a great lightness.

"If I hold position, I can inspire people to fight off the occupation, if necessary with my death," Biron said. It sounded like a stance and not a passion. Maybe he was coming to his senses now in Renat's absence. *Ren failed yet again. He could have been a better man.*

Tas felt himself slip away again. *Not now. Hang on.* But from the near darkness he heard his own voice speak.

"Your life can inspire a great deal more than your death," Seren said through his simage. "You're well placed to advise on rebuilding essential services. Go home now with honour and lead people to win justice for Claer and the Politaya."

Tas listened, unnerved to hear himself say words he had never spoken, but certainly would have spoken, as Seren worked within the simage she'd created from his old templates. Lucky for Biron it was her. Tas might be too sorely tempted to leave the damned man to his fate.

Biron stared from the comm display without speaking, a man with his back to the wall and the dogs at his throat. Now he had a way to extract himself without death and disgrace. Finally, his heat image nodded.

"No surrender. I'll hand off my command to Madame Kerkallec."

"Stand by while I advise *Phoenix*," said Seren as Kuhan. She knew his procedure disturbingly well, and for a hotheaded Claeran woman she made a cool negotiator.

Not a bad compromise. The Pacters would take note, though Maq's Sitkum ships and Parvin's new Claeran fleet were still badly outnumbered and outgunned by the small Pact flotilla. Now to send them all home.

Home. Tas dreamed that he stood beside his father on the riverbank at Pronoia as summer afternoon sun shattered on the water that flowed beneath rustling poplars. It was a quiet time on the farm north of Spartí, with two hay crops in and wheat ripening on the stalk. Moki Kuhan had chosen to accept his son's transfer to MitraCorps. *Go forth as a destroying fire. Destroy hate, ignorance, fear. Destroy darkness, and bring light.* Tas smiled at the memory, though he felt nskin and scar tissue split. By now he must look like a lesser demon shedding a skin.

Seren gasped his name, and he stirred to see a ship sear past their viewscreen riding the beam of its forward laser cannon, so close his infrared picked it up as a glowing blur. A fighter.

"Whose is it?" His neck hair lifted at the pilot's flamboyant flying.

No answer. He fumbled to load submunitions as another fighter came in, amber shifting silver on his infrared-corrected weapons display. Seren had set a nav subdisplay to shipcentric, so it looked like a classroom diagram of subatomic particles with the old Az as the nucleus. The Pact ships gave no sign of moving off-station yet, but he saw scores of new ships taking position. Tas slipped his hand into the weapons glove.

"Wait! It's Spartí."

Helli's voice crackled on a personal link. "Welcome back, Teak."

His own people—Helli Njau's people. He dropped his hand.

"Tas?" Seren laid cool fingers on his arm.

Tas stirred to answer. "Acknowledge only."

"*MC/So9* off Las Hermanas, Spartí. Anastasios Kuhan as acting director-general of MitraCorps negotiating for Claer and the Politaya," Seren sent under her own identity.

"MitraCorps and the focal of Mitra in support of the Politaya worlds," said Spartí's captain. "You can stand down, Lieutenant."

"Understood, Spartí," Seren said and signed off.

Understood but not agreed. *Good.* This wasn't over yet.

"What kind of support?" Seren scrubbed her hands over her face. "Who's paying? We can't afford MitraCorps, and it can't compromise its neutrality as an unpaid ally."

"Family. Second-wave cousins." Tas shrugged. "Now we'll hold the node. Keep the peace."

6

"Kuhan?" Parvin looked stunned by the exchange between her Spartí negotiator and Biron. "Kuhan is years dead."

"Now he's alive," Maq said. "You heard the man. Those Piñar clips I showed you—Kuhan spent years in deep cover after his murder. Qasri brought him back."

"Seren told me under stun. I thought she was rattling on about her old love." Parvin shifted gears smoothly. "Good. We need him now."

Then Qasri was on comm, advising Kerkallec that Biron would surrender.

Nur Davi, the blonde comms spec, ended her shift but stayed on the bridge, watching the viewscreens and boards far too intently. One of the Claeran government people, she'd turned up at his Tirion office a year or so ago, but Maq never pressed his refugees for details they didn't offer. Now might be the time to find out. He called a data search, predictably turning up no names, but a DNA match pegged her ID, and suddenly everything made sense. Any way he turned, a Qasri was one step ahead.

In the *Phoenix* bridge vri zone, everything shifted steadily. The Az rode way too close to the red giant, sitting in the Dead Gate's crazy node like a cork in a bottle. *Careful, kids. That fireball will burn you right back to ash.* Maq frowned at his relay sent from the Az nav board readout. Still in infrared, invisible to human vision, but maybe it made sense to the skookum new eyes Tas got after Piñar.

So Kuhan was back from the dead. For years Maq had a spooky feeling that they'd borrowed him from oblivion, and sooner or later oblivion would reclaim him for good. But maybe, once in an aeon, love truly could win a round with death.

"One last throw to do something worthwhile," he said half under his breath. "That's how it goes in the old songs."

"You listen to too many old songs," Parvin snapped.

"That's how we learn. Old songs. It's the only way we can tell our own story after defeat."

Biron's flagship *Marianne* came to life and moved out fast. So did *Seneca's* two fighters, which pulled a fancy burn into a new heading. *Intercept.* Biron's ship cut a shallower arc, running faster and closer than safety dictated to the larger sun. Running toward *Phoenix,* putting himself at Parvin's mercy. His other ships peeled out in his wake in close formation, and Maq had to smile—Pol hotspurs, turning surrender into performance art.

The Pact cruiser *Seneca* lit its positioners and poised like a javelin to intercept Biron's trajectory. At Parvin's word, *Phoenix's* new actuators throbbed online. Everyone on the bridge froze an instant, checking boards, then smoothly went into action. Maq eyed the vri display unhappily. *Phoenix* sat square in the middle of this mess, and if anyone missed a step, he'd have a ringside seat on a new disaster.

Maq swore in a language he hoped the lady didn't know as three more fighters scorched past the viewscreen. Silver on grey. *Trouble.* MitraCorps. Spartí. Who hired them in? Someone with deeper pockets than Maq. God knew he'd tried to hire all nine companies. Now the Greys would wait in the dark to witness the death of the Politaya.

7

Ships schooled like deadly minnows on the Grey side of the node, coming the long way around from the Broken Cluster. Seren's drone pinged as ships—a great many ships—triggered its proximity alert. She tapped magnify. Light cruisers, frigates, destroyers with full fighter racks, fast transports, a swarm of small craft. MitraCorps's lean and lethal hunters had arrived.

Seren wrestled with a temptation to wipe the comm file and burn, but it was no longer an option. Tas Damou could run for the Tripline with his lover, but not Teak Kuhan.

A drone image lit a display: it showed the black Landfaller, in a sequence recorded an hour ago. Von again. Seren sighed and scrubbed both hands through her hair, recognizing Tas's gesture. Then she sat up abruptly. Von's ship approached *Seneca* and vanished into one of its deep docking bays—she punched fast forward—only to emerge minutes later. Next it approached a Spartí frigate and settled into an empty rack. Soon it quickly lifted and burned.

Renat Von was trying to peddle his wares to the highest bidder. No takers. Then his Landfaller changed course and darted toward the red giant Gorda, vanishing into its glare. Suicide? Seren reached for compassion but fell short. Renat Von had hunted her since Arian and Tas for years. The man belonged

in penal restraint for life. But knowing Von, this might be just
another dramatic pose.

Seren tapped her slate to check Tas's vital signs. *Impossible.*
Defaulting her slate must have scrambled its medical scan. She
reset it, but it gave her an identical reading. His heartbeat had
slowed, his fever was down and his face had partially healed—all
in one hour. Even his colour looked better, no longer ashen. His
Grey-lab medical nano was doing its job. Her own face and arm
felt better too. Tas had told her at Samun, *This will transfer med
nano.* Now she was another Grey freak. *Good.*

Tas sat up stretching as if he'd enjoyed a good night's sleep.
"Still have the tree stone?"

Seren tapped her breast pocket. "Want it back?"

"Not yet."

Seren leaned in her chair and tilted the stone to the dimmed
boards so that its sinuous engraved pattern flowed with darkness.
A tree reflected in still water. Or fork lightning. A map. A sea
creature. *Hello.*

"What happens now?" Seren asked. Tas had received
multiple-encrypted, frequency-spread comms from Helli Njau
confirming Jaime Riordan's death and MitraCorps updates, but
no immediate plans.

"Now we wait till Parvin debriefs Biron. And we'll hear from
the Pacters. Meanwhile . . ." Tas tapped through different files of
his strange synthesized music, then lifted the tree stone from her
hand and laid it gently on a data port. Immediately the pattern
on it glowed bright blue. When it went dark after a minute, Tas
handed it back to her.

"Did you know it would do that?"

"No. I meant to try it earlier."

"What does it mean?"

"Let's find out."

"Your music sounds like an ancient canon, one theme
repeated in endless variations," Seren said, keeping an eye on the
controls.

"It's from Mitra." Tas leaned over the rerouted comm board
and set his music to transmit on open comm. Trying to irritate
the Pacters? It was a strange time to be concerned with music.

"New composer?"

"I extrapolated it from a moulder pattern like the one Maq showed you on Claer."

Seren had to ask, "What if they're not a million years gone? What if they're in human space right now?"

"We considered it." Tas didn't laugh at her vri-thriller question. "Nothing indicates present-day activity. The polar sites underwent centuries of natural erosion. Ancient."

The tree stone rested dark and solid in her palm. Art. Relic. Currency. Unknown tech device. Seren dropped it back in her pocket, ran an image search on her slate and tapped the first interesting choice, a screen from a paleoastronomy site.

A tree unfolded in the slate's small vri zone, a tree of spreading branches and many leaves like a Claeran wildwood beech. The scrolling text described the ancient unity of string-quantum mathematics that finally led to modern physics. Multiverse theory and string theory led to what the newsgrids called mirror physics, and mirror physics opened the doors to the universe, not over the vast lifespans of galaxies but on a human scale of days and years.

The ancients imaged this complexity as a tree with its trunk dividing fractally to branches and twigs and leaves, each leaf a universe that touched infinite other universes in infinite dimensions. The multiverse was like a stylized tree beside a still lake that showed its perfect reflection.

Interesting, but it didn't explain the tree stone.

Seren called up her nav board and started work on alternate flight plans to get them out of here once they were done. Dead Gate to Vritra, Dead Gate to Xanadu, Dead Gate to Gandhi Base by way of the Bight and onward to the Deep Outside. What would be easiest? She overlaid them together on the board in traceries of blue dotted lines. Pretty. And—*Gods.*

Seren dropped her slate and caught it midair, and her hand passed tingling through the vri zone tree. Not a high-country watershed, not branching coral, not static electricity, not the multiverse. It was—

The comm board flashed with a high-priority call from *Seneca*, but she only stared at it, not wanting to know.

"Give them a warning," Tas said.

Seren plunged in before fear could seize her. "MitraCorps ship

MC/So9, do not proceed, *Seneca.* The node is blocked and the approaches are mined."

"*Seneca.* Depart the area, *MC/So9.* You are in violation," said a woman with a slurring Nuevo Chubut accent. "Priority. Spread your transmission."

In five seconds the comm noise altered subtly, and the image shivered. A Pact general starched into a gilded uniform looked out; his square face had never seen the inside of a cosmod salon. Anton Rethel.

Tas took over using his Kuhan simage, mercifully, and gestured at the comm pad to relay the conversation to Helli and Maq. "We have an agreement from Captain Villandry Biron. His ships are now under Commander Kerkallec's orders." Tas looked straight at the comm pickup. If Rethel realized he was flash-blind and hanging on by a frayed thread, this would end quickly.

"Too late, Captain. Clear the node. The Interworld Accord requires unrestricted transit."

Seren checked to see that the Az captured every word, and her slate was recording just in case. *Precedent.* Rethel acknowledged the authority of the old Interworld Accord, surely not by accident, long after the Pact destroyed it. Strange man. But other Pact warships now crowded her display in a convincing show of force.

"Armed mines," Tas reminded him. "Three plasma warheads sequenced to destroy any ship that transits, then close the node. And no one knows the outcome if we detonate a world-killer into nonspace."

"A hit could breach us, but our bulkheads are double-sealed. Acceptable risk."

"No one passes, by Mitran order in council."

"You have no authority to speak for MitraCorps, and Riordan won't stir."

"As director-general elect of MitraCorps, I regret to inform you that Jaime Riordan is dead," Tas said formally, and keyed something quickly on his slate. "Transmitting authorizations."

"Mitra is years dead, Teak. You haven't the strength." Rethel glanced down at a board and shook his head. "Your agreement with Biron means Politayan ships are massed against us with clear hostile intent. And anyone else would take your warning as an open threat."

Seren activated her board translator, unable to follow their fast colloquial Peel; her hands shook so badly that she dropped the earpiece twice trying to fit it.

"You're in Grey space, Anton. You have no business here. Pull out now. MitraCorps has all nine companies fully deployed."

"Where? I don't believe you."

"Plus another fleet," Tas said far too soberly. "The quiet kind."

"You mean privateers—Tripline runners. Why would runners back you?" Rethel rubbed his lower lip with a thumb, spoiling the effect of the crisp uniform.

"Family. Friends. And piracy's rampant off Claer these days— no doubt Biron brought out a reserve unit to police the area. He should have notified your sector command. Tell him to tighten up his cardwork. Thank him. Mention him in a dispatch." Tas grinned alarmingly, showing his titanium teeth. In the vri zone, the Teak Kuhan sim presented a flawless smile.

"You should have stayed covert, Teak. New orders from Walden." Rethel shook his head, perhaps regretfully. "Destroy the polar sites on Claer. Release plague and nano. Clean sweep. The purchaser wants the resources, not a troublesome hostile population."

"Mitra again."

Rethel made a noncommittal grunt that seemed to be assent.

"How long do they think they can destroy and deny? This won't go away."

"It will go away—for a year, a generation, long enough that they won't have to face the final outcome. Others will." Rethel laughed without humour. "Your ship's damaged, you and your lady are hurt, and the charges against you both make you moving targets. Your people have a day to pull what you can from Claer. It will take us a while to deploy fully."

Listening to him talk calmly about the death of her world and the extermination of the last Mitran survivors, Seren couldn't make it seem real. But it had been real on Sitkum and Mitra. She reached for her comm controls, but Tas motioned her to wait.

"Spartí and Commander Kerkallec will oversee the safe return of Biron's ships to Claeran airspace. Keep your distance. Claer is under MitraCorps protection."

Seren guessed that was pure improv.

"I see a Politayan battle group, not a police action," Rethel said. "Play both sides and you'll be destroyed along with Claer. Other fleets back this one."

Why was Tas drawing this out? Seren gestured, *Let's go.* Tas's text scrolled on her display, *A little longer. Distract him. I need more time.*

"The Pact is already losing its grip on Politaya worlds if it's selling them off to criminal cartels," Tas said. "Do you really think Gabriel de Jong sent that command? Or was it Duri Balint moving Wilm Nolin's hand? Do you want history to remember you as the man who razed a world on forged orders?"

Losing control on its own worlds too, Seren texted back, seeing his intent. *News came in while you slept. Tox burned Havre council chambers yesterday. Jacked government files on prisoners of conscience and internal diplomatic memos.*

Tas picked up on her cue. "Rioters from the Havre slums have shut down the city council and released classified documents on diplomacy and opposition prisoners. There's a state of emergency. Anton, you have a conscience. Refuse your orders. They're illegal and unethical. Otherwise, you'll face a war crimes tribunal. Nolin and Balint are in custody; they won't be around to thank you. Save yourself and your people. You're needed at home."

Staring match, Seren texted. *Maybe he wants to but can't.* Tas didn't move. Rethel had bulled his way up the Pact military hierarchy, and he didn't answer to Greys.

Rethel said, "A few refugees won't make any difference in the long run. Lift as many as you can from Claer."

"Forget Claer. Go home and save Outlook and Walden," Tas tried again. "Let Kerkallec and Biron leave. They'll give you no more trouble."

"You think I can leave because you ask? Kuhan, you're about to learn a hard lesson."

"Not because I ask." Tas managed a deadpan. "Check your new scan target." He named co-ordinates above the ecliptic that defined the galactic core. Seren checked but found nothing.

"Scan ghost." Rethel looked aside for a moment anyway. "We sent a drone to check. It's nothing, a stray rock."

Seren typed, *Patrol ship launched from Seneca.*

"Captain, we're taking you into protective custody. Prepare to be boarded." Rethel nodded, and the comm link ended.

"Do we fight?" Seren asked.

"No. Take care of anything you need for security," Tas said.

"All done." She shrugged. "Bad ending. I'd never get away with this in a vri drama."

"It's not over."

Cedar had crept from her locker to listen to the exchange, and Seren put her arms around her guardian. "Do whatever the Pacters want, treasure, and ask to be taken to Rozenn Milosz. I'll come for you when I can."

Silently she clasped Tas's hand, now unscarred again thanks to his med nano. There really wasn't anything to say. Then she remembered. "Tell your scientists the moulder pattern isn't a watershed or a sea creature. Enter it into your ship's system as a flight plan."

"A fractal flight plan?"

"Many worlds, many destinations."

Tas gave her a look she easily interpreted: *I knew you could work it out.* He checked his chrono. "I'll try it later. After we're done on *Seneca.*"

Seren nodded as though she fully believed they would be doing anything after they were done on *Seneca*, but added in the same vein, "I'd like to use some of the Claer and Pamir images on your slate for a vri."

"Take what you want."

"I want you." *Never forget.*

The U-rings clattered as the Pact transport ship grappled the *Az.*

"Soon." Tas laughed soundlessly against her hair.

How did he do that, act as though they were heading off to a concert in the park? She told the hatch to open, since her hands shook too badly to trust the controls.

8

ES2742.117

Moving shot, animal view. Red lights and darkened displays lit a hellfire glow in *Seneca's* rider bay, dimly lit to preserve pilots' night vision, and steam rose from fissures in the deck plates. Seren and Tas descended into the vast space from the transport ship. *Entering purgatory, proceed at your own risk.*

A wall of silent Pact faces met them, clean and well-rested above crisp uniforms. The Az sat nearby where it had been deposited, looking like salvage scrap. Seren reached for her pocket cam, but the boarding party had taken it along with their slates and comms and weapons.

"Cedar, look and record," she murmured, knowing their captors might confiscate the cat's bead. Strangely they'd let Cedar curl at her feet on the patrol ship, and now she padded ahead, taking in her surroundings. They clearly didn't know much about Mitran augments.

Four Pact soldiers kept a closer watch on Seren and Tas despite their cuffs. Tas looked battered, but being Tas, seemed stronger than an hour ago. The hardsuited corporal and soldiers who'd taken them into custody reported to a lieutenant. She measured them coldly as she spoke into a hand implant, then turned to ask Tas something—they hadn't yet realized he was blind.

"Qasri, Seren, Lieutenant, Claer Defence Force, seconded to MitraCorps." Seren pitched her voice to Tas a metre away. He needed to hear that she was all right, nothing to fear. Yet.

"We know who you are, Lieutenant. You're not prisoners of war."

Keep talking. "What are we?"

The lieutenant barely hesitated. "Guests."

"General Rethel will need us on the bridge," Tas said, earning a glance of chilly amusement. Instead, the lieutenant nodded them toward a dark portal.

Seren took a deep breath, gathering courage. During the war the Pact ignored conventions on the handling of prisoners. Rethel would carry out Nolin's execution order on Tas. Seren was Pol intelligence, so she would probably die in interrogation— quickly, she hoped. Tas's captors on Mesa had allegedly tortured him long after he told them everything. After a point it had nothing to do with gaining information and everything to do with demonstrating absolute power.

Seren's guard nudged her forward, suddenly blinking in an overlit muster station. No one stopped her when she eased close to Tas and matched his long stride. Shoulder brushing his shoulder to keep him on course, she realized he was strung tight with tension. Not a bad actor.

Their security escort steered them into a passageway wider than some Tirion streets, lined with people. Ratings, a few officers and cadets, fairer and taller on the average than Pols. Curious and ready to be entertained, they looked like an opening night crowd.

In a narrower passageway they stepped into a lift that carried them upward a long way, then walked again. Seren managed to stay on her feet and keep Tas on track. Air was fresher on this deck, where the panelled passageway had big viewscreens and the doors bore gilt-lettered wooden signs, no common nano paint here. In the lounges they passed, Seren glimpsed fittings that were luxurious by Politaya fleet standards. Even on a warship these Pacters had so much power and wealth, and they didn't even know.

The lieutenant halted at a guard station to uncuff them, and a windowless reinforced door opened to her palmprint. She saluted a senior officer and marched out.

At an absurdly ornate desk, a man with a Pact captain's bars sat tapping a transtylus against his knuckles, taking his time to look them over. His too-regular features suggested heavy cosmod. A silent pair that could be brothers flanked him at ease. Portrait of executioner and staff. Seren couldn't have cast them better.

Let Tas know she was on the job. "We have a right to know the charges against us and to obtain legal representation. Abduction of a Neutrality ship's crew is in clear contravention of airspace law under the Interworld Accord."

"Not a protocol we recognize." The officer looked indifferent. "Piracy is a capital offence. You will be processed accordingly."

A dark-haired girl in a rating's plain coverall tried to snap a leash on Cedar's collar, but the cat edged back into a crouch and silently showed her diamond fangs and claws. An attack would only get her hurt, when they were outnumbered by several thousand.

"Peace, Cedar. Stand down." Seren got a moon-eyed glare of resentment for her trouble.

"The vri said you had a lynx," the girl said. "Tufted ears and a short tail."

"Woodcat." Seren reached for the Peel word. "Wildcat." Then she realized, "What vri?"

"That Outlook vri drama *Star and Shadow* about you and—" The girl blushed, as Seren would have ten years ago. "Is that really Captain Kuhan?"

Seren nodded. Teak Kuhan's return was public knowledge now anyway. So, he was still a legend in the Pact—and Pacters tore their legends limb from limb and ate them alive.

The girl whispered, "Thank you for *Poison*. My brother died in the water gangs."

Two guards pulled Seren away from Tas toward another unmarked door. She could go down fighting, but it would only make things worse.

"Get Qasri into a holding cell. And the animal. Separately," the captain said.

Her cell was three paces across in either direction; its fourth wall was carbon mesh that went solid and opaque when she tried to walk through it. Seren washed at the sink, loosely braided her hair, and sat on the bare shelf to wait. No one came, but she guessed she was under observation. Her heart raced, her hands felt icy, and she felt light-headed as the room darkened around her. What would Teak say? Then the humour of it struck her. Her virtual aide was gone, but now she could put her questions to the real man, if she saw him again. What would Tas say? *Breathe. Stay calm.*

Seren folded her feet under her to sit cross-legged as she would in a sanctuary meditation cell. She tried to empty her mind, but her thoughts swirled like trout in a riverbend pool. Think something useful then. Her vri *Return* was ready to beta on *Singularity* or another gridsite. And after that?

Let the dead speak to the living. Her next vri would showcase the terrible images from Louhi Takahara's report. No one needed another war story; this could be a peace story. *Marwnad*—she despaired of translating that into Peel. *Elegy* sounded fusty, and *Death Song* clunked. Maybe nonClaerans would just have to stretch their minds around three foreign syllables. *Marwnad.*

Open with centuries-old images of Sitkum from space—for all she knew, it was Maq who recorded them—as the world glowed from bright noctilucence to a searing fire that torched its atmosphere and all life. End with the greening world Tas described in the Deep Outside—

Faintly and far away, an alarm wailed.

9

Maq watched the Pact patrol ship grapple the Az. *Game over*. Let some newsgrid producer make an upbeat story out of that one. But Parvin Kerkallec sat head in hands at his *Phoenix* comm board, so he had to wonder out loud how long they'd wait.

"Wait for what? End of file."

Maq snorted. "Hell no, it's just started. I never named any ship for a cinder. Phoenixes come back from the dead, remember? Watch this."

Not that he had any idea what hope they might possibly expect now or any other time. Now they were back to another century of war and ruin, and it looked like the new songs were going to be about ghost lovers.

"What's the point?" Parvin didn't stir, even when Nur laid a comforting hand on her shoulder and Rozenn brought her rescued angel to lean at her knee.

Parvin was crap at lahal too; she didn't yet appreciate the fine art of bravado. But after a while she looked up and called for a motion scan of *Seneca*.

10

Low angle shot. Overhead light panels flashed as the guard station klaxon screamed, and people yelled orders out in the passageway. The security lieutenant returned at a run, shouting words that the alarms swallowed whole.

"General wants them on the bridge," she finally got the guard captain to understand.

Seren took Cedar's leash from a nervous subbie, wondering at the change of plan. Rethel might have decided to flaunt his vessel's speed and firepower. Pact thinking: show them death and they'll fall to their knees. It never worked, it only angered Pols and pushed Greys to the high ground. But for some reason, Tas was smiling.

Seneca's bridge was a black hole of matte carbonglass desks and soundless dark carpet, lit with a subdued gleam from the boards and a huge vri stage. It was deeply quiet.

At a station of midnight deadwood corded in gold, Anton Rethel stood by a specialist's shoulder, intent on the displays. When he glanced up, he looked wearier and less certain than on the *Az*'s comm display.

In the vri zone, local space rotated a slow three-sixty on its y axis and then on its x and z axes, showing the red giant and white dwarf at the centre, a protoplanetary straggle of dust and rocks in an eccentric orbit, *Marianne* and *Phoenix* and the other Pol ships clustered in visual range of the MitraCorps ships.

Rethel highlighted an area off *Seneca's* stern, above the ecliptic and out toward the Tripline. "Intelligence thought the first drone malfunctioned, so they sent a second. Same result. But something's jamming our comms and scans. A few hours ago, you said 'check your new scan target.' What did that mean?"

"Set a vri to display in infrared. Then overlay it with visible light," Tas said.

Rethel looked startled but gave the order.

Seren looked over his shoulder as Tas studied the display, slowly rotating and sectioning the area. Then he folded his arms, leaning on a desk. Ready to fall over. Waiting. Cedar leaped silently into an oversized chair that might be Rethel's and curled in a ball with her tail over her forepaws, the biosensors above her natural eyes glowing faintly in the bridge's deep twilight. It was a purely territorial move. Rethel scowled and decided to ignore her, so Seren left her there on safety. Anyone who sat on her wouldn't do it twice.

Rethel broke the thunderous silence. Seren still hadn't decided whether he and Tas were old friends or old enemies. Maybe they just understood each other. "All right. Now explain."

"My comm and slate," Tas said. "Turn the ship one-eighty and hold position."

The security lieutenant apprehensively sought Rethel's nod, then tipped a foil pouch onto the nearest chart desk. Seren gave Tas his things and pocketed her own.

Tas tapped his comm and checked his slate, then turned toward Seren. Cedar lifted her head and stared in her direction, ears twitching. In the dim cockpit a glow spread outward, and in a moment, she realized it came from her breast pocket. She lifted out the stone carved with the moulder pattern that looked only slightly like a tree.

In her palm the stone pulsed with a gentle blue light. An unnameable other sense tugged at her mind, but as she strained to catch it, a sound dropped through three octaves to a singing hum in cadences that made her think of Tas's strange music.

All heads had turned to the huge bridge viewscreen, and a distant pulsing core of light nearly twenty-five degrees above the ecliptic. Between the reddish twilight of Gorda and the distant white blur of Bella, a glowing shape appeared. Its complexity suggested a tree reflected in still water, dreamed and forgotten in a kinetichron's shifting probabilities. It grew into a vast star-shot cloud of brilliant blue-green and writhed with dark cords like night rivers in a wall of mist. Then it blossomed and wheeled a stately dance of great cloudy vanes, spat one brilliant flash from its lightless centre, and folded into itself like an anemone.

"What do you see?" Tas asked her quietly.

"Mist and starlight, the same as the Bight, as though a mirror node opened between the binaries." Seren reached for words. "Now there's nothing. Stars. Space."

Tas didn't answer. Instead, he listened to a hardsuited and armed sergeant take orders from an officer, orders that Seren thought included attack and destroy.

"Fire on it, and we'll all die," Tas said, "as your other ships died."

"You don't know that," Rethel challenged.

"I saw the cruiser *Providence* die in Herschel's Reach. I was taking fire from it, after I'd said I was an unarmed survey mission."

"*Providence* didn't fire on an unarmed ship," Rethel said too sharply.

"No witnesses, unknown Mitran pilot—who would ever know?"

Seren asked, since no one else did, "What happened?"

"A great billowing cloud of light, then a flash of directed high energy. *Providence* vanished. Ceased to exist, at least anywhere my sensors could detect. By the time I looked again, the cloud was gone too." Tas turned to the reset display. "Strip a launch of all weapons and send it out. You should scan an object the size of a large drone probe. Bring it in."

Rethel glowered at his back. "Do as he says."

"Then stand down all weapons systems on *Seneca*. Disable or jettison any that you can."

Rethel bit back a protest and nodded to another officer. "After that—"

Seneca shuddered as its powerful propulsion systems sighed to a halt. One blurt of the klaxon cut off sharply, and deep silence fell. One by one the ship's nav and comm and weapons boards dimmed, so that Cedar's ruby sensors and Tas's slate were the only points of light in absolute blackness. Even the stone had gone dark again. Tas silently eased closer to stand at her shoulder, and Seren took his arm. Crew members seized hold-downs as artificial gravity vanished. Seren kicked a foot into a floor hold-down. Discipline silenced the bridge as officers gave quiet orders.

Rethel said, "What's the technology, Kuhan? How are you doing this?"

"Soon." Tas didn't look up.

"Say the word and I'll call for approvals."

No one answered.

After a minute *Seneca*'s bridge reappeared as emergency power came on and partial gravity returned, but except for shouts in the passageway, the ship was eerily silent.

A board lit, and Tas turned toward it. At extreme range the drone probe image showed a grey object that looked like grownstone covered in ridged patterns. It was rounded at one end and tapered to three rounded points like the roots of a human molar. The probe slowed to circumnavigate it several times, and at a tech's command, the composite image rotated in a vri zone at full size, just over a metre on its longest axis.

"Is that what the one at Piñar looked like?" Seren asked quietly.

"Not much. It was more oval with no projections, but I saw one like this not long ago." Tas turned to Rethel. "Open full-vri mirror-comm links to *Rustam News, Walden Today,* and the Politayan arts site *Singularity.*"

Rethel glanced around the bridge and back to Tas. "Do I have a choice?"

"No."

Good, Rethel's face said plainly.

As the links opened, Tas sat at the nearest desk and nodded to Seren. She leaped to guess what he needed—unsure whether they were now captives or captors—loaded the simage she'd created and announced, "Anastasios Kuhan, director-general elect of MitraCorps, speaking for the focal of Mitra in exile and the parliament of Claer."

"An imminent threat to humanity faces us," Tas said to the cams he couldn't see. "Ten years ago, Pact ships encountered ancient artifacts in human space. President de Jong acted quickly—doing what he believed necessary—to force reunity of the three great branches of humanity in the most direct way. The way he chose was war."

The simage synched perfectly as he talked, better than she'd hoped with no time to finesse it. Seren loaded a playback of what they'd just seen, a low-res capture with rough transitions, but at least people could see an unsimmed original of the glowing mist shot with rivers of night and then the object expelled from it.

"Humanity will never reunite by force, but it can reunite. All hostilities in human space will end immediately. Occupations of Politaya worlds will end. Treaties will reopen to consider new evidence. Fleets will stand down."

Seren found images of the Pact's illegal weapons at Piñar on Tanna—ironically, in her haste, she pulled them from *Rain*—and loaded Louhi's terrible images of unburied torture victims and mass graves on Taiga and Claer. This could be a key sequence, the thought flashed through her mind, of her vri doc *Marwnad*.

A murmur of protest gathered on the bridge. *Lost his mind*, an officer muttered. Seren hoped the man was wrong.

"We live alone in the Local Arm of our home galaxy. We'll die alone and be forgotten—" Tas let it hang a moment. "—unless we rise above our differences. In three days on Sakai Station, we will begin talks on full interworld cooperation. All polities and peoples may attend."

Voluntary reunity, in other words. Neatly done. Sakai Station was the transfer point nearest to the boundaries of Pact, Neutrality, and Politaya space—but it lay within the Neutrality.

Tas nodded, and Seren thumbed the comm pad off. All around them, people turned in silence, uncertain whether they'd heard a bluff or madness or high diplomacy.

"Good try," Rethel said wearily. "You'll never make it work. Greens and Greys might turn up, but Wilm Nolin will make sure the Pact boycotts."

"Herra Flett," Tas said to thin air. "Your prisoner."

An image appeared on Tas's display and then bloomed in a vri zone. It was Wilm Nolin, not the sleek, expensively groomed

Wilm Nolin of Walden's world council meetings but Wilm Nolin in irideco and leather harness on Claer Arian a few days ago, surrounded by his prancing and snarling manimal playmates and his gangster ally Duri Balint in liveware and feathers—then a pale, trembling Wilm Nolin, guarded by Doll Sorrow and another fearsome chimera on *Phoenix*. The bridge murmur broke into argument, a few cheers and a rising wave of laughter. Nolin had few admirers here.

Tas fell back in his chair, exhausted. *Let's get out of here*, his glance at Seren said. But then he looked up from his slate.

"General, prepare to be boarded."

Rapid movement in the vri zone caught her eye. A silver spark dropped through it at impossible speed toward the gold spark that was *Seneca*. Seren touched Tas's shoulder, and he sat forward to watch. Silently, a sliver of darkness grew in the forward viewscreen until it swallowed suns and dust and stars and space itself. Its darkness took on faint gloss and detail and became a streamlined blade of composites and glass bearing the Mitran emblem of a silver star radiant on the horizon of a golden sun.

A portal in the ship's flank irised open, giving out bluish light, and a silvery dart leaped out from a rider bay. It flashed by the bridge viewscreen, and Seren caught a glimpse of a dim cockpit on a tiny craft much like Louhi's courier. *Seneca*'s bridge lights brightened abruptly and shipboard sounds hummed back to normality. Cedar rose from the general's chair with a dagger-toothed yawn and eased down to the carpet.

With calculated Mitran arrogance, the warship hanging in the viewscreen had sent its boarding party. Alone between four Pact soldiers, framed in the passageway portal, stood a boy in MitraCorps uniform.

Seeing Tas, the boy came forward and saluted sharply.

"Identify yourself to Captain Kuhan," Seren said in her sketchy Damotik to cue Tas.

"Cadet Cohen, MitraCorps/Spartí ship *Satya*," he said in a bizarre backworld accent, taking in Tas's blood-spattered clothing and nskinned face. "Captain's compliments, sir and ma'am, are you prisoners?"

"Guests, Suva." Tas looked in Rethel's direction. "A

MitraCorps crew will assist on your bridge, General. Follow us to Sakai."

A larger patrol ship had launched after the courier. In minutes a softsuited Spartí unit shadowed in with Parvin Kerkallec and her people treading on their heels, and a MitraCorps medic tried to get Tas onto a float gurney.

"Come with me." Tas found Seren's hand and drew her in.

"Go. I'll bring the Az to *Satya*." She kissed the one unscathed part of his face that she could find, high on his left cheek.

A woman detached from Parvin's group and crossed the bridge to them. Nur Davi, Maq's comm officer from *Phoenix*, held out a small case bearing the Claeran Senate seal, and opened it for a moment to reveal a single small object nestled inside. "Images and documents to support our Sakai deposition."

"It's a titanium high-security bead," Seren told Tas.

"Delun. Good work." Tas pocketed the case.

Mam? Now Seren knew why the blonde woman seemed familiar. She remembered to breathe, not yet trusting her relief, wanting to ask and say everything at once, tongue-tied.

Nur Davi embraced her tightly. "Look at you, my girl. We're all so proud of you." Then she straightened. "Teak, once again we are in your debt."

Tas nodded, wasting no words on it.

"And Cedar, good friend, you kept her safe."

"As you wanted, Delun." Cedar crouched on her forepaws, unruffled as always, but her ears-forward expression said she was happy.

Mam turned, still clasping Seren's hand. "I'll see you on Sakai, sweet. Be good to each other."

Then she was gone, swept away in a skein of people returning to *Phoenix* and *Satya* through a crowd of *Seneca* crew who called out or touched hands or stood in dazed silence.

The medic prevailed, scanning Tas as they walked for the passageway, and Spartí surrounded him to recover their own. At the portal the crowd slowed, and Tas turned to look in her direction. *Soon.*

Seren lingered at the forward viewscreen, ignoring the chaos around her, and Cedar came to lean at her knee. Once the crowd thinned, she could claim the Az.

Out in the dark, *Satya* rode in orbit, burning occasional corrections, as the patrol craft returned to it. At the farthest limit of visual range, Iqaluit and Bulawayo and Cuzco ships began to lift into the long night like cottonwood silk on a summer wind. They drifted from Las Hermanas orbits and the rider racks of *Phoenix* and *Satya*, heading in toward the Dead Gate or bound outsystem. The Grey companies were leaving the crisis point, ghosting back toward neutral space or the Deep Outside.

When Seren turned from the viewscreen and looked back, Tas had passed through the portal, and Parvin's four specials blocked her way.

IX
HOME

1

ES2742.311

Static shot. Summer rain in Tirion's citadel square blew cold with sleet all through the liberation ceremony, just hard enough to soak the chafing collar and cuffs of Seren's dress uniform. By dusk the rain dripped from the bare branches, fracturing the festival lights into a crazed stained glass on the wet pavement. In the end the great occasion of returning Claer to Claerans smelled of fireworks and wet cat hair. Cedar leaned at Seren's knee trembling with cold, and no matter how carefully groomed, shedding grey hair on her dark green number ones.

"Is your beau here yet?" Seren asked Anya. Her guard was hoping to steal a few minutes with her lover after the ceremony. Parvin Kerkallec would have them both in irons if she found out Anya had taken her eyes off the detainee, but Parvin was distracted elsewhere tonight.

"Under the rowans on the top level, next to the cider stand."

Seren waved at Anya's beau and in return saw the flash of his white teeth in the deepening twilight. "Go! I'll wait for you."

"Thanks, treasure." Anya vanished into the rain.

Crowds flooded the square as everyone escaped the interminable ceremony. Musicians and singers drifted out of the café-bars, and people gathered to dance. Three guitarists set up under a canopy to tune their instruments, and a famous actor

back from offworld exile was entertaining people with jokes that
were getting more risqué as the café-bars uncorked their hard
cider. The first notes of a gavotte whirled out into the drizzle, and
dancers filled the main square. An Ayiti teenager grabbed Seren's
hand and pulled her into the melee, but after a few rounds she
escaped to the shelter of a maple tree where she watched,
clapping and singing the refrains.

This flash festival rescued Seren's tiresome day of being
presented onstage as a pre-eminent artist and offstage returned
to custody. Once Anya finished her tryst, they were both back to
work. No escape. Seren had looked for Tas among the dignitaries
at the ceremony even though she knew he was leading the reunity
talks on Sakai. Their long hours at the Dead Gate and on the Pact
warship seemed half a lifetime ago.

Claer's party of the century would be going strong at daybreak,
but Seren stifled a yawn. This evening she'd have her head down
on her desk before she could put together the current
instructional vri for Parvin. Her sombre documentary vri
Marwnad was still barely begun, and Parvin had confiscated her
image and research files along with her slate and comm. Her
messages to Mam went unanswered, probably censored; Delun
was still on Sakai, assembling her war crimes case against Wilm
Nolin.

Seren shivered, wishing she'd been able to wear her heated
anorak. The dress uniform was elegant but, like a lot of Claeran
design, short on practicality and comfort.

"Wake up, Green, you're missing the party." A small man
stood on the cobblestones beside her maple tree with a mongoose
on his shoulder. At a discreet distance, a black Daimler-Morgan
limousine hovered silently.

Seren accepted the calvados bottle tucked under Maq's elbow
and took a drink while Hasi and Cedar touched noses on the
cobbles. Instantly she felt warmer; ten-year calva went down like
apple-flavoured flame.

"What brings you, Maq? I thought you were busy advising
Gabriel de Jong."

"Ayuh. Why you're here is the real question. Thought Tas got
you seconded to MitraCorps."

"No." Seren bit down on the rest. In three months, Tas had

never contacted her.

"Give him time." Maq was expansive with calvados and satisfaction. "Maybe at Sakai we'll actually agree on something for the first time in a century. We can't go back to the bad old days, thanks to your denial of passage stunt at Thermopylai."

"Thermopylai?"

"Don't you watch the grids? They say you two held the hot gates until *Satya* burned in to save your hides—*Satya* and Tas's moulder pals. How did he do that anyway?"

"Do what?"

"Ayuh, serves me right for asking. Tas hates all that hero crap, and I guess you do too."

Two chimerai stood near the hover until Maq waved them forward, and Doll Sorrow and Anubis came to touch hands with Seren. Most of the chimerai and runaway animals had emerged from hiding to seek amnesty, and there were two manimal seats on the new Politaya council.

Seren took another drink of calva. A story had spread that she'd negotiated at the Dead Gate under Tas's simage, and her vri dramas were in demand. Tonight, the new prime minister Danek Arwyn had lauded her as a cultural treasure, the heart and conscience of Claer, and the Anansians had given her a medal. They also gave Mihal one, which put things in perspective.

All she wanted was to get away. Parvin couldn't confine her to barracks for life. Once she was free, she would run for the Tripline. Crew for a freight service at first, then set up something on her own, maybe a vri studio. She wouldn't be working on the Tripline with Tas Damou, so she'd do it for both of them. Damou was gone, replaced by the famous and charismatic Kuhan, but it was Damou she missed.

"Come on, I'll give you a ride—where to?"

"Classified." She waved him off.

Maq laughed and ducked back into his sleek hover. "Come visit me on Walden."

"Soon as I can." Seren waved goodbye as the hover lifted.

The rain gave way to falling mist. Anya was taking her time, and Seren needed to leave soon or she'd be working all night.

"Can Tŷ Coed spare you this long?" she asked Cedar.

"Yes. Sanity requires," Cedar said crankily.

Seren and Cedar, with Parvin's grudging approval, had turned her old livewood tree into a cattery. A handful of litter mothers and a Mitran breeder occupied it, working with DNA from scores of Mitran guard cats. Now Tŷ Coed watched over the tumbling kittens and aloof young cats, allowing them to scratch its newly toughened bark and climb its branches. When Seren visited under escort, she found her tree happier than she'd ever known it, putting out new roots and shoots. It had even learned to purr.

Then a pair of stilt-walkers jigged past, and someone handed out hot honey cakes. As she licked honey from her fingers, a group of uniformed Mitrans crossed the square and joined the dancing Claerans to a noisy welcome. Mitrans could do no wrong at the moment, since Spartí and Palikir companies were overseeing the transfer of power from the Pact.

Seren heard the growl of a military craft under the music, and a gleaming MitraCorps patrol ship settled in the dark corner of the square's lowest level. Three men and a woman in casual clothing disembarked, though the shimmer of shock shirts at their necks gave them away. The woman and a stocky black man headed past the dancers and split up, and a man with a blond braid crossed the square to buy cider, positioning himself near the few Claeran security people on duty. The null-masked fourth man left the square. Special ops, by their smooth efficiency, probably taking in one of the criminals still at large. Leaning on the smooth maple trunk, Seren went back to watching the round dancing.

A vendor wheeled up a wagon, and someone passed her a hot handful of chestnuts and a cheese galette that she split with Cedar, and two Nevez women started singing rounds, and for this moment, life was quite livable.

In the crowded square, someone moved in close beside her right shoulder, close enough that in the cool evening she felt the warmth. When she eased left around the maple trunk, the warmth remained. Cedar rubbed around her legs, purring, quite unlike her fierce guardian. Then Seren went still. *Impossible.*

"Do not turn. This is an extraction," said a familiar voice quietly next to her ear. "There's no quick return if you leave. If you don't want this, walk away now."

Frozen where she stood, Seren looked out blindly at the

square. A smile found her face.

"Now walk around the outside of the square to the northeast corner. Rear portside cargo hatch on the Az opens to your palmprint. Your guard won't be back soon. I'll be behind you. Take the controls. Go."

Seren pushed away from the tree and threaded her way through the crowd, somehow in the process acquiring a crown of hothouse flowering apple branches and a handful of hazelnuts, expecting an alarm at any moment. It took forever to walk around the margins of the celebration, and she fought a temptation to run. Down a broad flight of grownstone steps, across the main square under a glare of festival lights and down another set of narrow, barely lit stairs.

Someone shouted not far behind as she reached the lower square, and she slowed. It could be pursuit or just the party. It took all her will to stroll calmly toward the darkest corner, expecting a stun net to fall on her at any moment.

Then an Az loomed up in front of her, and she ducked around the stern to slap her hand on the cargo hatch palm plate. The hatch hissed opened, the ramp extended, and Cedar bounded into the pitch-black cargo hold ahead of her.

Another rescue. Seren had no chance to say it. Tas was suddenly right there. For one happy moment they flew together like two magnets and she leaned to his familiar warmth. *I missed you so much. I couldn't reach you, even Anya tried for me—*

Anya.

Seren stepped back and turned for the hatch. "I can't go anywhere. I promised to wait for my guard. They'll ream her if I run." If she sprinted straight across the square, Anya might see her, and she could explain—but Tas held her back with a hand on her wrist.

"You can't go because they'll punish your guard?"

"Anya's my friend. And my shop steward. She's with her beau."

Laughter was a breath against her cheek. He spoke quickly in Damotik to his comm bracelet. Then he told her, "Asleep in her lover's arms. When she wakes, she won't remember anything, but a witness will say she was stunned protecting you."

"Thank you," she said too formally. Now that she'd caught her breath, she had no idea how to talk to him. Once again, she was a shy teenager in her mother's orchard with a handful of wet apples, and Teak Kuhan was a glamorous stranger.

He found her hand in the dark and pulled her forward. "Lift now. Your security people have just realized you're gone."

Seren threw herself into the pilot chair and found the boards live. She called for restraints as she lifted the Az slowly and hovered above Hafn Boulevard to the Tirion city limits, then burned upward. They soared above Claer's glowing night side until they met dawn spilling over the midnight green horizon.

"Take us to two hundred kilometres and orbit," Tas—Teak—said from the nav chair. "You have control. My eyes aren't fully regenerated yet. I'd fly us straight into a mountain." That must be why the cockpit was as black as a cave; he was still relying on infrared.

"Won't they pursue?"

"We're running dark in nanoflage, and they're chasing a stolen diplomatic hover instead."

Running dark like a privateer in Claeran airspace with Teak Kuhan—Seren should be scandalized, but instead she grinned. She hadn't flown since Parvin's security crew dragged her back to Claer from the Dead Gate. After they reached their altitude and burned into an orbit, Seren reset the ship to sim a scientific satellite of the same mass. Why were they orbiting? She badly wanted to get offworld, and Teak Kuhan must be needed somewhere.

"Power down."

Seren linked her trembling hands and waited.

"You have a choice," he said. "What do you want?"

Seren shook her head, unable to answer. *I want Damou. I want to run for the Tripline and the Deep Outside.* The Az burned a minor correction, and Seren assiduously checked the nav and engineering boards, anything to avoid looking at Kuhan.

"One choice is this. I can take you to Rustam or Vritra, get you a place to live and people to talk to about work. If that's what you want." He sounded formal now, perhaps starting to wonder if this was a good idea.

Thanks for the rescue, but I'll go now. Drop me anywhere, I'll find my way. But to ease his awkwardness, she said, "Unless this is a New Grove parable, there should be another choice."

Tas laughed as she'd hoped, not that it was much of a joke. *Friends.* But then he grew serious. "Seren, I had to find out for myself what this is about. Parvin Kerkallec said you had no response to my last message."

"I've been in detention for ten tendays. What did your last message say?"

"No chain of command issues if you're at the institute."

"Institute?" Seren shook her head. She'd dared to hope that he might want to be with her, but this sounded impersonal and official.

"Astrobiology Institute on Rustam. I thought you might . . ." Tas knew when to abandon a pointless discussion. "I see Parvin's version of damage control still includes brute force. The other choice is that we run for the Tripline."

Seren laughed, it was so unexpected and so exactly what she did want. By the time she collected her thoughts, he'd released his restraints and freed her from the pilot chair and discovered that her hands were still icy from the cool evening in Tirion citadel square, and warmed them between his own. Both talked at once, but they still managed to hear all that was important.

"I wanted you, I sent messages. I thought I'd looked back and you'd turned to shadow."

"Parvin said you needed medical care and didn't want to see me."

"You believed her?"

"No. I came to see for myself. I told you in the orchard that I'd return."

"Choices," she finally remembered to say. "I want it all."

"It's all yours."

In the dark cockpit he was only a blacker shape drifting near the viewscreen, but she turned to his familiar voice.

"Spare jacket under the pulldown?"

In answer he wrapped her in his own jacket, warming her in his subtle scent. His hand rested on her shoulder, and he leaned to murmur that he wanted her. Then everything was easy. His jacket floated away unnoticed. Love in freefall called for improv, but nothing had changed in his knowing touch or his warm voice. Afterward they drifted in each other's arms.

"We may have a minor detour before the Tripline," Tas said from a peaceful quiet.

"About twenty years?"

"If you like. We can live on Mitra, once the nanoform is done."

"Parvin will track me down, Tas."

"Parvin will respect Claeran law. Consensual sex is accepted as a personal contract."

"Archaic."

"Still on the books."

"Do you read law tracts for fun, Kuhan?"

"I read law tracts to get what I want, Qasri." He was laughing again.

"Is that what this was about?" Trust him to be three moves ahead.

"Seeing that I had to extract you first, I thought we might as well enjoy it."

"It's usual to ask your lover in advance about a major life commitment."

"It's reasonable to interpret passion as consent."

Seren drifted with her hands clasped behind her head, smiling. They could keep up this silliness for hours. Her hair was floating free, and she found her comb. "Lights, brighten."

"Cancel," Tas said.

"Does it bother your eyes?"

Instead of answering he drew her hands up to his face. The damaged side no longer felt like tree bark and seemed less twisted. He said too carefully, "They took a lot of shattered glass and composite out of my face. I don't look like Damou."

"Show me." Seren lightly framed his cheekbones.

Whatever they'd given him for a face couldn't be any worse than Damou's—but when the cockpit brightened at his word, Seren managed to look at him only long enough to flinch and glance away. *Far, far worse.* He'd healed uncannily like the simage she'd programmed, out there in the dark, to a Teak Kuhan who'd never lived until now, aged by ten years to a strikingly handsome man with faint scarring on his right cheek. His eyes were the same, direct and compassionate. Under her shocked gaze, he looked away.

Gathering her courage, Seren took a deep breath. It wasn't

important. A minor distraction. "When I saw you on the grids, I thought you were showing my sim."

"Wearing it. It felt right that you gave me back my name and my face."

"Tas. Teak." Seren lifted a shoulder. Saying it made it true.

He kissed her on the mouth, a first time, and drew her gently closer. As always, he was good to lean on, warm and steady. They floated together for a long time, holding each other like lovers long parted. Lovers and friends.

2

A Mitran's idea of a comfortable cockpit temperature was Seren's idea of a deep freeze. When she drifted free, she shoved her Clacr Defence greens into a locker. Tas handed her clean greys that looked like MitraCorps standard issue and showed her the thermal controls. She asked if she could get a ball gown like this, cozy but maybe a little more stylish, only to see him laugh.

"Detour now," he said.

The heading he gave her was almost due north. She flew it wondering and rotated the vri chart to follow the track to his coordinates. Nothing was marked at that location. She set autopilot and sat back to admire the night green world below until the altitude warning demanded her attention. At close range she saw they were heading for a small island that breasted the grey sea. Farther north there was only steely water and blue-white ice. Seeing no marked pad on the islet, she dropped slowly, and Tas pointed out a flat space with a flashing red beacon triggered by their approach. The maglevs sagged and took the ship's weight, and she cut the engines. Grit and dust swirled up around the Az.

The wash of waves and cries of seabirds were loud once she shut down, and a strong scent of seaweed blew in through the open hatch. Cedar was first out to explore the packed gravel pad under the ship. Seren pulled on a well-worn MitraCorps jacket that Tas offered. Outside, he checked his slate for direction and walked out with his hair ruffling in the sea breeze and his shadow slanting away in the late polar sunlight.

The rocky island was bigger than it looked from above, maybe two kilometres from shore to shore, but its only life seemed to be sparse native vegetation like lichen that matched the tan bedrock. Someone had come here to install that nav beacon, but otherwise this place was raw habitation-zone; it didn't offer much to humans beyond air and sunlight.

Tas came back and caught her by the hand, leading her toward the nearest shore, where the low sun picked out ridges and hollows. He walked into the pattern that might represent a sea creature or two mountain watersheds or the roots and branches of a spreading tree reflected in still water—or a multidimensional flight plan.

Seren recorded a minute of Tas walking in the pattern, then set her new full-vri cam to auto and went to join him at the centre where the two halves connected.

"I cited your flight plan theory in my Kalevala report," he told her. "Maybe the moulders travelled world to world across the local bubble while we were still chipping flints on Earth."

"What have you learned so far about their artifact?"

"Not much. No datable features, and we still don't know what it is. Our best guesses are communication device or territorial marker. But ancient."

Seren hesitated, knowing he'd laugh at the hunch she'd tried to shake for many tendays. "They were at the Dead Gate. Realtime. Watching."

"Qasri, you're a romantic. We triggered an ancient system."

"Kuhan, open your eyes. You called them with your fractal music and the tree stone. You expected them."

"Is that how it seemed?" Tas looked at her thoughtfully. "We can go now. You'll like Rustam. Good sailing on the Cinnabar Sea."

"Why did you warn of an imminent threat to humanity?" She wouldn't let him duck this.

"We needed a way to get Pact and Politaya and Neutrality working together instead of wasting lives and resources on conflict. I never said the threat came from another species," he admitted. "In my view the imminent threat to humanity is humanity."

"That's all?" Her cam beeped that it needed a recharge. Strange, since it had a new cell.

"I check every time I'm here in case there's some change."

Change didn't look likely. Seren glanced around the sinuous whorls of stony ridges, a few fingers high, that looked as though they'd lain waiting under the cool wind and blowing dust for millennia and would wait for millennia to come. The place had a haunting air of time and distance, and she felt its lightness. At the foot of the ramp, she looked around, pushing back the hair that the breeze tugged over her shoulder. Grey sea, deep blue Claeran sky, bare tawny stone at the end of the world. They'd come a long way for nothing, but she wasn't sorry.

Her cam chirped again when she was halfway up the ramp, so she stopped to turn it off. But when she pulled it out of her pocket, it was already off. She turned around so quickly that she bumped into Tas.

"Your slate's beeping." But his slate was silent. So were the ship boards.

"Seren!" Cedar sat near a forward strut. "Come. Look."

Together they walked back down onto the gritty tan bedrock, looking around. Cedar padded outward from the starboard bow support and dropped into a hunting crouch.

Seren spotted her prey and laughed. "Someone came here with her child."

"No. It's a restricted scientific zone protected by orbitals. They'd get three warnings, then flashes of blue light, then a patrol drone would be here in minutes."

A child's bright purple game slate lay just off the edge of the landing area. In the clear air over its display danced a vri of Baka-chan, the small animage lemur host of a children's show, singing in an unknown language.

On a barren world in the Deep Outside, Tas had said, Mei had traded her broken slate for a pretty carved stone.

Seren reached to pick it up, but Tas swiftly caught her hand. "Put a clean secure bead in your cam." He kneeled, and after a minute she joined him.

They watched as the playful voice transformed to instrumental progressions that seemed to tumble down a musical staircase, and the music became a complex sequence of beeps and clicks. The lemur morphed into a glowing blue tree of spreading branches that stood reflected on shimmering silver water.

It was broken. They wanted it anyway. But it was working now.

The End

AFTERWORD

This is an ancient story. A young woman is bitten by a snake and dies. Her grieving husband, a poet, travels to the land of the dead to bring her home. But he looks back to be sure she is still with him, and at his glance she fades to a shadow. *Death is forever,* the story tells us. *Let go. Get on with your life.* But what if love can somehow open forever's grip, and death is only another mask?

Stories and old songs, that's how we learn. Some of our stories become history. If history is written by the victors—in other words, by enemies—how do we tell our own stories after defeat? *Shadow Matter* answers that question.

Art for the benefit of humanity, art for the historical record, is a double-edged sword. It takes obsessive determination to produce unwelcome, transgressive art year after year, and even greater determination to resist the seduction of being declared a cultural treasure.

Art for art's sake? As the poet Pierre Reverdy observed, "For the primitive, art is a means; for the decadent, it becomes an end[1]." Humans have a long tradition of using art as a means,

---

[1] Pierre Reverdy, Le livre de mon bord (Paris: Mercure de

often to bring news or warn of impending disaster. Some would say such art is propaganda. It is, in the original sense of spreading an idea. But it may also be good art.

Science is not my academic background—classics and mediaeval studies claimed me first—so I approach science with the benefit of unlimited ignorance and curiosity. Much of my research was done in the pages of *New Scientist*, *Science*, and *Nature*, on the websites of CBC Science and BBC Future, in many books, and at science centres and events. In the end I drew on my interest in Late Antiquity as much as my reading on deep space to talk about the peoples of *Shadow Matter*'s Politaya, Pact, and Neutrality. Empires and their opponents haven't changed much from era to era.

The technology of *Shadow Matter* is not far beyond the reach of our 21st century science. Avatars advise and speak for us; full virtual reality informed by artificial intelligence is on the drawing board. Phones and tablets provide all-encompassing information and entertainment needs.

Already we culture and transplant human organs including skin. Cloning human beings is now possible but prohibited as a grave breach of bioethics. What if rogue future cultures decided body farms, cloning, and transgenic human-animal chimerai would be good for the sex trade?

Astronomers remotely assess atmospheric and surface elements, gravity, and probability of life on distant exoplanets. A space elevator and high station may soon lie within our capabilities, as may interplanetary spaceships. Quantum physics researchers have now put visible physical objects into a superposition of two states.

Today we know enough to practise low-impact sustainable agriculture, transportation, and industry. We can stop climate catastrophe, protect biodiversity, and let our planet heal through international co-operation—but instead we deny and delay. The inevitable climate wreck may throw us back into an anti-scientific, anti-intellectual era that will take centuries to escape.

France, 1948), quoted in Elias Lönnrot, *The Kalevala*, trans. Keith Bosley (Oxford: Oxford University Press, 1989).

Interstellar space travel is the most obvious technological difference between our 21st century and *Shadow Matter*'s 28th century. Even without considering the formidable challenges of propulsion, radiation shielding, and life support, let alone time dilation, at present we cannot overcome the sheer vastness of even one small arm of our home galaxy. Recent discussion of multiverse theory led me to wonder—now that we can put physical objects into quantum superposition—what if in a few centuries we learned to send physical objects through near-identical iterations of the multiverse? It could be like flying through a hall of mirrors.

Given that we now grow human organs and conduct gender-affirming surgery, we're not far from readily available consumer cosmetic modification to let people change the colour of skin, hair, and eyes as well as their physical structure.

In this book I wanted to write about cultures in which appearance is selectively mutable. What if 28th century humans didn't view others through a flawed lens of race, gender, and ethnicity but by their social affiliations and actions? And what if people in this diverse and morally complex future learned to use art and negotiation, not brute firepower, to settle their differences?

In *Shadow Matter*, first-wave emigrants fled the toxic Earth in ships travelling slower than lightspeed to settle and exploit the nearest exoplanets. The monoglot cultures of the Pact of Human Worlds descend from today's rich G7 nations; they speak Peel, a form of English derived from PL or plain language.

Second-wave emigrants escaped in hastily built, untested mirror transit ships. Driven off Pact worlds at gunpoint, they settled prime earthlike worlds out beyond the Pact, where they survive more sustainably. The multilingual cultures of the Politaya and its offshoot the Neutrality descend from poor non-G7 nations left to die on a poisoned and climate-wrecked world.

In thinking about the 28th century Politaya, Neutrality, and Pact, I faced a problem of not knowing enough languages to create place names or personal names, let alone essential concepts and philosophies. Invented languages seem pointless from anyone but a linguist like J.R.R. Tolkien. So I pulled together fragments of a few languages I know slightly and researched a few more to create a patchwork of cultures.

The Damotik language of Mitra derives from Ελλενικά (Greek). The Tavod language of Bryniau Claer comes from "y tafod" or Cymraeg (Welsh). The Tariqan dialects derive from Pashto and Arabic. Ayitien Kreyol is an offspring of Caribbean French. The lost dialects of Sitkum derive from the Chinook Trade Jargon of Canada's West Coast.

Private military companies have long been regarded as a scourge; they answer to no one, and the governments that hire them believe no one can hold them accountable. If unpaid and left to themselves, they murder and pillage at will. Most recently they worked in Ukraine, Iraq, Syria, Afghanistan, and especially Africa with predictable outcomes.

But what if the 28th century gave rise to well-regulated, ethical companies that provide dependable war-fighting and peacekeeping services to smaller polities? It might break the cycle, or it might not. All it takes to spark disaster is an internal power struggle.

When is science fiction? In a future time? Now? In the unknown past? Some of my other writing considers historical events. This story could as easily chart the aftermath of a terrestrial calamity of the past or present, but writing about a possible 28th century frees me from known history to create imaginary people and places. In the end, what's important is the story.

In *Shadow Matter* I wanted to write about how human cultures might evolve and prepare to meet the larger cosmos. But mostly I wanted to write about love and loyalty that defy great loss, and the restorative power of art in our lives.

S.W. Mayse
Vancouver Island, 2023

GLOSSARY

animage—animated moving images

augmented animal—animal with artificial intelligence and often speech, or enhanced with superior strength, speed, or other attributes, usually to aid or entertain a human owner; illegal on some worlds, bioethically controversial

Azande AirSpace—a Mitran spacecraft manufacturer

The Bight – a remote, dim region of space with scattered dwarf stars and dust lanes at the edge of Politaya space out near the Tripline

body farm—an illegal organization in which indentured, imprisoned or unlawfully detained persons are used as hosts for replacement body parts, often sold on the black market

brother-friend, cousin-friend, sister-friend—blighted by a fatally low birthrate from a still uncorrected immigration-era mutation, Claerans form loosely defined quasi-familial relationships; sister-friends, brother-friends, and cousin-friends are personally contracted to aid and support each other

burnskin—gel applied after minor burns to protect skin and aid healing

The Cantons—settlements of Mitran refugees from the destruction of their now-quarantined world, grouped on the northern-hemisphere continent of Tariqa on Claer

cat's cradle—a child's game of looping string around the fingers to create complex patterns

chimera—a transgenic creature or person crossbred from different species

Claer—a mainworld of the Politaya

comm bracelet—small, multifunctional data storage and communication device with the same capabilities as a data implant but worn externally as a bracelet

cosmod—cosmetic modification of hair, eyes, skin, shape of face, or other features

data bead—small data storage device, often carried in a case or worn ornamentally on a chain

data card—a palm-sized plastic card providing more storage than a data bead

deadwood—lumber from felled trees, usually nonsentient

Damotik—the language of one of the founding cultures of Mitra

The Deep Outside—space beyond the Tripline; it was declared a prohibited zone by the Interworld Accord of the Pact, Politaya, and Neutrality worlds, except for unarmed survey and rescue missions

Derw Sanctuary—a healing and spiritual centre of the New Grove order, heavily populated with sentient trees, known for its healing springs and livewood chapel

ecodebt—damage to an environmental system reckoned as a restoration cost

exo suit—a robotic exoskeleton for construction or military use

focal—the world council of Mitra

freestanding sim—a visual deception, sometimes deployed as a nonlethal weapon, often introduced into others' electronic systems via a tailored computer virus

glitz—a highly addictive narcotic

glop—to attack a structure with nanoscale devices or chemicals, reducing it to formless gel

Greens—slang for people of the Politaya worlds

greenway—a travel route for pedestrian and small wheeled traffic, usually surfaced in grass, moss, other ground cover plants, or their local analogues

Greys—slang for people of the Neutrality worlds

grownstone—extruded or moulded composites created from

local materials for construction; self-replicating nanoscale machinery can grow a building or other structure from human instructions or templates

hewnstone—natural stone sawn or lasered into various shapes for human construction use

hexlock—a six-sided shipping or storage container

hovertune—a small music-emitting device controlled by an individual or commercial enterprise

humanic—humanlike beings, including transgenic human-animal crosses, often enslaved, illegal on many worlds but widespread on most; may serve humans as child-minders, bodyguards, vermin hunters, domestic servants, and sex slaves

implant—data storage or communication device implanted under the skin, usually linked with retinal overlays, communications grids, databases, and other functions

irideco—a cosmetic application of colour, jewels, metals, textures, or occasionally living components under the skin of face and hands

kinetichron—large kinetic sculpture of moving vanes that evoke interdimensional mirror travel; some claim kinetichrons actually break the barriers of space and time as mirror transit does, permitting people to glimpse past and future lives; more likely the shifting kinetichron vanes have a hypnotic effect that encouraged flights of imagination

lahal—a game of guessing which hand holds a stick or other object, usually played in groups or lines of players facing each other

'Line deco—slang for Tripline decorative arts used in buildings, public spaces and spacecraft, known for its colourful and exuberant forms

livewood—transgenic tree or woody perennial, sentient and often capable of limited data processing and speech, grown into a desired shape such as furniture for human use; larger trees may serve as chambers for human occupation

The Long Dark—a period following emigration from old Earth when the human worlds abandoned technology and nearly ended the species; it took two centuries to redevelop science and technology once taken for granted on pre-migration Earth

luzard—one of Claer's surviving native lifeforms, a small leathery-skinned quadruped with a long tail, an analogue for an old Earth lizard

maglev—magnetic levitation used for transportation including trains and semi-autonomous hovering pods available for public use

manimal—a chimera created transgenically from human and nonhuman DNA, highly illegal on many worlds

mirror drive—propulsion for spacecraft employing multi-dimensional space

mirror node—unreal navigational point that enables mirror drive

Mitra—a mainworld of the Neutrality, now dead and quarantined

mourning cloak—a hooded cloak worn to indicate a person is mourning and requests no contact from others; if a cloak is not available, most Claerans respect a shawl or wrap drawn over the head in the same way

nanobot—nanoscale robotic machine

nanoform—to alter landforms and built structures using self-replicating nanoscale machines

nanowire—a nanoscale strand of a material such as silicon or metal, used in construction or as an assassin's weapon to slice through human flesh and bone

natural animals—animals not augmented with artificial intelligence or enhanced with superior strength, speed, or other attributes

neodar—a genetically adapted tree common in Claer's temperate zones, derived from the old Earth deodar species

Neutrality—alliance of worlds and star systems settled by second-wave emigrants from Earth, originally part of the Politaya

New Grove—a natural-science based healing and spiritual order of the Bryniau Claer region

Nskin—a protective coating to aid healing of minor wounds applied as spray, gel, or peel

Ntex—a Mitran-made explosive putty

null mask—a thin holographic envelope that protects identity by blurring facial features; usually controlled by subskin implant, communications bracelet, or slate

Pact of Human Worlds—alliance of worlds and star systems settled by first-wave emigrants from Earth, mainly from wealthy and powerful former G7 nations

Peel—PL or plain language, the common speech of the first-wave Pact

Poison—a satirical vri drama written and produced by Seren Qasri of Tirion y Bryniau, Claer

Politaya—alliance of worlds and star systems settled by second-wave emigrants from Earth, mainly from resource-poor or politically weak former non-G7 nations

Rax—a Politaya entertainment kidgrid popular with Claeran teenagers

Rain—a vri documentary about the Tanna massacre written and produced to exonerate MitraCorp/Spartï Captain Teak Kuhan, by Seren Qasri of Tirion y Bryniau, Claer

reunity—a plan to regather the divided second-wave worlds back into a greater Politaya informed by Neutrality ethics

retinal overlay—virtual display technology that projects an image directly onto the retina of the human eye

scaremod—cosmetic modification of hair, eyes, skin, shape of face, or other features to create a frightening or distasteful appearance

senselink—to join in virtuality to share senses with another person or group, available to audiences of some vri productions

sensorium—the array of human senses considered as a whole

serpentine—a chimera derived from reptilian and other genetic sources, often limbless

shock shirt—a garment that can protect against ballistic and energy weapon fire, usually covering the upper body and hips and worn under civilian or military garb; more advanced types retract or expand to fit individual wearers

simage—simulated image, usually a portrait of a human subject

Singularity—an arts gridsite that showcases avant garde works and supports radical politics

skookum—strong or brave in one of the languages of the destroyed second-wave planet Sitkum

slate—small, multifunctional handheld portable data storage and communication device

softsuit—lightweight, flexible one-piece spacesuit with attached hood, faceplate and breather

Sphinx, Dragon's Gold—vri games played via implants or external devices

Tavod—the language of Bryniau Claer, one of the founding cultures of Claer

tox—the toxic poor, disadvantaged and sometimes enslaved residents of poor districts

The Tripline—the outward boundary of human space, as agreed under the Interworld Accord

unsect—small native flying animal, an analogue for flying insects of old Earth

vri—virtual reality imaging device, projects retinal or freestanding 3D-seeming images

Walden—a Pact mainworld

ABOUT THE AUTHOR

S.W. Mayse is a professional writer of fiction, nonfiction and drama who worked long ago as a cannery hand, sailmaker's helper, reporter, disk jockey, photographer, television researcher-writer, book scout, and editor.

Her books include a historical novel *Awen,* inspired by a ninth-century Welsh poetry cycle; *Ginger: The Life and Death of Albert Goodwin,* a historical biography of a BC labour socialist shot in 1918 by the Dominion Police; and a political thriller, *Merlin's Web,* exploring internal colonialism, direct action, and state terrorism in Wales. Short fiction appeared in *On Spec* and *Space Illustrated.*

Awards include the Edna Staebler Award for Creative Non-Fiction (*Ginger*), the Arthur Ellis Award for Best True Crime (*Ginger*), and the Arthur Ellis Award first novel first runner-up (*Merlin's Web*). *Awen* was shortlisted for the Georgette Heyer Award for Historical Fiction.

Her work in Western and Northern Canada and Wales finally brought her home, and she lives on Vancouver Island with her family and two cats.

www.ingramcontent.com/pod-product-compliance
Lightning Source LLC
Chambersburg PA
CBHW030745030726
47497CB00001B/142